WHEN FEDERAL AGENT$
NO GOOD CHOICES, WILL THEY BE GUIDED BY
PRINCIPLES AND A SENSE OF JUSTICE, OR
VENGEANCE AND DESIRE FOR RETRIBUTION?

When three women rise to the forefront of the male-dominated field of drug law enforcement, they face the gravest threat in a generation. The drug war in Mexico has taken a sinister turn when 2000 kilograms of cocaine are secretly laced with a lethal amount of Fentanyl prior to being dispensed in Southern California.

With thousands of American lives at risk, Victoria Russo works to stop the cocaine from reaching American streets. Together with Special Agents Ana Lucia Rodriguez and Remi Choylia, their involvement results in an unprecedented opportunity to dismantle Mexico's largest drug cartel. The investigators also uncover linked crimes of a human sex trafficking ring led by a US Congressman and an attempted mass murder of a group of 30 children.

To be successful, or to avoid disaster, the agents must turn to ghosts of the past for help. Difficult decisions are made, often in situations where the only options to choose from are bad ones.

Editorial Reviews

" Total adrenaline rush from start to finish. MUST READ!"—*Scott Eichenberger, retired DEA Special Agent*

"Non-stop action. Realistic, difficult decisions. Tough, gritty characters."— *James Chappell, retired US Probation Officer*

i

NO GOOD CHOICES
Scott Nickerson

Moonshine Cove Publishing, LLC
Abbeville, South Carolina U.S.A.

Moonshine Cove Edition Apr 2023

ISBN: 9781952439551

LCCN: 2022904354

Cover images public domain; cover and interior design
by Moonshine Cove staff.

About the Author

Scott Nickerson worked as a DEA Special Agent for 13 years, spending 9 years in the Los Angeles Field Division. He worked closely with members of the District Attorney's Office in Los Angeles County, San Bernardino County, and Riverside County, authoring dozens of search warrants and affidavits requesting telephonic interception during a five-year period. He also worked a 9-month federal wiretap investigation with the US Attorney's Office in Los Angeles.

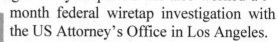

He developed an area of expertise in the field of telephonic interception, and he worked closely with several agents that were exceptional at the recruitment and development of informants. He developed a close working relationship with several local police departments in Southern California, to include Pomona PD, Santa Ana PD, and Beverly Hills PD.

Currently, Scott works part-time as a Sportswriter for the *Elmore Autauga News*.

His debut novel, The Informants, was published in February 2022.

Scott is a 2003 graduate of Auburn University, where he obtained a bachelor's degree in Criminology.

More at: <u>https://www.amazon.com/stores/Scott-Nickerson/author/B09RZDSX6M?ref=ap_rdr&store_ref=ap_rdr&isDramIntegrated=true&shoppingPortalEnabled=true</u>

CAST OF CHARACTERS

CARTEL DE CULIACAN

Juan Montoya – Leader of Cartel de Culiacan following the death of Julian Rodriguez, aka: El Jefe. Previously coordinated with American authorities to arrange for the downfall of El Jefe and the release of his son, Carlos Montoya, from American prison

Carlos Montoya – son of Juan Montoya. Previously witnessed his sister, Maria Montoya, raped by El Jefe's son, Victor. He killed Victor and as punishment was exiled from Mexico and forced to surrender to US authorities. He was released as a result of the deal between his father and the American authorities.

"Pelon" –Montoya's personal bodyguard/enforcer.

"Vaquero" –works for Juan Montoya by meeting with cartel customers and suppliers, coming to agreements and reaching contracts.

Teofilo – head chemist responsible for producing Cartel's meth

DEA

Special Agent Victoria Russo – Senior Special Agent from DEA's Office of International Sensitive Investigations Unit

Special Agent Ana Lucia Rodriguez – Recently transferred by DEA HQs from the El Paso Field Division to the Imperial County District Office in El Centro, California. Only remaining agent still in the field following Operation Raging Bull

Special Agent Remi Choylia – Special Agent from Los Angeles Field Division Enforcement Group 5. Less than two years on the job

Special Agent Bear Johnson – Senior Special Agent from the Los Angeles Field Division Enforcement Group 5.

Stan Paston – Special Agent assigned to Los Angeles Field Division Enforcement Group 5, former military officer.

Johnny Nguyen – Special Agent assigned to Los Angeles Field Division Enforcement Group 5. Parents immigrated from Vietnam.

Cheri Edmonds – Deputy Administrator of the DEA, 2nd in command. Former supervisor of SA Victoria Russo

Dennis Haskell – Administrator of the DEA. Appointed by the President despite limited knowledge of drug trafficking and drug trafficking investigations

CIA

Toby Phillips – Case Officer

Sergio Ramos – Undercover for CIA, works for major telephone company in Mexico that gives information to Cartel de Culiacan

OTHERS

Toro – notorious former assassin that worked for the Cartel de Culiacan. Killed El Jefe when he discovered that his sister that was kidnapped years before was ultimately given to El Jefe, who then married and had a child with her, and threatened to kill her family if she left him. Toro's niece accidentally died as a result of the operation to kill El Jefe.

Leon – former cartel assassin that worked with Toro.

Chapter 1
Hong Kong, China

"Today is a very important day for the future of our organization."

The new leader of the Cartel de Culiacan did not mince words. He was always known as a straight shooter and would not change his ways now.

"Any time a criminal organization such as ours has a change in leadership, there will undoubtedly be a challenge in the beginning. A test to determine the strength of the new leadership. In order to pass that test, we must solidify our agreements with suppliers and customers around the world, which is why we are here."

Juan Montoya looked in the eyes of the three men standing in his room on the 7th floor of the Hong Kong Ritz Carlton.

"Each one of you must be successful in your individual assignment today for the agreement to be solidified. I trust you will."

The room phone rang.

Vaquero, given the nickname for the cowboy boots and 10-gallon black cowboy hat that he always wore, walked over to answer the phone. He listened and nodded his head before giving an update.

"Pelon is ready with the vehicle. El Chino's man is already downstairs. I'll make quick introductions, and then we will follow him to the warehouse." Vaquero looked at Montoya, who nodded and walked out.

The two were followed by Montoya's son, 28-year-old Carlos, and 42-year-old Teofilo, a chemist and family friend for over two decades.

The four men rode the elevator in silence, contemplating their individual roles in the pending meetings. As the elevator doors opened to the spacious lobby, Vaquero exited first and walked toward Li Wang, who raised from a seat as the quartet from the Cartel de Culiacan approached.

Vaquero shook the man's hand, and in English, introduced Montoya.

"Senor Juan Montoya, this is Li Wang."

The two men shook hands and nodded at each other, both realizing they were unable to speak the other's native language, considerably restricting the level of communication.

"Follow me," Wang said in heavily accented English, as he immediately turned and walked out the door and past Pelon, nicknamed for his shaved head, the man in charge of security for Montoya and the delegation from the Cartel.

Pelon's eyes did not dart everywhere, but it was clear that he constantly was assessing his surroundings. The slight nod to Montoya signaled all clear to exit the hotel and proceed to the waiting bulletproof SUV parked outside.

Vaquero grabbed the door as Pelon walked out, scanning the area for possible threats. The head of security was followed by the elder Montoya, with the younger Montoya behind him, and Teofilo third with Vaquero bringing up the rear.

The black Lincoln Navigator was pulled in front of the lobby, and Pelon walked to the front, giving a hand signal to Li Wang that he knew which vehicle to follow.

Once the doors of the Navigator closed, Teofilo glanced at Pelon in the driver's seat, and asked the question that was rumbling around everyone's mind.

"What are the odds that the Chinese are going to turn on us? Or that they just allow some of our rivals to ambush us once we get to the warehouse?"

Each man leaned closer to the leader of the Cartel de Culiacan, who was sitting in the backseat of the Navigator beside Teofilo and his son, Carlos. Vaquero, in the front passenger seat, leaned back to hear the boss' response.

"El Chino has had a deal with the Cartel de Culiacan in place for the last decade. Of course, that was when Julian was the leader. Now that Julian is dead, there is always the chance that they could refuse to deal with us and go with our competitors at the Guardianes del Golfo.

"The previous agreement has made both of our organizations very, very rich. It is true, 90 percent of the methamphetamine sold in the United States today is produced in Mexico, but the chemicals come from China. That is why we are here. We need confirmation the Chinese are going to continue to honor the previous agreement they had with Julian. The market for methamphetamine in the United States is booming, and it is vital that we maintain a supply of methamphetamine.

"But the market here in Hong Kong for cocaine is equally booming, and that is where the Cartel comes in to play. The Chinese triads need our cocaine for the market in Hong Kong. Once these Triads receive the cocaine, they will also transport it to other countries such as the Philippines, Taiwan, Vietnam, Cambodia, and Thailand. It is a mutually beneficial agreement."

Vaquero looked at the three men in the back as the Navigator stopped in a traffic jam on the busy Hong Kong freeway. "Just to be clear, Senor Juan, El Chino does understand a limited amount of Spanish, but he is fluent in English. When I met with him two weeks ago to confirm this meeting, we communicated exclusively in English. I did not get the feeling that he was trying to set us up."

"Let us hope you are right, Vaquero," Juan said, patting him on the shoulder. "You have a natural ability to speak with people, and an even greater ability to get them to agree with you. You know people all over the world. People like you. I like you. Let's hope the Chinese like you, and your natural charisma will make it easier to come to the agreement that needs to be made."

"I hope so, Senor Montoya."

As the vehicles slowed to a crawl, inching along the freeway, they entered underneath an overpass, realizing that the cause for the slowdown was a white Chevrolet Suburban that was stopped in the middle of the right lane, blocking traffic, and causing all the vehicles to merge to the left to move past. All the drivers moved over except Pelon, who pulled the black Navigator right behind the stopped white Suburban.

The security chief looked back at the occupants with dead seriousness. "Everybody please exit the vehicle and enter the white SUV in front of us."

Nobody made a move until the boss said or did something. "What's this about, Pelon?" Montoya asked.

"Pre-arranged vehicle swap, sir. To protect against possible ambush by our rivals, or the rivals of the triad, as well as against aerial surveillance of law enforcement that might be following us. I apologize for not mentioning it, sir, but I considered that it was essential to ensure there were no leaks, intentional or unintentional, that might betray our position, and those of our Chinese counterparts."

Montoya nodded his head approvingly. "Very smart. I like it," and opened his door, quickly moving to the same position in the white SUV. The driver of the white Suburban exited the vehicle and entered the driver's seat of the black Navigator.

Once everyone was in the white Suburban, Pelon quickly drove away.

Moments later, with the assurance that they were not being followed by law enforcement, the contingent from the Cartel de Culiacan walked into a large warehouse, to discuss the deal that would hopefully solidify their future as continued suppliers of methamphetamine in the US market.

* * *

Zang Yin stood as tall as his 5 feet 5-inch frame would allow. Dressed in the finest dark gray Italian suit money could buy, he looked very much the powerful businessman. His control of a powerful criminal gang, or Chinese Triad, as it was known, was not immediately apparent based on his appearance and eloquent speech. The 55-year-old leader of the Chinese Triad 14K offered a warm smile and extended a hand to Vaquero as the men from the Cartel approached.

"Very nice to see you again," Vaquero said, embracing the leader of the 14K.

"The pleasure is mine," Yin said, without a hint of accent. "I trust your travel and accommodations were nice."

"Yes, they were. And I brought you a little something," Vaquero said, unzipping the backpack that he brought into the warehouse, and pulling out a black leather cowboy hat. "Made in Guadalajara. From the very same company that made the hat that I wear."

Yin's smile was genuine and wide. "I love it, my friend. Your offer is very kind. I will value this for a long time," he said, rubbing his finger along the outer rim of the hat, and turning it around in his hand, marveling at its craftsmanship for several moments, before handing it to a worker standing by his side, instructing him to place the cowboy hat in his car so that he could take it home after the meeting.

"Now, shall we get down to business? You gentlemen came a long way."

"Yes, of course," Vaquero said. "First, Mr. Yin, I would like to introduce you to another man that I admire greatly. Juan Montoya is the new leader of the Cartel de Culiacan."

Montoya stepped forward, shaking hands with Yin as the two leaders of their respective organizations met for the first time, sizing the other up while they did so.

"Senor Montoya, I assume these two individuals will be the ones to go offsite?"

"Yes. My son Carlos will take your men to his container at the Port of Hong Kong. As was previously discussed with Vaquero, our good faith offer sealing this agreement will be 2,000 kilograms of cocaine. These will be free of charge. All future transactions obviously will be at a price. That price will depend on the number of kilograms ordered. Any further transactions, if you are satisfied with the product and wish to proceed, will be coordinated with my son."

"Very well," Yin said, nodding his head toward two of his men that walked off with Carlos. "The precursor chemicals that have been collected by 14K are in a nearby location as well. I can have my men take your representative there now."

Montoya turned and waved his hand. "This is my trusted friend, Teofilo. He is a chemist retired from work at the University of Guadalajara. He will be responsible for inspecting the chemicals and manufacturing the production of the product that will go into America."

With another nod of his head, two of Yin's men went out of the warehouse with Teofilo.

"Perhaps we can speak privately while we wait on their confirmation?" Yin asked.

Montoya nodded. Vaquero took the signal and walked to the corner of the large warehouse, where Pelon was silently observing everything, watching for any type of threatening movement towards Montoya. Pelon felt uneasy about this situation but had agreed to it at Montoya's insistence of the necessity to meet in person with the leader of the Chinese Triad 14k.

Once they were alone, Yin spoke up once more. "14K had a long and profitable arrangement with your organization for over 10 years while Julian was in charge. I understand you were his right-hand man during that time, but our paths never crossed."

"I was mostly responsible for coordinating the cocaine shipments, with not only the suppliers in South America, but also the transportation cells in Mexico and the distribution cells in the United States. I honestly had very little involvement in the methamphetamine side of things for our organization. Yet I realize how profitable it is for my organization due to the tremendous appetite the Americans have for the drug."

"The Americans are always a tricky bunch," Yin said. "American law enforcement extends worldwide now, yet it is only because of their citizens that men like us become so wealthy."

"I agree."

"Over the course of time I have been in this position, several of my associates have been arrested on drug related charges. Some of those are still in prison. So, I find it funny now, as we meet, while many of my associates remain in an American prison, that I have seen with my own eyes your son Carlos. The very man who turned himself into American authorities, and received a prison sentence, only to escape while being transferred from a prison in California to a prison in Colorado."

"Are you aware of the details of why my son turned himself in to the American authorities?"

"I have heard rumors. I am not sure which are true, and which are not. Something to do with a disagreement with Julian's son, Victor."

Montoya nodded. "Carlos was once best friends with Julian's son, Victor, until one night at a party he walked into a room and found Victor raping his sister. My youngest daughter. Maria.

"Carlos beat Victor to death. Only because of my friendship with Julian was my son's life spared. But Julian demanded that Carlos turn himself in to American authorities. He spent five years in American federal prison before he escaped."

"I find the timing of that escape somewhat suspect because it occurred at the same time Julian was killed. Did one have to do with the other?"

The tension in the room had grown considerably, and the tightness in Montoya's posture caught Pelon's eye, despite his inability to hear the conversation with Yin. Knowing the eyes of the security chief were on him, and that he needed to choose his words carefully in response to Yin, Montoya replied, "From the information I have collected, Julian was killed by a former cartel assassin named Toro. Evidence collected at the scene of the crime indicates that Toro was there, and he has since disappeared. Toro's murder of Julian was not connected in any way to my son's escape from American prison."

It was the most important lie that Montoya had ever told. Years of playing cards had given him an incredible poker face.

Yin shrugged his shoulders, giving the impression that the question had been more of a fishing expedition than an actual accusation.

"You can never be too careful when dealing with new business partners. Especially those who were recently confined in American prisons and are fugitives of justice. The Americans are well known for turning many drug traffickers into rats, snitches, informants, whatever you would like to call them."

"I assure you that my son is not a snitch or a rat."

"Very well then. As I understand it, Julian's nickname throughout the world was El Jefe, so since you are the new leader, I assume that makes you El Jefe Novo?"

"I suppose that is what I will be called for a while. My nickname is not important."

"So, there has not been any trace of this individual named Toro that killed Julian? I considered Julian a friend. I am most willing to see his killer brought to justice."

"No, there is no sign of Toro, but I assure you that we will be looking for him."

"From what I understand about Toro, he was a very accomplished assassin, and had worked for your organization for many years, eliminating thousands of competitors and corrupt government officials, which makes his turning on Julian all the stranger. But by any accounts, having such a man in your employment is very valuable. Without his presence, who does the Cartel de Culiacan have to take care of the duties that Toro previously handled?"

Montoya had not suspected the direction of the conversation to change toward this area. Furrowing his brow before giving an answer, Yin interjected, "I only ask because having someone such as this Toro, was obviously a very stabilizing force for Julian for many years, until Toro's betrayal of course. But when Toro was loyal, there was never a hint of any type of rebellion against Julian. Will the Cartel de Culiacan have any similar type of stabilizing force in their midst? Because as a business partner, stability is vital."

"Toro is gone, yes, but for what it is worth, someone has stepped in to fill the void left in his absence."

Yin's eyebrows raised. "Really? Who?"

"It is an individual that has remained anonymous, known only as Omega."

"Omega?"

"Yes. It is the last letter of the Greek alphabet. Often used to indicate the end of something. I assume the name comes because when Omega arrives, it is usually the end of that person's life."

"I like it."

"But since Julian's death, reports of Omega have run rampant throughout Mexico. In each instance, as with Toro, our competitors have been eliminated, or those corrupt within our own organization, or perhaps police officers that did not uphold their end of an agreement."

"Just in the last few months?"

"Yes."

"Any chance this individual is Toro?"

"Unlikely. Each operation undertaken by this individual has been posted to social media sites, on different platforms each time. Toro barely knew how to use a cell phone. Also, from watching the videos posted to social media, and the few witnesses at the scene that have described this person, the physical characteristics do not match those of Toro."

"How so?"

"Well, the individual is slighter in build, and moves...differently."

Montoya thought before making the next statement, but ultimately decided it could not hurt. "It is believed that this person, fighting on our behalf, was trained in martial arts, somewhere in Asia."

"That is most interesting," Yin said. "If the identity of this individual is ever revealed, I would be most pleased in a meeting."

"Perhaps that could be arranged."

The conversation was then interrupted by Vaquero. "Just wanted you to know, that Teofilo just called. He said that everything that he looked at is good. Everything necessary to make a considerable amount of meth. The chemicals all check out."

"Very good," Montoya said.

Yin took charge. "One thousand tons of these chemicals will be loaded on a container today and are being shipped to Mexico. They will arrive in a couple of weeks. As a sign of good faith, after speaking with Vaquero previously, I have already arranged for 50 tons of these same chemicals to arrive early. You should have them very soon. They will be landing at the Port of Manzanillo."

This obviously pleased Montoya and Vaquero, as it was a definite sign that the meeting was going well, and the agreement was close to being complete.

The last thing needed was confirmation that the Cartel had provided 2000 kilograms of cocaine as previously agreed upon. The wait did not last long, as someone walked up to Yin and whispered in his ear.

Yin smiled and approached Montoya. "Your son upheld his end of the bargain. All 2000 kilograms were provided in a container. We are thankful for the sign of respect that you have shown us and our people while you have been here."

"Thank you for your time, Mr. Yin."

Vaquero approached the two men respectfully. "Senor Montoya, I apologize for interrupting, but before we leave, I wanted to remind you that I need to travel straight to the private airport in order to make the appointments in California tomorrow. I don't believe there will be time if we go back to the hotel and then I return to the airport."

"Then feel free to take one of my vehicles. I will have Li take you to the airport now," Yin told them.

"Thank you, Mr. Yin," Montoya said. "It is most important that Vaquero make his scheduled appointments tomorrow. He is meeting with many of the different customer groups around Southern California, renewing our agreements and contracts, much like we have done today."

"No need to explain. I understand. Business is business."

"Yes, it is." Montoya looked at Pelon and waived him over. "Mr. Yin, I hope you don't take this the wrong way, but I would like to send my security guy, Pelon, with Vaquero to make sure he gets on the plane safely."

"That is perfectly fine," Yin assured him.

"Sir," Pelon said, "my job is to protect you."

Montoya turned to his security chief. "This agreement is confirmed. Our mission to China has been successful. The next part to ensure the survival, and future success of our organization, is to renew these agreements with our customers based in California. The GDG in the east, and what's left of competing rival cartels in the west have been known to try to intrude on our customer base at times.

"Vaquero must get to California, and he must be successful. I need you to make sure that he gets to the airport. If Vaquero does not arrive on time and safely, then everything the Cartel has accomplished here is worthless. Carlos, Teofilo and I will enjoy one more night in Hong Kong before returning to Mexico on another flight."

"Of course, sir."

The leader of the Cartel de Culiacan turned once more to the leader of the 14K. "It was a pleasure meeting with you. I believe this agreement will be beneficial to both our organizations."

"I agree. The pleasure was mine. We will be in touch Senor Montoya, but I must be leaving." Like a politician with a busy schedule, Yin turned around without any further chit chat, and walked out of the warehouse.

* * *

Since Pelon was escorting Vaquero to the airport, the leader of the Cartel de Culiacan allowed his son Carlos to drive the white Suburban back to the Ritz Carlton while he relaxed in the back with Teofilo. With the stress of the meeting behind them, all three men looked forward to a night of relaxation and fun, dining at a nice restaurant and later taking in the sights, sounds, and women that Hong Kong had to offer.

Once again, traffic in the major city slowed down their return to the hotel. Carlos pulled the vehicle to the valet in front of the hotel so the hotel employees could park the vehicle at a more secure location.

All three men exited the vehicle. As Carlos was handing the keys to a hotel employee, he heard the rev of a nearby motorcycle. Turning his head and walking around the front of the vehicle toward Teofilo and his father 15 feet away, Carlos saw a man on a small motorcycle weaving its way toward their position.

"Father!" he yelled, as Juan looked directly into his eyes.

"Montoya!" screamed the man approaching, heard even over the noise of the nearby traffic and bustle of people on a busy city street.

Juan Montoya turned to look at the approaching motorcycle. From a black bag attached to his back, the man on the motorcycle pulled out a samurai sword. If Montoya had not seen it for himself, he would not have believed it, but the man raised the sword over his head, and swung it with ferocity as the motorcycle rushed by. Montoya, who previously prided himself on quick reflexes, was slow to react at the most important of times.

The motorcycle rushed by Montoya and then his son Carlos. After it passed by, Carlos ran forward to catch his father's body as it fell backwards.

It did not matter, because Juan Montoya's head was no longer attached.

Carlos fell to the ground holding his father's body, and turned around looking for the motorcycle, which was trying to disappear in traffic. In his line of vision, lying on the ground six feet away, was the decapitated head of the leader of the Cartel de Culiacan.

Chapter 2
Burbank, California

"Today is a very important day for the future of our agency."

The same words that were spoken by the leader of the Cartel de Culiacan hours earlier in Hong Kong were now spoken by the Deputy Administrator of the Drug Enforcement Administration through a laptop during a Skype meeting. More than a dozen federal agents were gathered in attendance in a briefing room in Burbank, California. All eyes were on the computer placed at the front of the room. Despite being physically located at DEA Headquarters on the east coast, the Deputy Administrator wanted to provide support to her star agent and the remainder of the team about to embark on one of the most important operations of any during her career.

Cheri Edmonds had risen from the ranks of a Special Agent, all the way to Deputy Administrator of the DEA, second in charge of all DEA. Only one other woman in the history of DEA had gone from Special Agent all the way to Administrator, but Edmonds was determined that she was going to be the second. While she was proud to have achieved such a lofty position within the agency, it was on a somber note, as the promotion only occurred after the gruesome murder of the previous Deputy Administrator by the infamous cartel assassin Toro, in the incident now commonly referred to as the Chinatown Massacre.

Still, some factors were in play against Cheri, mainly the fact that the DEA was long considered a man's world with Type A personalities. Women in power at DEA that were case makers were usually saddled unfairly with the reputation of being a bitch, high maintenance, or a psycho, even when making the same arguments and pushing for the same standards as their male counterparts. But Cheri had defied the odds, delivering case after case as a Special Agent in the New York Field Division, and becoming one of the most be-loved agents in the Division. That popularity had only increased after she had risen through the managerial ranks of DEA, transferring to the New Jersey Office, and promoting from a Special Agent to Group Supervisor to Assistant Special Agent in Charge, Associate Special Agent in Charge. Finally, Cheri had taken over the top spot of the New Jersey Field Division, as the Special Agent in Charge.

With five years to go before the mandatory retirement age of 57, Cheri received the promotion to her role as Deputy Administrator. It was only a matter of time before the President appointed her as the Administrator, leading DEA worldwide. Everybody knew that was coming at some point down the road, and as a result, agents fell over themselves trying to appease her.

While she was not able to be in Burbank for the operation due to obligations at Headquarters, Cheri knew that a little motivation from the future Administrator would go a long way in making sure that all the agents in attendance followed the case agent's directions in every little detail.

Cheri continued. "As I am sure Victoria has briefed you already, it is not very often that a target comes into our path that provides the opportunity to identify so many different drug trafficking organiza-tions, yet that is exactly what is happening today. DEA intelligence obtained from several different sources throughout the world has indicated that an employee from the Cartel de Culiacan known only as Vaquero, will be flying into the Burbank airport. Vaquero is com-ing to Southern California as a representative of the Cartel and is go-ing to meet with every different criminal organization in Southern California that has a contract with the Cartel either for methamphet-amine or cocaine. There has never been a better opportunity to identify so many targets at one time. It could truly dismantle numer-ous drug trafficking organizations throughout Southern California and the west coast.

"You guys are the best at your job. That is why only a handful of agents were selected to join the first ever International Sensitive Investigations Unit. You were chosen for your integrity, as well as your proven success at handling complex cases under stressful circumstances. This group was designed precisely for operations like this which can potentially be highly sensitive and very important, with a chance to shape the entire drug trafficking map in the future.

"Now I will leave you with some words of encouragement. The Administrator and I have a meeting with the Senate Chair of the Intelligence Committee tomorrow at 8:00 a.m. Senator Dylan Prescot is from Arizona and personally wants to be briefed on this operation. So, be successful! It will make my life a lot easier! Good luck and be safe!"

Deputy Administrator Edmonds leaned forward and ended her portion of the teleconference before any questions could be asked. She did not want to usurp the authority that Special Agent Victoria Russo had in the field operations, by answering questions that would cause those in the field to question who was really in charge. Edmonds knew how important it was for there to be one person in charge. Soon, that would be her role for the entire DEA. But for now, on the street, she trusted no one more than Victoria to get the job done.

Special Agent Russo stood at the head of the small room and regained the attention of the audience. Victoria handled herself with confidence that came from her father's side, a long lineage of successful Italian businessmen.

"We all knew the importance of this operation before Deputy Administrator Edmonds spoke to us on the teleconference. The only difference now is that we know a Senator is interested in the outcome. I would not approach this any different if it were for an ounce of crack.

"I cannot stress enough the importance that we do not burn surveillance. When Vaquero lands at the airport in his private jet, he is likely going to be accompanied by several representatives from the Cartel. If we want the opportunity to flip Vaquero and make him a DEA informant, it will only be successful if he is alone. If there is somebody with him, there is no way he will flip. To get him alone, we must not burn surveillance when Vaquero leaves the airport. We must follow him to whatever hotel he is staying at.

"Once we follow Vaquero to a hotel room, I'll take a stab at flipping him. I'll bring David with me," she said, pointing to David Morales, a Hispanic DEA agent recently assigned to the new group based out of DEA HQs.

"In case Vaquero refuses to speak English, David will speak to him in Spanish. However, we know Vaquero is fluent in English. It is fine if he wants to play that game initially; we will play it. But David, we will have to be careful when speaking with Vaquero. He is very suave and good with words, which is the reason that the Cartel chose him to meet with many of these organizations to confirm their contracts. Let us not forget, Vaquero was able to turn one of our very own DEA agents, Reuben Valdez from the Los Angeles office."

The story of Reuben Valdez over the last year was a black eye for the DEA, and it was likely the reason DEA Administrator Haskell was on his way out, to be replaced by the more capable and knowledgeable Cheri Edmonds. Almost a decade earlier when Reuben was a struggling DEA agent, he had been recruited by Vaquero, a cartel representative, and ultimately provided Vaquero information on certain DEA intelligence and locations from Southern California. Reuben's cover had been very effective. Vaquero provided Reuben information on small shipments of money and drugs that Reuben officially seized in his capacity as a DEA agent. But while DEA assets were allocated in one position, Vaquero made sure the Cartel used their own resources to transport bigger shipments of drugs into California, and bigger shipments of money out of California. The loss of 10 kilograms of cocaine in San Bernardino was acceptable when the Cartel was able to move 300 kilograms into Riverside. It was a reasonable loss, and the Cartel had used it many times, moving in tens of thousands of kilograms of cocaine while Reuben became a legend in his own right for dozens and dozens of smaller seizures.

"We're going to flip Vaquero just like he did with Reuben," Victoria said confidently. "I suppose it is some kind of irony."

* * *

An hour later, Victoria stood in the Burbank airport at the Hertz rent a car counter with a 28-year-old male employee. The individual was a source of information, not officially a confidential informant. He provided occasional information to law enforcement for monetary reward.

"That's him, right there," the Hertz employee said, pointing out the window at a Hispanic man that was walking down the stairs of a private jet. Vaquero put on his large black cowboy hat as he walked down the stairs, confirming to Victoria that the source's identification of the Cartel employee was correct. Victoria slid him a $50 bill and walked away, speaking into her hand radio.

There were eight DEA agents from the ISIU group on surveillance waiting for Victoria's confirmation that Vaquero had arrived. "I've got the target in sight. He is getting into a large black Chevy Suburban. Wait...several men just exited the rear of the Suburban, all armed with what appears to be AKs. They patted Vaquero down before he got into the vehicle. The Suburban has a California license plate, last three digits are 987, be on the lookout!"

Victoria rushed outside the airport and hopped into the passenger seat of a GMC Yukon driven by Morales.

Morales updated Victoria as she got into the vehicle, "Surveillance picked up the Suburban. It's just ahead on the road outside the airport perimeter."

"Moment of truth," Victoria said.

As the different DEA surveillance vehicles moved into place in the lanes behind the Suburban, Victoria watched in disbelief as a black SUV with tinted windows pulled in front of Vaquero's Suburban, slamming on brakes. Another black SUV that looked just like the first one came up quickly behind the Suburban.

"Who the hell is that?" Victoria yelled. "They are going to burn down this whole surveillance! We just talked about not burning surveillance!"

Morales looked over at Victoria. "Those vehicles aren't with DEA."

Victoria looked ahead. "Then who are they with?"

Before Morales could answer, the Suburban containing Vaquero reversed, ramming into the black SUV behind it, using all the horsepower it had to push it backwards, giving it just enough room in the front to break away from the obvious trap. By that time, the occupants of the unknown SUVs had already started exiting to approach Vaquero's Suburban, unable to get back into their vehicles.

The Suburban lunged forward, striking the rear bumper of the SUV in front, spinning the vehicle. The Suburban rushed forward and found freedom in the lane to the right.

"What do we do?" Morales asked.

Unsure of what was going on, Victoria knew there was only one thing they could do. "We have to follow Vaquero. But somebody must stay behind and find out who was in those black SUVs."

"Rival cartel maybe?"

Almost in an answer to that suggestion, the driver of the black SUV managed to get back to the vehicle, and promptly hit a switch that turned on red and blue lights from the front, confirming that the vehicle's occupants were law enforcement. The question remained, which law enforcement agency?

Attempting to swerve into another lane to evade the law enforcement vehicles, the Suburban turned quickly, hitting the lane divider at over 40 miles per hour, jumping the divider and landing on two wheels. The momentum of the vehicle caused it to land on its side, skidding another 50 feet as it stopped in the middle of the lane.

"Oh my God, this isn't happening," Victoria said. "We are so screwed."

It got worse. Five men armed with AK 47s crawled out of the Suburban. The men formed a protective semi-circle between the oncoming law enforcement vehicles and the overturned Suburban, which was 100 feet from the fence surrounding the perimeter of the airport. Nothing stood between the Suburban and the fence.

"Flank them to the right!" Victoria ordered David. They were met with a burst of fire from an AK-47, which demolished the grill of the Yukon, one bullet grazing Morales' neck, leaving blood spurting out as he attempted to cover the wound with his hand. In shock, with Morales unable to move, Victoria leaned over and slammed one hand on the brake. With the other hand, Victoria threw the vehicle into park. She tore off the left sleeve of her shirt and gave it to Morales to press against the wound on his neck, which did not appear to be life threatening. She left her phone and dialed 911, putting it on speaker so that Morales could direct first responders to their exact location.

Victoria slid out the passenger side, using the vehicle as a shield. They were stopped 75 feet from the Suburban in front of them. She looked over the hood of the Yukon at the shooters who were focusing most of their fire on the two black SUVs that had tried to stop them.

Then she finally saw Vaquero. Running toward the fence. The semi-circle of armed men formed by the Cartel shooters were protecting Vaquero's dash toward the fence, with nothing between them and the perimeter of the airport.

Victoria looked at the airport, trying to figure out Vaquero's play, when she saw it. A private jet was moving down the tarmac, towards the edge of the airport. Vaquero was going to hop the fence, get on the jet, and try to escape.

"Oh, hell no," Victoria said to herself. Looking to her right, she knew that running after Vaquero towards the fence would leave her without any cover or protection from the Cartel shooters. She would be running away from them but would not be able to lay down any suppressing fire. It was a risk she would have to take.

Before darting out, she peeked behind the door and got a read on the Cartel shooter closest to the fence. Bullets were coming fast and

furious in all directions, but Victoria put her training and marksman-
ship to use, leaning out quickly and placing one deadly accurate .40
caliber shot to the chest of a Cartel shooter from 50 yards out.
Without waiting another second, Victoria dashed toward the fence.
Vaquero was already climbing it and was almost halfway over. The
end of the runway was another 100 meters from the fence. There
was no way she was going to catch Vaquero without a miracle, but
Victoria did not let that stop her, and took off, using the long legs on
her 5-foot 10-inch frame to move as quickly as possible.

She kept her eyes on Vaquero, who had jumped down from the
10-foot fence, and seemed to twist his ankle, as he was noticeably
limping while running toward the jet. Maybe this was the miracle she
needed. Vaquero, unaware he was being pursued by Victoria, had
even taken the time to grab his famous cowboy hat which had fallen
to the ground when he jumped off the fence. Vaquero was gripping it
in his hand as he ran toward the jet. The jet's engine was on and appeared ready for takeoff as soon as Vaquero boarded.

When Victoria was within 20 yards of the fence, she heard bullets
whiz by her head. The Cartel employees had spotted her and were
directing fire toward her. She had no protection.

As she leaped onto the fence to begin the desperate climb over,
Victoria looked behind her, to see a black Dodge Ram truck roar
onto the grass, stopping between her and the Cartel shooters. Victoria realized that her survival would be determined by which side the
driver of the Ram was on.

While the passenger side of the Ram took in the vicious rain of
Cartel gunfire, the driver of the truck, a stout black man just under
six feet tall, jumped out of the vehicle and made direct eye contact
with Victoria even as she was scaling the fence. Leveling her gun at
the newcomer to the party, Victoria saw him pull something from his
pocket and toss it over the top of the truck toward the Cartel shooters. Moments later, the stun grenade went off.

Victoria re-holstered her weapon and turned away from the newcomer, looking back toward Vaquero, who was still hobbling along

toward the jet waiting for him at the end of the runway, now just 30 meters away. She took off with all her speed and energy, willing herself to stride longer and run faster, refusing to let Vaquero get away to never be seen again. Ignoring the burning in her lungs and maintaining a laser focus on the man gripping the cowboy hat, Victoria failed to notice the co-pilot of the jet standing in the doorway with a rifle aimed at her, when another gunshot rang out.

Victoria's eyes temporarily moved off Vaquero and towards the jet, where the co-pilot holding the rifle dropped it to the ground and fell backwards, clutching his chest. Looking behind her, Victoria again noticed the black man, who was apparently a guardian angel. The man had hopped over the fence and was also running in the direction of the jet. He had noticed the co-pilot aiming a rifle at Victoria and had dropped him from a considerable distance away. Whoever the guy was, he was on her side, so Victoria continued her pursuit. The man did not shoot Vaquero, and he obviously wanted Vaquero alive just like she did.

When Victoria was just 30 meters away from the jet, the remaining crew inside pulled Vaquero into the safe confines and immediately closed the door. The jet began accelerating even as Victoria closed within the last 15 meters, but it was a race she could not win. She watched helplessly as the jet moved away from her at a fast speed, and she finally stopped at the edge of the runway, realizing that her chase had been in vain.

While Victoria's chase had ultimately proven unsuccessful, it was not without an effect.

A disastrous effect.

In the jet's attempt to escape, the one pilot, unassisted by his co-pilot that had been shot, was desperately trying to get the jet in the air and out of Burbank airspace, hoping to disappear and find a hidden, friendlier location, for its prized passenger, Vaquero, to disembark. But confusion in the control tower prevented the escape. As Vaquero's jet rushed down the runway, attempting to gather the needed speed to lift and take off, another private jet that had landed was attempting to stop.

Victoria watched in horror, with the guardian angel that had reached her side, as the two jets collided. The sound of the crash of two aircrafts traveling hundreds of miles an hour was stunning, forcing the normally stoic Victoria to turn her face away.

When she looked back, Vaquero's jet was in flames. The left side of the jet had taken the impact. The wing was broken, and it leaned on its right side. The chance that anybody had survived the crash was minimal, but Victoria had to be sure. She and the man at her side took off toward the crash, hoping that Vaquero had survived, if for no other reason than to bring him to justice for his role in the cartel's drug trafficking operations. But this was also personal. Vaquero had turned a DEA agent. If he wasn't going to be an informant, he had to serve time behind bars. Death was the easy way out.

* * *

Victoria and the black man, whose name she still did not know, approached the plane at a full sprint. The door of the jet was at her chest level. Using her momentum and speed, Victoria used a flying sidekick to break the door in. The 4th degree black belt in Tae Kwon Do had no trouble with the door and landed like a cat on her feet on the inside of the jet.

"Pull him out! I'll cover you!" the man at her side yelled, as he hopped into the jet as well.

The man had his gun out, but it was obvious that nobody inside was conscious. Victoria immediately found Vaquero, and grabbed him from behind underneath the armpits, gripping his shoulders, and pulled him out of the jet and onto the ground.

Victoria did not worry about the others still on the Cartel jet. She looked up and noticed medical personnel already at the other jet helping the innocent victims, so Victoria refocused her attention on Vaquero.

He was not breathing. She started CPR and continued for several minutes, but it was to no avail.

He was dead.

On her knees, she leaned back on her heels and looked up at the sky, until finally looking at the man beside her. He seemed to be equally upset about Vaquero's death.

"We might still salvage this," he said to her, but the look in his eyes was the look that this operation had been royally screwed up, and he was in trouble.

"We?" Victoria asked. "Who is we? And why the hell did your team swoop in there and try to arrest Vaquero so close to the airport with so many innocent people that might have been caught in the crossfire? Not only that, but you let him get away. This is your fault!"

"That wasn't my team."

"Then who was it?"

"FBI."

"If that was the FBI, and you're not with them, then who are you with?"

A short silence, and then, "I'm Toby. With the CIA. You're DEA I guess?"

Victoria nodded. "You said we can salvage this?"

"Maybe. You must get Vaquero inside the lobby. There is a small storage supply room on the inside by the women's restroom. Use this cart," he said, flashing his identification and weapon and commandeering the cart from an airport employee.

"What are you going to be doing?"

Toby put on Vaquero's black cowboy that that he had swiped from the jet.

"Is that Vaquero's cowboy hat? What are you doing?"

"Trust me."

"Why would I do that?"

"Because I saved your life twice in the last five minutes. And I didn't even know your name." He tried to deliver the message with a slight smile.

"Ok."

"I'll meet you in that room in 10 minutes," Toby said, and took off running.

* * *

Ten minutes later Victoria stood inside the small room, along with Toby and the recently deceased Vaquero. Frank Dixon from the FBI was also in the room.

"Our time here is limited," Toby said. "Just to make things clear, Frank is FBI, Victoria is DEA. Both of you know who I am."

Looking at the FBI agent, Victoria did not try to hide her disdain. "So, the FBI was responsible for that pitiful attempt at an arrest? I guess the FBI doesn't bother checking to see if other law enforcement agencies are conducting operations in the same area or on the same target?"

Dixon, in a dark blue suit, attempted to puff out his chest. In his mid-30s, the tall, athletic looking white male was not used to being spoken to that way, most especially by a woman, and he noticeably took offense. "The FBI had an arrest warrant for Vaquero. It was based on our investigation when we identified that DEA agent that was working for the Cartel. You know Reuben Valdez, the one we arrested and is in jail now."

The last words were spat out. An insinuation. DEA agents were dirty.

"The bodyguards from the Cartel were captured, and all the FBI agents are safe. Thanks for asking," Dixon said sarcastically.

"Okay," Toby said, trying to place peacemaker. "The FBI had an arrest warrant for Vaquero from their previous investigation. I think that answers some questions. What about you Victoria?"

Staring a hole through Dixon and refusing to break eye contact until he looked away, Victoria said, "DEA intelligence indicated that Vaquero was coming to Southern California as a representative for Juan Montoya, the new leader of the Cartel de Culiacan, and was going to meet with every single criminal organization in Southern California that previously had an agreement with the Cartel when Julian Rodriguez was in charge. It was going to be the best opportuni-

ty in the history of law enforcement to identify every criminal organization in this area. Now that Vaquero is dead," she said looking at
Dixon accusingly, "that will never happen."

"Not our fault," Dixon said defensively. "We had no way to know
that information."

"Yeah, because the FBI thinks their work is always more important than anything anybody else is doing."

"Maybe it is. More so than DEA for sure."

Victoria stared daggers through Dixon, for one time in her career
wishing she could take a swing at a fellow law enforcement officer.
The smugness of the entitled FBI agent was repulsing, and only a
good old-fashioned butt kicking might make her feel a little better,
but it was not the time or the place.

Seeking to divert attention away from himself, Dixon finally asked
Toby what business the CIA had with Vaquero. In her focus and
determination in detaining Vaquero alive, Victoria had not asked
Toby that question.

Both federal agents turned to Toby. "And why did you want
Vaquero's dead body in here?" Dixon asked.

"And why did you take off with Vaquero's hat?" Victoria asked.

"There is going to be a very delicate situation that needs to be
handled very soon, and we were hoping that Vaquero would be able
to help with it," Toby answered.

"What situation is that?" asked Victoria.

"We have a case officer that has been undercover inside a major
telecommunications company in Mexico. He has been there for
years and provided very valuable information, all which has been
verified. After the death of Julian Rodriguez, it seems that the leaders
of the GDG are going to make a power play against their rivals from
the Cartel de Culiacan. They want to take over the drug trafficking
routes for the entire country, taking away the power held by the Cartel de Culiacan in western Mexico. Since a new leader is in place,
they think they have the opportunity to do so."

"How is the GDG planning to take over? And what does Vaquero have to do with it?" Victoria asked. "He's with the Cartel de Culiacan."

A serious expression clouded the face of the CIA case officer as he gave the explanation. "The GDG has coordinated with the Cali Cartel in Colombia that supplies Mexico with cocaine. The GDG is going to intercept all incoming shipments somewhere in Central America and lace each kilogram of cocaine with lethal doses of Fentanyl. But only the kilogram shipments destined to come to the United States. We do not know how to figure out where those shipments are in Central America, or Mexico. Because Juan Montoya just took over as leader, it is not yet clear where he is going to store his narcotics or who he is going to use to distribute the narcotics to the United States. We hoped by locating Vaquero, we would be able to flip him and get him to work with us before all those poisoned and lethal kilograms of cocaine get to the US."

Dixon did not understand. "Why would the GDG intentionally poison all those kilograms going to the Cartel de Culiacan?"

Victoria shook her head, realizing the awful truth. "Because if thousands of kilograms of cocaine are laced with Fentanyl, then criminal organizations will not trust the Cartel de Culiacan and they will not want to use the Cartel de Culiacan as their cocaine supplier. They will rebel and reach out to the GDG. And there might even be a civil war in the Cartel de Culiacan."

"Right," Toby said, "and that's not even the worst news."

Victoria finished his thought. "When this poisoned cocaine gets into the US...tens of thousands of Americans are going to overdose and die."

Toby looked at Vaquero's lifeless body, "and now we *might* not have any way to stop it."

Chapter 3
Los Angeles, California

Four Special Agents from Los Angeles Field Division Enforcement Group 5 sat at an upstairs table in the famous Phillipe's restaurant, known for its delicious French Dip sandwiches. The community style tables were mostly cleared out from the lunch crowd as the time crept past 2:00 p.m. and neared 3:00 p.m.

With no active cases to devote their time and attention towards, the agents were content sitting at the restaurant, away from the office at the nearby Los Angeles Field Division so they could discuss the reported events of the shootout in Burbank the previous afternoon. Reports were suspiciously vague, failing to list the names of the victims or even the law enforcement agencies involved. Eyewitness accounts ran rampant through the local Southern California television stations, telling of a wild-west style gun battle complete with AK-47s and stun grenades.

"You think the DEA was involved?" asked Remi Choylia, one of the newer agents to the group, a 28-year-old whose parents were Google employees that migrated to the US from Malaysia. Remi didn't have much law enforcement experience, but she could tell that something wasn't adding up.

The question was asked to Bear Johnson, a senior DEA agent recently assigned to Group 5 to bring it back to relevance. Group 5 was the former group of Special Agent Reuben Valdez. Following his arrest by the FBI for corruption several months earlier, all the agents in Group 5 were questioned extensively by the internal affairs investigators with the DEA Office of Professional Responsibility. Although each other agent from Group 5 had ultimately been cleared of any involvement, they were all transferred to different groups. The new Group 5 was made up of agents that had never worked with

Reuben Valdez. Bear Johnson was the only one that had ever spoken with Reuben, doing so when he was previously making cases for DEA's Group 1.

"I'm not sure what to think. If DEA was involved, they are keeping a tight lid on what happened. I know people in every group around the Los Angeles Field Division, and nobody said they were involved."

"FBI maybe?" asked Johnny, a Vietnamese-American agent in his mid-30's, with long black hair that came down to his waist when it was not pulled up into a ponytail.

Bear shrugged. "Maybe, but—"

The conversation was interrupted by the vibration of Bear's cell phone, which he had left on the table during the meal. Bear took the call, and a few minutes later, hung up. There was a sparkle in his eyes.

"We might have a case guys," he said with a hint of excitement.

"Who was that?" asked Stan, a quiet, reserved military veteran that had served in combat in the Middle East, but refused to speak about it. Out of respect for Stan, his co-workers never brought it up.

"That was Ana Lucia Rodriguez, from the Imperial County Office in Calexico, at the border with Mexico."

"You know Ana Lucia Rodriguez?" Johnny asked with amazement.

"Who is that?" asked Remi. "I know I've heard that name before."

Bear explained. "She was a Special Agent in El Paso. Had an informant that was crossing the border from Juarez to El Paso. Supposedly the CI was working for the GDG, and a hit team from the Cartel de Culiacan found out. Shot and killed the CI when he was in his car waiting to cross into Texas. A DEA agent from the Juarez office was shot and killed. Ana Lucia and her partner saw it all go down. She ran into the Mexican side to try and help, but she got blindsided by some other members of the hit team, a famous killer named Toro. They knocked her out, took off back into Juarez, and

34

found a tunnel that got them into El Paso. While everybody was looking for her in Juarez, she was being held in El Paso. Long story short, she made it out alive. The hit squad passed her off to somebody else, and some meth head was about to kill her, but Ana Lucia got the drop on him and managed to survive."

"I did hear about that," said Remi. "Wow, sounds like she went through a lot."

"She did. They were going to give her the DEA Administrator's Award for bravery."

"What happened?" Johnny asked.

"And why did she get transferred from El Paso to Imperial County? Who did she piss off?" asked Stan.

"She went to Headquarters and accepted the award. During her acceptance speech, she blasted management for how they treated the other agents involved in the case. One got fired, one got transferred to Training, and one committed suicide. Not to mention the agent that died in the shootout in Juarez."

"I heard about that," said Stan. "Wasn't that the same case Reuben Valdez was involved with?"

"It was, those agents were the ones he was betraying...or so I've heard, but that is all gossip. You know DEA, long on gossip and short on details."

"So, you trust Ana Lucia?" asked Remi.

"With my life," Bear answered.

"Where do you know her from?"

"I was a DEA counselor at training when she went through the Academy ten years ago. She was assigned to my group. Aced every class. Aced every firearms test. Every PT. I kept in touch with her over the years even though we never had any cases cross over. This is the first one. You guys interested?"

"Anything beats sitting around listening to more stories from the glory days," Johnny said. "What does she have?"

"She is in the Los Angeles area now. Said she wants to meet at the Commerce Casino at 4:00 p.m. I say we head straight over there."

The Group 5 agents did not need convincing. They left for the Casino, eager to meet the modern-day legend with the DEA, and see what kind of case she had to offer.

* * *

As is often the case with the buildup to meet someone of a legendary status, Remi expected Ana Lucia to be a physical specimen, and not a 5-foot, 4 inch, 110-pound Hispanic woman. But there was an undeniable fierceness in her eyes, a fierceness that came out as she spoke, that demanded respect from her audience.

"Bear told me that Group 5 has not had much work lately," Ana Lucia started.

"None," Johnny and Remi both confirmed, with Stan shaking his head.

"There's a reason for that. As you all know, the leader of the Cartel de Culiacan was killed a few months ago, and his best friend has assumed the leadership and taken his place. The Cartel de Culiacan's contract with all the American based criminal organizations was made when the old leader was in charge. Now that the new leader, Juan Montoya, is in charge, they are working on deals with their suppliers for cocaine and meth. The Colombians supply the coke, and the Chinese supply the chemicals to produce the meth."

"Sorry to interrupt," Stan said, "but how do you know all this?" He only had five years on the job, but combined with his time in the military, he had heard plenty of people talk about how much they knew and speak confidently as if it were the verified truth, although it was nothing more than speculative belief.

"I'm getting to that. We have an informant. Someone you guys will see in ten minutes." Johnny and Remi nodded, excited at the opportunity. Bear looked at Stan and nodded, giving him the non-verbal cue to hear Ana Lucia out before a decision was made.

"Back to what I was saying...our informant tells us that there are not any drugs coming out of Mexico right now, and there will not be any until the new contracts are confirmed between Montoya and the

Cartel, with the Colombians and the Chinese. But when it does, it is going to be like an avalanche, and we will quickly get overwhelmed."

"So, the DEA isn't really winning the drug war like the bosses in management want us to believe?" Stan joked dryly. "The lack of drug flow is nothing more than a delay in the agreement between the Mexicans and their sources."

"That's correct," said Ana Lucia, again looking at Bear and noting Stan's dry since of humor. Ana Lucia's reputation had not yet won him over as it had Remi and Johnny, the two younger agents. She preferred that, and even respected it.

"So, if there are no drugs coming into the US, or drug money leaving the US, then what does your informant have?" Stan asked.

Ana Lucia smiled. It was the question that made this operation so interesting, and one she was waiting to see who would ask and when.

"That's what we want to find out. The informant is nothing more than a money collector. He lives in Los Angeles, and frequently picks up money in Southern California and drives it to the border and gives it to the Cartel in Mexicali. We picked him off months ago, just after I got transferred, and he has been working with us ever since. We have done two operations with him and identified two additional money guys in Mexicali. We are in the process of going up on wiretaps now.

"There are a couple of interesting things about this case," Ana Lucia said. "First, as Stan mentioned, if there is no drug money coming out of the US, then why is my informant being requested to drop off money? If the money the informant is picking up is not drug money, then what kind of illegal activity is it from?

"The informant has already received money this morning out in San Bernardino. The second interesting thing is that the informant was not instructed to deliver the money to Mexicali like normal. He was instructed to provide it to somebody in Pasadena."

Remi asked the obvious question. "So, all he is doing is driving money from San Bernardino to Pasadena? That is less than a two-hour drive. Why didn't the guy in San Bernardino drive the money to Pasadena? Or vice versa? And how much is it?"

"It's half a million dollars," Ana Lucia answered. "And I don't know the answers to those questions. All I can think is that the people in San Bernardino and Pasadena do not want to risk being stopped with that money because of whatever illegal activity it was derived from. That is what we want to find out. Our goal is to cover the informant as he drives the half a million dollars to the parking lot of a grocery store in Pasadena. We want to follow whoever receives the money, and identify that individual, and where he or she takes the money. We want to figure out why couriers working for the cartel are being asked to transport this money since we know it is not drug money? What makes this money so important?"

Ana Lucia looked at Stan and smiled. "What do you think?"

His facial features rarely revealed his true feelings. He always appeared stoic, with what might be misconstrued as skepticism.

"Sounds good to me. Like Johnny said to Bear before, anything beats listening to his old glory stories," another dry joke, this time eliciting laughs and back pats from Remi, Johnny, Bear, and Ana Lucia.

* * *

An hour later, the five DEA agents watched as Ana Lucia's informant provided a bag containing a half million dollars to a Hispanic male driving a Toyota Camry. After a brief handshake and minimal chitchat, the meeting ended and the new target entered the Camry and traveled to a nearby residential neighborhood in an area bordering Pasadena and South Pasadena.

Johnny happily took over watching the residence for any movement. Surveillance was what he loved most about the job. He promised that he would let them know as soon as the money left the house. Ana Lucia had expressed her desire for the money to leave and go to its next destination.

Remi and Stan knew without being told to take positions around the neighborhood so that the money could be followed away when it left the house. Remi took the north and east and Stan took south and west.

With all necessary positions taken by the younger agents, the two older agents met in the parking lot of a gas station a few blocks away. Bear pulled next to Ana Lucia, and the two rolled down their windows.

After 10 minutes of light conversation, Bear decided to dig a little deeper. "What really happened while you were kidnapped? Those bastards didn't...you know...try to screw around with you, did they?"

The question was extremely personal, but Ana Lucia knew that it was asked by Bear not to be nosy but more from a place of checking on her mental well-being. Bear was one of the few people in the world that would not be on the receiving end of Ana Lucia's sharp tongue.

"No. They didn't touch me other than right at first when they knocked me out. Weirdly, the leader seemed to be protecting me against the other guys on his team. I don't know what would have happened if he wouldn't have been there."

"You mean that guy Toro?"

"Yeah."

"The same one that later killed his boss, the leader of the Cartel de Culiacan, and then disappeared?"

"The same one."

"Well, I'm glad he didn't hurt you."

"Thanks."

Their conversation ended as the squelch of the DEA radio came through both of their cars.

"Guys, we have an issue," Johnny said. The usually dependable surveillance agent sounded unsure of himself. Bear had never heard that in Johnny's voice.

"Five guys just came out of the house, *all* with bags. All five are getting in five different cars in the driveway. Which car do we follow?"

Bear nodded to Ana Lucia in deference. She answered, "Follow the biggest bag."

"They're all the same size."

"I guess just pick one vehicle, and we will follow it. We'll have to let the other four go."

Johnny picked a silver Honda Civic as it traveled toward Remi's location. She pulled behind the vehicle and deftly moved behind without being noticed, as the remainder of the DEA team did the same.

It did not take long until the Civic reached its destination, a local bank just two miles away from the residence.

"Well, this is something I didn't expect," Ana Lucia admitted. "Johnny, you don't look like a fed. Follow the guy in that bank and see which bank teller he speaks with and how much money he deposits."

Johnny did not need to be told more than once. He exited the car and followed the Hispanic male into the bank.

He walked out five minutes later, and immediately got on the radio. "The target went up to the bank teller on the right. I actually know the guy."

"What? Are you serious?" Bear asked.

"I'm serious."

"Where do you know him from?"

Johnny paused, perhaps embarrassed to admit it. "I know him from the clubs."

Ana Lucia laughed, realizing what the other Group 5 agents already knew. "You go clubbing in Hollywood?"

"Yeah! I do!" he said. "Just because I'm a fed doesn't mean I don't know how to have a good time. And let me tell you, the Hollywood girls can't get enough of a hot Asian guy with killer dance moves."

"Hot or homeless Asian guy?" Stan joked again dryly. "You look like you haven't had a haircut or beard trim in years."

"Okay, let's get back on track guys," Bear said. "Johnny what do you think? I see the Honda Civic guy walking out now."

"I know that bank teller is desperate around women. Does anything for them. Whatever they say. Remi and Ana Lucia goes in there, flash the badge, maybe flirt with him a little, they'll do whatever he asks. Guaranteed."

"Let's do it," Ana Lucia said. Providing her last instruction on the radio before getting out of the car, she said, "You guys follow the Civic and see where it goes while me and Remi go inside and talk to the teller. Good luck."

* * *

Remi met up with Ana Lucia in the parking lot of the bank as soon as the Honda Civic left. While Ana Lucia had more of an athletic frame, she prided herself on hitting the gym at least four times a week, she could not deny that Remi was a looker. Long black hair and dark eyes, with a slender frame and toned legs, Remi surely had her suitors. However, as Ana Lucia had experienced herself, many men were scared off by a successful woman, especially one that excelled in a man's world like the DEA. The two would use their womanly wiles to their advantage.

Walking in with a snug button up shirt, Ana Lucia suggested Remi unbutton the top two buttons to provide the slightest hint of cleavage. A young agent willing to do anything to help the case, Remi willingly complied.

Ana Lucia considered herself an advocate for women's rights and was usually the first to express disgust at young women that used their physical assets alone to woo shallow men.

In this instance, she had no problem with doing what was necessary to get the job done. If that meant showing a little skin, then that is what they would do. It was one of the few instances in drug law enforcement when she had an advantage as a woman.

Twenty minutes later, the duo walked out of the bank, armed with the information they had been seeking, and unable to contain their smiles.

"Good job back there," Ana Lucia smiled, giving Remi a fist bump as she pulled out her phone. "Let's find out where the guys are."

They walked over to Ana Lucia's car and waited for Bear to answer.

He was clearly driving and on the move when he answered.

"What did you find out?" he asked.

"The guy deposited $9975 into an account for a legit business, a soybean company. It was an obvious attempt at avoiding the $10,000 threshold which requires the bank to report the deposit."

"That would make sense," Bear said. "We just followed the Civic to two other banks. He must have been making more deposits under $10k. Another thing, as we were leaving the last bank, Johnny saw one of the other cars that left the house pull into the same lot. I think all those cars that left the house are doing the same thing."

"Where are you right now?" Ana Lucia asked.

"Another bank. This is the fourth one."

It was not the last. In all, the Civic was followed to 10 different banks, the driver carrying the same sized bag each time.

Ana Lucia directed the Group 5 agents to continue following the Civic after she and Remi caught up. Finally, after a long day of surveillance, they saw the meeting they had been waiting for.

The Civic pulled into the parking lot of a Whole Foods grocery store. The driver met with a white male driving a Toyota Tundra truck and handed over the receipts from his various bank deposits.

Stan quickly ran the license plate of the Tundra and relayed that it was registered to a man named Romeo Sheffield. A picture of Romeo's DMV photo was emailed to Stan, and he was able to confirm that the white male they were watching was indeed the very same Romeo.

"I can say this because I'm not a white boy and I'm not Hispanic," Johnny joked, "but with all the Hispanic drug dealers in Los Angeles, how does a Hispanic DEA agent bring us a lead and the target ends up being a white guy? Am I the only one that finds this ironic?"

Even the stoic Stan cracked a smile at this remark and offered his own attempt at humor. "Maybe Ana Lucia just has something against white guys?"

"Actually...the opposite. I think white guys are hot."

"Maybe you got a shot Stan!" Johnny said over the radio.

Stan did not answer. He was notoriously private about his personal life. In the five years he had been with the DEA, he had never once spoken about anyone he dated. Further, he never salivated at other women as many of his co-workers frequently did during an operation on the street. Realizing that Stan seemed to have an unbreakable armor that concealed his private life, his co-workers from Group 5 enjoyed finding any opportunity to discover something about Stan's likes and dislikes.

Before anybody had a chance to say something else, Romeo was on the move. The Group 5 agents, along with Ana Lucia, followed the Tundra as it traveled south on the 110 freeway and into the heart of downtown Los Angeles, traveling down Figueroa Avenue. Romeo made his way to the LA Live entertainment center, and valet parked his vehicle, going into a new steakhouse that had just opened around the corner from the former Staples Center, where the Lakers and Clippers held NBA games several times a week during the year in the winter, spring, and early summer.

Ana Lucia told the Group 5 agents that she wanted to see who Romeo met with. If it was clear that he was on a date, then they would leave. But if not, perhaps he was meeting with someone important.

It was not obvious at the time, but Ana Lucia's desire to maintain surveillance and not go home, and the Group 5 agents' willingness to continue, paid off in a way that would have ramifications for years to come.

Johnny and Remi went inside the restaurant hand in hand, pretending to be on a date. The Vietnamese and Malaysian pair were the least likely of all to be mistaken for feds. After waiting for 20 minutes, Romeo finally met with a tall white man in an expensive looking black suit. The men shook hands and briefly chatted before Romeo handed over an envelope with all the receipts that had been provided to him earlier that day.

Remi was able to slyly get a picture of Romeo handing the envelope to the man in the suit. It was a perfect shot, with a clear photo of the face of the man in the suit. She sent the photo in a text to the agents in Group 5, along with Ana Lucia.

"This guy in the suit looks familiar...can't place him. Anybody?"

Stan, the former military man, was the first to reply to the text.

"That's Bobby Lightfoot. Congressman Bobby Lightfoot."

Chapter 4
Hong Kong, China

The instructions were simple. Inflict as much pain as possible prior to death. What the Chinese triad 14K had started, Pelon would finish.

Eduardo Rodriguez stood in the middle of a large warehouse on the outskirts of Hong Kong. His hands were bound together and raised above him, tied around a pipe on the ceiling. He was forced to stand on the balls of his feet, barely touching the floor. That was painful enough because every toenail had been ripped out as part of the initial round of interrogations by the 14K.

Yin, the leader of 14K, had assured Carlos Montoya that his father's killer would be found within 48 hours. True to his word, the killer was discovered, attempting to board a boat to Thailand.

The identity of the killer was not questioned by Carlos, who had decided to keep his father's death a secret until such a time that he was able to gather his wits and decide what was the best course of action. Carlos knew that his life likely depended on that decision, not to mention the lives of the thousands of people working for the Cartel de Culiacan.

Carlos heard the killer yell the name Montoya, prior to his heinous act. It came from the tongue of a Hispanic killer. In Hong Kong, that drastically reduced the number of suspects. It also helped limit the search.

Yin's promise to have the killer identified and standing in front of Carlos was something that the new ruler of the Cartel de Culiacan would be eternally grateful for. Since his own resources were limited in a foreign country, he had been reliant on Yin to do what he said he would do. He had. Now was the time for Pelon and Carlos to confront the killer.

Carlos remained seated in a chair in the shadows while Pelon moved forward to approach the young man.

"Eduardo Rodriguez. Bastard son of Julian Rodriguez. Killer of Juan Montoya. Do you deny any of these statements?"

Resigned to his fate, and determined that he would not beg or plead for mercy, Eduardo simply said, "No."

"Prior to his death, Julian Rodriguez was married twice. He had two *legitimate* children, Victor and Esmerelda, both of which are dead now. He did however, father 31 *illegitimate* children from a variety of different whores. That much is well known."

Eduardo's facial features changed slightly, but he remained silent.

"Were you unaware that you had 30 other brothers and sisters?" Pelon asked.

Eduardo did not answer.

"You are the oldest of El Jefe's remaining children," Pelon said, referring to the nickname that the old leader of the Cartel was known by. "Just like you were taken care of, your father made sure that all the other 30 bastards were well taken care of financially. Your siblings are in private schools all around Mexico. Whether or not they know their true parentage, I don't know. I can only assume the woman that was raising you told you of your father's identity."

"It didn't take much to figure it out," Eduardo spit out. "My mother never had a job, and we lived in a huge house and I went to the most prestigious and expensive academy in Mexico City. My father provided for his son, even though my mother was not his wife. My father did not deserve to die."

"And you blamed Juan Montoya for your father's death?" Pelon asked. "Did you know that they were friends since childhood? That Juan was second in command of the Cartel for the entire time that your father was in charge?"

"Juan had that animal Toro kill my father because he was jealous and wanted to be the leader himself. It is Juan's fault my father is dead. I had to avenge my father's death."

"There are many things that you do not know and are incapable of realizing without more life experiences. But I promise you, in the short amount of life you have remaining, I will give you plenty of life experiences."

Pelon walked behind Eduardo and took out the first instrument of pain that he planned to use on the young man, a good old-fashioned baseball bat. Nothing too complicated.

Both knees and shins received ten whacks. Nothing more was left than broken and crushed bones. The man's screams echoed loudly throughout the warehouse after each swing.

The ropes holding Eduardo overhead were cut, and he fell to the floor in a heap.

Pelon again moved behind Eduardo. "Since you will never walk again, what's the point of even having your feet?"

With one swoop, Pelon used the sword that had been found with Eduardo, the very same one that had killed Juan, and sliced off the young man's feet.

Sitting in the back, Carlos smiled at the level of pain that was being inflicted on his father's murderer. He had only one request: "More."

Tourniquets were wrapped around Eduardo's legs to stop any bleeding that would cause a premature death. The ultimate disgrace was still to come.

Over the next 30 minutes, a series of ungodly measures were performed on the individual that had decapitated the leader of the Cartel de Culiacan.

After breaking his legs and cutting off his feet, Pelon used a sharp butcher knife to pluck out Eduardo's left eyeball. He left it dangling from his head by one of the nerve endings still attached.

Eduardo wished for death, but Pelon made sure that none of his injuries would grant his request. Not yet. Pelon then tore off Eduardo's pants, grabbed a hold of Eduardo's genitals, and sliced them off. But still his torture was not over yet.

Pelon grabbed a can of gasoline, and poured a small amount on Eduardo, who was lying on the floor, unable to move, drifting closer and closer to unconsciousness. A flame from a cigarette lighter was tossed on Eduardo, and he went up in flames. Despite his mouth being taped shut, the sounds that came from Eduardo revealed that he was still very much alive.

Again, Carlos smiled from the corner.

After 10 seconds, Pelon put the flames out. They had ravaged the man's body, melting away much of the skin from his head, face, and arms. But still he lived. Barely.

Finally, Carlos rose out of his seat and walked over to El Jefe's oldest living son.

"You have killed my father," Carlos told Eduardo. "That has forever changed my family. Now, I will forever change yours."

Carlos paused for effect, and circled Eduardo before speaking again. "Your mother will be the first to die. But do not worry, before she dies, she will be raped repeatedly by anybody that wants a piece of her. Then, her head will be cut off, along with her legs and arms. The rest of her body will be burned. It will be like she never existed.

"But the damage caused by your treachery will not end there. Your brothers and sisters, all 30 of them, will be dead by the end of the month. Yes, I know they are mostly teenagers and young kids. It does not matter. They might grow up to be like you one day, seeking revenge, and I will not take that chance. 30 kids are going to die because of your reckless and foolish actions. And I am going to make sure they suffer, just like you have today. Goodbye Eduardo. Say hello to your father tonight when you see him in hell."

48

Chapter 5
Lompoc, California

The thick metal door shut behind them as Victoria and Toby sat in plastic chairs at the side of a brown wooden table. Victoria placed her backpack on the table and pulled out her laptop as they waited. It had taken a considerable amount of pull to receive approval to bring the laptop into the inner corridors of the federal prison, and also to reserve a large private room. At the instructions of the CIA case officer, Toby made sure everything was removed other than the table and three chairs. Two were on one side of the table. A single chair was on the other side where the prisoner would sit.

"I really appreciate you coming along. I know my agency does not work with your agency very often...at least not in the field on domestic operations. I really hope this works," Toby said, glancing at Victoria.

"The way I see it, this is the only play we have left. Otherwise, tens of thousands of American citizens are going to die, not to mention the huge cartel war that it will incite in Mexico."

"You think he'll want to do it?"

Victoria shrugged. "All we can do is ask. I read his file. No family. Really no friends other than co-workers, and almost all of them abandoned him after his arrest. No one will ever know if he leaves here. It is on us to convince him. My question is, if he's been in solitary confinement 23 hours a day for the last six months, how do you know that he's lost 30 pounds?"

"Contacts on the inside," Toby answered simply.

"But he's still going to be 20 pounds too heavy, and three inches too tall."

"I know, but he's the only person we have access to with any knowledge of Vaquero."

"Well, we are about to find out."

The CIA case officer and the DEA agent looked up as the metal door opened. The prisoner had a bright orange jump suit and was shackled at the feet and arms. The shackles were removed, and the prison guards exited the room without saying a word.

Sitting across from them was disgraced former DEA Special Agent Reuben Valdez.

* * *

"Hello Reuben, my name is Victoria. I work with the DEA's International Sensitive Investigations Unit out of DEA Headquarters. This is Toby. We have some critically sensitive information that needs answers, some of which we hope you might have. Would you be willing to speak with us?"

Reuben stared at Victoria. "You said you're with DEA, but you didn't say who he is with." Reuben looked at Toby. "Who do you work for?"

Toby smiled politely. "Hi, Reuben, I'm with the CIA."

Victoria noted that Reuben was still mentally sharp, at least sharp enough to catch that she had not disclosed who Toby was working for. Six months in solitary confinement had not drained his mental faculties yet, which was a good thing.

Reuben's eyebrows raised slightly, but otherwise did not show any emotion. "What do you guys want with me?"

"Before we get to that, I personally want to hear some answers directly from your own mouth. Is that okay?" Victoria asked.

Reuben shrugged his shoulders and gave a quick head nod.

"We never worked together, or had any kind of communication to my knowledge, so what I know of your work ethic and reputation is limited to reports and people that I know that knew you. But like I said, I want to hear directly from you, to judge where you are mentally. I know you pleaded guilty to corruption. You requested, and received, an expedited sentencing. 18 years in prison, knowing you were going to get solitary confinement must have been difficult to accept. Why did you expedite the sentencing request?"

"Because I was guilty. The longer I held out, the more negative publicity that came out against the DEA and my co-workers, none of which were involved. I didn't need a trial to tell me everything the FBI had. I know what I did." Reuben's raspy voice revealed a man that had said very few words, to anyone, for almost half a year.

"I knew solitary confinement was coming. I put a lot of guys in prison. I knew they wouldn't let me in general population."

"Fair enough," Victoria said. "I read your file. I know that your cartel contact, Vaquero, gave you information about shipments of drugs and drug proceeds, some of which you lawfully seized. But by doing so, you knowingly directed law enforcement personnel away from other locations where much larger shipments of drugs and money were. Do you feel like the means justified the ends? I mean it is not like you did not get anything. You were seizing *some* dope and money."

Victoria was giving Reuben the chance to justify his unlawful actions. By acknowledging some of his good deeds, she wanted to see where the man's morals were. Was he truly remorseful for his actions, or would he attempt to minimize his crimes by explaining all the success he had experienced?

"I broke the law. That's all that matters. Nothing justifies a federal agent making a deal with the cartel."

Victoria breathed a small sigh of relief. That was what she had hoped Reuben would say.

Toby leaned forward to ask his next question. "How many times did you meet with Vaquero prior to your arrest?"

"In person, about a dozen times. Most of our communication was through text. He was the go between for me and the Cartel, so I never had to speak to anyone in the Cartel."

"We are aware of that," Victoria said. "Vaquero's previous role in the cartel was as the point of contact for multiple people in Southern California. He was in that role when the Cartel was led by Julian Rodriguez. Would you be surprised to learn, that after Julian's death, and Juan Montoya assumed leadership of the Cartel, that Vaquero began working for Montoya? In fact, he was the only Cartel member that previously worked for Julian and that is now working for Juan."

"Not surprised. Vaquero was always very smooth with his words. He had a country twang to his speech. It caused some people to let their guard down around him. Also, he was very...eloquent the way he spoke. Very persuasive. So no, I'm not surprised."

Victoria continued. "Vaquero's new role in the Cartel is to contact the different criminal organizations in Southern California and arrange a new contract between them and the Cartel now that Montoya is the leader. Vaquero flew into the Burbank airport two days ago. He was supposed to meet with all the different criminal organizations in Southern California and the Western United States. The Crips and the Bloods in South Central. The Mexican Mafia in Inglewood. The Hell's Angels in San Bernardino. Other groups in Riverside, Palm Springs, Vegas, and Arizona. In all, he was supposed to meet with 32 different groups over a seven-day period."

"What happened to him?" Reuben asked, picking up on Victoria's use of Vaquero in the past tense.

"He died in an accident at the Burbank airport."

"An accident? What kind of accident?"

"Well, DEA's goal was to follow him to his hotel, and when he was alone, approach him and try and flip him. Make him become an informant for DEA. But unknown to us, the FBI swooped in and tried to arrest him. Vaquero had security with him that got into a shootout with the FBI agents trying to arrest him. Vaquero tried to escape back to the airport and leave on a jet, but the jet was hit by another plane. Vaquero didn't make it and died at the scene."

"That's too bad," Reuben said. "He deserved jail. But what does that have to do with me?"

"We're getting there," Toby said. "But just so you know, eyewitness accounts saw a man running away from the scene of the accident wearing Vaquero's infamous black cowboy hat, so there is speculation that he survived."

"You just said Vaquero died."

"That's right."

"So, the person that ran away with Vaquero's cowboy hat was not Vaquero."

"No."

"You ran away with Vaquero's cowboy hat?"

Toby nodded.

"Why did you want it to appear Vaquero was alive?" Reuben asked, before a sudden look of realization swept over his face. Reuben shook his head. "You want me to impersonate Vaquero because I'm the only one that knows him. It won't work. I'm taller and bigger than Vaquero, even though I've lost 30 pounds."

"We know," Toby said. "Vaquero was almost 6 feet tall and weighed 190 pounds. You are 6' 3", and I am guessing now weigh about 210." Toby placed Vaquero's cowboy hat on the table. "Like Victoria said, Vaquero was preparing to meet with a bunch of organizations from Southern California and the West Coast, all for the first time. None of those guys had previously met with Vaquero. They do not know what he looks like. If a Hispanic male shows up with a cowboy hat, is dressed like a cowboy, and speaks with authority, they will believe that man is Vaquero."

"You want me to pretend to be Vaquero so that you can identify these organizations and arrest their leaders."

"That's right," Victoria said. "You have more knowledge of Vaquero than anybody else. You know how he dressed. How he walked. How he talked. How he texted. His slang words. You will only work in the US. Obviously, you would not go to Mexico where somebody might recognize you are not the real Vaquero. Interested?"

"Possibly. This explains why the DEA is involved in this operation. It doesn't explain why the CIA is involved." Reuben turned toward Toby. "Why are you here?"

Vitoria was hoping to get an answer from Reuben before revealing that thousands of lives potentially hung in the balance. Doing so would take away leverage they might have. Who knows what Reuben might request in addition to release from prison? Again, she noted that he still appeared mentally sharp.

Victoria had to admit, many times she came across rigid and by the book, a fed in its truest form. By contrast, Toby carried himself casually. His smile was friendly and not forced. His physical stature was not imposing. He was 5'10 and 200 pounds. A little excess weight but not fat. Not too tall. He spoke as if he were talking to a buddy and not a suspect. His intelligence and aptitude for language were even bigger pluses. Fluency in Spanish, Portuguese, and Italian offered him his pick of many desirable foreign CIA offices, and he had chosen Mexico. If Toby could not convince Reuben to join them, then Victoria did not think anyone could.

"There is another reason the CIA is involved. You were correct to suspect more. To put it simply, thousands of American lives are at risk, and we need your help to save them. As you know, the Cali Cartel from Colombia supplies both the two major cartels in Mexico, the Cartel de Culiacan, and the GDG. With the change in leadership at the Cartel de Culiacan, the GDG is trying to take over the drug trafficking corridor through Western Mexico. They made an agreement with the Cali Cartel to lace 50,000 kilograms of cocaine with lethal amounts of Fentanyl. They are hoping with so many deaths, the Cartel de Culiacan will lose control. Customers in the US will stop dealing with them. Law enforcement in the US will increase efforts to go after the Cartel de Culiacan and put pressure on the Mexican government, and their own workers might start rebelling against them when they realize the cause is hopeless."

"I understand that part. It is not surprising. Why doesn't the CIA or DEA just use a snitch or undercover in Mexico to stop the dope somewhere in Mexico before it gets to the US? I want to get out of prison, but obviously using a snitch already in the field with knowledge of the situation would be the best play."

"I'll answer that," Victoria said. "When Montoya took over as leader, he made a wholesale change. New contracts, new workers, new stash locations. Right now, nobody knows who Montoya is going to use in Mexico to move his dope, so there is no one to target to try and convince to cooperate. Nobody knows where he will stash the dope in Mexico when he collects it, so there is nowhere to initiate surveillance. We are in a tough place. With your help, we hope to identify the different criminal organizations in the Southwest US, and intercept the dope before it gets to them, saving the lives of all the people they would distribute the dope to."

Reuben took in the information, rubbing his face, deep in thought. "How long has it been since Vaquero died at the airport in Burbank?"

"Two days," answered Victoria.

"And there was not any information released that he died?"

"None. There were five deaths reported. The five security members of his team."

"How would I even contact the criminal organizations in Southern California? Or Montoya?"

"Vaquero had his phone on him when he died. We have his phone in our possession."

"Is Montoya blowing up Vaquero's phone up trying to find out what happened? This could be over before it gets started."

Victoria and Toby looked at each other. "Actually, there has been radio silence from Montoya for several days. Not sure why. It is possible Montoya suspects Vaquero was captured by law enforcement. If you text him as Vaquero and let him know that you-Vaquero- survived, spent the last two days avoiding law enforcement and getting out of the area, then maybe that will work. It is the least we can try. Go ahead and let Montoya know that Vaquero has reached out and contacted the gangs in LA. Montoya is desperate to get the contracts made. He'll go for it."

"And if Montoya wants to speak or communicate by video?"

"Then make sure he doesn't."

"What about all the groups Vaquero was supposed to meet with?"

"They ARE blowing up Vaquero's phone."

"What's the plan for use of his phone? Will I be given Vaquero's phone?"

Victoria took the lead on this question. "DEA will provide you with a phone. Obviously, we will be able to monitor all the conversations and text messages coming and going. There will also be tracking on the phone in case you get in trouble and we need to rescue you."

Reuben smirked and leaned forward, responding in his deep, raspy voice, "You mean in case I run, and you need to find me."

"It serves both purposes," Victoria said.

"So, you want me to risk my life to save a bunch of drug dealers and drug addicts in the United States that will be snorting and ingesting poisoned cocaine in the next few weeks. That is ultimately what this is coming down to, right?"

"The lives of Americans are at stake," Victoria said. "Yes, they might be drug dealers and drug addicts. But they deserve the right to live, do you agree? A chance to redeem themselves and restore their reputation, much like you are getting to do now?"

"Yeah, but nobody will ever know about my efforts. If this is successful, it will be covered in the news cycle for about a day, before the next big thing comes along. Drug addicts around the world will forget within a month."

"Yes, that's possible," Toby conceded. "But at the end of the day, with the information that we have, the best thing to do, the right thing to do, is to try and stop all those people from overdosing and dying. Do you agree?"

Reuben did not tip his hand. "Does the FBI know you are going to let me walk out of here? How in the world would this get approved?"

Victoria clicked a button on the laptop that was on the table. She turned the laptop around so that it was facing Reuben. In a live video conference meeting was the Deputy Administrator of the DEA, along with the Attorney General of the Department of Justice, Steve Whittaker.

"Hello, Mr. Valdez," Deputy Administrator Edmonds said. Since he was fired from his position with DEA, Reuben had always noticed that he was never referred to as former Special Agent Valdez. It was a small slight, but a slight, nonetheless.

"I have spoken with Special Agent Russo, and she has updated me on the details of the investigation. Together, we have discussed this situation with Attorney General Whittaker, and in the interest of public safety, the Department of Justice has decided that the potential benefits of your release outweigh any benefit the US government may receive from maintaining your incarceration."

"That's correct," the Attorney General said. "Just this morning, I spoke with the President of the United States. He signed your pardon, pending your agreement to work with the DEA and CIA. If you abide by the rules they set forth, then the agreement will be honored."

"What if I abide by the agreement, but the operation is still unsuccessful?"

"Then the pardon will be upheld."

Reuben noticeably rolled his eyes in disbelief. He had seen promises made and broken by government employees, especially those in power seeking to maintain that power. Reuben knew that the moment something went wrong, one if not both the people on the computer screen in front of him would disavow all knowledge of his actions. They would claim that he was working without their authority, and that the mission he had partaken was reckless and dangerous. He smirked at this realization, as he looked at Victoria and Toby, realizing that they were going to be the ones having to answer these questions. Reuben was already a convict. What more could they do to destroy his reputation?

Victoria met Reuben's glare with a steely one of her own. Her dark green eyes bore deep into Reuben. He sensed in her a determination that he had only seen in one other agent during his DEA career. And he liked it.

"I've made my decision. That last question was more of a joke. I am not going to even pretend to believe that the DOJ will uphold their end of the agreement if this thing goes sideways. But the way I see it, the chances are highly likely that I will not live to see my freedom. There are too many variables that are uncontrollable."

"We don't want you to die, Reuben. That is not why we are here. I will do everything I can to make sure that doesn't happen." Victoria seemed sincere. Reuben trusted her. He liked Toby. In different circumstances, they could have worked together and been friends.

Reuben waved his hand in dismissal. "Don't worry, I'll do it. I would rather die out there in the world than live here in solitary confinement. But I do not want to die. I'll try to make this work...but on one condition."

Here it was. Victoria knew this was coming. Some condition that had to be upheld for Reuben to agree to work with them. Likely some unreasonable agreement like a million dollars or a house in the Alps. She was genuinely surprised by Reuben's one condition.

"If you read my file, you know that one of the last things I did was meet with Toro in Tijuana. I had to pass on information in person that was provided to me by Vaquero. The meeting in Tijuana ended when the Mexican Federal Police stormed in. I got caught in the line of fire and took a bullet in the side. Toro and his team of assassins wiped out the Federal Police team that came in, which gave all the bar patrons time to escape. I thought I was going to make it back to the US safely, but one of Toro's workers, this huge goon named Leon, came after me. Tried to track me down and kill me. And he would have, but an agent that I worked with from San Diego came and rescued me."

"Tyler Jameson," Victoria said.

"That's right. Tyler had a wiretap. He discovered that I was dirty, working with the Cartel, but he did not know how. But Tyler also heard on the wiretap that the Cartel had sent Leon to kill me. Tyler took a wiretap monitor from San Diego that spoke Spanish, and they went into Tijuana and rescued me, saved me from Leon. I was moments away from being murdered when Tyler saved me. After I was arrested by the FBI for corruption, the DEA decided to get rid of Tyler. He was suspended immediately, but he was officially terminated several weeks ago. I know that because Tyler is the only person left in this world that still writes me. Everybody else has abandoned me. Everybody except Tyler."

"So, what's the condition Mr. Valdez?" the Attorney General asked.

"I will work with Victoria and Toby. I will impersonate Vaquero. I will try to save all those drug addicts from overdosing. I will try to identify all those criminal organizations that have contracts with the Cartel. But I will *only* do it if it is promised that Tyler Jameson will be reinstated as a DEA Special Agent. He should have never been fired. I deserved what I got. Not Tyler. He is a good man and was the best agent on the west coast. What the DEA did to him because of me was a miscarriage of justice."

Deputy Administrator Edmonds leaned forward. "I appreciate your loyalty to your old co-worker, but re-instatement isn't that easy."

"Sure, it is. Tyler reapplies. You accept it. Without your word that will happen...I do not agree."

Edmonds looked at the AG. They held a brief discussion before coming back to the screen. "It's a deal," Edmonds said. "Tyler will be reinstated at the end of the operation."

Reuben smiled. "Thanks Deputy Administrator. But honestly, I do not trust you, or any other person in DEA management. Your promises mean nothing to me. Less than nothing. Reuben turned to Victoria and said, "I do trust her. I can see it in her eyes. She's not like the rest of you."

Reuben directed his words at Victoria, forgetting Toby and the attendees in the video conference. "Give me your word that you will make sure Tyler gets reinstated at the end of this, whether or not I live. If you give me your word, then I will do what you ask. I'll impersonate Vaquero."

Victoria maintained Reuben's stare. She did not look at the Deputy Administrator for confirmation before agreeing. "You have my word. Now we need to get started. Immediately."

Chapter 6
Long Beach, California

The four members of Group 5 gathered in a corner booth of the small, privately owned restaurant feet from the Pacific Ocean. Specializing in fried and grilled seafood, Bear's favorite was the grilled shrimp, but he had tried everything on the menu, and knew that it was all delicious. It was a good place to bring the new group and enjoy a lunch on a beautiful Southern California day, which was the pretext for the meeting that Bear gave to DEA management. Long Beach was not exactly a hop, skip, and a jump away from downtown Los Angeles, where the DEA management worked in the Federal Building.

Bear wanted to get out of the office to discuss their latest findings. Group 5 had their first case and Bear knew that it was important to be successful to establish confidence. However, based on the circumstances, he also knew that they would have to be very careful the way they approached this investigation.

Since it involved a United States Congressman, it was possible, maybe even likely, that DEA management would shut down the investigation before it started. An investigation of an elected official brought with it an inherent risk. If the investigation was successful in identifying the politician as a criminal, then public ridicule would follow. But the mistrust many had in all government officials would also bring with it a public spotlight on the DEA, in an attempt to portray DEA agents as hypocritically targeting politicians as criminals when some of their co-workers were committing equally bad or even worse crimes. And every agent knew, bad press for the DEA hurts individual careers. Nobody is more concerned about careers than those in management climbing up the ladder, so while it might just seem like a regular investigation to the other agents, Bear knew it was something more serious that required delicate handling. It was why he brought them to this location, more than 30 miles away from the LA office, where the group could discuss what they had found over the previous two days.

After the entrees had been brought to the table, Bear got down to business. "Since we saw Congressman Lightfoot meeting with Romeo the other day, each one of you were tasked with some digging to find out whatever information we can on this business that the two of them are involved with that received half a million dollars from couriers working for a drug cartel. Since there are not any drugs flowing through California right now, the question is what in the world was that money for? There are two main reasons we can assume the half a million dollars was illegal gotten gains. First, it was delivered to Romeo by couriers known to be working for the Cartel. As far as I know, the Cartel is not doing any legitimate business these days. Second, the courier we followed in Pasadena was obviously smurfing the money. The deposits in increments of less than $10,000 are designed at avoiding detection from the bank and law enforcement. If the proceeds were legitimate, then they would not have gone to that trouble. So, what do we have? Stan, why don't you start."

With five years on the job, Stan was not a veteran agent, but Remi and Johnny both had less time on, and Bear could tell that they both seemed to look up to the former military man and take his lead.

Stan approached the task in a very matter of fact manner, much like when he had to make presentations in his military career. Speaking clearly and loudly enough to be heard at the table, but not loud enough to be overheard by a passerby, he began.

"My job was to find what I could about Romeo. The Congressman is cut and dry. He has been vetted. There was no point in looking deep into his past to see what this connection is. Whatever connection the Congressman has to these drug couriers delivering money is likely through Romeo. That is what we all thought after speaking with Bear, and after doing some research, I am even more convinced.

"Romeo and the Congressman have been friends since childhood. Both experienced privileged upbringings in the Orange County area near Laguna Beach. Both attended private schools through high school. Then, both attended Pepperdine University in Malibu."

Bear whistled. A native Californian, he knew that Pepperdine was one of the most beautiful college campuses in the country. Nestled on a hill overlooking the Pacific Ocean, it was sometimes hard to tell the difference between the sky and the ocean. It was also very expensive, far out of the price range of most normal citizens.

"So, they come from money?" Bear asked.

"They do," Stan replied. "And lots of it. Romeo's father and the Congressman's father were partners in a multi-million-dollar technological business. Paid for them both to go to Pepperdine, which is where the paths of the two started to take a turn. The Congressman made excellent grades. He was a part of several different honor societies when he graduated with a bachelor's degree. Romeo, on the other hand, never graduated.

"He was arrested three times in a six-month period. Two DUIs and one felony possession of narcotics that was later pleaded down to a misdemeanor that resulted in a hefty monetary fine but no jail time. It was during that time that Romeo started earning his name. Slept with hundreds, maybe thousands of women. Beautiful women. Not sure what they saw in a loser like Romeo, but that's normally the way it works."

Stan took a break to take in some fried popcorn shrimp and a sip of ice water. Johnny took the moment to broach the subject that Stan was notoriously private about. "Not finding success with the ladies?" he asked with a big smile. "I think Ana Lucia was into you dude."

"You're a horn dog. You think everybody is into everybody...and you go to Hollywood clubs, so your judgement obviously can't be trusted."

Johnny smiled and nodded in agreement while rubbing his long beard. "It's true. I take no offense."

"Finishing up, Romeo worked off and on, as best I can tell, never finding success, while the Congressman went to law school at USC and really flourished, ultimately marrying and becoming one of the youngest Congressmen in the nation. The only link I possibly found that might explain all this, was that Romeo was arrested again, several years after he failed out of Pepperdine. This time for breaking and entering with a weapon. His parents refused to bail him out this time, and he spent time behind bars. I called the jail, and his roommate was a guy from the Ukraine, arrested for illegal arms selling. How the two of them ended up in a cell together, nobody knows. The two men have remained in contact since that time."

The four agents looked around at each other. "This may be a silly question," Remi said, "but as the newest agent to the group, I was just wondering how you found all that personal information?"

"I am a Criminal Investigator," Stan joked. "There are a lot of means and methods to finding this information, but I always take the easiest path. Two little words will help you when you search for personal information: Social Media. You will be amazed at what idiots will post to social media. Basically, their entire life story. Makes our jobs easy."

* * *

The four agents decided to finish their meals before addressing the other two angles that were investigated over the previous couple of days. In her four months on the job, Remi had not had the opportunity to lead any kind of briefing. She wanted the first time she presented information to her co-workers to be a success, with the information appearing clear and concise. It helped considerably that it was in such an informal setting like the booth of a local Long Beach restaurant. Eager to impress, she took a deep breath and began explaining what little she had been able to find.

"Bear asked me to check on the bank account we identified where the couriers were depositing the money. I know a good deal about the banking industry from my parents. I also used one of Bear's contacts over at the IRS to help. They had an informant working in the Wells Fargo bank. As we know, those money couriers deposited the money directly into a bank account of a soybean company, which Johnny will talk about later. Any deposits made into this account are automatically and immediately transferred into another account, which I will call Account 2.

"Account 1 will always have a balance of $0, other than for a few seconds after money is initially deposited and prior to being transferred to Account 2. This protects the funds in Account 2 from immediate seizure by law enforcement in case one of the couriers depositing money into Account #1 is arrested while he is in the process of smurfing money into Account #1. It is smart, but basic stuff.

"Account #1 was set up five years ago, by none other than Romeo. Suspiciously, the account was set up on the same week that his best friend Bobby Lightfoot was elected Congressman. Not much other stuff on Account #1.

"The second account is the one we are going to focus on. It was opened by an individual named John Smith. About as fake and unassuming a name as possible. No identifiable information about this John Smith. Opened 1 day before Account #1."

"So how much money does Account #2 have in it?" Bear asked.

"Over 10 million dollars."

Stan's eyes bugged out. Bear whistled. Johnny stood up and leaned on the tables with his hands. "Are you serious? Any chance we can seize that money?"

"Not right now. We must figure out the source of the rest of the money in Account #2, without spooking them and getting the money split up and transferred to different accounts around the world. What we do know, is that Account #2 makes monthly deposits of $50,000 into seven different accounts. I would assume at least one if not all those accounts are used by Congressmen Lightfoot, all under the guise of profits from this soybean company. What makes it extra suspicious, is that all seven of those accounts belong to shell companies. Companies made for the sole purpose of moving money to other reputable accounts, or perhaps set up for future use should the account be needed. Shell companies in and of themselves are not illegal, but they are frequently used by money launderers. The fact that the money from Account #2 is being sent to seven different shell companies...these guys are trying to hide something. Lightfoot is being very careful. I'm not sure how they have $10 million in this account, but I assume it's safe to say that it isn't from some Congressman selling soybeans."

* * *

Johnny rubbed his long black beard and pulled his black ponytail from the seat behind him. He was eager to explain what he had found. Just because he had a fun life away from the office did not mean that he could not get the job done. When it was time to work, Johnny focused on the task at hand. He just did it with a more carefree demeanor than someone like his Group 5 co-worker Stan, who always seemed serious and rarely smiled.

"Bear asked me to check on the business associated with the account, and I found some interesting stuff. The soybean business was formed the same time the accounts were made, right around the time Lightfoot was elected to Congress. The business has a website that indicates it has a base of operations in several locations in the mid-west, which is primarily where soybeans are grown. The business address lists an address here in Long Beach that claims it exports tons of soybeans each year to China. Soybeans are one of the top exports from the US to China each year according to Google, so that checks out, at least up front.

"Digging a little further, it gets fishy. The company was founded by a guy named Bill Davis. Kind of like the bank account, it seems like they picked the most common white guy name possible. No way to find out more information about that guy without a date of birth, or address, or picture, or anything like that, but none exists."

"What about the address here in Long Beach?" Stan asked.

Johnny shook his head, "It's just an office, seemingly where they coordinate the exports to China. I went by there yesterday and did some digging around and got in good with a Vietnamese guy down at the Port of Long Beach. Spoke with him some in the native language, and the guy was willing to tell me his life story. When I finally got around to asking about the soybean company, he recognized Romeo and said that he comes around once a month or so and over sees shipments that are placed in containers and then sent off by ship to Hong Kong. He remembered that specifically because Romeo was particularly careful about one shipment of soybeans," and Johnny used air quotation marks, "that apparently came from Arizona...not the Midwest. The shipment from Arizona was placed in the container and marked as soybeans going to Hong Kong. He was even able to get me a copy of the paperwork of the guy authorized to receive the container in Hong Kong. I have the Hong Kong recipient's name, but I have not run any checks on him yet. I'll do that when we get back."

The four agents looked around the table at each other, interested in the possibilities of the case. Stan spoke up first, "I think it's safe to say that Romeo is not receiving soybeans from Arizona that are being exported to Hong Kong. It is not drugs, because everyone knows that there has not been any cocaine come out of Mexico in the last two weeks. If it is not drugs, or soybeans, what did Romeo send to China?"

Remi picked it up from there. "And who is it being sent to *in* China and *why*?"

Johnny continued. "And what does all this have to do with the money that was illegally deposited by drug couriers into a bank account belonging to Romeo? And why were the receipts given to Congressmen Lightfoot?"

Bear smiled for one of the first times on the job in a while. The thrill of the hunt excited him. "Looks like we have more questions than answers. I have a former co-worker that is currently in the DEA Hong Kong office. I'll send him the information we have on Romeo's shipment to Hong Kong but will do so without mentioning anything about Congressmen Lightfoot. In the meantime, we might have to do some good old-fashioned surveillance and follow Romeo for a week or two and see if he meets with any other couriers and deposits money into that same account. We'll work both angles and see which produces fruit."

"Since you've had us digging up all this info, what have you been up to, Bear?" Stan asked. He could get away asking that since he was not the newbie.

"I may or may not have put a slap-on tracker underneath Romeo's car yesterday while he was at the grocery store. I have been tracking it everywhere he goes. Give it the weekend, and we should have a pattern for him. Then first thing next week, we will get out and follow him around, see where he goes and who he meets with. Hopefully, the DEA Hong Kong office will be able to shed some light on this shipment from Arizona in the meantime."

The four agents got out of the booth and went to pay the bill. "I hate politicians bro, they're all dirty," Johnny said to Stan as Remi and Bear were paying.

"Not all, but probably most," Stan responded.

"I know one thing, bro. We're taking down Lightfoot."

A steely look of determination came over Stan, and he nodded in agreement.

Chapter 7
Guadalajara, Mexico

News of Juan Montoya's death was all that anybody could talk about. Official sources were claiming his death was the result of a gruesome automobile accident, but everyone secretly wondered if he was murdered, just another tally in the ongoing violence between competing Mexican drug cartels. If Montoya was murdered, then it was only a matter of time before there was a vicious response, which would undoubtedly result in a significant amount of bloodshed. For some reason though, none of the rivals of the Cartel de Culiacan had claimed responsibility for Montoya's death, which caused further doubt about the situation, and created greater intrigue into the real reason behind Montoya's sudden death.

Was a war coming to the streets of Guadalajara, Culiacan, and many other cities in Mexico? If so, then the people, especially the young people whose lives were going to be affected, needed a respite from the coming violence. For some, that respite came in the form of late-night street fighting.

Street fighting in Guadalajara had long been a staple of the late-night crowd, and the most feared champion in history had returned to his roots, taking on younger challengers eager to test the champion's hard-earned reputation.

Pelon walked with the organizer of the event, a 20-year old young man, as they left the crowd of 2000 people behind, and walked into a nearby local furniture store which served as the preparation room prior to the night's event. The bell attached to the door jingled as Pelon entered.

Seated in a chair with a small coffee table in front of him was the fearsome Leon. The man rose from the chair, sniffing his nose as he wiped away the white, powder residue from underneath his nose.

Pelon took a mental note of the man's cocaine use, and temporarily reconsidered if he had chosen the correct individual to carry out Carlos Montoya's wishes. He could not use an unreliable drug addict. Was this indicative of a bigger drug problem, or was it an occasional stimulant used for preparation that did not have a negative effect on Leon's physical abilities?

Leon looked past the event organizer with disinterest. It was the confidence and air of authority of the man at his side that garnered Leon's attention.

"I know there is only five minutes before the fighting starts," the event organizer said, "but this man insisted that he speak with you prior. He is a representative of Carlos Montoya."

Leon nodded, and waved the man away. "That'll be all. Leave us."

Pelon represented an organization from Leon's past, sandwiched in between his rise as a fearsome street fighter during his late teens and early 20's, and his current status as the returning champion in the same arena more than 10 years later. It was the period in between when he was employed as an assassin with the Cartel de Culiacan that had defined his life up to that point, giving him the most fulfillment.

He had worked in the assassin group with Toro, the most well-known assassin throughout Mexico. Leon had been Toro's right-hand man for years, occasionally bumping heads due to differing opinions and competing Alpha type personalities, but ultimately always working together successfully. Leon did not mind if Toro was the most well-known assassin, so long as he was the most feared.

His physical stature was only part of his reputation. Leon towered over most at 6 foot 5 inches tall, weighing in at 220 pounds. He had lost over 20 pounds since...the incident that ended his employment with the Cartel, and almost his life. The long scar down the middle of the back of his head was the reminder of what had been taken from him. It was why he fought with such viciousness now.

The last thing he remembered was being tasked by Juan Montoya, then second in command of the Cartel de Culiacan, to find and kill the corrupt DEA agent, Reuben Valdez, after Valdez had been in a meeting with Toro at a bar in Tijuana. When he finally awoke from the hospital several days later, Leon was informed that his brain had suffered serious trauma after being struck from behind by a metal object. The weapon had been left in the back of Leon's head. Nobody had dared face him. The cowards had left him to die on the street. The fact that he would never be able to confront the coward had left Leon temporarily depressed. That, along with the fact that he had to slowly regain movements of many extremities caused him to fall into a self-pitying despair that lasted several weeks. But he recovered remarkably fast, and with his return, was eager to again prove himself, and his strength and toughness.

With the return of that desire, came the second trait that made Leon one of the most feared men in Mexico: his viciousness and lack of a moral compass. When he worked with Toro, he did not just kill people. He destroyed them, personally enjoying making victims unrecognizable to families and friends.

Was this perhaps the opportunity for him to regain a semblance of who he was? What he was made to do?

* * *

Once the young event organizer had walked back outside to the waiting crowd, Leon finally addressed Pelon, a confident and formidable man in his own right.

"I work for Carlos Montoya. As you probably know, Juan Montoya recently passed, and Carlos is now the new leader of the Cartel de Culiacan."

"I'm aware."

"A need has arisen for a man with special talents and a willingness to perform several...tasks that might be considered cruel. There is also a requirement for secrecy. This is not the normal task where murders are meant to send a message. El Jefe Novo wants this done without anybody knowing."

71

"El Jefe Novo? Is that what Carlos is calling himself? El Jefe has been dead six months. Carlos' fathers' body is not cold yet, and he is already calling himself El Jefe Novo. Seems like that might be a cursed position. He might not want the title. Might not be long for this world." Leon smirked as he looked at Pelon. His eyes were dancing, and his fingers were twitching as he began to feel the effects of the cocaine he had snorted moments before.

"I am the head of security. Anybody that wants to harm El Jefe Novo, will have to come through me. It won't be a pleasant experience." The two men, both very used to things going their way, stared at each other in the dim store light.

"What is it that El Jefe Novo wants me to do?"

Pelon handed Leon a piece of paper. "This list has 30 names and locations on it. Your job is to find these people and kill them. Quietly."

"Shouldn't be a problem. It isn't too different from my old job."

"It isn't. But you should know, most of the names on this list are teenagers, some even younger than that. Boys and girls. Do you have a problem with that?"

Leon whistled. "30 kids huh? Any chance these are all El Jefe's bastards? The ones that he didn't allow to live with him, but still provided for financially nonetheless."

It only showed for a split second, but Pelon was surprised that Leon had figured it out so fast. He was obviously a man of considerable intelligence in addition to overwhelming strength. "I'm not like most of the other assassins that had no other job to do because they were stupid. I went to college. Could have done anything I wanted. But I wanted to be an assassin. I loved it. It did not take a genius to figure this out. El Jefe dies suddenly. Juan Montoya takes over, then he dies suddenly. Now Montoya's son wants all El Jefe's children killed? Hmmm, let me think why," he said, breaking into a smile.

"Do you accept the job?"

"Why me? Of all the people working for the cartel, why pick me?"

"I knew of you when you were on Toro's team. I worked for Juan Montoya and monitored your team's actions. Also, I am from Guadalajara, and have friends in the crowd tonight, friends that told me about your return. I thought who better than someone that has been through the battles, knows what is expected, and is trying to get his old job back. This is your chance to prove you still have it."

"And you need someone okay with killing children."

"That's right. Did I choose the wrong person?"

"No, you didn't," Leon said after a pause.

"Good, here's $20,000," Pelon said, throwing the bundle of cash down on the table Leon had just used to snort cocaine. "Use it for travel and expenses. When the task is accomplished, you will be given $100,000. Of course, we will need proof of each death. Send confirmation to the phone number at the bottom of the list with the names on it."

"Of course. Now you should stay for the show."

Pelon walked out the door without another word. He did not like dealing with people that had such an inflamed ego, whether it was justified or not. After speaking with Leon for five minutes, he decided that while he did not like the man, he was most definitely the right person for the job. Only a true psychopath would have no reservations about killing so many children.

* * *

The crowd was abuzz as Leon waked into the area designated for fighting. All the bets had been placed, and a lot of cash swapped hands as money was thrown around, most of the participants in favor of the undefeated champion. But this was different than any regular street fight pitting two men against each other.

Since Leon had shown that nobody was able to physically match his speed and strength, some fun had gone out of watching the fights. The thrill of not knowing who might win a certain fight was replaced with the anticipation of how long it would take Leon to knock out whatever poor individual decided to challenge him.

Pelon watched from the corner as the event organizer walked into the middle of the designated fighting area. "The time has come for the main event!" he yelled, as the crowd replied with a roar of readiness.

"Since his return two months ago, Leon has posted a record of 30-0, with 30 knockouts. His longest bout was barely three minutes. Now, we have decided to up the ante. Tonight, Leon will have 30 minutes to knock out five different men. If he can do that, then he will win $10,000! If not, $10,000 will be divided between the challengers. Are we ready to see if Leon can do it?!?!"

The crowd again roared their approval and circled around Leon and the first challenger. The other four men were standing shoulder to shoulder at the front of the semi-circle, ready to go in when the first challenger was incapacitated.

Leon observed the first man as he stretched his arms and did a few squat jumps. His blood was flowing, and he was ready to pounce from the stimulation provided by the cocaine, but experience had enabled him to harness that energy until the right time.

The first challenger was barely six feet tall and weighed only 170 pounds. The man showed an impressive array of speed kicks and punches as he warmed up. Common sense suggested the smaller, perhaps quicker man, would try to use speed to his advantage, striking intermittently, all the while making sure to not get too close to the larger champion. But in times like these, where men were eager to prove their courage and strength, Leon knew that these fighters often did the opposite of what was expected.

It was why Leon was not surprised, and even ready, when the much smaller challenger charged at the beginning of the fight, attempting to deliver a punishing jump side kicked aimed at his head. What was surprising, was the quickness and speed with which Leon moved, falling to the ground, and rolling underneath the man as he flew over him trying to land the jump kick.

Before the man had the chance to turn around, Leon had both of his huge hands on the man's ankle. With all his might, Leon stood up, swinging his arms up and away. The force of momentum caused the challenger to fall to the ground with a thud, face first. Before he had the chance to roll over, Leon brought all 220 pounds down on the man's head with an elbow strike. The crunch from the elbow that connected with the man's head was as traumatic as the splat of the man's head against the pavement.

The fight lasted less than ten seconds. Despite the man's unconsciousness, Leon stomped on the side of the man's face, crushing the cheek and jaw bones on the right side.

Event security quickly ran in to remove the man before he was killed.

Leon turned around to the challengers. "Next?" he taunted, as one cautiously entered the ring, weary of suffering the same fate as the man before him. Seizing on the second challenger's indecision, Leon rushed the man and cocked his right hand back, feigning that he was about to land a punishing blow. Predictably, the second challenger attempted to side-step the attack by moving three steps to the champion's left side. It was right where Leon wanted him. Planting his left foot, Leon showed surprising balance, quickness, and explosion for a man of his size, especially a man that suffered a potentially deadly head injury a few months earlier. Spinning around and cocking his right leg, Leon lunged toward the second competitor with a ferocious jumping side kick.

Despite having seen Leon fight previously and knowing that he was capable of such a move, the quickness and power which he delivered the blows could not be estimated. Only when it was too late, did one have a proper understanding for the suddenness in which the fight could get out of hand.

Leon's jumping side kick landed in the man's chest with a loud thud. The unexpected impact launched the man into the surrounding circle of onlookers that let out, "Oooooohs," and "Ahhhhhs," with every significant blow that was landed.

75

The crowd of onlookers somewhat cushioned the man's fall from landing on his back, but the people immediately parted as Leon approached with bad intentions.

The second challenger landed on his butt, and with the breath knocked out of him, valiantly attempted to rise. He was too slow. He put one knee on the ground and steadied himself from falling over with one hand in the ground. He never saw it coming.

Breaking through the parted crowd, Leon pounced, delivering another bone crushing kick, this time kicking his leg in an upward motion, catching the second challenger as he looked at the ground, and snapping his neck back with such ferocity that the crunch of a broken nose was heard as the man's teeth flew out into the street and landed on several bloodthirsty onlookers who reveled in savagery.

Leon looked unmercifully at the man lying on the ground and considered continuing the attack, wondering if he was paralyzed after his neck had snapped back so quickly. Only a strong hand on Leon's left bicep stopped him. Leon spun to face the man that dared place a hand on him, only to realize it was the event security, a strong and burly young man with a terrified look on his face, nonetheless.

"Two down, three to go," the man told Leon, attempting to get him back to the middle of the fighting area. Leon returned to the middle, his back to the third oncoming challenger, when he made direct eye contact with Pelon, standing several rows back. The look between the two men was brief, with each giving a respectful nod.

Pelon turned around to leave. He had seen enough, confident in Leon's abilities. He walked around the block to his waiting SUV, noting the continued "Ooooooos," and "ahhhhhs," from the crowd, followed by the chanting, "LE-ON! LE-ON! LE-ON."

Chapter 8
Los Angeles, California

Victoria recognized the look in Reuben Valdez' eyes when he walked out of federal prison. It was a look of someone that would never again be confined. She just hoped her instincts were right and that Reuben could be trusted to carry out the duties had had promised as part of the conditions of his release. Despite Victoria's belief that Reuben was being honest with his agreement to help, Victoria would have been derelict in duty had she not assigned a small group of co-workers to monitor Reuben when he was not in her presence.

The first full day of Reuben's newfound freedom was spent holed up in a CIA Safe House in Los Angeles, compliments of Toby. Victoria knew she could not bring Reuben to the DEA office, or anywhere public for that matter, that would risk her being observed in the presence of the corrupt DEA agent sentenced to 16 years of federal prison. The chances of being seen by somebody that recognized them both were minimal, especially given Reuben's weight loss since going to prison, but it was a risk that Victoria was not willing to take. She gladly accepted Toby's offer to make a location change so they could game plan their first move.

That first move was altered considerably by the news leaking out of Mexico that Juan Montoya, the leader of the Cartel de Culiacan, had died suddenly. Reuben was going to be impersonating Vaquero, and Vaquero was known to be so loyal and trustworthy to Juan Montoya, that the leader of the cartel had picked Vaquero, as opposed to Juan's own son Carlos, to travel around the Southwest United States confirming contracts with different criminal organizations. Now that Carlos had presumably taken over for his deceased father, would the younger Montoya continue to use Vaquero in the same role? Would he call Vaquero back and send someone else? Or would he refuse to contact Vaquero, after learning that Vaquero had narrowly escaped his own capture and death when the FBI attempted to arrest him at the Burbank airport? There were a lot of unknowns, and Victoria and Toby sat down with Reuben to discuss the options.

Fortunately, Victoria had the wherewithal to swipe Vaquero's phone after pulling him out of the burning jet at the airport days earlier. To her incredible luck, the phone was unlocked and accessible. Before Toby and the FBI agent had gotten to the room back at the airport, Victoria had found a charger and forwarded all the contacts and conversations to her own phone. Reuben was given his own cell phone, with the acknowledgement that all calls and text messages would be monitored by the DEA, as well as the GPS location of the phone which was automatically displayed. Victoria directed Reuben to send a text message in Spanish to Carlos Montoya.

"This is Vaquero. I got a new phone in case I was being monitored. They tried to arrest me at the airport, but I was able to escape."

"I'm sorry to hear about your father. He was a great man."

"I found shelter with a friend and am preparing to meet with the first contact tonight."

After the three messages were sent, Reuben paced the safe house while Victoria and Toby waited for a response. Three hours later, a response finally came. Not from Carlos, but the bodyguard, Pelon.

"Call now."

Reuben looked at Victoria. "What do we do?"

Victoria shook her head. "Tell him it's too dangerous to speak. You think that is how the feds tracked you to the airport. You have a new phone that is clean, and you will only use it for text messages. For his safety and yours. Make up something about it being hard to prove in court who is sending text messages, but they can play recorded calls during a trial."

"Okay, Okay," Reuben said, continuing to pace the room. "Let me think of how to say it."

"Don't hit send until we read it," Victoria said.

Moments after Victoria approved the message to be sent out, the new phone dinged with another message from Pelon. "*What happened in Burbank?*"

Reuben looked at Toby and Victoria. He was not used to being on the receiving end of instructions, but he knew the game, and waited for their direction.

"The feds tried to arrest you. There was a shootout. You climbed the fence at the airport and disappeared into a hanger. Escaped in a vehicle dressed as an airport employee."

"Remember," Toby said, "we made sure the *LA Times* carried the story about an eye-witness observing a man running away from the scene in a cowboy hat. It's online. Here, I'll send it to you."

Toby forwarded the link to Reuben, who then wrote his message and included the link to the article.

Finally, a short time later, another message from Pelon. "*Who are you supposed to meet with first?*"

Victoria scrolled through all the messages from Vaquero's phone and determined that he had arranged to meet first with Big D from the Crips gang in South Central Los Angeles.

The reply of, "*Big D*," was sufficient. If it was meant to be a test, then Reuben, or the new Vaquero, had passed.

"*Carry on like initially planned. You will be contacted in three days.*"

Victoria looked at Toby, hopeful that perhaps they had pulled off the first important stage of the rouse. "Looks like he bought it," Victoria said.

Reuben offered his own two cents. "The part about not using the phones to be safe was smart. Normally, if the feds are trying to set someone up, they always want to get the bad guy's voice on a recording. Assuring him that I did not want that probably convinced him I was really Vaquero.

"Very good," Toby said. "Now let's call Big D."

* * *

Deep in the heart of South-Central Los Angeles, a black SUV pulled onto the street of a densely populated residential neighborhood. Reuben exited the rear passenger seat of the SUV, dressed as Vaquero, with a button up blue jean shirt and dark blue Wrangler jeans. He completed the ensemble with snakeskin cowboy boots, a giant silver belt buckle depicting the flag of the Mexican state of Sinaloa, and of course the infamous black cowboy hat.

Before he moved away from the vehicle, two other men exited. The Hispanic undercover CIA case officers were chosen as Reuben's security for this meeting. One walked ahead toward the residence designated as the meeting place.

Victoria was the last to get out of the vehicle. Her eyes searched the area for possible threats, which were everywhere. The neighborhood was filled with individuals dressed in blue shirts, jerseys, and bandanas. She assumed each one was armed. The house they were walking into was in the middle of a neighborhood controlled by the Crips gang. Although Victoria knew that Toby had a CIA drone overhead monitoring the situation, she knew that if something happened inside the house, it would be very difficult for a rescue team to get inside in time to protect them.

The fact that the meeting took place inside the target's residence, in addition to the fact that a former DEA agent convicted for corruption was working undercover pretending to be a Mexican drug dealer, were the obvious reasons that Victoria had agreed to not involve DEA resources in this operation. It violated just about every rule the agency had, and if something bad went down, then she would not risk the negative attention that would come down on the DEA.

However, DEA would need some form of documentation of the meeting, if for nothing else than to prove that Reuben was upholding his end of the agreement and doing exactly what he had promised to do. If he did not, then that too would be used to send him back to federal prison. The problem was that Victoria knew that a recording device could not be taken into a meeting between a South-Central Los Angeles gang and representatives from the Cartel de Culiacan.

The Crips gang would monitor each person with a device to determine if any of the participants were recording the conversation. The meeting would not end well if they discovered someone was wearing a wire. The agreement would be broken, and they would likely all be killed. Since Reuben nor the CIA case officers posing as security were DEA agents, Victoria knew the only answer to the situation was to include herself in the meeting with Big D and the leaders of the Crips. She hoped that her reason for being there was okay with the guys with the guns on the inside of the house.

Reuben, Victoria, and the two CIA case officers posing as security walked through a small fence and into the front yard of a house that was not otherwise noteworthy. Victoria noted the address number and the layout of the house for future documentation on a Report of Investigation...if she survived to that point.

* * *

"Good evening, good evening," Reuben said as he entered the home, offering up a big smile in his attempt to convince the armed black men around him that he was the real Vaquero. Reuben shook hands and went around the room until ultimately getting to the biggest individual in the room, who he assumed was Big D. As expected, the man at the door waved a wand over each guest, a device designed for detecting recording devices.

"Call me Vaquero," Reuben said, as he shook the man's hand and tucked his cowboy hat under his left arm. "Thank you very much for inviting me into your residence tonight. I very much hope we can come to an agreement on the terms of the contract between our two organizations."

Victoria knew that she was not the only one in the room uncomfortable. The gang members seemed on edge, and that worried her. She counted at least five inside the living room, one of which was blocking the door. There were another five guys outside the residence in between the front door and the fence.

Being the only female in the room, Victoria received the stares of several of the men in the room. She tried to look ahead at the individual that Reuben was speaking with, but another man answered instead.

"Actually, I am Donte," said another man, stepping forward. "Better known as Big D." Victoria looked at the man. He was under six feet tall and not 200 pounds. She did not ask the obvious question about why he was referred to as Big D when there was a much larger man in the same room. Reuben was smart enough not to ask as well.

His face blushed with embarrassment. "My deepest apologies," Reuben said, lowering his head in deference. "On behalf of Carlos Montoya and the rest of the Cartel de Culiacan, we are honored to be in the presence of your organization. We look forward to a long and profitable relationship for both our groups."

"Are you representing Carlos Montoya, or his father Juan?" Donte asked. "When you came to California, technically, you were working for Juan Montoya right?"

"That's correct, but unfortunately, Juan Montoya passed recently, and his son Carlos has taken over and given me the go-ahead to continue representing the Cartel."

"Is that so?"

"It is." A quick flicker of seriousness in Reuben's eyes was replaced by the softer, friendlier tone that Vaquero would have shown in the same situation. So far, Victoria was impressed with Reuben's acting skills. She eyed the other men in the room and noted that each one had their hands near their sides. Victoria was sure that each of them had weapons. She could even see the bulge in the side of the pants of the big man that Reuben had mistaken for Big D.

"Even if Carlos did send you, I guess there is no way I would have to know that, seeing how we never met before." Victoria knew Big D's icy coolness and calm demeanor was designed at unnerving his guests. At best, it was an attempt to obtain any psychological advantage possible that might get them a better deal. At worst, it was the prelude to a massacre. Had another rival cartel got to the Crips gang first?

Big D's gaze finally rested on Victoria for a while, before returning to Reuben. "Introduce me to your guests."

"These two guys are my security, Oscar and Raul."

"And the woman?"

Reuben and Victoria's eyes locked, and she nodded her head. "This is Vickie."

"And why is she here?"

Victoria stepped forward to answer. Enough letting the men play their little game. "I'm Vaquero's gal on the inside. I tell Vaquero when and where law enforcement is going to be. To keep him out of jail."

"You brought a narc into my house?" Big D asked unbelievingly. The big guy pulled out his gun, prompting the two undercover CIA officers posing as security to step forward, but it was Victoria that tried to smooth over the situation.

"I've worked with Vaquero for years. While I am here, he is safe. If he is safe, then you are safe. You should be relieved I am here, not angry. This is the big leagues. Not coach pitch. Don't be so...scared," she said in disgust, staring at Big D while she said it.

Not used to having someone speak to him like that, much less a woman, Big D crossed the room to confront Victoria.

"Are you calling me a coward?"

"I didn't have to. You just did."

"You know I have killed people for saying a lot less to me than you have."

Reuben tried to take back control of the situation. "With all due respect, Vickie is here at my request. And as such, she is a representative of the cartel. Those that have made threatening comments to representatives of the cartel have suffered equally gruesome endings. If you touch Vickie, then a whole host of guys in blue clothing will be swaying from bridges in El Paso or dumped in plastic bags in Tijuana in less than 24 hours. Nobody wants a war."

Big D stepped back momentarily to consider the threat, and for a second it looked like he was going to strike Victoria. She assumed a defensive position, but Reuben again attempted to salvage the situation.

"I did not mean to surprise you or disrespect you by bringing a fed in here, but she's been in my pocket for years. I had a big buffoon I used for a while, but he got arrested by the FBI and is in federal prison now."

The irony that Reuben was talking in such a way about himself, while pretending to be the very man that caused him to be arrested, almost made Victoria smile, and shake her head in amusement, despite the precarious circumstances.

"She is a fed?! You brought a fed in here?!" Big D exploded, causing all the men in the room to pull their weapons and level them at the contingent claiming to be from the Cartel de Culiacan.

"Yes, but she's cool, I swear!" Reuben said, doing his best to win over the hostile host.

"Why do you think nobody has busted in here yet?" Victoria asked coolly.

"What?"

"Yes, I'm a federal agent. You've leveled a weapon at a federal agent. If my people, the feds, knew I was here, then they would have busted in as soon as all your men started pointing their weapons at me. The fact that you are not dead or in handcuffs right now is all the proof that you need. Think about it!"

Big D considered that, and realized that she might be right, but decided to press further. "If you are really looking out for Vaquero, then how was he almost arrested the other day in Burbank? Everyone heard about it. Supposedly...his security was killed, but he was able to escape. Those security would not have died if feds were really providing him information and protecting him. I think you're a liar."

Victoria did not back down, step back, or look away. It was the last thing you did with men like this, especially when lives hung in the balance. She stared at him and answered. "Well, I think you are an idiot. I am amazed you haven't been arrested yet. Use what little brain you have, *Big D.* How do you think Vaquero was able to get away? He would have been killed at the Burbank airport or at least captured if it had NOT been for me. I got him out of the airport. I gave him a place to stay while police everywhere were looking for him. ME! It was the FBI that tried to arrest him. I did what I could when I found out. My job is to keep Vaquero safe...not his security team."

Big D was the first to look away, convinced. He looked at the Vaquero imposter. "I see why you like her," he said, waving his arms for his men to lower their weapons. "You always need somebody willing to tell you what all the 'yes men' are unwilling to say."

"Vickie definitely does that," Reuben said. "Now, can we get down to the reason we are here? We have a deal to make, and we have other meetings to attend."

Big D looked at Reuben and then Victoria. "Let's do it."

Chapter 9
Long Beach, California

The four agents that made up DEA Group 5 had followed Romeo from his residence in the San Fernando Valley to the business office in Long Beach. They could sense that something was about to go down. After days of surveillance produced no results, each agent hoped this was the day that their efforts would finally pay off. Before they had time to think about what Romeo was doing in the business office, he left again, this time driving to the nearby Long Beach airport.

Several planes from Jet Blue were arriving, along with a private plane that taxied to the runway farthest away from the parking lot. Remi was chosen for mobile surveillance. She exited her car and walked into the airport lobby, doing her best to track Romeo. As an attractive Asian female in her 20s, Remi looked more like a Hollywood hopeful than a federal agent, which made it easy for her to blend into her surroundings and not arouse suspicion.

When Remi's phone rang, she thought it was likely one of her coworkers calling from outside with an update. She was surprised to hear Ana Lucia on the other end, calling from her office in El Centro.

"Bear isn't answering," Ana Lucia said, sounding rushed. "But I have something that can't wait. Can you talk?"

"I'm following Romeo through the Long Beach airport to see who he meets with, but I can talk."

"Of course! You can multi-task. You're a woman. Good thing the boys chose you."

"Right?!" Remi said, smiling at the compliment.

"Okay, quickly, I wanted to tell Bear, but I followed up on the guy that delivered the $500k to my informant. Remember he had

86

already given my informant the money and we didn't get a chance to identify him or follow him."

"Yeah I remember."

"Well I did some digging based on the guy's phone number and license plate, which the informant memorized. The guy that gave my informant the half a million is a Panamanian guy that was arrested in Dallas three years ago for Human Trafficking, but his attorney found some loophole and got the charge dropped."

"He wasn't a drug dealer?"

"Not that we know of. A human trafficker. Even worse than a drug dealer."

"So, you think the half a million dollars that went to your inform-ant, and was then deposited into an account that was associated with Romeo and the Congressman, that money was likely a product of human trafficking and not drug dealing?"

"We can't be sure, but it definitely looks like a possibility."

"Okay, thanks Ana Lucia, I'll let Bear know. Let me let you go because it looks like Romeo is meeting with somebody now."

"Good luck," Ana Lucia told the younger agent. "Don't forget to take pictures of who he meets."

* * *

The earpiece in Remi's ear that connected with the rest of her fellow DEA agents immediately came to life with news from Bear. Remi could tell from his tone that he was excited.

"Just got off the phone with my old partner that is now assigned to Hong Kong. The guy in China that received the so-called shipment of soybeans is a known lawyer representing one of the biggest gangs out there, or what they call triads. The Sun Yee On. These guys are known for drug dealing, kidnapping, human trafficking, and a whole host of other things."

Human trafficking. That was twice in the last minute that word had come up. It made Remi's skin boil that young women were get-ting used like that. Was it possible that an elected representative from Congress was involved in that?

"My old partner thinks the Sun Yee On is about to go to war with another triad named 14K, so the shipment from the guys here in the States was likely weapons...not soybeans."

Stan could not hold back a sarcastic dig. "Human trafficking and weapons? The people of the great State of California obviously made a stellar choice by electing Bobby Lightfoot."

"Now we need the evidence to prove it," Bear said.

"You have to be kidding me," Remi said, mostly to herself. "Well, we might get that evidence. Lightfoot's best friend Romeo is escorting about 20 young Asian women to a private area near the back of the airport. Looks like they are going to take the rear exit. One of you needs to get back there to see what vehicle they leave in. I'm not going to be able to without being seen."

"I'm on it!" Johnny said.

"Twenty women? You mean like human trafficking victims?" Bear asked.

"Surely he isn't audacious enough to bring them in to the Long Beach airport during the middle of the day," Stan wondered out loud.

"This guy thinks he's untouchable," Bear said.

Remi started jogging through the lobby of the airport and back to her vehicle as Romeo led the gaggle of women to two large white vans outside the airport terminal. She listened as Johnny called out the license plates of the two vehicles the women entered as they immediately left the lot.

Remi got to her car quickly and did not fall behind in the surveillance. Despite her relative inexperience, she knew it was of utmost importance that they keep the vans in sight.

The two white vans maintained all traffic laws as they went in and out of the infamously busy Southern California traffic, until eventually landing at a large compound in Brentwood. A ten-foot stone fence prevented the Group 5 agents from seeing where the white vans went and what happened with the women inside.

"What do you think the chances are that Lightfoot is in there right now?" Stan asked over the radio.

"Impossible to know unless we get an airplane up and look down. That fence is too high," said Bear.

"He's back there," Johnny answered. "I've got a feeling that he's back there."

As if an answer to his question, less than a minute later, from the five acres in the rear of the property, a helicopter rose above the neighborhood. From her position on the street beside the residence, Remi was the only Group 5 agent with a good view of the passenger side of the helicopter. She saw at least five women in the back of the helicopter, but it was another face that had her attention. Staring down below, almost making eye contact with her, was the unmistakable face of Congressman Bobby Lightfoot.

* * *

Two hours later, Remi and Bear sat in front of Dave Brown, an Assistant United States Attorney in the Central District of California based in Los Angeles. They spent the meeting explaining the intelligence collected over the course of the investigation. From Remi's viewpoint, it was more than enough for a search warrant at the estate in Brentwood, and at the very least warranted a questioning of Romeo and Congressmen Lightfoot. But then again, Remi was one of the newest agents in the entire field division. As Bear explained to her prior to the meeting, it was the opinion of the attorneys, and then the DEA brass, that was important. Especially if it led to the arrest of a United States Congressman for Human Trafficking charges.

Bear had been through this process many times but knew that it was the first for Remi. He took the lead on several issues, but nudged Remi or gave her a nod when it was her turn to provide input. His impression of the young agent was that she was articulate and intelligent, ready to take on the important task of convincing the federal prosecutors of the need for a search warrant and possibly arrest warrant.

The two agents went back and forth, explaining how the investigation started with a lead from a confidential informant directed by Ana Lucia, the DEA agent in Imperial County, California. The informant, a cartel employee that was used to transport drug proceeds, had picked up currency which was not from the sale of drugs due to the lack of drugs available in the market at the time. Remi explained how the money was then illegally deposited into the accounts in increments of less than $10,000, a blatant attempt at concealing the depositing of the money and the money's origin. She also explained the information learned from the account, which showed Romeo's involvement in opening the parent account, but the dead end that resulted from the other accounts that were all under fake names and businesses.

The kicker, at least in their opinion, was that Romeo had been observed receiving the receipts from all the different deposits, and that Romeo then went directly to meet with Congressman Bobby Lightfoot.

At the mention of an elected official, the AUSA noticeably shifted uncomfortably in his seat, looking at the window. Remi looked at him, wondering if the federal prosecutor was contemplating the fame that would come from taking down a US Congressman, or if instead he was deathly afraid to go down that trail, the end of which would likely result in the end of his career if it failed to result in a conviction.

Bear continued to explain about the suspected shipment of weapons from Arizona to Romeo's company in Long Beach that then went to China under the guise of soybeans, a highly popular export from the US to China. He also pointed out that the individual in China that received the shipment from Romeo's company was a lawyer for a powerful Chinese gang.

Remi then took over the conversation, explaining the information relayed by Ana Lucia earlier about the source of the money to the informant being a man previously arrested for human trafficking. Surely that intelligence was further validated when Remi was at the airport and saw Romeo exit with 20 Asian women that were likely human trafficking victims. The vehicle then traveled to an estate in Brentwood that had high fences preventing anybody from seeing what was going on inside the walls.

The stake in the heart, no doubt, was when Remi confirmed that she saw a helicopter leave the property moments later with several of the women, along with Congressman Lightfoot.

Remi smiled and looked confidently at Bear. She was sure they had articulated the evidence well enough to convince the AUSA of the probable cause that existed to search the residence in Brentwood where Remi had observed Lightfoot with suspected Human Trafficking victims. The AUSA's uncertain look suddenly made Remi doubt herself. Bear's uncertain look was because he could tell that the Federal Prosecutor was not convinced.

He told them he was not convinced, much to their exasperation. The fact that the investigation was targeting a US Congressman no doubt complicated matters, but as the ASUA told them prior to leaving, "The only way Lightfoot will ever go to jail for this is to catch him red-handed. Not with just speculation. Not with a source that is a drug dealer, or some third-party information. You will need a wiretap, which you will probably never get, or you will need an undercover or an informant. And even then, Lightfoot will hire a defense attorney that will absolutely tear apart any poor strung out, drug addicted, woman that you can put on the stand."

Remi looked at Bear in disbelief. "I'm sorry the news isn't better," the attorney said, exiting the room without another word.

* * *

"I can't believe they are just going to let Lightfoot get away with this, when we know he's guilty!" Remi said.

"I agree. They're scared. They do not want to prosecute a case that is not assured of a conviction. Especially a high-profile case involving a US Congressman. But the AUSA was not wrong. The defense attorney would tear apart any witness we put up there, even if we did have one. He'd pick apart every little thing."

"So, we're stuck? We don't have anything else to move forward?"

"Well, my old partner in Hong Kong did mention that he has an informant that is into the Sun Yee On triad. A female informant. She is former law enforcement in China. Her sister was a previous human trafficking victim. Chinese government will not do anything, so she went to FBI. They linked up with DEA because of the drug angle. This chick wants to take down the entire Sun Yee On triad. I think it's the same triad that is delivering girls to Lightfoot."

"But you just said yourself that Lightfoot's defense attorney will tear apart anyone that goes on the stand," Remi reminded him.

"I know. An informant is good, but I do not think it will be good enough. Sometimes you got to admit when you have lost. And it looks like we've lost."

"No," Remi said with surprising conviction. "That prosecutor said the only way Lightfoot goes to jail is to get caught red-handed, but an informant won't work."

"That's right."

"Well, what about an undercover federal agent? That would hold up on the stand."

"Right, but that would mean...no way that won't work. It looks like this group captures girls in China that are then sent to the US for sex trafficking. You'd have to go to China, find the right person, get captured, and then get sent to the US, hopefully to Lightfoot in Southern California."

"It will work," Remi said assuredly, trying to convince herself as she said it. "And you know it's the only way. We should go to China to meet with your friend under the guise of discussing other details of the investigation. The weapons angle with the attorney for the Triad that received the shipment from Arizona is a perfect reason. We will claim that he is our main target. Meanwhile, I will meet up with the female informant; we will figure out who and where to get noticed and be more than willing to go to Southern California. We'll coordinate to meet up with their guys back here in Southern California. I'll catch the Congressman red-handed. That is what the prosecutor wants, that is what he will get."

"It might work, but it will be very risky. Meaning we couldn't tell DEA management the *real* reason we are going to China."

"I know. It's the only way. And I'm offering to do it."

"If something goes bad in China, our careers could be over. I have enough time, I can retire. You're just starting out on the other hand. Are you sure you want to take that risk?"

"I'm sure."

Bear smiled at Remi. He liked this girl. She had fire and guts.

"Let's do it."

Chapter 10
Quepos, Costa Rica

Over 100 security forces from the Cartel de Culiacan were in the area outside the private villa where Carlos Montoya stood. He would not make the same mistake in Costa Rica as his father did in Hong Kong. If somebody took him out, they were going to have to also take out a bunch of armed security forces. But Pelon was the only one that he trusted to remain in the room with him while they waited for word from the Colombian based Cali Cartel that their leader, in a nearby villa, was ready to meet to discuss an agreement that would immediately send hundreds of thousands of kilograms of cocaine from Colombia into Mexico.

He scrolled the online Mexican news from his I-phone and saw two internet articles that made him pause. Carlos showed Pelon the phone. "Is this your guy's work?"

Pelon looked at the article describing the home invasion and murder of a family of four in Hermosillo. The particularly gruesome nature of the deaths had made the news. Two parents, and their two adopted children, a boy, and a girl, were stabbed multiple times. Their heads were taken off and left on the fence outside the small house as a warning of the carnage that was inside.

The boy, 15 years old, was one of Julian Rodriguez' 31 children that had been placed in private schools around the country. The boy had the fortune of being adopted by a loving couple. Little did they know that their generosity would lead to their murder over a decade later after Leon tracked the boy down as being one of the biological sons of the former leader of the Cartel de Culiacan.

"Are you concerned about the collateral damage?" Pelon asked. "The deaths of the mother and father might have been avoidable."

Carlos shook his head. "It has to be done. Julian's line must be wiped out. If other people must die to ensure that, then so be it."

"I understand boss."

"Have you spoken with Leon?"

"He sends me proof of death. This is the third so far. The first one went under the radar, but the last two have made the news."

"So, he has 27 to go?"

"Yes."

"Very well."

Carlos was quiet as he patiently waited for the call from the leader of the Cali Cartel. While he waited, Carlos continued reviewing the website.

"Have you heard about what happened in Durango?"

Pelon shook his head.

"Twelve men were found lying on the road in front of a small house. Each man had been cut from base to sternum and hung, their insides spilling out on the ground below them while they choked to death. The dead bodies were laid out on the street in front of the houses where they lived. On the street, below the bodies, a message was spelled out that said: Beware: Knights Templar. Rebellion will be punished."

"Message? Written in what? Blood?"

"No. With guts and intestines."

"Wow. That is sick, even for our standards."

"But it sends a strong message. It tells me two things." Carlos stood and walked to the window, overlooking the ocean. "First, it tells me that former rivals like the Knights Templar, that were previously taken out by Toro, are trying to re-establish themselves after the deaths of Julian and my father. There are other groups as well. I've heard of our people being killed in Chihuahua, Juarez, and Tijuana."

Pelon nodded. He had heard the same news and come to the same conclusion. Old cartels such as Tijuana, Juarez, and Knights Templar were clearly making a power grab for control of the drug trafficking routes from Western Mexico into the US. The grip the Cartel de Culiacan had on the western portion of Mexico had never been more perilous. The GDG was in firm control of the drug trafficking routes in eastern Mexico. Perhaps they too would try to take over the entire country. Between all the different groups vying for power, Pelon could sense it was only a matter of time until something dramatic happened. Something that gave control to one of the organizations, and result in countless deaths for the losers. Pelon had aligned himself with the Cartel de Culiacan, and his fate would be determined by whether or not Carlos maintained power.

"What is the second thing it tells you?" Pelon asked Carlos, eager to judge the man's insight, to determine whether the Cartel de Culiacan had a chance to come out on top.

"We have somebody fighting on our side. The article says it was posted to social media by this unknown individual named Omega. There are plenty of questions. How did Omega kill 12 people from the Knights Templar with no help? How did Omega know the people in that residence were Knights Templar? Most importantly, who is Omega and why is this person on our side, fighting for the Cartel de Culiacan?"

Pelon stood silently by his boss' side. Those were answers he did not have. They were questions he had asked as well. At least Carlos Montoya was asking the right questions. They were answers that needed to be discovered to determine how to move forward once the agreement was in place with the Colombians.

"I don't know what's more worrying," Carlos said. "That these old cartels are rising from the ashes to challenge the Cartel de Culiacan, or that the person that is taking them out on our behalf is completely unknown. This person's motives are unknown. It could be anybody."

A knock on the door interrupted the thought. A man peaked his head in, "It's time."

* * *

Pelon led a group of ten men that flared out in a semi-circle around Carlos, creating a protective shell as they walked the quarter mile distance that separated the two villas. The remainder of the security forces from the Cartel de Culiacan created a further barrier, ensuring that nobody or nothing could get to Carlos without first going through them. It was very clear that in the event of Carlos' death, there was nobody left to reasonably assume control of the largest drug cartel in Mexico. It would throw the entire country into chaos, a bloody Civil War. Nobody wanted to go down that road.

With Teofilo hard at work back in Mexico cooking methamphetamine that was almost ready to be distributed, the only thing left in the way was securing the supply contract for cocaine with Cesar Escobar, a distant cousin of the infamous Pablo Escobar, that had seized control of his own Colombian cartel by relying on the power and mystique that came with the famous last name. Carlos would have to reassure Escobar that the Cartel de Culiacan was in good hands with him at the top, and most importantly, that Escobar would receive payment for every kilogram that was provided. In the end, money ruled.

Carlos strolled confidently toward Escobar after being introduced by Pelon. The two men shook hands, looking each other in the eyes. Escobar even looked somewhat like the former drug kingpin in his last days. Under six feet, with wavy black hair and an ever-increasing belly from nights of drinking beer, the Colombian had serious looking piercing black eyes.

"Hello, Carlos, my deepest condolences for your father's death. I previously dealt with him on several occasions when Julian was still considered El Jefe."

"Thank you very much, my father was a good man."

"A very good man."

"But I want to assure you that the Cartel de Culiacan remains in good hands. You have my guarantee that every dollar owed to the Cali Cartel will be paid."

"That is good to hear from you, as the representative of your organization. I do understand that there has been some...*unrest* recently. I trust that you have a plan for keeping that under control?"

"Of course, Senor Escobar. We will respond appropriately. In fact, we already have."

Escobar looked at Carlos, considering his words. "I have seen the reports. Who is this individual, Omega, that seems to be single handedly taking out challengers to your throne? It is not the infamous Toro, is it?"

Even the leader of the Cali Cartel in Colombia had heard the legendary stories of Toro.

Carlos smiled and shook his head. "It is definitely not Toro. This individual is much more technologically savvy that Toro ever was. Toro has not been seen since Julian's death. It is possible Toro died with El Jefe, although that could not be confirmed. To be honest, I have not invested the time and resources in identifying Omega, but I do plan on doing that as soon as I return to Mexico. I am grateful for the results, for sure."

Escobar ran his hands through his hair. "The stories are very impressive if they are true. Have you considered a partnership? Perhaps something that might solidify your hold on this mighty organization?"

"Everything is under consideration."

"That's good to hear," Escobar said, pacing back and forth across the room. "A strong and solidified Cartel de Culiacan is good for my business as well. It keeps the cash flowing to Colombia. Which is why I have an offer for you. One that I think you should consider very carefully before immediately rejecting it."

Carlos looked over at Pelon in the corner, who expressed a look of uncertainty about what was coming next.

"What kind of offer?"

Cesar Escobar waved his hand, and a door opened. Through the door walked several armed security members followed by Luis Hernandez Castillo, the leader of the GDG, the most powerful drug cartel in eastern Mexico.

Carlos recognized the man by sight. Pelon moved between the leaders of the two biggest Mexican drug cartels and looked at Escobar for an explanation. "What is the meaning of this?"

"It is literally an offer that you cannot refuse," Escobar said, looking past Pelon at Carlos. "I think you should hear out Mr. Castillo."

The leader of the GDG looked the part, with a power suit directly imported from Europe snugly fitted over his athletic features.

The GDG leader spoke first. "A pleasure to meet you Carlos. As you know, I came to an agreement with El Jefe prior to his death. The agreement."

"I know the agreement. It was a peace agreement to not infringe on the other's territory."

"That is correct," Castillo said. "I never got to speak with your father, but I am offering you an olive branch. I will provide extra security to your forces. I will help put down any rebellions that might be started by the remnants of the old cartels wiped out by Toro several years ago."

"I'm not sure that we will need that help, but I am interested in finding out what you are willing to offer. Like any good businessman, if the offer is too good to refuse, then I would not be a good leader if I did not at least consider it."

"That is very good to hear," Castillo said. Escobar nodded in agreement beside him. "Well after you have the chance to consider my offer, I'm sure that you will not hesitate in accepting it."

Carlos was surprised. An offer of help from the GDG was not what he had expected from his meeting with the Colombians.

In the room walked a woman whose beauty took away everyone's breath. A white sun dress modestly contained her large breasts and shapely rear. Toned legs and sculpted arms were matched with long and radiant black hair and beautiful brown eyes.

"This is my daughter, Fernanda," Castillo told them. "I am offering her to you as your wife. Any children you have will be the heir to the Cartel de Culiacan. The GDG will provide unending support in making sure that power structure is not affected in any way, beginning by assuring your protection, but only when needed."

Carlos heard what Castillo was saying, but his eyes remained locked on the gorgeous woman staring at him. There was no way he would turn down any deal involving the chance to marry a woman like that. He was a man, first and foremost.

"We most definitely have a deal," Carlos said with conviction.

All three men smiled as Escobar poured liquor into three small glasses, and they raised the glasses in a toast.

"To new beginnings," Escobar said, as the glasses clinked happily.

Chapter 11
Mexicali, Mexico

The sound of boots walking down the aisle of the Catholic Church caused the priest that was looking at the front altar to turn around to give the visitor a warm welcome. The visitor, however, was not there to speak with the priest and confess his sins. Nor was he there to speak about the saving grace of the Lord Jesus Christ, as Father Jose was accustomed to doing with his flock. The visitor had one goal in mind, and that was to find a 13-year-old boy that was scheduled to arrive soon and participate as a member of the youth choir.

The intelligence Leon had obtained on the teenager only included the boy's involvement with the church choir, and nothing to do with his family life. Leon thought the boy might be living at the church. As a devout atheist, Leon looked forward to this job more than the others. He had a particularly sickening defilement planned for this boy at the church and smiled just thinking about it.

The priest looked at the inquiring man, searching his eyes and attempting to look in his heart to determine his true intent. Despite the seemingly pleasant exterior, Father Jose sensed darkness.

"May I ask your name, young man?" Father Jose asked.

"I haven't been a young man for a long time," Leon answered.

"When you are as old as I am," the 70-year-old priest laughed, "a much larger portion of the population is considered young. That includes you."

"My name is Leon."

"Well good afternoon, Leon. I am Father Jose. I am glad you are in the house of the Lord. May I ask why you have come here for?"

Having expected this question, Leon was ready with a response. "I am looking for a 13-year old boy named Diego. It is regarding his inheritance. His birth family recently passed away and he is the only living relative. They left a sizable sum of money. All for Diego. Of course, for your help, I will obviously offer a portion to the church."

Surely, Leon thought, the offer of money would be sufficient to disclose the location of the teenage boy. "Very interesting," the priest said. "May I ask how much money he has been left?"

Leon smiled, believing that he had the man exactly where he wanted him. "Over seven million US dollars."

"May I ask how you are able to give away money to the church if it does not belong to you? If it is legally bound to Diego, then he should receive the full amount. If Diego wants to give some to the church, then that will be up to him." The priest smiled at Leon, waiting for a response.

"I'm sure Diego has enjoyed the life that he has here," Leon continued, fishing for information. "I'm on a tight schedule. When do you expect him?"

Father Jose looked at Leon, his gaze suddenly growing serious.

He knew. Leon could sense it. His hand went to the gun at his hip, but before he made a move, a voice called out to him. It was a voice from his past. One that he had not heard in months, but one that was nonetheless recognizable as soon as the first words were uttered.

"The long scar down the back of your head indicates that somebody finally got the best of you. The Leon that I know, would have never allowed that to happen."

Despite recognizing the voice behind him, confusion briefly flashed in his eyes as he turned around to face the man whom he had worked with for so long.

Leon's hearing had not deceived him. It was exactly who he thought it was; he smiled, and said one only word, "Toro."

* * *

The most infamous cartel assassin in the world had disappeared off the grid since the murder of Julian Rodriguez. Wild speculation had resulted about the extent of Toro's involvement in the death of the former leader of the Cartel de Culiacan, a man he had worked for honorably for more than a decade. But what could not be refuted was that the assassin disappeared as soon as Julian was killed.

What was known only to Juan Montoya previously, and now lost to the world with his death, was that many years earlier Julian Rodriguez had taken for his wife a young teenage girl that had been kidnapped by sex traffickers. The event had also resulted in the murder of the young girl's adopted mother. Those events had a devastating effect on the girl's younger brother, the individual that grew into the killing machine known as Toro.

Toro had spent many years working diligently for Julian Rodriguez and the Cartel de Culiacan, all the while not knowing that his own kidnapped sister was the man's young wife. Only after the woman's death by poisoning did Juan Montoya reveal the truth, that Julian had married the young teenage woman kidnapped by sex traffickers that was Toro's long-lost sister. At that point, it was only a matter of time until Toro would kill his boss Julian. Nothing could have stopped that. What was not planned, was the death of Julian's youngest daughter, Toro's niece and only living relative in the world.

Distraught by realization that he had killed his own flesh and blood, the daughter of the woman whose absence he had grieved for so long, Toro had given up the role of assassin and vanished into the Mexican countryside, vowing to retire from killing once and for all.

Despite the change in employment, the look in Toro's eyes remained the same. It was one that Leon had seen many times previously. It was an intense stare. The man said very little. And what was said, was well thought out before spoken.

The fact that Toro was in the Catholic Church in Mexicali of all places, could not be a coincidence. Both men knew. And they both knew that the other knew. But what Leon did not know was why Toro had come for the boy, Diego, and who had sent Toro.

"I wasn't sure you were still alive," Leon said as the words echoed in the church.

"I am."

"Where have you been hiding? After killing El Jefe that is. The question everyone wants to know is why? Why kill Julian just to disappear afterwards?"

"I am not here to talk about the past."

"Then why are you here?"

"Same as you. For the boy." Toro looked at the priest and knowingly nodded his head in recognition.

"You plan to murder him just like you did the boy's father, Julian Rodriguez? El Jefe?"

The question came out accusingly, like a dagger. But Toro did not answer.

"I don't care which one of us kills him," Leon said, "but I need proof of death. A picture will suffice."

Leon turned around to look at the priest behind him and noted that the man did not look surprised at the fact that Leon had admitted to being there to kill the boy.

Did he know that Leon was there to kill the boy? If so, had Toro told him?

"The boy is coming with me," Toro said. "There will be no pictures."

Leon's eyebrows furrowed as he looked at his old boss, the man that had been the leader of the most vicious assassin group in Mexico. Together, with Leon at his side, they had killed thousands of rivals of the Cartel de Culiacan. But still, despite their history and success, the relationship between Toro and Leon could never be confused for a friendship. It was a working relationship and nothing more. But Leon, ever competitive, had always considered himself the Alpha male among Alphas. He had always thought that one day, at some point down the road, he would confront Toro for the right to lead the group. Since neither were in the assassin group any longer, there would be no battle for leadership of the group, but the confrontation had finally arrived.

Leon had always wanted to test himself against Toro. Having never tasted defeat, he could not begin to grasp how the smaller and lighter man would overcome his power, but he had seen the man fight on numerous occasions, and he knew not to discount Toro based on size alone. That had been the fatal mistake of many that had come before him. Leon would not make the same error in judgement.

"I always knew this moment would come," Leon said, "I just pictured it happening under different circumstances. I hope you're ready." And with that, Leon quickly withdrew the pistol at his right side and fired it at Toro.

* * *

Toro's anticipation of Leon's actions caused him to spring to action even as the larger assassin was pulling his gun out. Quick as a cat, Toro moved forward on the balls of his feet, jumping left and right, while withdrawing the metal asp from his side pocket and swinging it out so that it was a fully extended metal stick two feet in length. Toro felt the air rush by his face as the bullet shot from Leon's gun went by inches to the left side of his face, impacting the wood of the church pews behind them.

Leon tried to point his gun at where he thought the moving target of Toro was going next, but by that time Toro had made up the distance between the two men. Leon pointed the gun left, preparing to shoot, just as the tip of the metal asp hit his hand holding the gun. The force and upward strike of the motion caused the gun to fly to Leon's right, toward a wall with a spectacular stained-glass window.

In one fluid motion, after knocking away Leon's gun, Toro flicked his wrist back attempting to strike Leon in the face with the asp. The hulking giant barely was able to duck the metal tip, but by that point Toro was already beside and then behind Leon, delivering a striking blow to the back of Leon's head. The strike opened a gash in the scar that ran down the back of Leon's head, and blood dripped to the floor of the church as Leon turned to face Toro.

After wounding Leon, instead of attacking, Toro waited, facing the man. Toro stood in the same spot of the church that Leon had occupied moments earlier.

"I'm disappointed in you, Leon. As much as you talk about being a ferocious fighter, when you finally faced me, you pulled your gun instead of settling this without weapons."

Leon's face flushed with embarrassment, which quickly turned to anger. "You're going to die either way. One is just quicker than the other." From his right hand, Leon flicked the switch to release his switchblade. He approached Toro, and the men circled each other like lions on the plains.

At that moment, a door near the front of the church opened, and a group of young boys walked inside. Closer to the priest and the boys that entered, Toro instructed the man, "Grab Diego and get him to the bike and send him to the location I told you about."

Toro stood in between Leon and his target, but Leon knew that he would not be able to snatch the boy while Toro remained there. Not waiting any longer, Leon charged, extending his arms so that they would take whatever blow was delivered by Toro's asp.

The blow came down hard on Leon's left arm. Just as quickly, Toro dropped to the ground, leaving his right leg in front of Leon, but swinging his left leg around. Rotating his hips, he tripped Leon, who fell to the ground, also losing his grasp on the switchblade.

Toro quickly stood, attempting to use the asp to deliver another debilitating blow to the back of Leon's head, but the large man rolled on his right side and delivered a punishing kick to the chest of Toro that caused him to stagger backwards, immediately losing his breath.

"If you're not here to kill the boy, then why do you want him?" Leon asked as the two men gathered themselves prior to resuming the fight.

"Enough have died," Toro gasped, regaining his breath. "He doesn't deserve to die for his father's sins."

"Ironic coming from a man that has killed thousands for much less."

"That doesn't mean I have to continue down that path."

"So, what, you're a savior now? Why do you even care?"

"I'm not a savior. I am just protecting the life of a boy that does not deserve to die. Especially not at your hands. I have seen what you have done with the other three children of El Jefe. I knew it was you and that you are coming for the children of Julian Rodriguez. Children do not deserve that fate."

"Some of those children grow into men. Men that kill. The oldest of Julian's bastards is the one that killed Juan Montoya."

The two men continued to circle each other. "It doesn't mean that Diego deserves to die, or any of the rest for that matter."

"Yes, it does. Especially when the request is made directly by the boss of the cartel, Carlos Montoya. Even if you are successful, and stop me from killing Diego today, I have the entire weight of the cartel behind me. We will come for the boy. We will find him and kill him."

"You'll have to get through me first," Toro said, assuming a fighting stance.

"Gladly," Leon said, as he rushed toward Toro, throwing combinations of jabs, hooks, elbow thrusts, knee blows, and reverse kicks. The attempted strikes were fast and furious, but Toro repelled each one. Having stood side by side with Leon for years, observing the man's tendencies and traits, his feigns and rushes, nobody on the planet was better able to withstand the withering assault of the ferocious Leon. Toro was forced to primarily play defense with occasional offensive strikes.

Leon's frustration rose as his normal tactics that had worked so well in street fights were deflected time and time again. He was ready to end this fight. He had to track the boy down. Having made up his mind that there was no more time to waste, Leon finally moved for the gun that remained on the ground near the wall of the church. He had wanted to end the fight with his fists but waiting any longer only increased the likelihood that Diego was going to escape.

Leon was several feet closer to the weapon, and landed on his right-side rolling, attempting to shoot Toro. Once again, Toro was on him, kicking the barrel of the gun straight up at the same time

Leon was turning. The impact of Toro's kick caused the gun to fire overhead, hitting a chandelier above, bringing it crashing to the ground between them as they rolled apart. The gun flew against the wall and landed on the floor in front of the stained-glass window.

Having sworn off using guns, Toro knew that he had to keep the gun on the ground and away from Leon, so Toro lunged for the weapon, but he was too close. Leon tackled him in stride, sending the two men crashing through the beautiful and historic stained-glass window. Leon landed advantageously on top of Toro as they hit the ground outside. Toro knew how precarious his situation was with him weakened considerably from the fight, and Leon on top. The situation grew worse when Leon sat up on Toro's chest, wrapping his giant hands around the man's throat, slowly choking the life out of him.

Toro bucked his hips as best he could to no avail. Leon was too big. Too strong. His vision started to blur, and he fought against unconsciousness, knowing that he would never again open his eyes if they closed. Toro's hands reached out beside him, searching for something, anything to use as a weapon, but finding nothing except for the dust and dirt on the ground outside the church, until...finally he found something.

His fingers came across the corner of the jagged edge of a broken piece of the stained-glass window. Even as his vision was blacking out, Toro gripped the sharp glass in his right hand. With his left hand, Toro grabbed the outside of one of Leon's wrists that was slowly choking him to death. But Toro wanted to make sure Leon's hand did not move. With his left hand, Toro held Leon's wrist, while he brought his right-hand underneath and slashed the wrist deep from one side to the other.

Leon let out a deep, painful scream, as the pressure from the cut wrist immediately subsided. Instinct caused Leon to release Toro's throat with the other hand and use his free hand to support the deeply cut wrist. Leon realized something had to be done to stop the blood flow quickly, or he would bleed to death.

With the release in pressure around his throat, vision slowly returned to Toro's eyes. Still lying on his back with the jagged piece of glass in his right hand, and Leon sitting on his chest but now clutching his own injured hand, Toro threw up his right hand, stabbing Leon in the left side of his neck.

Toro's vision returned just enough to see the look of shock in Leon's face as he realized the piece of glass was now embedded in his neck. Toro's goal of puncturing Leon's carotid artery was millimeters off, but the shock was just enough to allow him to buck his hips one last time and throw Leon off balance onto the ground, the larger man not sure which of his wounds he needed to staunch first.

Toro rolled onto his stomach and looked forward. In the parking lot 50 meters ahead was the motorbike he had arrived on. He willed himself to get up, stumbling and moving one foot in front of the other, desperate to get away from Leon and back to the rendezvous location to meet with Father Jose and young Diego.

Climbing on the bike, with his senses slowly coming back, Toro gave one last glance over his shoulder, hoping to see Leon sprawled out dead on the ground from blood loss, but expecting to see him charging toward the bike. But Leon was gone, nowhere in sight. Not waiting any longer, Toro turned on the bike and raced away from the church.

Chapter 12
Palm Springs, California

It was not the three consecutive 20-hour workdays that fatigued Victoria, it was the amount of time dedicated to paperwork documenting the meetings that had taken place as Reuben impersonated Vaquero. The circumstances could not have worked out better since Vaquero had yet to meet with any contacts in Southern California, and Reuben did an admirable job impersonating the Cartel businessman. Victoria was convinced that Reuben was atoning for the prior sins that had landed him in prison.

Under other circumstances, the collection of such a vast amount of intelligence on so many DEA targets would have been cause for celebration. However, with the looming threat of so many American citizens dying from fentanyl laced cocaine, Victoria did not feel like celebrating. And she did not let her team celebrate. In fact, reinforcements from D.C were called to help with the surveillance of so many of the recently identified targets. Victoria also had to employ local DEA teams in San Diego, Orange County, and Riverside. She would not provide those groups with intelligence on the targets her group had identified until Reuben was long gone. She would not risk him being recognized.

Still, the DEA needed additional information on these individuals that were identified. What other locations do they visit? What vehicles do they drive? Who else do they associate with? And most importantly, where is their stash location once they receive the cocaine? Once Reuben had confirmed the individual that would receive the dope, and that information had been documented in a DEA Report of Investigation, only then would Victoria give the green light to another DEA group to follow the target. Days and days of surveillance were not fun, but it was a necessary evil in the investigative process.

This investigation did not focus on one specific racial or ethnic group. Whites, blacks, Asians, and Hispanic criminal organizations throughout California were all waiting on the Cartel de Culiacan to release their dope. And after waiting for so long, Reuben had been able to calm fears, assuring each group that the cocaine would be in their possession within the week. Victoria only hoped that they could coordinate all the details perfectly so the DEA could seize as much poisoned dope at one time as possible, thereby saving as many American citizens as possible.

In the early morning hours as Victoria documented her 12th Report of Investigation, this one for their UC meeting late the previous night with a Hispanic gang based out of Coachella, her progress was stopped by a knock on the door. Looking at her clock, and seeing it was not yet 6:00 a.m., Victoria grabbed her Glock firearm that was on the desk beside her and walked to the door, asking who was there. When she heard Reuben's voice on the other end, she let him in, surprised to see that he was already dressed and ready to go for the day.

"You're getting an early start," Victoria said as he rushed in.

"Have to. I received a message at 5:00 a.m. It is from somebody that Vaquero knows named Teofilo. He stated that the *crystal* is ready and that it is pending delivery to the white biker gang we are scheduled to meet with at 9:00 a.m. Do you know this Teofilo? Is he legit?"

"Yeah, he's legit. We don't know much about him, but his name and contact information were in Vaquero's phone, along with a few text messages between them. We are not sure what his role was though. I guess he's the meth contact."

"Right. I told Teofilo that we are scheduled to meet with the Renegade biker gang today. He already knew. He gave me the phone number of the courier from the Cartel driving up 100 pounds of methamphetamine. What do you want to do?"

Victoria rubbed her eyes as she considered the options. "We can't blow off the delivery of meth, because if we do, then the Cartel will become suspicious about you before they agree to send the poisoned cocaine. Then we might never find out where it's going and when it's going to arrive."

"Right, but as a DEA agent, you can't knowingly let 100 pounds of crystal meth go without seizing it."

Victoria sat in silence for several moments, thinking about the two options, until she finally realized there were no good choices, just one less bad than the other. "As bad as it is to allow 100 pounds of crystal meth to hit the streets, it would be even worse to allow poisoned cocaine to hit the streets that would kill tens of thousands. We are going to have to let the 100 pounds of meth get to the Renegades. If we don't, then the Cartel de Culiacan won't trust you and they won't deliver all the cocaine to your contacts. I'll call the Deputy Administrator and let her know that is my decision."

"I agree that is the best thing to do. But if this goes bad somehow, and the press finds out that you let 100 pounds of meth hit the street, then you can bet that the DEA will deny that they ever gave you approval to do it. I don't want you to end up in a cell beside me for facilitating a drug transaction."

"Maybe Toby and our friends at the CIA can facilitate the transaction. They don't have to operate by the same strict rules regarding drugs as we do."

Reuben smiled, "Now you're talking. I like the way you think."

"I'm glad," Victoria said with sarcasm. "Now let me make some phone calls. I'll see you in a couple of hours."

* * *

Victoria and Reuben stood together in a spacious warehouse east of the resort city of Palm Springs, 100 miles east of Los Angeles. Since their initial speed bump with Big D in South Central, there had not been any trouble or pushback regarding Victoria's presence. That was partly due to Reuben letting each group know ahead of the meeting that he was going to be bringing a dirty fed with him that would keep the heat off. Victoria considered that the reason there had not been any complaints or side eyed glances.

The conversation with DEA Deputy Administrator had gone as planned, with her trusting Victoria's judgement, so long as she was not personally involved in allowing a criminal group to receive 100 pounds of crystal methamphetamine. It did not matter if the CIA carried out the deal, so long as Victoria could truthfully swear in court that nobody from DEA was personally involved.

Victoria felt more tense than normal as Reuben began the meeting with the Renegades. She was not sure if it was because the DEA was going to allow meth to hit the streets, something that went against everything she believed, or if the tension was for another reason.

The leader of the Renegades, a white man in his 50s, led the way, followed by three other men working in a subservient capacity.

Reuben tipped his cowboy hat in respect. "Mr. Dennis Johnson. I am Vaquero. Pleasure to finally meet you."

The leader of the Renegades looked at him before finally extending his hand. "I think we have met before, VA-QUE-RO," he said, slowly pronouncing the syllables in a condescending manner.

Victoria froze. Had Dodd met with Vaquero before in another capacity? Or what if Reuben had interacted with Dodd during a DEA investigation prior to going to jail? She was not sure what angle Dodd was playing. She glanced sharply at Reuben, who did not look back at her, but instead maintained eye contact with Dodd.

"I don't believe so, Mr. Dodd. I'm sure I would have remembered somebody of your status."

Reuben had called the man's bluff.

Dodd turned around to his cronies and laughed. "Yeah, you're probably right. My mistake."

The man nearest to Todd, a lean and sickly-looking white man with unkempt hair and an unshaven black beard patted Dodd on the shoulder. "It's hard to tell all these wetbacks apart, ain't it Dennis?"

The insult earned laughter from the other two cronies, but only a smile from Dodd. Reuben neither laughed nor smiled but stared at the man before looking back at Dodd.

"You'll have to excuse my brother. This is Scott."

Reuben just nodded at him but failed to extend his hand. It was not clear if Reuben was genuinely insulted by the comment, or if he were playing the part of an insulted Cartel employee that simply wanted to get the deal completed so he could move on to his next meeting.

"And who is this fine little thing?" Scott asked, looking Victoria up and down.

"I'm Victoria, but you needn't worry about me. Somebody like you would never get the pleasure." The jibe was intended to direct Reuben's anger away from the rednecks.

One of the other cronies moved forward. "I'll take you if I want to, and you won't do a damn thing to stop me." The man then swung his left hand around to get a handful of Victoria's rear.

Moments later he was on his knees, squealing in pain, after Victoria used lightening quick reflexes to grab the man's wrist and jerk it behind his back at such an impossible angle that it would have immediately snapped if he had not fallen to the ground in submission.

Scott attempted to intervene, but Victoria just increased the pressure, making the man squeal louder. Reuben looked at Dodd imploringly. "Are you going to get your men under control so we can complete this deal? If not, then we will walk out right now. I'm sure there are other groups that would gladly accept the first shipment of methamphetamine that has crossed the border in several weeks."

Dodd shrugged his shoulders. He seemed like a man that did not want to appear too needy or anxious. "Looks to me like the lady you brought needs to get herself under control before we can start."

"She'll release him, but if any of these guys lays a finger on her, then the weight of the cartel will come down on you. There will be bike parts and body parts from here to Montana. We can find another group that needs the product, that won't be a problem."

Victoria released the man and pushed him face down to the ground as she stepped back.

"Well, maybe we can find another group to deliver us the product," Dodd shot back. "I've heard the stories. I know some of the old cartels are trying to get back in the game. Maybe they already have. Maybe I've talked to some of them."

Reuben stared at Dodd, and then turned to look at Victoria.

"We'll be on our way," Reuben said. "You gentlemen have a good day."

Once again, the big guy had called the Renegades' bluff. Victoria walked beside him. "They'll wait until we get to the door," she whispered, as Reuben nodded. Just as she suspected, as soon as Victoria opened the door to the warehouse exit, Dodd called out.

* * *

Victoria drove a black Ford Explorer to the parking lot of a nearby shopping center, and met with several men, secretly working for the CIA at Toby's direction. Three duffle bags were loaded into the back of Victoria's Explorer. After a brief conversation, she started driving toward the warehouse where Reuben remained.

Before exiting the parking lot, a large pickup truck screeched to a stop in front of her, blocking her exit onto the main road. Behind her, another large pickup truck stopped so closely so that she could not reverse. A loud motorcycle screamed into the lot and stopped feet from the driver's side. All three drivers got out of their vehicles and approached Victoria with guns drawn. The trio of Renegades, led by Scott, approached the Explorer quickly but cautiously.

"Pop the trunk," he demanded. Victoria did as she was told. Scott leaned down in her face while the other two men went to the trunk. "The only thing worse than that wetback Mexican with a big cowboy hat, is a dirty wetback Mexican cop."

"I'm half-Italian, not Mexican, although I'm sure you don't know the difference," Victoria responded, despite the gun in her face.

"You look Mexican to me. We're just going to be taking this 100-pounds of crystal meth. You can say it was stolen from somebody else. That way the Renegades will not be needing to pay you Mexicans anything. It's the penalty you get for embarrassing my buddy back in the warehouse."

Victoria shook her head. These guys really were as stupid as they sounded and looked. They were willing to risk the complete and utter annihilation of their entire organization because one guy got offended in front of his buddies. Lucky for them, Victoria had anticipated this exact scenario as she looked into Scott's eyes before leaving the warehouse.

"Uhhh, Scott," one of the guys mentioned from the back of the vehicle. "There ain't no crystal in here. Just a bunch of clothes." Scott took his eyes off Victoria, looking at the back of the vehicle, in disbelief. In that moment, Victoria reached through the open window and snatched the handgun out of his grasp. She quickly opened the door and slid behind Scott as she held the gun to his head, while the other two cronies looked on in amazement.

"I never had the meth you idiots. I knew exactly what you were going to do. I could tell by the look in your eyes. The dope is currently with Vaquero and Dennis in the warehouse right now. If you want to make this a big deal, I can put a bullet in Scott's head and do all the women of Palm Springs a favor. My guy in that Escalade right there can finish off you two bozos."

The two men turned around to see a couple of men sitting in the Escalade with their rifles trained on them. The UCs from the CIA looked convincing in their role as Cartel security. "But don't worry," Victoria continued. "You two will probably be dead before you hit the ground."

The two men did not need to be convinced further. Both lowered their weapons and fled to their vehicles, leaving the area. Only after they were out of sight did Victoria lower the weapon from Scott's head, and push him back toward his bike.

She got back in her Explorer and left the area. She detested leaving guys like that to roam free, but it was necessary if they wanted to identify the poisoned cocaine coming into the US. "I will be seeing you again. I'll put the cuffs on you myself," Victoria promised, watching Scott's bike fade away in the distance.

* * *

Half an hour later the trio of Victoria, Reuben, and Toby were traveling southwest towards Lake Elsinore and on to Temecula for more meetings. Victoria had her laptop out, typing a report as Toby drove down the freeway. She liked to write the report of investigation while the meeting was fresh on her mind. While she composed the ROI, Toby gave a rundown of the next group they were meeting, a Hispanic gang that had moved from San Diego. They were large, but they controlled the flow of cocaine in the Lake Elsinore and Perris area, and they were anxious to get their hands on a shipment of 40 kilograms of cocaine that was two weeks overdue.

Toby's briefing, and Victoria's report writing, were both interrupted as a message dinged on Reuben's phone. After reading the message, Reuben's facial expression betrayed the fact that something was wrong.

"What is it?" Toby asked.

"This is a message...directly from Carlos Montoya." Up until that point, Montoya had been careful not to include himself on any communication with who he believed to be Vaquero, leaving that task up to his trusted bodyguard, Pelon.

"What does it say?" Toby asked.

"Good news and bad news. It says that the cocaine should arrive in the US within 48 hours."

"That's great news," said Toby, "it means this is almost over. What's the bad news?"

"His father's funeral is the same day the cocaine is scheduled to arrive in the States. Carlos expects to see Vaquero at the funeral. He has already purchased plane tickets for Vaquero to leave out of San Diego tomorrow night."

All three looked down at the floor, knowing what that meant. If Reuben showed up at the funeral, it would be obvious to those that knew Vaquero that Reuben was most definitely not Vaquero. Common logic would indicate that the situation would be resolved if Reuben just did not go to Mexico. But each one knew that if he did not go, then Montoya and others would get very suspicious, and perhaps delay sending the poisoned cocaine into the United States. If Montoya did not trust who he thought was Vaquero, then another individual would be used to coordinate when, where, and to whom the cocaine was delivered, which would leave the DEA unable to seize the poisoned cocaine prior to it getting into the hands of its eager American consumers.

"I have to go," Reuben realized. "Otherwise, all this will have been for nothing."

"You don't have to go," Victoria told him. "You've upheld your end of the bargain."

"The cocaine is going to arrive in California on the same day as Juan Montoya's funeral. If I go through with it, then maybe you guys will get the cocaine before I am discovered as a fraud at the funeral. Anything is better than nothing. It is the only way this will work. Some things are bigger than one person. Plus, if this will restore my reputation among those that I respected my entire professional career, then that only adds on to the reason why I should do it."

Reuben sent the message to Carlos: "See you soon."

Chapter 13
Tecate, Mexico

The quinceanera of Flora Fuentes-Lopez was as grand as any that had been held in the ballroom of a recently renovated community center in Tecate, a border town located 50 kilometers east of Tijuana just off the federal highway connecting Tijuana to Mexicali. All the customary Mexican traditions had been observed, and the best part of the night, the fiesta, was finally under way. Flora's father, Rodrigo Fuentes-Lopez, had spared no expense in the celebration of his daughter's 15th birthday. Her arrival at womanhood was something that he had promised would be as memorable as any that had ever occurred in the history of the family. He was not wrong that it was one that she would never forget, and Omega smiled as the man made the promise yet again on stage as he introduced a popular local Mexican band. The music and joyful noise brought young and old alike to the dance floor.

Dressed as a servant providing food and drinks to the partygoers, Omega had managed to mingle among the crowd, unrecognized by some of the very people who had recently committed themselves to overthrowing the Cartel de Culiacan's stronghold in Tijuana and re-viving the now defunct Fuentes de Tijuana cartel. Rodrigo's life had been spared when Toro and his crew went on their murderous rampage almost ten years earlier, but only because he had fled the country with his family like a coward. Now he was back to reclaim what he thought was rightfully his, and what better time to do so when your opponent has experienced such recent upheaval to include the loss of its leader? The death of Juan Montoya after Julian Rodriguez' death had only increased Rodrigo's resolve, and many of his former family and friends had flocked to him upon his return, pledging their loyalty.

The rebellion was only regional but had started with ambushes of local Cartel de Culiacan representatives in Tijuana and the surrounding areas. Several assassins had been captured and tortured, along with money movers and drug couriers. Their gruesome deaths displayed in the public for dramatic effect were combined with the efforts of several other cartels that were doing the same thing in other parts of the country, all of course which were propped up and funded significantly by the GDG in the east section of the country.

Looking at Rodrigo, it would have been impossible to know that he was recently responsible for planning and executing the murder of so many young Mexican men. His laughter and dancing gave the appearance that he did not have a care in the world.

After 20 minutes on the dance floor, Rodrigo walked to the bar to get a drink. Omega walked over to the bar at the same time with a tray and laid the server's tray on the counter. With his heart still thumping from so much physical activity, and the blare of the music from the stage, nobody noticed when Rodrigo lurched backwards, surprised by the prick in his hand. Not knowing what happened, he looked at the server beside him, and then at the bartender in front of him before his eyes got glazy and he began to stumble. Fortunately, Omega helped direct him to a chair, and Rodrigo was laid gently against the wall.

With most from the party enjoying the dance floor, nobody noticed Rodrigo in the chair. With one quick motion from behind, Omega plunged a long knife into the back of his skull near the neck, immediately killing him. Now, it was time to sit back and wait for the hysteria. It was the moment of realization, and the panic that followed, that Omega truly enjoyed. The best part was, that the moment, and what was planned afterwards, would be captured, and broadcast out for the whole world to enjoy.

* * *

While Rodrigo remained in the chair, his death unknown to the partygoers, Omega waded through the crowd, marking the other four targets. The location of each was confirmed when a scream shattered

120

the joyous atmosphere. Omega turned to see Rodrigo face down on the floor, having fallen forward when pulled to the dance floor by a family member.

The silence that had followed the scream was broken as Omega immediately hit a button, causing the sound of an intense barrage of gun fire and windows breaking to play over the loudspeakers. In an effort of self-preservation, every person hit the floor or scrambled toward the nearest exit. Omega was the only person standing among the people in the room.

The rest was like shooting fish in a barrel. Walking up to Rodrigo's lieutenant and right-hand man, a middle-aged man that had landed on his chest but was slowly rising attempting to determine what was going on, Omega placed the silencer equipped pistol directly against the side of his head and put one bullet through his brains.

Most people were still trying to save themselves and had not looked up to notice that a man was shot in the head by a servant. That included the next two men that were standing beside each other. One reached for a gun at his side as he laid on the floor to return fire, but he had no clue where to shoot at, as the speakers around the room gave the impression that the bullets were coming from every direction. Without remorse, Omega double tapped each man in the head, dropping them immediately.

The fifth and final target of the day had risen to his feet and was standing across the room. He led a group of people that were determined to rush to the exit and escape from the hell that was inside. With the aim of an expert knife thrower, Omega pulled out the blade that had just been used to kill Rodrigo and tossed it the length of the room. The blade landed hard and deep in the neck of the fleeing final target, its impact throwing him against the wall as he clutched at the blade and realized that he was quickly bleeding out. The death did not deter the stampede of partygoers out the door, as they fled outside to their vehicles.

Omega made one final sweep of the room after all the partygoers had fled the community center in terror. Each of the five dead men were dragged out the door, their feet tied to a chain at the back of a dusty black SUV. Although each man was dragged and tied up one by one, it took no longer than three minutes before the five bodies laid attached to the SUV.

Hopping in the driver's seat, Omega put the car in drive, and looked up at the drone above that was recoding the entire incident as the men's dead bodies were pulled along the dusty road for several miles until the vehicle arrived at a small shack, little more than a roof with four walls. It would serve the purpose for which Omega needed.

Setting up a live stream to all the latest social media sites, Omega used a voice altering device to describe how the five men that had been killed were all trying to revive the Fuentes-Tijuana Cartel. One by one, Omega laid out the evidence that had been collected, proving each person's guilt of fighting against the Cartel de Culiacan.

After proving the case and showing the video of the five deceased men being dragged several miles, the five bodies were pulled into an overgrown ditch. Omega doused them in gasoline, lit a match, and tossed the match on the pile of bodies.

Omega finished with a stark warning. "The message is clear. If you try to use this perceived moment of weakness to overthrow what belongs to the Montoya family and the Cartel de Culiacan, you will meet a fate worse than the five men behind me. For those that have already rebelled, your fate is sealed. I'm coming for you."

Chapter 14
Hong Kong, China

The bustling passengers coming and going from the Hong Kong International Airport took no notice of the three DEA agents walking to the exit, plotting a risky, yet potentially rewarding move designed to expose an American Congressman involved in the same human trafficking of Asian women that he railed against on television airwaves.

Remi traveled light, with a strap over her shoulder pressing a duffel bag close to her back. Bear walked in the middle, rolling a small suitcase with four wheels. The LA agents were led by Bear's former partner, Hong Kong DEA Special Agent Kevin Young, a first generation American whose parents were born and raised in Wuhan before moving to California and having Kevin, who they gave an American name in hopes to improve his ability to fit in with American classmates. The plan worked, and Kevin became popular, while still maintaining the strong work ethic installed in him by his parents. Kevin Young was a man that Bear trusted as much as anyone in the world. If Kevin thought this plan could work, then Bear did too.

Walking out the airport to his car, Kevin explained what had to be done before they got to the real reason for the trip.

"Okay, you guys are going to meet with all the DEA bosses at the office tomorrow morning. Wear your suit, shake hands, tell everybody what a great job they're doing, stroke their ego so they go back into the cushy chairs in their air-conditioned office and wait to get the notification from me that you guys are back on the plane to the US in three days."

"Those guys really aren't going to care what we are doing?" Remi asked in surprise.

"As long as it isn't something that is dangerous that could unravel and potentially threaten their career, then they could not care less."

Sitting in the front seat of the SUV, Remi looked at Bear in the back. "But isn't that exactly what we *are* doing?"

Kevin turned the ignition on the vehicle, put it in drive, and hit the gas. "Yes, it is very risky. Which is exactly why we won't tell them. As far as they know, you are meeting with some local counterparts that have a lead on the attorney from the Sun Yee On triad that received the shipment of weapons from Arizona that your group identified last week. That's *all* you're doing."

* * *

The next afternoon following the mandatory meetings and handshakes with DEA personnel at the Embassy, Kevin led Remi and Bear through a labyrinth of streets in and around an outdoor market. Finally, after walking more than 20 minutes, Kevin ducked into a small coffee shop and spoke with the owner for a short while, before placing money on the counter and walking to a back room, concealed from the main area by two wooden double doors.

Inside the room sat Chen Zung, a 28-year-old woman with shoulder length black hair and an athletic build. Chen, a Hong Kong native and former member of the People's Armed Police of China, was responsible for security, riot control, law enforcement, and antiterrorism. Chen was a rising star in the ranks but had taken on this mission as a private citizen, knowing that her country would not let her work together with the Americans in such a sensitive case.

Kevin made the introductions. "Chen, this is Bear and Remi. They are from the DEA in Los Angeles. You are going to be working with Remi. Bear is an old friend and colleague of mine. We worked together in California. He can be trusted."

As the lone non-Asian in the room, Bear could sense that Chen looked at him with doubt, but that look in her eyes went away with Kevin's assurances. "We're here for introductions, but most importantly, Remi and Chen need to get their stories straight. You guys need to make a bond to watch each other's backs during the next few days. If everything works, then we are going to identify a human trafficking ring from China that delivers women to a human trafficking group in California. As a DEA agent, I expect both Chinese and American organizations to have a number of illegal drugs. These drugs are used to pacify the women and give them what they want, while at the same time creating the dependency on the drug that will assure that the women will not leave. From what I have heard, and from the information Chen has as well, the triad, here in China, does not administer the drugs. They provide the drugs to the women because they know the women are addicts. If you two cover each other's backs, then neither will have to be injected with that poison."

"So, what's the plan?" Remi asked, anxious to get started.

Kevin nodded at Chen. Her English was fluent and impressive. "The People's Armed Police recently carried out several arrests and seizures. During the operation, I was able to identify and flip a scout for the Sun Yee On triad. He looks for needy women desperate for drugs and money, and if he suspects that the women can earn top dollar, he sends them to his boss. His boss has a contract with some Americans. They send the Americans beautiful Asian women that are addicted to cocaine or heroin, and the Americans make money off all the perverts in that country that have a thing for young Asian women."

Chen's delivery was concise and effective, but it was noticeably delivered with an edge. It was something more than just work and the desire to catch bad guys. It seemed personal. "Do you mind if I ask, do you have another reason for doing this, other than to catch bad guys?"

Chen locked eyes with Bear. "It *is* personal for me. These same guys grabbed my childhood best friend two years ago. The last I heard she was shipped to the States. We lost contact for more than a year, until I was finally able to track her down. Or at least what happened to her. She was found dead in some ditch in New Jersey. Cause of death was listed as overdose. Somebody literally just threw her out like the trash. I may not be able to find the exact guy that left my friend like that, but I'm going to take down as many people re-sponsible as I can in the mean-time."

"Works for me," Bear said. "Look, you and Remi are the ones putting your lives on the line. It is incredibly brave going undercover in this capacity. Remi is the youngest agent in my group. She is smart and decisive, and I think you two will be able to get the job done."

Kevin took back over the conversation, his anxious personality leading him to talk faster and faster to relay the urgency he lived by. "It's very important that when the scout takes you in, that you two are together, and that you both go to the same location in California. How long do you think you will be here in China before they want you in California?"

"Depends. Could be 24 hours, it could be a week. But I'll press my guy to do it as quickly as possible."

Bear grimaced, and Kevin knew why. They could get away with Remi being MIA for 24 - 48 hours. Anything much longer than that would raise eyebrows. It was important for the girls to make an im-pression, and express their desire to get to California, without tipping their hand.

"You trust this scout?" Remi asked Chen.

"I do."

"What kind of leverage do you have on him?"

"He is dating the daughter of a rival triad, the 14k. If either were to find out, then he would be tortured and killed. And then they would go after the girl. It would get real nasty, really quick."

Bear and Remi both nodded, looking at each other.

"We'll both be on surveillance and monitor as best we can," Kev-in said. "We won't have eyes or ears inside, so you two are going to be responsible for your own well-being, at least until you get to the US."

"And before that, you promise to identify and work up everyone involved from here in China?" Chen asked, looking at Kevin for as-surance.

"That's the deal. All that information will be handed to you as soon as you get to California and the individuals there are identified."

Satisfied, Chen turned toward Remi again. "You're a new agent?"

"Less than two years. But I can do this. I want to do this."

Chen half-smiled. "I believe you. I see it in your eyes. We will watch each other's backs."

"And like I said," Bear went on, "Remi is smart and trustworthy, I wouldn't risk her life and career if I didn't know she could do it, or if I thought there was another way to expose the guys back in California."

Chen continued sizing up Remi. "I believe she can do it. Not because I have any knowledge of the type of person that she is, but..."

"What?" Remi asked, curious to find out why Chen held this belief in her that they would be successful.

"There are three things I know the Americans want. First, they like Asian women. Second, they like young Asian women. Third, they like hot, young, Asian women. You check all three boxes."

Remi smiled at the compliment. Kevin stood up and patted Bear on the shoulder. "Okay you two," he said to Remi and Chen. "Bear and I are going to step outside for about half an hour. Get your stories straight. How you know each other. What your drug of choice is. How much and how often. How you plan on faking it. Why you want to go to California, without seeming too obvious or desperate. The meet with the scout is later tonight."

Kevin walked outside the coffee shop and lit up a cigarette.

"What do you think the odds are that we are going to be successful?" Bear asked his old partner, who blew out a long stream of smoke before providing a response.

"With the end goal of arresting an active US Congressman? Not sure. It is entirely dependent on those two women. One of them has less than two years in law enforcement." He shook his head as he took another long drag of his cigarette and looked around anxiously. "But if they are successful, it is going to create a firestorm."

127

Chapter 15
El Centro, California

The peaceful pre-dawn hours always prepared Victoria for the mania that came with the rise of the sun and the start of a new workday. She had given up on sleep shortly after midnight and sat on a bench outside her motel, content with nothing more than her thoughts and the sounds of nature. Those thoughts were consumed with the outcome of the DEA Special Agent's carefully crafted plan. She walked through the plan step by step, from the team and team leader assigned for each location, to the plan to transport the poisoned cocaine to the Southwest Lab in San Diego. A police escort would travel with vehicles transporting the dope from areas nearby. For the locations further away, such as Victorville and San Bernardino, Victoria had coordinated with Stan from Group 5 in the Los Angeles Field Division. The former military man had experience flying in helicopters and was comfortable in that capacity, so it was decided that he travel to each location as the passenger of a DEA owned helicopter, pick up the cocaine seized from each location more than 150 miles away from San Diego, and then fly to the lab. Doing so would eliminate the risk of that much dope being in vehicles on the street for such a long period of time.

Despite the thousands of kilograms of poisoned cocaine that were scheduled to enter the US later that day, potentially killing tens or hundreds of thousands of Americans, at the forefront of her thoughts was Reuben, who was at a hotel in Culiacan at that same moment.

He had sent a message a couple of hours prior to midnight, letting her know that he had arrived at the hotel in Culiacan as arranged by Carlos Montoya. Nobody had yet recognized that he was not in fact the real Vaquero because he had not seen anyone prior to check in. Hopefully by the time the realization was made, the DEA would be in possession of one of the largest seizures of cocaine ever to come across the Southwest Border. The seizure itself was not the only thing that hung in the balance, but also the lives of those that would be lost if the poisoned kilograms of cocaine were consumed. Was Reuben's life worth sacrificing for the lives of those abusing illegal drugs? Victoria was sure that the life of one was worth sacrificing for the lives of so many others, especially if those others were drug addicts or users. Who knew what one of those lives saved might end up doing? What if one of the people saved ended up turning their life around and found the cure for cancer?

Still, now that the moment of truth had arrived, Victoria felt an undeniable sense of sadness and regret. Today was going to be the day that Reuben Valdez died. And several hours of torture would likely precede his death. The work the former DEA Special Agent had put in to get to this point was as honorable as anything Victoria had ever been a part of. But the fact remained that Reuben Valdez was a convicted criminal, and that was how he was going to be remembered by many after his death.

Victoria played back the conversations in her head between Toby and Reuben prior to Reuben's departure, trying to remember if anything had been left out. If there were any last-minute pearls of wisdom that might help Reuben.

Keep the cowboy hat down low over your face as much as possible. There had been a discussion about whether he should go without the hat. But the hat was his ticket into the event. Everyone knew Vaquero because of the hat.

Sit down as soon as you get there so that his height will not be recognized.

Try not to talk much. If you do, give only short answers.

Most importantly, try to avoid those that had known relationships with Vaquero, mainly Carlos Montoya, his bodyguard Pelon, and the meth trafficker and chemist Teofilo. Pictures were provided of each person so that Reuben knew to avoid those specific individuals. But what about somebody else not on their radar? It was a crapshoot. Reuben's ploy was to extend this as long as possible, so as many of the deliveries as possible of cocaine could be made to Southern California. It was not lost on Victoria that Carlos was holding his father's funeral on the same day, at the same time, as more than 2000 kilograms were being transported across the border and into Southern California. It was a sign that he was in charge. Carlos Montoya was running the show.

More than 300 law enforcement members were on standby in 21 different locations across Southern California. All over Los Angeles, San Diego, San Bernardino, Victorville, Riverside, Lake Elsinore, and Coachella, DEA agents and other federal personnel were watching the locations where Reuben had been instructed to deliver the cocaine. Each location had a team leader that had to get clearance from Victoria before being allowed to descend on the location and seize the dope. She wanted to get seizures from as many of the deliveries as possible. Lives hung in the balance.

Finally, at 3:00 a.m., Victoria went to the DEA Imperial County Office in El Centro. The moment of truth was at hand.

* * *

The first two deliveries of the day were scheduled to two different locations in El Centro. Both deliveries were 200 kilograms, a substantial shipment, but one that Montoya had felt was necessary due to the length of time since the previous shipment.

Victoria was designated as the team leader for Alpha Team. She walked into the meeting room and was met by the Team leader for Bravo Team, Ana Lucia Rodriguez.

Having thoroughly studied the file of Reuben Valdez prior to recruiting him to go undercover as Vaquero, Victoria had analyzed every single relationship he had. She had also reviewed all the different agents that were involved in the case that had such amazing results in terms of seizures of drugs and money, but calamitous effects in terms of lives and careers lost. In addition to Reuben's imprisonment for corruption, Victoria knew that one agent had been killed during a shootout in Juarez, another agent leaped to his death from a residential building in Mexico City out of drunken humiliation and shame, while Reuben's friend from San Diego was fired and an El Paso agent was transferred to Headquarters. The only DEA agent to make it out was Ana Lucia Rodriguez, who was now standing before her as the Team Leader for the Bravo Team.

The two headstrong women offered the other a strong handshake and smile as introductions were made by the Supervisor of the El Centro office.

"You have all the information and instructions?" Victoria asked.

"I do. We are going to begin surveillance at 04:30 at the warehouse receiving the second delivery of cocaine. A vantage point from an empty business across the street has already been arranged. I will be there myself. The delivery of cocaine is supposed to arrive at 7:30 a.m., 30 minutes after the delivery to your location at 7:00 a.m. But unless the dope moves from the warehouse, we are not going to take any enforcement action until I hear from you."

Victoria had not informed the other DEA agents involved in the takedown operation that all the kilos of cocaine had been laced with a lethal amount of fentanyl, designed to cause a rebellion against Carlos Montoya and the Cartel de Culiacan. It was extra information that would not change the tactical aspect of the investigation, and it would likely draw more questions than necessary about the origin of the intelligence.

"Right. There are 21 deliveries that are supposed to take place across Southern California from 7:00 a.m. – 12:00 p.m. today. If one of these first few deliveries are hit immediately by law enforcement, then there is a significant chance that the other deliveries will be cancelled. We must be patient, and not swoop in as soon as the cocaine arrives. The cocaine will likely sit at the warehouse for hours. If not, then you will need to follow any vehicle that leaves, while also maintaining surveillance of the warehouse. We want to get the most bang for our buck."

"I understand. We are going to have a helicopter overhead, so if any vehicles leave the warehouse, we will follow it as far as possible."

"Good. All of the dope coming today is likely going to be separated into smaller shipments before being distributed to the consumers. Hopefully, that will buy us the time that we need until noon. If all 21 deliveries are made by noon, we will hit everything at the same time."

"Sounds good," Ana Lucia said. Before they parted, Ana Lucia looked at Victoria. "Whatever intel you have that got you to this point, at the end of all this, I would appreciate it if you would throw some scraps my way. I'd love to get something big going down here."

Victoria smiled sadly, realizing that the source of intelligence was going to dry up sooner than anyone realized. "If I can, I will."

* * *

While most federal agents coordinating such a large takedown considered it necessary to be in the controlled environment of an office setting to handle any obstacles that came up among any of the different 21 locations being surveilled by law enforcement, Victoria held a different viewpoint. She wanted to be in the field, overseeing the first location. If something screwed up the first transaction, then the entire operation would fall apart. Hopefully, if the first delivery went through as planned without any hiccups, then the other deliveries would likewise go smoothly and none of them would be delayed.

Victoria sat in the driver's seat of her black Ford Explorer, parked on the street, three houses away from the residence where the very first delivery of cocaine was going to arrive. She had her lap top open and sitting on the passenger's seat, with an interactive map of all 21 locations across Southern California, with the name and contact number for the team leader of each location. She would be able to update the map, which was being simultaneously viewed by the DEA Administrator and the DEA Deputy Administrator back in Washington DC, as soon as confirmation was given that the deliveries had been made.

Search warrants had been drafted and were given to a Federal Judge in the Southern District of California. All that needed to be updated was the time of the delivery. As soon as that information was obtained, the judge had given his assurance that the warrant would be signed. 21 different warrants sat in the judge's chambers as he awaited word from Victoria.

At 7:00 a.m. sharp, Victoria observed a Honda Odyssey van with California license plates pull into the driveway of the residence. These traffickers were punctual, which was a good sign that hopefully the remaining deliveries would be punctual as well. With the aid of binoculars, Victoria wrote down the license plate of the Odyssey. She snapped a couple of pictures of the van as it pulled into the garage, and then she waited. This was it. The first delivery was finally being made.

Knowing the van would be there for about a half an hour as the courier took the time to open the hidden compartment and remove all 200 kilograms from the trap, Victoria updated the laptop to confirm that delivery was being made to location one. She then grabbed the cell phone that was dedicated for communication with Reuben and Toby and advised both that the first delivery had been made. Reuben replied a short time later, passing along the information that he was coordinating on his cell phone while still pretending to be Vaquero.

Reuben texted. *"Going smooth so far. Next delivery at 7:30 a.m. at location 2 should be on time. Driver is about to cross the line. From there it will only be 10 or 15 minutes."*

"What time do you leave for the funeral?" Toby asked.

"Five till 9. I'll get there about a quarter after."

Victoria thought about sending a reply, but what was there to say to the man that was essentially going willingly to his own execution? As soon as Carlos, Pelon, or Teofilo realized that Reuben was not Vaquero, then he would be captured and tortured, and the deliveries stopped. But if Vaquero failed to show for the funeral, then suspicions would arise, and the remaining deliveries would also end. It was a no-win situation.

As Victoria continued to mull over the different scenarios, she was not able to come up with one in which Reuben survived to see the end of the day. Her train of thought was finally broken after receiving a phone call from the Bravo Team Leader, Ana Lucia.

"F-250 just showed up at our location here at the warehouse. Mexican plates. I'll see who the registered owner is and will text the info."

"Sounds good, thanks."

"Has your guy come out of the garage yet?"

"Not yet. I'm sure it's taking a while to pull out those 200 kilos."

"You think there's a chance the dope doesn't leave the residence until noon, when all the deliveries have been made?"

"Let's hope so. Let me know when the truck leaves your location. If any other vehicles leave from the warehouse, give me a call, and we'll have a decision to make."

"Copy that," Ana Lucia said, ending the call.

Victoria updated the interactive map on the computer, and said to herself, "Two deliveries down, 19 to go."

Chapter 16
Culiacan, Sinaloa

The 48-hour wake for Juan Montoya ended at 9:00 a.m., and the procession moved from the community center to the large Catholic Church where Montoya had been a regular attender. Having missed the wake in lieu of his approved business obligations in the United States, Vaquero was expected to be present for the funeral. Maintaining the façade that he was Vaquero was easy when Reuben was in the US meeting with people that had never met Vaquero and did not know what to expect. Plus, he was protected by the strength of the federal government, both the DEA and the CIA. Now, here in the heart of cartel territory, Reuben was on his own.

As the cab stopped in front of the Catholic church, Reuben looked at the front doors, unsure if the individuals standing at the doors were friends of Vaquero or not. His phone had been busy all morning, pinging with messages from both the cartel's couriers delivering cocaine, and the drug recipients in Southern California receiving the dope. Reuben stole a glance at the phone to see if there was an update. Other than a few last-minute location changes, everything had gone smoothly. Nine of the 21 deliveries had been made. Reuben had done his best to urge the customers in Southern California to be very careful before transporting the "product" away from the initial location where it was delivered.

Give it time to cool off.

Watch for law enforcement.

This is the first delivery of cocaine in almost two months. The feds will be anxious.

Make sure the coast is clear before you move the "product."

Reuben hoped those suggestions to the different organizations, whether it was the white biker gangs in San Bernardino, the Hispanic gangs in San Diego, or the black gangs in South Central Los Angeles, would afford Victoria and Toby the time that they needed for all 21 deliveries to be made before the takedown started.

It was 9:03 a.m. The message from Pelon came as he was waiting to get out of the cab. "*I am here with Carlos. We are waiting in a room to go in and will be seated in front. See you after the service. Carlos is very interested to hear how the deliveries are going this morning.*"

There was no more time to delay. Reuben opened the door, keeping his head low to the ground, and placed Vaquero's famous cowboy hat on top of his head, beginning his walk toward the church.

* * *

Reuben walked up a series of steps as he came to the entrance of the immaculate church. It was a spectacle to behold, and under other circumstances, he would have taken the time to marvel at the beautiful architecture and decoration.

Cautiously eyeing the people welcoming attendees of the funeral, Reuben noticed one was a clergy man of the church. To his side was a bodyguard, likely from Pelon's staff protecting Carlos. The man had a device checking for weapons. Even in church, that was something that had to be done at a cartel funeral.

But it was the woman standing beside the two men that caught Reuben's eye, and likely the eye of every warm-blooded man nearby. Dressed respectfully in a knee length black dress that was tight around a slim waist and snug against her chest, Reuben wondered who this woman was that had captivated the attention of so many men coming for the funeral for the leader of the Cartel de Culiacan. She was not included on the list of people that Carlos and Victoria had briefed him on.

Reuben tried to keep his eyes at his feet as he came through the door, but they had already made eye contact with the woman, who caught Reuben's gaze as he looked away. Approaching the bodyguard, the man looked at Reuben and held a hand up, waving the metal detector over his body as he looked at the woman for confirmation allowing the man to enter. The woman gave a quick nod of her head, and then spoke.

"Based on your famous cowboy hat, I assume you are Vaquero. Carlos has told me much about you."

Reuben nodded his head respectfully. This was the first test. This woman had obviously never met Vaquero, but how much could Reuben say without being burned? "Yes," he said in a deep voice, with an attempt at a country twang, "and you are?" Reuben picked up the woman's left hand and kissed it ever so gently.

"Carlos was right. He said you were quite the gentleman. I am Fernanda Castillo."

Castillo. Why did that name sound so familiar? But then, he knew. "Castillo...your father is the..."

"The leader of the GDG, yes," she said confidently. "But I am here now as the fiancé of Carlos Montoya. We are planning a wedding ceremony immediately after the funeral. We want this day to be remembered positively. Juan Montoya might be gone, but his legacy will live on. This marriage will unite the two most powerful...business organizations in our country. There will not be any more fighting or warring between groups."

Suddenly a light bulb went off inside Reuben's head. *That was how they were going to do it.* Castillo's father, the leader of the GDG, had made secret arrangements with the Colombians to poison the cocaine that was going to the US today under the umbrella of the Cartel de Culiacan. After it was apparent that the kilograms had been poisoned, and so many people died, Carlos, as new leader of the Cartel de Culiacan, would be considered responsible for killing so many of its customers. He would be captured or more likely killed. And who better to take control in the power vacuum, than the daughter of the next most powerful cartel in the country. The Castillo family was not content with being the most powerful drug cartel in eastern Mexico. The Castillo family wanted it all. They wanted the routes in the western portion of Mexico, which would give them control of not only the customer base in the western United States, but also international consumers from around the Pacific. The Cartel de Culiacan's contract with organizations in other countries such as Canada, Australia, Japan, and many other East Asian countries, was well known.

If Fernanda Castillo assumed command of the Cartel de Culiacan upon the death or arrest of Carlos Montoya, it would exponentially increase the business dealings for their family. They would be the most powerful, and wealthy organization in the western hemisphere, if not the world.

Reuben did not say anything as these thoughts rushed through his brain, instead focused on keeping his head down and blocking his face from anybody walking by that might potentially recognize the man under the cowboy hat was not the real Vaquero.

Fernanda broke the silence, and put her hand under Reuben's chin, raising his face so that their eyes met. "I know that you, of all people, must be suffering greatly from the death of Senor Montoya. Other than his own family, I cannot imagine anyone he was closer to during his lifetime. He obviously trusted you a great deal, since you were the only person that previously worked for Julian Rodriguez that he kept in his employment when he assumed control. That tells me that you are a very, very loyal man. I trust that you will express that same loyalty to his son, and my soon to be husband, Carlos."

"Of course."

"Excellent. Now, walk with me," she said, looping her arm inside his as they walked away from the door. "I'm sure Carlos will be pleased to see you are here so the services can begin. He and his sister are in a room near the front, about to walk in and take their place."

Reuben's body noticeably stiffened as Fernanda indicated that she was taking him to see Carlos, but he continued to be led. He could not stop in his tracks, or could he? Should he just leave the church now? He was walking to his death for what? To help the same government that threw him in solitary confinement. To save the lives of a bunch of drug addicts, or spoiled rich kids mooching off mommy and daddy's money to fuel their drug habits?

He had known this moment was coming prior to coming to Mexico, and he knew the answer to those questions, and reminded himself of his convictions, and the desire to restore his reputation that he thought had been forever ruined by agreeing to work with Vaquero and look the other way as a DEA agent in Los Angeles when the Cartel de Culiacan had large shipments of cocaine and money coming and going through Southern California and Mexico.

Fernanda continued to walk with Reuben, arm in arm, as they went around the side of the church, and down a hall. "The door is just there on the left," she mentioned, seemingly eager to get the ceremony started. The sooner the funeral was over, the sooner that she married Carlos Montoya, Reuben thought as they approached the door. At this point, there was nothing left to do except accept his fate. He had hoped that he would be able to extend this moment until the end of the funeral, or at least another hour or so, giving Victoria the time that she needed back in the US.

With no family back in the States, and all his friends avoiding him like the plague except his old partner Tyler that wrote him weekly, Reuben had nobody that he cared about seeing again. His emotions changed from questioning why he was doing what he was doing, to accepting that this was how it was going to end for him. And he was okay with that.

"Vaquero!" a voice shouted from behind them as Fernanda put her hands on the doorknob. Instead of opening the door, she turned to look at the man approaching them.

Reuben turned around slowly, looking into the eyes of the man, waiting for the realization that he was not Vaquero. But that realization never came.

"Ms. Castillo, I am very sorry to interrupt you! Please accept my sincerest apologies, but a situation has come up that requires Vaquero's attention."

Fernanda's hand dropped from the doorknob. "I'm sorry, I am still learning everyone and their roles. I am afraid I do not know you. Is everything okay?"

The man looked at Reuben's eyes, and then turned to Fernanda. "I'm sure it will be. My name is Sergio. I have worked for the Montoya family for several years, inside the headquarters of Telcel."

Telcel was the largest cellular telephone communication company in Mexico. Reuben should have known that the cartel had somebody on the inside in all the major organizations in Mexico, but still the revelation was surprising. It explained how the Cartel was often so able to avoid detection from law enforcement, and it surely gave them an advantage on other rival drug traffickers in Mexico.

Fernanda nodded. Reuben sensed that she was a woman in total control, playing her role as a loving spouse until the moment came to seize power for herself. As the oldest child of the leader of the GDG, she was used to giving commands, and having them followed, but she was playing a careful game until she married Carlos. She would not do anything to jeopardize that.

"Yes, Carlos mentioned a contact with your company. What is the problem?"

"I'm sure you're aware of the deliveries being made today," Sergio said.

"Yes, business has finally resumed."

"Right. Well, I've just been made aware that one of your drivers might be compromised by American law enforcement."

Before Reuben had a chance to respond, Fernanda said, "Based on what intelligence?"

The man smiled uncomfortably as he looked at Vaquero, and then back to Fernanda. "I've been monitoring not just the phones for cartel drivers and workers, but also those individuals they are in contact with from the different organizations in the United States. There is a back door to check certain things with the American cell phone companies. I only use that back door during significant operations, as to not draw too much unwanted attention. I figured that with the amount of product being distributed today, that it was an appropriate step to take."

"Of course," Fernanda answered. "What information did you learn?"

"One of the customers in Coachella is being investigated by the DEA. The feds are listening to his phone. He doesn't know."

"Has Vaquero been in contact with this person being intercepted by American federal law enforcement?" Fernanda asked.

"No, but a cartel driver has been intercepted in contact with the Coachella customer. The American authorities are investigating two brothers working together in Coachella. Vaquero has been in contact with the older brother. That brother's phone is clean and has not been intercepted by the American federal agents. But the cartel driver delivering cocaine today contacted the younger brother. The younger brother *is* being intercepted by the feds. Vaquero needs to immediately call the older brother in Coachella and the cartel driver and warn them both to change locations. He also needs to pass along the instruction for the younger brother to dump his phone."

Fernanda nodded, giving approval. "Business calls. Do what you must, I'm sure you will be able to find a spot in the back of the church after you handle the call."

"Yes, ma'am," Reuben responded, his head abuzz with everything he just heard.

"Make the phone call. We will get the service started." Fernanda opened the door to walk into the room as Sergio grabbed Reuben by the shoulder and started walking down the hall toward the front of the church, away from the room where Carlos was waiting.

Sergio looked back over his shoulder and called out to the fiancé of Carlos Montoya, "Please let Senor Montoya know that Vaquero is here to pay his respects. Perhaps it will provide him some comfort."

Fernanda just smiled, as she entered the room, and closed the door behind her.

* * *

"Don't worry," Sergio assured Reuben, "I work with Toby."

Reuben's eyes bulged out. This guy was undercover with the CIA!

"I was able to get you out from going into that room with Carlos, but there is security posted at every exit of the church. You couldn't leave if you wanted."

"Is there really a problem with one of the customers being intercepted by American law enforcement?" Reuben asked.

"No, I made that up. But I really do work for Telcel. I've been there for years, so I knew it would work."

"So, you've never met the real Vaquero?"

"No, which is how I knew I could get away with it. He is famous for the big cowboy hat. I'll just say I didn't want to bother Carlos before the funeral."

"Your cover won't be burned?"

"No."

"And you've been undercover for how long?"

"Too long. Years. The lines start to get blurred at times as to who I really work for, but the information I have been able to provide has been valuable, which is the only reason I am still here. Toby told me about your situation. It is a very valiant thing you are doing. I wanted to do what little I could to help. At the very least this just bought you an extra hour, until the end of the funeral."

"What's going to happen next?"

"They'll go to the graveside and then there will be a gathering of family and friends. I assume Carlos will want to speak with Vaquero. At that point, I'm not sure if there is anything that I can do. If I can, I will."

"I understand. I knew the outcome coming here."

"How many of the deliveries have been made?" Sergio asked.

"As of 9:00 a.m., nine have been made. Four more each hour for the next three hours."

"Good. Well, at least these next four should be made without any interruption. As for the last two hours, that is anybody's guess. My advice would be to hang in the back of the church. Take a long bathroom break. Whatever you can. As for now, hunker down in the back of the church, near the middle of an aisle, so that Carlos will see the cowboy hat if he looks back, or maybe when the family is walking out of the church and going to the grave side. It will buy some more time. Good luck." And with that, the undercover CIA case agent walked away, having bought Reuben an extra hour of life. But he realized that the intercession had likely not changed the result.

* * *

Once Fernanda entered the room, she approached Carlos while he stood talking to Pelon. Carlos was talking while looking at a local newspaper.

"As soon as this is over, Pelon, I want you to find out who this Omega is." Carlos held up the newspaper article explaining the killer's most recent escapades in taking out members of the Fuentes de Tijuana Cartel before continuing.

"Of course. I'm glad that Omega is on our side. But who is he? And why is he fighting on our side? We need to figure that out as soon as possible. It makes me look foolish."

"I will look into it immediately," Pelon said.

Carlos' sister, Maria, recently arrived to attend her father's funeral, stood up from the chair. "Why does it matter, brother? This person is doing your bidding. Be grateful. I'm sure the intent is not to make you look foolish."

Carlos hugged his sister and kissed her on the forehead. All the recent events, to include the deaths of the two most recent leaders of the Cartel de Culiacan, had been put into motion when Carlos walked into a bedroom to witness the son of Julian Rodriguez raping Maria, the daughter of Juan Montoya. Seeing his sister being raped, Carlos beat Julian's son to death, and the relationship between their fathers was forever altered. Ever since that moment, Carlos went out of his way to make sure that his sister, Maria, was protected. His heart ached for her as she struggled with depression. He worried that he would never see her again. While Carlos was forced to turn himself in to the American authorities, he had heard that his sister, Maria, had left Mexico, traveling the world in search of herself, anything to distance herself from the painful memory of the traumatic event at the hands of Victor Rodriguez. Despite everything, here they were, brother and sister, back together again against all odds, but without their father. Carlos would do anything to protect his sister, and he wrapped his arm around her as he looked at his fiancé.

"Yes, of course you are right, Maria."

Fernanda smiled at them both. "Vaquero is here. He is handling some business that just came up. Something immediate that required his attention, but I advised him to take a seat in the back of the church, and you will meet with him after the graveside services."

"Excellent," Carlos said, using his free hand to grasp the hand of Fernanda, as the trio exited the room and walked into the church, sitting down on the front pew. Carlos and Maria both could not take their eyes of the casket which held the lifeless body of their father.

In the back of the church, former DEA agent Reuben Valdez found an open spot in the middle of an aisle, just as the funeral was beginning.

Chapter 17
Hong Kong, China

The guard outside the downtown Hong Kong club gave a nod to the two attractive women in their mid-late 20s. The women were on the outer limits of the young crowd that usually frequented the establishment. But dressed in tight black dresses that showcased enough cleavage and an enticing back side, he would not get any grief from his bosses with the Sun Yee On triad inside the club.

Passing through the front door was a good sign to Chen. It signaled that her new informant, Yao, a human trafficking scout for the Sun Yee On triad, had provided his first bit of truthful intelligence. He had assured Chen that the guys out front had a soft spot for women in tight black dresses. Knowing how to look the part was essential to get in. Now she had to find the other scout. It would not have looked normal for Yao to go outside the club and bring her in, but the man's information had gotten them into the club. Chen and Remi hoped that the rest of his intelligence was accurate.

Inside the club, the dark dance room floor was illuminated intermittently with quick bursts of bright colored rays. Orange, yellow, red, green and all other kinds of mixtures of lights pulsated through the club with the beat of the music. The pounding of the music through the overhead speakers contributed to an overall festive atmosphere, at least on the surface. Underneath that surface, a far darker game had been at play for a long time. Several men, designated as owners or managers of the club, were on the payroll of the Sun Yee On triad. They were on the lookout for desperate women that frequented the club and were suspected or known to have little or no male companionship, so that their disappearance would go unnoticed by local authorities until the women were long gone. It was even better if those women had a known dependence on drugs, because their actions could be controlled much easier by offering something they knew the women could not refuse.

Remi's long ponytail bounced as she walked hand in hand with Chen through the club, directly past the man that Chen had recently developed into an informant. Several club goers gazed longingly at the two attractive women as they made their way across the room, but the two women had one plan in mind.

Yao nodded approval and led the two women down a hallway and away from the dance floor. Opening a door into a private office, Remi and Chen both entered. Their law enforcement instincts immediately caused them to look in the corners of the room and behind the door for any unseen threats.

"Just us," Yao said to Chen in Mandarin. He looked approvingly at Remi. "Does she speak the language?"

"Some," Remi answered.

"Good. You both look good."

"We didn't come here for your approval. You know why we are here. Do what you said you would do, and the information I have stored in my desk that could have you killed will be destroyed. If you do not, then there are arrangements for that information to come out to the very people that you don't want it to go to."

Usually in a place of authority over women, Yao seemed uncomfortable being spoken to like that by Chen, but he held his tongue, eager to get the night over.

"I'm going to have to transport you two, along with other women, to a more secure location two hours away."

"What kind of secure location?" Remi asked.

"It's a warehouse, close to a private airfield. You will have to stay the night. Two nights at most. But then the women will be loaded onto a large jet and you will be taken directly into California. From what I understand, the contracts have already been signed. The Americans are anxious to get another delivery. Their demand for Asian women is very great."

"You're sure it's the same American group in California?" Chen asked.

"Yes. I know what kind of girls they like. The politician and I have the same taste in women. Part of the agreement was that I supplied all the girls."

"You know the politician?" Remi asked, wondering if he meant Congressman Lightfoot.

Yao looked at Chen unsure of how to answer. "We're not going to use this as evidence, or for testimony," Chen said. "We just want to make sure where we are going."

Yao nodded. "Okay. Yes, the Congressman from California. The white guy."

"How do you know him?" Remi asked.

Yao looked at Remi a while before answering. "I met him in a club much like this one, a year before he was elected. He already had contacts with the Triad. He knew what I did. We were introduced, and the rest is history."

"How many girls have you sent over to the Congressman since you met him?" Remi asked.

Yao scoffed and shrugged his shoulders. "Hundreds, maybe thousands."

Remi shook her head in disgust. Chen looked at her and asked, "Are you sure you want to do this? This is your last chance to back out."

"I'm sure."

Yao walked to another door in the back of his office. Opening the door, he led Remi and Chen into a room. Sitting in chairs and on sofas, or standing around, were 12 other Asian women, all young, skinny, and attractive, but with one noticeable difference, the defeated look of a recent drug addict that had no other place to go.

* * *

The 14 women exited the building from a door in the back of the club. Parked just outside was a large black Mercedes Sprinter van. Remi and Chen were in the back of the line of women willingly entering the van. Remi looked to see if there was any chance that Bear and Kevin were in position to see them getting into the vehicle, but she realized that their location was concealed and out of view. Realizing the same thing, Chen shrugged her shoulders. "They'll catch up," she assured her as both women entered the vehicle and found a seat.

Before the back door closed, one of the pitiful women looked pleadingly at Yao, begging him for a snip of coke before the trip started. Yao looked at the other women that all had their eyes on him, including Remi and Chen. "Wait here," he told the woman, as he went to the front of the van, and retrieved a small duffel bag from the front seat. Throwing the bag to the back of the van, Yao said, "Have at it," as he started the vehicle and left the employee designated parking lot.

Remi looked on in astonishment as the women in the back of the van fought over possession of the duffel bag. More so, the fight was over the contents inside the duffel bag. Before the fighting got out of hand, the van stopped hard, with the women that were fighting tumbling over each other toward the front seat. When everyone looked up, Yao pointed a gun at the women. "No more fighting. The next one of you to make a noise, I'm going to leave on the side of the street with a bullet in the head."

The warning had the desired effect, as the threat of death overtook their desire for a quick fix. One of the women ended up with the bag and sat down in a seat while she pulled out a small glass frame that was used to hold the powder, as she snorted the powder up her nose. After finishing, the woman passed the bag to her side. "Plenty in there for all of us," the woman said happily.

A little unnerved by the up close and personal effects of human trafficking and drug addiction, Remi shifted in her seat, crossing her legs at the ankles as she looked at Yao. She felt a hand on top of her right hand and was comforted by Chen. Despite her tough exterior, the Chinese officer was doing her best to comfort her American friend.

As the journey began, Remi's nerves started to calm. She told herself that Kevin and Bear were behind them, following the van from a safe distance. Bear and Kevin would monitor their every move until boarding the plane to California. According to what Yao had told them, they would be at the warehouse one night, two at the most, which was as good as they could hope for. Remi was going through the plan of communication once she got in California, when her thoughts were abruptly interrupted by shouting from the driver's seat.

His screaming at an oncoming driver did nothing to impede its path. Yao's attempts at evasions were too late, and even as the van swerved left, a large truck coming from the other direction plowed into the front passenger side at a speed of over 40 miles per hour. The impact of the crash and the momentum of the large van caused it to spin completely around, unable to stay on all four wheels as it first rolled onto the driver's side, and then completely upside down.

The screams of scared women echoed in the van as it spun and rolled. Most of the women had on seat belts, which kept them safe for the time being. Two of the women, one of which was the first person to grab Yao's duffel bag moments before, were without seat belts, and knocked unconscious as they flew forward into the windshield.

Temporarily stunned by the accident, Remi realized that she was alive and conscious. With mounting fear, she realized that what she thought was ringing in her ears, was instead the sound of rifle fire. Quickly gathering her wits, Remi knew that she and the other girls were sitting ducks in this immobilized vehicle, and if the rifle fire was being directed at them, then none of them would make it out alive unless decisive action was immediately taken.

Unbuckling herself, and falling to the roof of the van, which was now on the ground, she looked at Chen, who was dazed after her head had hit hard against the wall. Remi unbuckled Chen and kept her upright, as some of the other women in the van that were still conscious began unbuckling themselves.

Knowing that the only weapon in the vehicle was likely with Yao in the front, she looked ahead, and saw him unconscious and slumped against the driver's seat. She rushed behind him as more rounds started hitting the front of the van. The incoming rounds were noticeably striking the front of the Sprinter van, and not at the rear, almost as if the gunmen were intentionally trying to keep the cargo in the rear safe.

Reaching into Yao's side pocket, she felt the Smith and Wesson, and pulled it out, just as a gunman arrived at the Mercedes, screaming demands. Appearing at the passenger door, the gunman shot fatal rounds into Yao and the two women that had been flung to the front on impact. From the separation in the back, Remi waited no longer, and used Yao's Smith & Wesson to fire two rounds into the gunman, dropping him as he climbed inside the vehicle. Thinking quickly, Remi grabbed the man by the back of his shirt, and pulled him farther inside, so she could have access to his rifle.

Just as Remi confirmed there were over 20 rounds of ammo left in the rifle, the rear door of the van opened. Not waiting to determine if they were going to shoot or take captives, Remi fired as soon as she saw the whites of the gunmen's eyes, dropping two of them with headshots.

Beginning to believe that she was going to make it out of the situation alive, Remi was suddenly grabbed from the back of her dress, and pulled backward, on top of and over the deceased Yao. She tried to grasp the rifle, but as a large hand closed around her throat and pulled her out, she lost grip.

Flat on her back and looking up at her captor, the man, irate at the loss of his partners, lifted a large right boot and tried to come down with it hard on Remi's face. She rolled with the grace of a dancer and was on her feet opposite the man before he could realize that she was not like the other slower reacting drugged women in the back. With all his might, the man swung with a right hook that connected with nothing as Remi easily dodged him and moved behind. However, still without a weapon, and unsure of how many other gunmen there were, Remi hesitated in attacking. Facing her with a newfound respect, the man pulled a large knife out from his side pocket, muttering something that Remi could not understand. She took two steps back as the man reared back with the blade in his right hand, and started to rush forward, when another gun shot rang out, this time from behind.

The man with the blade fell at Remi's feet, a bullet hole in the back of his head. Kneeling, Remi rushed to grab the blade out of the man's hand and looked up to see Bear. When the adrenaline had started rushing, Remi had completely forgotten about Bear and Kevin, instead focused solely on her own survival. With the senior agent now rushing to her side, she felt a great deal of comfort.

"Remi, I'm so sorry!" Bear exclaimed. "I got here as fast as I could. How did you take out all those guys?"

Before she had the chance to answer, Kevin yelled at them from the back of the van. "We have to get out of here now! Reinforcements are on the way."

Remi noticed Bear's eyes go wide as he looked out to the horizon at numerous headlights heading toward them, no more than a kilometer away. Bear helped Remi up as they rushed to the DEA vehicles that had come to a stop behind the van. Remi had been so consumed in her own ordeal that she had not heard the DEA vehicles arrive.

With the overturned van in the street, Kevin's Land Cruiser had pulled in first, pointed toward the direction where the van had been traveling. Bear pulled his Land Cruiser behind and turned it, blocking the street from any approaching traffic. The side rails on the street would prevent anyone from going around.

Kevin was loading the other women in the back of his Toyota Land Cruiser, so Remi ran for the Land Cruiser that Bear had been driving but stopped dead in her tracks when it was riddled with bullets from the oncoming barrage of reinforcement vehicles.

"No time! We have to go!" Bear yelled, pushing Remi toward the only vehicle still operable. As Remi rushed toward Kevin's vehicle, he turned to grab the one last woman exiting the van.

The thud of the bullet impacting Kevin's head shook Remi to her very soul. She turned to her side in horror as his lifeless body fell to the ground.

With the back seat filled with screaming women, Bear pushed Remi toward the middle of the front seat of the Land Cruiser, as he turned to help the last woman, who they only then realized was Chen.

She was still stumbling as Bear thrust her into the front seat, on top of Remi. "Come on Bear!" Remi screamed as he scrambled for the driver's seat. When he threw his head back in a loss of breath, and then moved forward, crashing into the driver's seat, Remi could not believe her eyes. When she looked down at Bear's shirt, she saw that it was soaked with blood from a shot to the back. Remi hugged Bear and refused to let him slide back out of the driver's seat and to the ground, pulling him with all her power into the vehicle. "You have to get us out of here!" he urged her.

Remi rolled underneath Bear, and with everyone packed tightly in the vehicle, she pulled the door closed and sped off into the night, as the backups arrived at the scene, attempting in vain to move the shot up DEA Land Cruiser that blocked their path. A few got out on foot and ran toward the fleeing Land Cruiser, letting out bursts of fire from their automatic weapons, and screaming their promises that they would not be far behind. With Kevin dead and Bear wounded, Remi looked to Chen for any kind of direction of where to go and what to do, but she was still suffering the effects of what Remi assumed was a concussion.

Remi was on her own as she raced to the outskirts of the poverty-stricken villages around Hong Kong. For the first time in a long time, Remi felt two different emotions. She had not known it was possible to feel both emotions at the same time; she thought they were mutually exclusive. First, she felt the sense of terror and fear that was in her bones at that moment, feelings that had not been felt since nightmares had consumed her early childhood years in grade school. But the second, puzzling emotion that she felt at the same time alongside that fear, was the feeling of confidence.

Confidence that SHE was in control.

Chapter 18
El Centro, California

All the lights on the interactive map glowed green from Victoria's laptop when she took the phone call from the Deputy Administrator.

"Special Agent Russo, I have Administrator Haskell on speaker phone. How is the situation in the field?"

"Well, ma'am, I've been sitting in my vehicle for 11 hours since the first delivery was made to the garage of this residence in El Centro, a small town near the Mexican border. No vehicles have left from here or any of the other locations."

"Were all 21 deliveries made?"

"Yes ma'am."

Administrator Haskell spoke. "Why do you think that there hasn't been any movement yet? I thought all these organizations were very eager since they haven't received any dope in a while."

"They are very eager, sir," Victoria said. "But our undercover, former Special Agent Valdez who was posing as Vaquero, did a very good job convincing the local criminal organizations that they needed to be patient with the first load, because any mistakes would be taken advantage of by the feds."

"You're confident that all of the poisoned dope is in those locations?"

"I am."

"Then what are you waiting for? Why haven't the search warrants started yet?"

"Every location has a team suited up and ready to execute the warrants. All the warrants have been signed. They are waiting on my word."

"Why haven't you given it yet?" asked Haskell. "Wasn't the last delivery over six hours ago?"

Victoria shifted uncomfortably in the front seat of her vehicle, sweat dripping down her head from the stuffy air in the parked car which had been turned off for several hours. She kept the car off during the busiest parts of the day when pedestrians could have realized that she was inside the vehicle.

"I was hoping to receive some kind of notification about the status of former Special Agent Valdez."

"When is the last you heard from him?" Deputy Administrator Edmonds asked.

"It's been a while. He sent me a text from the funeral about 10:00 a.m. Pacific time."

"Eight hours?" Haskell asked. "I think it's safe to assume that what everybody suspected was going to happen has happened. Mr. Valdez knew the risk he was taking. We should go ahead and start these search warrants."

Victoria's face did not betray her true feelings, but inwardly she was disgusted. She knew the Deputy Administrator likely felt the same way. Haskell was more concerned about looking good on the news. He would claim that it was all about saving lives, but the real reason was known.

Still, Victoria knew it was time. It would be dark within two hours, and she did not want the entry teams executing search warrants in the darkness unless absolutely necessary. While the cover of darkness would hide their approach, she was more concerned about the entry team missing a hidden weapon that could be used to hurt a law enforcement officer.

"I'm going to give the order as soon as our conversation is over," Victoria said, "but I do think it is vitally important to withhold releasing this information to the media for at least 48 hours."

"Very well, Special Agent Russo," Deputy Administrator Edmonds said. "Good luck."

Victoria ended the call, and before sending out the message to execute the warrant, she attempted one last call to Toby.

"Where are you?" Victoria asked.

"I'm back at the Embassy in Mexico City." Assigned to the Mexico City office for the last few years, Toby considered it home, at least until his next assignment.

"You haven't heard from Reuben?"

"No, I'm sorry I haven't."

"Any idea where he might be? Is there anything we can do?"

"We have a UC that was at the funeral. He confirmed that Reuben was in the church during the funeral, so he at least made it through the first hour. The ceremony then went to the graveside, so Reuben should have been okay there as well. After that, we're not sure."

"How long was the UC able to stay at the funeral?"

"Not long, he actually met with Reuben prior, kept him from going into a meeting with Carlos Montoya before it started."

"Wow."

"Yeah, and get this, it appears that the leader of the GDG has given his daughter to Carlos Montoya to be married. They were planning to marry immediately after the funeral!"

"Are you serious? The GDG? The same cartel plotting behind Montoya's back to overthrow him by poisoning this cocaine?"

"Yeah. It's brilliant. Once thousands die from OD'ing, Carlos will either be overthrown and killed or put in jail. Who else to step into the power vacuum and take control than Fernando Castillo, the wife of the leader of the Cartel de Culiacan, and the daughter of the leader of the GDG? The Castillo family will control every drug trafficking route in Mexico."

"Jesus, that is diabolical."

"I've got my ear to the ground. I'm trying to find out now if the wedding happened, or if perhaps it was delayed by the discovery that Reuben was not Vaquero. I have not been able to get confirmation either way. Once I do, I'll let you know."

"Okay. Just so you know, we are about to execute all 21 search warrants."

"Thanks for the heads up. Good luck."

If there was some chance that Reuben was still alive, 21 search warrants being served at the same time in California would seal his fate in Mexico. Vaquero would be sought out, and if found, and discovered to be Reuben, he would surely be put to death. However, that might have already happened, and Victoria could not wait any longer. She gave the order that went out to 21 different teams of law enforcement officers, in 21 different locations.

"Execute."

* * *

Special Agent Ana Lucia Rodriguez was relieved when the instruction finally came to carry out the search warrant. Sitting in a chair inside an air-conditioned building, she had been much more comfortable than Victoria had been in her Official Government Vehicle, but she was ready to get the show on the road. Ever since the delivery had been made to the location she was watching more than 10 hours earlier, Ana Lucia had seen three different men walk in and out of the warehouse, looking up and down the streets and in the parked cars. It was obvious they were on the lookout for law enforcement. Fortunately, the trio of men never thought to look inside the empty building across the street. The former offices of a real estate agent in El Centro, the area had more than served the purpose for what was needed that day.

For a while, Ana Lucia was worried that one of the three men were about to leave with some or all the 200 kilos, especially how often they continued to come outside and look down the street. But the hours had come and gone. Nobody left the warehouse, and nobody showed up.

When the order to execute the warrant flashed on Ana Lucia's phone, she threw on her bulletproof vest, grabbed her handheld radio, and told the other ten members of Imperial County Group 2 that she would fall in the back of the line when they entered the warehouse from the door on the side. She reminded the perimeter team, made up of some of the younger agents to the group, to maintain their weapons on the rolling door to make sure it did not come up and a vehicle leave while the entry team was gaining access.

A well-placed strike of the 40-pound metal battering ram opened the warehouse door on the first swing, and the swarm of DEA agents entered the warehouse, screaming in both English and Spanish at the three men to show their hands and get on the ground.

The three men were standing in different parts of the warehouse. Only one vehicle was inside, a Honda Odyssey Van, which was parked right at the large rolling door. For a moment, Ana Lucia thought that the three men were not going to be compliant, but when they quickly realized that they were outnumbered and outgunned, they put their hands over their heads and laid on the ground. With a few of the team members checking out the bathroom and private office located in the back of the warehouse, and two law enforcement agents going to detain each trafficker, Ana Lucia ended up in the position to handcuff the third member of the three-man crew, a slightly overweight Hispanic male with thick black hair and the beginnings of a mustache. She estimated that he looked to be in his early 20s.

Under Ana Lucia's instructions as Bravo Team Leader, which were passed down from Victoria, the team knew to immediately separate all three men, so they could not see or hear each other. If one of the three men decided to spill his guts to law enforcement, he would only do so if his other co-workers were not there staring at him. The only problem was there were not many places to take the detainees that were out of sight and earshot of the others. She decided that one detainee would remain on the ground against the wall in the warehouse. Another would be seated at a chair in the office, with the blinds drawn, and the third would be taken to a SUV outside and placed in the back seat.

Ana Lucia grabbed the man she detained by his arm and walked outside. "What's your name?"

"I want my lawyer," was the only response.

She did not say another word as she put the man in the car and instructed one of the young agents nearby to stand by the car while the suspect was inside. "I'll be back after we find the dope. Then maybe he'll be willing to talk."

The search did not take long, because the only obvious place of concealment in the large, empty warehouse was the van parked by the rolling door. After ten minutes of maneuvering, prodding, and pulling, Ana Lucia found the combination of actions necessary to open a hidden compartment underneath the carpeted rear passenger seat. The carpet spread apart nicely, and the hidden compartment moved upward, and remained at an incline.

"We were instructed to be very careful pulling these out and wear gloves," Ana Lucia told her co-workers. "They don't even want us to conduct the field test to confirm it is cocaine. Once the evidence is counted and collected, get photographs of the kilograms and the hidden compartment. Once the search is complete, we will transport these guys to the DEA office, and I'll get with Victoria and see what she wants from there."

"Let's get to work so we can get out of this dump," Ana Lucia said, as she walked outside to speak with the individual that she had placed in the SUV. The other two men were being questioned by some of the more experienced members of the group that were seasoned interrogators, so she felt comfortable things were under control.

She opened the back door to the SUV and pushed the man over to the rear passenger seat, while she sat in the rear seat behind the driver. She closed the door so that their conversation would be private. Before beginning, Ana Lucia realized that she had not been alone with a bad guy since being kidnapped by Toro and his team of assassins. Of course, she had been in a house with the entire team until Toro had convinced Leon, his second in command, and the remainder of the team to go back to Mexico for another mission. During that time, she felt like she had gotten close to breaking the armor that Toro had placed around him, protecting the infamous

159

assassin from the pain of emotion. Obviously, something had damaged the man mentally at an early age...Ana Lucia shook her head to get rid of the cobwebs. She found herself sometimes...lost in memories of the shootout at the El Paso/Juarez border that had resulted in the death of a DEA informant and a DEA agent from Juarez, as well as her capture and kidnapping. So many things went wrong. She was determined not to make that mistake again.

"We found the 200 kilograms in the van." She sat there quietly and waited for a response.

"I don't know anything about it. It's not mine," the man responded after sitting in silence for almost half a minute.

"What were you doing in the warehouse?"

"I was just there with one of my friends. I told him I'd help with some work."

"Which friend?"

The man cut his eyes at her and refused to speak.

"If you won't answer that, then tell me what kind of work you were here for."

"I don't know."

"So, you decided to come to this warehouse with a friend to do some work that you didn't know what it was going to be?"

"That's right."

"How long have you been at this warehouse?"

"A couple of hours."

"You might want to rethink that answer. How long have you been at this warehouse?"

The man was silent again. "I told you, I want a lawyer. I'm not saying anything else."

"That's fine," Ana Lucia said. "One of your buddies is already spilling the beans. We know you got 200 kilograms of cocaine."

"I don't know anything about that."

"You were here when the delivery arrived."

The man was silent again, judging whether Ana Lucia was bluffing. Sensing that he was trying to figure that out, Ana Lucia pulled out a camera, and held it out so that he could see the pictures. "You see, I've been sitting across the street watching this warehouse since 5:00 a.m. I saw the vehicle arrive at 7:30 a.m." She showed him the picture.

"I know that it left about an hour later." She showed him the picture of the truck leaving.

"And I know that you were here the entire time." She showed him the picture of himself, walking out of the door of the warehouse 45 minutes after the vehicle left. "You were here when the 200 kilos arrived, and when the truck left. Do you deny that?"

"I want my lawyer!"

Ana Lucia pretended that she was about to leave the vehicle when she heard a cell phone vibrating on the front passenger seat. She realized that the man's phone had been placed in an evidence bag on the front passenger seat. She caught the man eyeing his cell phone in the seat in front of him. Did she detect worry in his expression for the first time?

"Let's just see what we got there," Ana Lucia said, reaching into the front seat, and pulling the phone out of the bag.

"What's the password to unlock the phone?"

"I'm not telling you anything."

"Oh really? Well let me tell you something, Octavio." She waited for the man to realize that she knew his name after all. The dawning in his eyes was the kind of moment that Ana Lucia lived for, the realization that the agents knew a lot more incriminating information than they had revealed.

"That's right, I've known your name for a while. You see, while you were sitting in that warehouse counting the kilos and providing security to make sure the cocaine was not stolen before it was sent to another location, I had a team out here tracking down everything possible on this warehouse. All the vehicles outside, all the cell phones inside." With that last tidbit, Ana Lucia smiled, just to make Octavio worry some more. "So yes, Octavio, I know who you are. I also know that you are trying to provide for your wife and son that live in a little house three miles from here."

She waited again to let this information sink in before she delivered the line that worked nine times out of ten. "So, if you tell me how to unlock your phone, then I will promise to not have your wife arrested for conspiracy, which would end up sending your son to Child Protective Services, forever separated from both of his parents, only to be lost in the shuffle of American kids looking for a home. Is that what you want?"

"My wife had nothing to do with this."

"That's not what my report will say."

"There's no evidence she's involved. You're bluffing."

"I work for the federal government. You think the judge will believe a federal agent or a known drug trafficker?"

Octavio looked down at his feet. He could not take the chance. He gave her the password.

* * *

Ten minutes later Ana Lucia walked into the warehouse to check with the Group Supervisor, the only member of the group that outranked her, although she was still considered the Bravo Team Leader. Ana Lucia's attention was now focused on something else entirely, the message that she observed on Octavio's phone.

"We're all good here. I think everybody is just about finished up and ready to leave," the supervisor told her.

"That's good," Ana Lucia said. "We might have another problem. A big problem."

"What's that?"

She held up the cell phone in her hand. "This is Octavio's cell phone, the guy I just questioned. He started receiving text messages while I was talking with him. Something big is about to go down."

"What?" the supervisor asked, already weary from a long day.

"I'm not sure who sent this message, but there has been a message sent out, basically like an amber alert for drug dealers. They're looking for a group, and they think that this group is on our side of the border."

"I don't understand," the supervisor said.

"I don't know all the details, other than what I've read on these messages. But the gist of it is that a lot of local drug dealers have been called to conduct an ambush of a group. It is not clear why this group is being targeted by the Cartel de Culiacan, or who is in the group. But it's going to be a massacre unless we stop it."

"How are we going to stop it? We don't know who it is."

"No, but we do know where they are going. They just put out the address."

"Where?"

"A gas station in the middle of the desert, somewhere between the 8 freeway and Highway 98."

"Why is the group waiting there?"

"They're likely waiting to get picked up and taken away."

"Well, if the drug dealers have the address where the group is waiting, then why are the drug dealers waiting to attack?"

"The address just got put out. This individual is trying to go around collecting people to help with the assault. And plus, they probably want to wait until nightfall to attack it under the cover of darkness."

"We don't have much daylight left. Call the District Attorney. Tell him what you are doing. And call the case agent for this seizure. Let her know what's going on. It might have something to do with this operation. And for God's sake, call the El Centro PD and get them out there with you."

Ana Lucia nodded as the texts continued to roll in on Octavio's phone. The person organizing the ambush had just texted the group. "They have 20 confirmed going to that location."

"That's a lot of guns."

"Yeah, and..."

"What?"

"The guy organizing the ambush...his name is...Leon."

"How do you know him?"

Ana Lucia breathed deeply. "He was on Toro's team the day I was kidnapped in Juarez.

Chapter 19
Mexicali, Mexico

Padre Miguel had been estranged from his adopted son for a long time, and had heard all the rumors about Toro, the infamous killing machine, knowing that the young boy he had tried to raise was gone, replaced by a murderous killer that took life without thinking twice. Nevertheless, Padre Miguel prayed for his son every day since the boy left more than two decades before. He prayed even more earnestly following their encounter at his wife's burial place a few months earlier which resulted in Toro confirming his new identity and his continued rejection of the notion of a loving God. Padre Miguel never questioned God's reason but had resigned himself to the fact that perhaps during his lifetime he would not witness Toro repent of his sins and receive forgiveness or redemption. So, when Toro arrived at the door to his small cottage in Chihuahua asking for help, Padre Miguel considered it the answer to years and years of prayer.

The long-awaited reunion was far from perfect. Toro admitted his misdeeds and acknowledged that he had been fighting for something that he no longer believed in, but he still, stubbornly, refused to repent of those sins to the Lord. He refused to ask for forgiveness, despite Padre Miguel's pleading. Despite the refusal to acknowledge his sins before the Lord, Padre Miguel felt like he could see into his adopted son's soul. The older man could tell that Toro was now living for a new reason. The cause for that inside change was something Toro refused to speak about. Still, Padre Miguel sensed that something had damaged Toro far beyond anything since the awful moment in Toro's childhood when his sister was kidnapped by human traffickers and Padre Miguel's wife was murdered. Padre Miguel was content to let Toro speak about his trauma when it was the right time.

Months had passed as Toro came and went, keeping to himself at all hours of the day, but always coming to the table for breakfast and dinner to spend with Padre Miguel. For that he was grateful for the company of his son. Finally, one day recently, Padre Miguel was stunned by the outflowing of information his son provided about a situation that required his intervention, lest dozens of children under 18 be murdered. The outpouring of information came one morning as Toro sat at breakfast and read a national newspaper that he brought home the day before. Reading the article about the death of a child, which was believed to be linked to the murder of another child in a different location, Toro knew the connection despite not being revealed in the article.

The children of Julian Rodriguez were being hunted down and killed.

After making inquiries into the situation from people at the scene of the first three locations, one witness claimed to see the murderer and gave a description that could only be Leon, Toro's former right-hand man when both worked for the cartel as the most dangerous assassin group in the country. Toro knew that Leon was killing Julian Rodriguez' children, one by one, and would not stop until the very last one was gone.

Memories of Toro's final actions as a sicario, actions which unwittingly caused the death of his own niece, the last remaining blood relative on earth that he knew about, had scarred his soul. There was not some dramatic turnaround that caused him to be a crusader against the very people that he previously worked for, but he most definitely sought some type of internal redemption by rescuing other children from the violence of the drug trafficking world. While Julian Rodriguez was a drug kingpin in life, his children did not deserve death. Much like Toro's niece did not deserve death because of his actions.

Toro knew that saving these children would not bring back his niece, and it would not undo all the harm and violence he had inflicted on others, but in this moment, it was the right thing to do, and the only thing that made him feel like he had any kind of a purpose remaining in life.

Always one to advocate for the safety of children, Padre Miguel offered his services. For once, his son had not dismissed his claims immediately, a telling sign to Padre Miguel that he could be useful. And for several days, Padre Miguel had been most busy. Making phone calls. In person meetings. Urging the necessity to flee for survival.

Between the two of them, Toro and Padre Miguel had gathered almost all of Julian's surviving children, until Toro ran into Leon at the Catholic Church in Mexicali. Toro's encounter with Leon was as difficult and dangerous as he had expected, and he was unsure if Leon was dead or alive. But there was no doubt that even if Leon was dead, there would be others coming for the children. Padre Miguel agreed to keep the children at a house in Mexicali until all the Rodriguez' children were accounted for. Once Toro arrived with the last Rodriguez child, the wheels of their plan would start into motion.

* * *

The kids were restless. For well over 24 hours, 26 of them had gathered inside the basement of the small residence in the Mexican border city of Mexicali. The last two of the 30 children of Julian Rodriguez were delivered to the residence by Toro, having come from San Luis Rio Colorado, not far from Yuma, Arizona, and Puerto Penasco, a small town on the Gulf of California. Most of the older kids knew why they were there, and they comforted the younger kids that were confused and wanted to return to their normal life. A return to normal life was something that would never happen while Carlos Montoya was leading the Cartel de Culiacan.

All the kids knew the narco ballads of years past invoking the name of Toro, and naming off some of his most famous accomplishments, such as eliminating numerous corrupt law enforcement, or finding and killing so many of his cartel's competitors that the drug war was essentially over out of lack of competitors to the routes in Western Mexico. So, when the legendary Toro called for all the children to be silent, for once, they listened without being told twice, out of fear and nothing more.

Toro looked at the children, ranging in age from 4 - 17. The hard life he experienced caused him to lack pity for their situation. The lack of empathy however did not mean that these children deserved to die, especially not at the hands of a monster like Leon. He had experienced enough murder and would not be responsible for any more deaths. This was his first attempt to save lives, instead of taking them.

"Most of you know why you are here." Some of the older boys nodded, but many looked on with confused and scared expressions. "I want to go home!" cried an 8-year-old girl.

Not experienced with children, and not sugarcoating their situation, Toro spoke the truth. "If you go home, then you will die, as will your family. If you stay with me, then your family will live, and you will be safe."

"Who is going to kill our family?" one child yelled.

"Why? What did we do?" another hollered.

"Enough!" Toro said. "You all are brothers and sisters. You each have the same biological father, but different mothers." A whisper of excitement and disbelief went among many of them.

"No way!" one of the teenage girls said.

"It is true," Toro told them.

"Who was our father?" another asked.

Toro had thought long and hard about whether to reveal the truth to the children, but he realized that eventually, if they really wanted to know the truth, they would find out. The oldest of Julian's sons had found out and tracked Juan Montoya to China and killed him, which is how this entire fiasco started and also why there was now a standing order from Montoya to kill every remaining child of Julian Rodriguez. So, there was no reason to lie or tell half-truths.

"Your father was Julian Rodriguez. He was the leader of the Cartel de Culiacan." Toro failed to mention that he killed their father. It was not that he regretted doing so. The way he saw things, Julian Rodriguez deserved to die for taking as his bride a young girl that had been kidnapped by sex traffickers, Toro's own sister. But these children did not deserve to die *because* of their father's sins. And whether each one of them lived or died was ultimately going to be up to Toro's ability to get them to a safe location.

The children could not contain their surprise and excitement about the revelation of their father, until one finally spoke up, "Does someone want us dead because of who our father was?"

"Yes," Toro answered.

"Why? What happened?" This question came from Diego, the teenage boy that Toro had barely saved from Leon a few days before at the Catholic Church. "Obviously, something bad happened. What was it?" His question was met by all the kids agreeing that they wanted to know the reason they were being hunted.

"There are 28 of you here. There were 31 children of Julian Rodriguez that were not officially recognized as his children, but he provided for your schooling and housing nonetheless." He let the statement hang in the air as they processed the meaning.

"What happed to the other three?" Diego asked. "Were they killed?"

Again, refusing to lie, even though some of the younger ones probably should not hear it, Toro told the truth. "Two of your brothers were killed by the man that Diego saw at the church a few days ago. That man came to kill Diego. I know the man well. He is evil, and he enjoys inflicting as much pain as possible on his victims before they die."

"I saw the man," Diego confirmed to the others.

"What happened to the other person?" one kid asked.

"Yeah, you said there were 31. 28 of us are here, two were killed, what about the last one?"

"That is the reason we are here. Your oldest brother killed Juan Montoya, the leader of the Cartel that took your father's place."

"Our brother killed Juan Montoya? The newspapers said..."

"The newspapers were wrong."

Diego, showing himself to be the most vocal of the bunch, and possibly the leader of the group despite several other older siblings, stepped forward. "You fought the man that came to kill us. You are standing here now. Did you kill him?"

"I'm not sure," Toro answered honestly. "Even if I did, there will still be people coming after all of you. We must go to a safe location."

"Where will we stay? We won't have any money!" one of the younger boys said.

"I have a place, and I have money," Toro said. Having never spent anything on himself during his employment with the Cartel de Culiacan as an assassin, Toro had collected a large sum of money, several million US dollars. He had already decided that he was not going to use the blood money for personal comforts. He would put it to use by looking after the innocent children of the last man that he had murdered.

"If the killer was in Mexicali, then why are we still here? Shouldn't we be going somewhere else?" This question was asked by Veronica, the oldest female.

"Now that you are all here," Toro told them. "It is time we leave."

"Where are we going?" Diego asked.

"I know of a tunnel that will get us into California. We will wait at a gas station on the other side and get picked up tonight by someone trusted by Padre Miguel, and from there we will spread out and leave California."

The kids looked at each other, all stunned at the sudden change in the direction of their lives but realizing that Toro was their only hope for survival. Some of the younger children instead clung to Padre Miguel, sitting in a chair in the corner of the room while he listened to his son answering questions.

Toro ended the meeting and walked over to Padre Miguel. He had yet to even embrace his adopted father, but he used this moment to do so. "I appreciate all you did for me in my childhood, and all that you are doing now. I know this won't right my wrongs."

Padre Miguel smiled with the satisfying knowledge of the parent of a prodigal son. "You are very welcome, my son," he told Toro, "but what I did in between those two seasons of your life are what you should truly be thankful for."

For a moment, Toro was confused. "What was that?"

"While you were lost in despair, and taking your grief out on the world, I prayed for your safe return. Without ceasing. I prayed for your redemption, and for peace for your soul. I am proud of you, my son."

Toro looked at the man in astonishment. Even with the darkness of the basement, he could still see the pride shining in the man's eyes. "You realize I've killed thousands of people? Nothing I can do now will ever make up for that. Not even this."

"I know. Which is why I prayed so hard for you every night you were gone. The grip of the evil one is strong, especially when he gets someone that is willing and capable to do his work."

Toro nodded. He was still not in a place to speak about God, but he did respect Padre Miguel for his steadfast faithfulness. For the first time since leaving his father's house decades ago, Toro felt a semblance of regret for all the time that he had missed spending with this remarkable man. The feeling was exacerbated by the realization that this might be the last time they would see each other. Before he had the time to experience any more emotion, Toro patted Padre Miguel on the shoulders, and went through the house, collecting the children.

* * *

Toro decided that they could not wait another night to leave Mexicali. He knew better than to consider Leon dead since he had not seen Leon's body, and he did not want to wait any longer for the chance that Leon might track him down. Toro had been very careful by paying cash to rent the house for a six-month period, doing so without providing a name. Having carefully planned that the best chance for the kids' survival was to get them into the US undetected, Toro knew that they could not just drive across the border. Leon would have lookouts there. He also could not use a smuggler to get them across, Leon had lookouts with them as well. Toro would have to get the children into the United States himself. And he would do so by using some of the very same tunnels from Mexico to the US that he had used in the past, crossing the international border undetected.

He hoped leaving Mexico that night would be slightly safer because it was the night after Juan Montoya's funeral. Perhaps any requests Leon made for help would not be available due to the observation and period of mourning for the former leader of the Cartel de Culiacan. Not that it would stop Leon, but hopefully it would stop anybody else in Mexicali that was requested to participate.

Just getting to California was not enough. He also had to get the kids out of California. He thought they could disappear somewhere like Wyoming, Nebraska, or South Dakota. Toro did not know much about those locations, but he determined that those were the three states where the kids would go.

Padre Miguel called a friend in California that agreed to pick up Toro and the children, and take them wherever he wanted, once he was assured that he would receive $10,000 for travel expenses. By this time tomorrow, Toro hoped that he and the rest of these kids would be hundreds of miles from the border.

* * *

Unfortunately for Toro and Padre Miguel, Leon was now aware of those exact same plans. Having used his belt as a tourniquet to stop the bleeding of his wrist after the fight with Toro, Leon managed to get himself to a hospital to survive the night, before escaping into the hot Mexicali afternoon the following day. Suspecting that the priest at the church had been tipped off by Toro's adopted father, a man that Leon knew was an old priest, Leon determined that the priest, Toro's adopted father, was likely one of the only ways to find Toro. Leon called his contact at Telcel, demanding the identification and interception of any numbers belonging to Padre Miguel. The priest had been foolish enough to keep the cell phone number in his name, and even more foolish to use the number to make a call on Toro's behalf. Armed with the knowledge of Toro's arrival at the gas station in El Centro with the Rodriguez children, Leon was going to have a big surprise waiting for him. This matter was going to be settled, once and for all.

Chapter 20
Hong Kong

With no knowledge of where she was going, and nobody to tell her which direction to go, Remi just drove. The darkness of night, and the rain that started to come down only added to the dire circumstances. Not sure how she got there, Remi ended up on one of the only streets with an English name, Clear Water Bay Road. She was able to determine that she was heading east. Knowing that she was already an hour east of downtown Hong Kong, her memory of the geography of Hong Kong told her that they were likely approaching the eastern limits of the city, heading directly for the bay that fed into the South China Sea.

As the street they were on turned south near the water, the Land Cruiser let out a last gasp and died. A bullet hole had punctured the gas tank, draining the gas as they traveled down the road. Chen had started to come around and was showing signs of awareness, but Remi had avoided looking at Bear.

He died soon after getting into the vehicle.

There was no point looking for a hospital. What if the people that ambushed them were waiting? She had no idea who those people were or why they attacked. Even if she had known those things, Remi did not know where the hospital was or how to get there.

The road was deserted and eerily quiet, other than the sound of falling rain. As the girls exited the vehicle, everyone other than Chen was crying. Nobody knew what to do or where to go. Remi did her best to keep them together while she tried to figure out what had to be done. They had escaped from whatever group was trying to kill them. But now what were they supposed to do? Bear was dead. Kevin was dead. The mission was a total disaster. She grieved as she looked down at the lifeless body of the field training agent that had placed so much trust in her with this operation.

"Anything I can do?" Chen asked as she moved beside Remi.

Before Remi could respond, despite the noise from the rain, they heard vehicles approaching from their previous direction. Hoping it was a regular motorist, her hope turned to dread as she realized she was looking at the same type of headlights that had tried to kill them. The people that had ambushed Yao in the van earlier and killed him as well as Bear and Kevin...they were coming, to finish the job.

* * *

Two trucks pulled up to the abandoned Land Cruiser. Having split up over 10 different reinforcement vehicles, the two that approached on Clear Water Bay Road knew immediately that they had chosen correctly. They would be rewarded for bringing back the heads of whoever was responsible for killing some of their compatriots during the attack on the van being driven by the Sun Yee On triad member. Four men exited each truck in the pouring rain, cautiously approaching the Land Cruiser with their weapons out.

The nearest gas station, building, or any sign of life was a kilometer south. A quick inspection showed that the Land Cruiser was empty, but suddenly they stopped as one person discovered the deceased body of an American. Four of the men gathered around the body while the other four spread out in both directions toward the sides of the road. Both sides had a fence protecting the pedestrian sidewalk, with densely covered trees and brush behind it. The four men spread out as they assessed the area and looked for survivors.

Back at the Land Cruiser, one man reached down to check the American for identification. As soon as he pulled Bear's DEA credentials from his front pocket, the man's head snapped back, and he dropped to the ground, a rifle round in the middle of his forehead. Three rounds took out the other men gathered around Bear's body. The four dead Chinese triad members joined the dead American surrounding the Land Cruiser.

Each of the four remaining triad members that were spread out began firing their weapons indiscriminately into the brush despite having no clue from where the rounds had been fired from that killed their associates. After shooting more than 100 rounds into the brush and trees on each side of the road, the firing stopped, and all was quiet as the men listened.

And then they heard it. The whimpering. Or crying. A woman.

The four men turned to look at each other. The crying was coming from the brush on the left side of the road.

Each man went into a crouching position, leveling their automatic weapons at the spot as they approached. The men took turns jumping over the waist high fence until all four were on the sidewalk, less than 20 meters from the crying woman. The enemy had proven to be very dangerous, and killed several of their friends and brothers, so they approached cautiously, with guns aimed at the sound.

A burst of automatic gunfire from behind cut down each man.

Chen walked down the middle of the street with an AK-47 in hand. "It's okay, you can come out now." Walking behind Chen was a few more of the women that had come with them in the Land Cruiser.

From behind the largest and thickest tree in the area, Remi stood with one of the other women. She picked up Bear's rifle that had been in his Land Cruiser. Fortunately, he and Kevin picked it up prior to the mission, and it worked flawlessly when she took out the four men that had gathered around Bear's body. That, along with the other girl's crying, had done precisely what she expected, drawing the remaining members of the attack team to her location. They were completely oblivious to the threat Chen posed from behind.

"Your plan worked," Chen told Remi as the DEA agent hopped the fence back onto the road. "Thank goodness we found the rifle and AK-47 in the Land Cruiser. We killed eight of those bastards and they didn't get one of us."

"That's what they get for underestimating us."

Before they started back to the vehicles, one of the men let out a groan, and begged for a quick death. Not realizing anyone was still alive, Remi and Chen approached the man. They told the remaining women to go back to the Land Cruiser. Remi had a plan and would get everybody to their next location safely if they listened. Each woman obeyed, following her directions.

"We need answers from these guys," Remi said, with a knowing look toward Chen.

Remi and Chen both kneeled so they were directly in the man's line of sight. Although he was still alive, he was moments from death, having suffered several shots throughout his body. The man looked up at the two women in surprise. They were still dressed in their tight black dresses that were now smeared and stained with blood and guts of friends and enemies.

"Who are you?" he asked in Mandarin.

"We ask the questions," Remi said.

Chen followed. "Answer them, and we will not prolong your pain," she said, digging her finger into the bullet hole in the man's thigh. He howled in pain as he begged for Chen to stop, assuring her that he would tell her whatever she wanted to know.

"Who do you work for?" Chen asked.

The man took some deep breaths. Remi was not sure how many he had left.

"14K," was all he was able to get out.

"Rivals of the Sun Yee On," Chen said, "who we were meeting."

She looked back at the man and continued in Mandarin. "Why did you do this?"

The man looked like he was not going to answer, but when Chen moved her hand toward the bullet hole in the leg, he started speaking again. "When the Mexican was here, he was under their protection, the protection of 14K, when he was killed. It was an insult to 14K. The person that killed the Mexican ... was helped by the Sun Yee On."

"Which Mexican are you talking about?" Chen asked.

"The leader," was all the man was able to gasp. When Chen translated for Remi, her eyes got wide. "Juan Montoya was killed here?"

"Apparently so," Chen said, "by somebody that was assisted by the Sun Yee On. Montoya was under the protection of 14k, so his murder embarrassed and dishonored them."

Chen looked at the dying man. "So, this attack was payback to Sun Yee On?"

"Yes," the man whispered softly, his last words before closing his eyes forever.

"What do we do now?" Chen asked.

"I have a plan. Let's take their vehicles. Can you get us to a location where we can meet and discuss some things for a couple of minutes?"

Looking around, Chen nodded, having regained most of her senses. "Yes, I know where we are and where we can do that. I will take one of the trucks from the 14k. We need to load the ladies up."

"Okay, but first help me move Bear's body to the sidewalk. Call the police so they will come out here. We can't leave his body out here like this."

* * *

Several of the women ran off into the night while Remi and Chen had laid in wait to take out the 14K triad members, but five women remained, each broken, scared, and afraid to do anything other than exactly what Remi and Chen told them to do.

Finding a place off the main road without being spotted by passing cars and trucks, Remi instructed the girls to wait while she spoke with Chen outside of earshot. They found cover in a small and abandoned shelter near the side of the road. The penniless occupant that had called that location home, with nothing more than a cardboard sheet overhead, had long since passed away, with nobody coming to claim that pitiful spot of land.

"Look," Chen said. "I know this mission is over, but I will see it through to the end. I will give it another shot down the road when the opportunity presents itself. I must at least try and hold everyone accountable that was responsible for my friend's death. I will drop you off at a hospital or the embassy if you prefer. You can say that you were involved in a shooting. Bear and Kevin died, and you barely escaped. Maybe they'll get you out of Honk Kong as soon as possible."

Remi looked at the ground as she considered her options.

"Did you say you had another plan?" Chen asked.

"Yeah," Remi answered. "The Americans at the Embassy are going to keep me for questioning since I was present when two American citizens were killed overseas. During the time that I am here, if the government finds out that some rouge American DEA agents were on an operation that resulted in the deaths of more than a dozen of their citizens, even if they were gang members, it will create an international incident. The local government will demand answers. I could be arrested and thrown in a foreign jail."

Chen knew that it was possible that her government would demand Remi's arrest if they found out she was responsible for killing so many local citizens. "Well, even if you go back to the Embassy..."

Remi finished the sentence. "I could still end up in jail later. Jail or dead."

"So, what's the plan?"

Before answering, she was interrupted by the sound of sirens on ambulances and police vehicles rushing down the main road toward the scene where Bear's body remained with the bodies of the eight members of the 14K. Feeling like they were being closed in on, Remi looked at Chen. "There is only one way I get out of Hong Kong safely, and we still identify the men responsible for the human trafficking ring back in the United States."

Chen looked at Remi like she was crazy. "You can't mean..."

"Yes. I know how to find the warehouse where Yao was taking us."

"How?"

"I swiped Yao's phone during the shootout. He was following the directions when the ambush started."

Chen shook her head, impressed at the young DEA agent that had proven to be a warrior. "So, you're telling me that you want to..."

"Go back to where the Sun Yee On were taking us. Get on the jet that they were going to put us on. Stress the need for it to leave immediately because of what happened with the 14K. Also stress the amount of money they will lose if they don't uphold their end of the bargain and get us to California."

"After everything that's happened, Bear and Kevin dying, Yao dying, some of the girls dying, not to mention all the people that we've killed from the 14K, don't you think it's probably best if we just stop the losses now?"

"I don't think so. I don't want to end up in a foreign jail for killing Hong Kong gang members, and I'm not convinced the American government would protect me since I lied about the real operation. The only two other people that knew about the operation are dead. Plus, you will get what you want too."

"If we do this, how will you communicate with someone in California when we get there?"

"I have phone numbers memorized. I will just need to get a cell phone at some point. It will work."

Chen breathed deeply. She did not want to give up, but even she had not considered the possibility of going back to the Sun Yee On that same night. But Remi was right, it might be the only way she avoided a foreign jail cell. Not to mention that Chen would still get what she wanted.

Chen looked back at the truck with five women still sitting there too scared to do anything. "If we do this, then we are going to be responsible for putting all those other women back in the human trafficking world. We might not be able to protect them."

"I know. There are no good choices. But I don't...I won't let Bear's death be in vain."

Chapter 21
El Centro

The barrel of the Glock .22 was the first thing out of the hole in the back of the wall. Toro realized the necessity of picking back up a handgun, which had once been an extension of his body, was required on this occasion. When Toro was sure that nobody was waiting in the room to ambush him, he slowly crept out from the tunnel while leading the remaining children of Julian Rodriguez through to the California side of the border.

The gas station where the tunnel ended was only occupied by one person. It did not get much business and was merely acting as a front for the more profitable reason of being one of the pedestrian tunnels from Mexico into the United States. The door exiting the tunnel opened to a room in the rear of the gas station. Toro led the way, walking to the front of the store, making eye contact with the young man behind the counter.

The young man did not say anything other than giving a nod as Toro approached.

"I need you to leave," Toro told the young man.

"I'm supposed to work until 10:00 p.m.," the man said.

Toro placed two one-hundred-dollar bills on the counter. "Nobody else is coming here tonight. Take this money and go spend it, but I need you to leave. Now."

There was no mistaking the fact that it was not a request. The look in Toro's eyes did not need to be verbalized, so the man took the $200 and left the gas station without hesitation.

Once the man was gone, Toro went to the back room and told Diego and the rest of the Rodriguez children that it was now safe to come into the gas station. Each one entered, setting foot in the United States for the first time.

Each kid clung to one bag of clothes and personal items. Diego, seeming to be the only one brave enough to speak directly to Toro, asked, "How much longer until the pickup arrives?"

Toro looked at his watch. "12 minutes."

Diego's eyes slanted as he looked outside the gas station. A SUV rolled into the parking lot. "Is he early?"

"No," Toro said. "He knows how important it is to not be early or late. Too risky to get caught." Seeing the SUV in the parking lot, Toro again removed his firearm and kept it by his side as he opened the door and leaned the left side of his body outside while keeping the right side of his body, with his right arm holding the gun, inside the store and out of view of whoever was in the SUV.

"We just closed," Toro yelled out to the SUV, as he flipped the sign on the door from opened to closed. The driver's side door of the SUV opened nonetheless, and the driver stepped out. Toro put a bullet on the ground at the feet of the driver. "I said we are closed. The next one will not miss. You need to leave now."

The driver leaned back into the vehicle, and for a moment, Toro assumed the vehicle was going to leave the area. Quickly, for no more than three seconds, the red and blue police lights flashed from a visor inside the SUV. Toro thought about trying to shoot his way out of the situation, however unlikely that might be. But then he saw a couple of other SUVs traveling down the road toward the gas station.

The presence of law enforcement would not keep these kids safe. They would all eventually be found and executed by Leon or one of Montoya's other henchmen. If American law enforcement found out they had the infamous assassin Toro in custody, then he would likely face the death penalty. That is what happened to someone that had murdered several federal agents, but Toro would not kill any more law enforcement officers. Turning around, he closed the door and started rushing the crowd of children back to the tunnel. Before he reached the back room, the front door of the gas station opened. "Stop!" a voice yelled. "Police! We have intelligence that you and the children with you are going to be targeted by a group that will be here any minute! We have to get you to safety!"

Toro froze. He recognized that voice. It was a voice from his past. "Wait," he told the children before they went back into the tunnel. He opened the door and came face to face with the voice of the person yelling at him.

Ana Lucia Rodriguez, the DEA Special Agent that he had kidnapped in Juarez the previous year, and then taken through the tunnels to El Paso while the entire world looked for her in Mexico.

Ana Lucia stared at Toro in stunned silence. Then, she drew her gun and pointed it directly at Toro's head.

* * *

Victoria came to the second location in El Centro to get a glimpse of the 200 kilograms of cocaine seized by Bravo team. She arrived on scene just as Ana Lucia was getting in her vehicle to drive to the gas station and warn the group of children to turn around or leave quickly. Both women had already coordinated with members of the El Centro PD to provide security while the DEA agents transported the fentanyl laced cocaine from El Centro to the DEA Southwest Laboratory in San Diego, creating a shortage in law enforcement bodies available to help Ana Lucia.

The Group Supervisor determined that they could not leave that much cocaine on the street, unguarded, for a long period of time. The chances that the drug dealers or another criminal element would mount some type of response to reclaim their dope and then escape across the border to Mexico multiplied with each passing minute. But then again, he could not exactly let Ana Lucia travel by herself to the gas station with no assistance. He was relieved when Victoria offered to back up Ana Lucia if he made sure the dope was safely escorted to the lab.

Victoria knew that something was out of the ordinary when she pulled up behind Ana Lucia at the gas station and saw her partner's gun trained on the man in front of them. "What's going on?" Victoria asked, with her weapon drawn and pointing at the man standing in the doorway.

"Show me your hands!" Ana Lucia yelled.

"I have a gun in my right hand."

"Then drop it."

It went went against everything Toro believed in to lay down a weapon when a weapon was pointed at him. But he had put himself, and these children, in this situation, and he wanted to get them out.

Toro placed the gun on the ground in front of him.

"What are *you* doing here?" Ana Lucia asked. The man stared at her, and then turned to look behind him.

"I have 28 children here," Toro answered. "They're being hunted. I'm trying to get them to safety."

"Do you know this guy?" Victoria asked.

Ana Lucia nodded. "This is Toro, the guy that kidnapped me in Juarez last year. He killed Special Agent Daniel Benson during the shootout at the border. Took me along with his team to a house in El Paso and threatened to kill me unless the DEA revealed who was responsible for killing Julian Rodriguez' wife. Julian had put out a $10 million reward for the information, so Toro used me as bait to get the information that he needed to get $10 million. Once he got the information, he left me with some local attorney while he went to collect his reward."

"You were not harmed in El Paso. I made sure of it."

"The attorney hired some punk with a long rap sheet that tried to kill me. In case you didn't know."

"I did not tell him to do that. I told him not to harm you."

"You think I believe that? I saw you murder a DEA agent. I also saw your goon Leon murder my informant as he was waiting in line to cross the border. Oh yeah, by the way, we have information that Leon is actually on his way now planning to kill everyone here."

"Leon knows we are here?"

"Yes."

"We must leave immediately. I have to get the children to safety."

"Who are these children? And why do you care about their safety? You kill people for a living."

"There's no time!" Toro said, raising his voice, "we have to leave now, or they will all be massacred. Including you two. Leon will not leave witnesses."

"NO!" Victoria yelled over the two of them. She looked at Ana Lucia. "I know that you really want to put a bullet in him right now. Maybe that will happen down the road. But for whatever reason, he is leading this group of children, and someone is coming to kill them all. We have to get the children to safety, even if the man did murder a DEA agent last year."

"Right," Toro said, looking at Diego, "now go."

"NO!" Victoria yelled again. "This guy Leon and his team are on the way. Will he know that this place has access to a tunnel back to Mexico?"

"Yes."

"Then he will know exactly where to find you back in Mexico. He will call somebody across the border in Mexicali, and they will be waiting for you when you get there. You will be trapped either way. Your only choice is to come with us."

"No way," Ana Lucia said. "This guy has killed multiple federal agents. He kidnapped another DEA agent, and has murdered thousands of people in Mexico. We're going to let him come with us?"

"If that means saving these children...then yes," Victoria answered.

Ana Lucia grimaced. The trauma she had suffered from the ordeal had been carefully hidden beneath a playful and light-hearted exterior, but deep down the wounds were still there, and with Toro unexpectedly in front of her those wounds had returned to the surface. Ana Lucia's finger remained on the trigger of her Glock.

"I know you want to put a bullet in him," Victoria said. "But these children won't come with us if you kill the man that brought them here. Then they'll be killed when Leon arrives."

"You don't understand who this guy is, if we do not stop him now, then he will find a way to disappear and escape. He's like a ghost."

"I've heard the stories of Toro," Victoria said. "I just don't have the personal experience with him that you do. There are no good choices. We can either save these children, and let Toro leave here, with the knowledge that he might escape in the future, or we can take Toro into custody or even kill him, knowing that will also sign the death warrant for these children."

"They are the children of Julian Rodriguez," Toro told them. "Carlos Montoya has given the order to have them all killed. Leon has already killed three children. The rest are here, and I am trying to get them to safety."

"You killed their father!" Ana Lucia cried. "Why do you care about them? And why would they trust you?"

"You killed our father?" Diego asked, genuinely surprised, as a murmur of anger and disbelief spread among the children.

At that moment, an F-250 truck pulled up in the parking lot, and three men hopped out, armed with handguns. Victoria looked down the road. She saw a long line of headlights approaching their direction.

"We're too late. They're here."

* * *

As soon as Sergeant Lopez from the El Paso Police Department received the call from Ana Lucia that she would need some men to respond to the gas station, he got up from his desk and walked through the office to see who was available. More than half of his officers had been assigned as security to escort the DEA agents transporting the recently seized cocaine to the laboratory in San Diego. He was not sure why, but for some reason the feds had been much more anal than normal about protecting this dope. He was sure they had intelligence they were not sharing, but he had learned long before not to let that bother him and get in the way of doing his job.

A couple of his officers were returning from the DEA search warrants, having not been required to provide security for the dope transportation to San Diego. As they were his most experienced officers available, he tried to raise them on their radio, but there was no response. He called out and asked if anyone knew where the officers were. One officer responded that he had seen two vehicles pull into the lot a few moments earlier. Another said that he thought they were parked out front, so Sergeant Lopez hurried outside to tell them to turn around and report to the gas station immediately. A couple of the newer officers followed the Sergeant outside at his request, grabbing their patrol keys on the way.

As they got to the door, Sergeant Lopez stopped, gazing at a backpack lying against the brick wall outside the building. A discarded bag on police property was a huge security risk, and Sergeant Lopez approached the bag to make sure it was not dangerous. When he picked the bag up and heard ticking, he knew it was too late. Moments later, the bomb inside the backpack detonated, blowing a hole in the side of the building of the El Centro Police station.

The DEA request for police assistance at the gas station was forgotten as the remaining surviving police officers scrambled to try and put out the fire and pull their co-workers from the rubble.

There would be no cavalry coming for the DEA agents at the gas station. The El Centro PD had their own problems.

* * *

Seeing the three gunmen approaching, Victoria rushed down the short hallway and slid behind a counter to her right. Leaning out to the right, she waited for all three of the gunmen to enter the door before she dropped the first two with shots to the chest. The third jumped behind rows of sodas and snacks as he fired indiscriminately while trying to find cover.

At the sound of gunfire, all the children in the back room started screaming and crying. Toro did not wait for permission to pick up his gun. He grabbed it, and ran down the hallway, but Ana Lucia had already moved to her left to confront the third shooter. Moments

187

later, at the sound of two shots, and trusting that it was Ana Lucia that had shot the third gunmen, Toro rushed toward the door, grabbing the handguns from the two men that Victoria had killed, and put them in his back pocket. He grabbed the two men and slid them out of the doorway.

Seeing that Toro had gathered more weapons, and fearing the worst, Ana Lucia yelled for him to stop.

"Do you have any more weapons in your vehicles?" Toro yelled back.

"Yes, there is a rifle in the back of both of the SUVs!" Victoria said, realizing that Toro was trying to gather as many weapons as possible for the coming battle. The approaching line of vehicles were now less than a quarter mile away from the gas station. Leon had sent the vehicle with three men ahead as nothing more than guinea pigs to see if they were taken out by Toro.

"Cover me!" Toro yelled as he rushed out the door to the SUV parked 20 feet from the front of the store. Both Ana Lucia and Victoria stood at the door frame of the gas station as they fired at the approaching vehicles.

The approaching hit squad were two vehicles wide as they came down the road. The windshield of the lead vehicles shattered, as one of the vehicles veered off to the right and continued off road into the desert until bumping downhill and flipping, while the other continued straight past the gas station before eventually coming to a stop on the side of the road.

Ana Lucia and Victoria immediately set their sights on the next two vehicles, emptying their 15 round capacity magazines into the front windshield, until finally both vehicles stopped less than 50 feet from the gas station. The other vehicles in the conga line of gunmen spread out off road, creating a barrier between the gas station and the gunmen. As they did that, Toro sprinted back from the second SUV, spraying rounds of bullets in the directions of the gunmen, giving him enough time to make it back inside the gas station.

Once back inside, Toro tossed one rifle to Victoria and another to Ana Lucia. He also pulled out four extra 30-round rifle magazines that were loaded to capacity. "Take these," Toro said. "I'll make do with these three guns."

Ana Lucia looked at the man, very conflicted. Toro had risked his life to get them two more rifles. The same man that killed SA Benson and kidnapped her a year earlier.

"TORO!" a voice boomed over a loudspeaker from behind the wall of vehicles protecting the gunmen. "TORO! I have a proposition for you!" Leon's voice was cocky, and arrogant as always. "Do you hear me in there? Cowering in fear?"

Toro yelled from inside. "What is your proposition?"

"There is one way that I will allow Julian's children to live. One way only!"

Victoria shook her head. "He's lying."

"What is that?" Toro asked.

"You come out here and face me man to man. Our only weapons are our hands. The last man alive, wins. If that man is you, then I have instructed my men to allow the children to leave."

"There are two federal agents here, Leon. They have called the El Centro Police Department. They will be here soon."

"In case you didn't hear," Leon said, "there was an explosion at the El Centro PD a few moments ago. Safe to say that they will not be responding any time soon. It's just us."

"I don't believe you. Why did you bring all these people with you if you don't intend to use them to shoot us?"

Leon smiled from behind the truck. "Because I wanted witnesses to tell the story of the man that finally killed the infamous Toro."

"Release the federal agents and the children now, and I will fight you to the death. Right here. Right now."

"The deal wasn't for the feds, Toro. The deal is for the children."

"Then no deal."

"Are you really working with the Americans now, Toro? Are you not ashamed?

"I'm not working with them. They knew you were coming here and tried to warn us."

"That didn't work out too well for them, did it?"

"No deal. The only way you will get what you want is if you assure me that they will be able to leave here."

"After we fight, the feds can leave *if* you win. If I win, then I will rip them limb from limb, after they watch me do the same to every one of Julian's little bastards."

Victoria looked at Toro. "If you do not make it, then we are not giving up. We are fighting."

Toro looked at the two women intently. "I won't lose."

Chapter 22
Hong Kong

Using the GPS from Yao's phone, it took less than an hour before Chen and Remi pulled the vehicle in front of the warehouse, still east of the downtown metropolitan area. The darkness of the night was confounded with the still present dark and ominous clouds from the rainstorm that continued to drop sheets of seemingly unending water.

Remi, Chen, and the other five women looked nothing like the made up and attractive women that had walked out of the club several hours earlier. Makeup was gone. Hair stuck to their head was wet from the pounding rain. The most noticeable element that had not been present before was the blood that stained the dresses of each woman, and the look in their eyes that things had been seen which could not be unseen.

Upon arrival at the warehouse, Remi wondered what they would do if the contact at the warehouse was not there. Fortunately, Remi did not have to worry about that. One member of the triad named Zhang was there for security reasons. Chen did most of the talking, and translating, but the meaning of the man's intent was clear and did not need to be translated when he told Chen, "You girls look awful! The Americans will call my boss if you show up there looking like that. And there is only seven of you! What happened to the other girls?"

Chen's response was very measured, as she tried to control herself. "It's not our fault that the 14K ambushed Yao on the way here. But we survived. It is also not our fault that this monsoon started as soon as we tried to make our way back. Give us time to gather ourselves, and we will soon look hot like normal."

"Are you sure it was the 14K that ambushed Yao?"

"That's what they told us."

"Why did the 14K attack us?"

"The 14K is obviously rivals with the Sun Yee On."

Zhang shook his head. "We are. But still, this was a designed attack. It was for a reason. What reason?"

"It was payback for the Sun Yee On helping someone kill the Mexican cartel leader. The Mexican was protected by the 14K."

"How did you women survive an attack from the 14K?"

"By killing them."

The man looked at Chen, openly questioning how the women in front of him had the capability of taking out members of the rival triad. He shook his head in disbelief. "How? You had no weapons. And...you're women."

Chen let the remark slide. She did not even translate that to Remi. "All that matters is that we are here now. And we want to go to the US. We want to get out of here and go to America."

"Even if you did. You look horrible. I don't have any clothes for you to change into. I can't put you on that plane."

Chen decided to shift tactics, and Remi caught on. "What's your name?" she asked.

"Zhang."

As seductively as she could, Chen walked around Zhang, letting her fingertips brush first on his chest, and then to his back. Remi walked directly to Zhang's front, placing both hands on his chest and rubbing her hands gently down his front until she gripped the top of his pants, tugging on them ever so much and giving the impression that she was very willing to pull them down. Chen walked back around in front of Zhang, who was now standing very still. She moved her head close to his neck, breathing in his scent, and then smiling as she looked back into his eyes. "Have you ever been with seven women at once?" Chen asked.

"No."

"Make the call. Get us on the plane, and it will happen."

Zhang closed his eyes, anticipating the pleasures that he would receive from seven different women. It was almost more than his mind could bear. But soon his eyes opened, and he shook his head. The threat of an unhappy boss, and what would happen as a result of that unhappiness, outweighed even Zhang's desire to be satisfied by seven women at once. He shook his head and pushed Remi and Chen both away. "I've given you my answer. No woman is worth my pride, nor my life. I won't sacrifice that for you...or for all of you."

Chen looked away, disappointed that the ruse was unsuccessful but refusing to admit defeat. Despite being convinced that the women in front of him had managed to kill several members of the 14K triad, Zhang still did not seem the slightest bit concerned with their presence. After all, they were women and he was a man, and in his wildest imagination he could not imagine a scenario in which he was overpowered by a woman, even if there were seven of them.

It did not take seven women to take control over Zhang. Just one. The one whose childhood best friend had likely been kept in this exact warehouse by this exact excuse for a human being. That is what Chen told herself as she snatched a large wrench off a nearby table and smashed it into Zhang's unsuspecting face. Stunned, he stumbled backwards and covered his nose with his hands to stop the blood gushing out. Tripping over Remi's outstretched leg, Zhang fell onto his butt.

Remi had already spotted Zhang's handgun that was on a nightstand beside a pair of handcuffs. Remi swiped both and tossed the handcuffs to Chen as she kept the gun aimed at Zhang's head. Chen grabbed the man by his hair and dragged him to the nearest wall, as Remi stood with a gun aimed at his head.

"I am no longer asking. I am telling," Chen said. "Make the call."

Zhang looked up at Chen and Remi with hatred in his eyes.

"Bitch," he said as he spat blood on Chen.

The boom of the handgun surprised even Chen, as the sound echoed through the warehouse. Two of the five girls screamed in fear, even though they saw what was going on and knew they were not in trouble. Zhang's scream was delayed about two seconds, as his brain attempted to process the immense pain that was shooting through his leg and up his body. Looking down at his left leg, there was no kneecap remaining, having been blown off by the close shot. He leaned back on the wall and screamed, but Chen quickly stuffed a cloth into his mouth and tied it around his head to quiet him. Zhang chomped down on the cloth in pain as Chen kneeled in front of him.

She pulled his phone out of his pocket and held it in front of him. "Tell me exactly where to go to send the message for the plane to get here. Still defiant, the man shook his head, and then proceeded to beat his head against the wall behind him. The resistance suddenly stopped when Remi placed the gun directly into Zhang's crotch.

Chen smiled. "We're not going to kill you, Zhang. Just disfigure you enough so that you will be dishonored forever. Your face will always bear the evidence of a wrench to the face. You will never walk the same again because your knee is forever damaged. But hey, at least you still have your manhood. You will be able to hire some whore to satisfy your sexual needs."

Remi turned the gun counterclockwise and pressed it deeper into Zhang's crotch, while Chen continued. "But if you do one more thing, other than telling me who to text to get here with the airplane that will take us to California, then you will never get to experience the pleasure of a woman again, no matter how much money you pay. Do not make me do that, Zhang."

* * *

Two hours later, Remi, Chen and the five women that survived the night walked across the tarmac of the private airfield, and onto the waiting jet. The pilot and the co-pilot stood outside the jet as one member of the Sun Yee On Triad stood at the door welcoming the ladies on board.

"Where is Zhang?" he asked as Chen led the way on board.

"He wasn't feeling well."

"And yet you still came?"

194

"Yes."

"You will not regret this decision," the man said very smoothly, confident that these women were so desperate that they boarded the plane out of their own desire to pursue a different, more exciting life. "As I informed Zhang in the text message, there is plenty of stuff inside for all of you to freshen up and change clothes. I am sure everyone will soon look much better. Wait to start until we are safely in the air. With everything that happened last night, I want to spend the least amount of time possible on the ground."

Chen nodded. "I'll tell the girls."

She and Remi continued to speak in English in hushed tones as the jet began its taxi down the runway. As the jet started ascending into the sky, both women sat back in their seats, glad to be leaving Hong Kong.

Remi looked out over the huge metropolitan area, with sadness in her heart as she wondered what was going on at the Embassy at that moment as they had recently discovered that Bear and Kevin were dead, and she was missing. Surely there was a huge manhunt for her at that very moment, as well as a search for whoever was responsible for killing the two Americans. Remi wondered what the local authorities would think had happened since the other members of the 14K were dead along with the two DEA agents.

Beside her, Chen looked out the other window, smiling to herself that she had started to enact her revenge against those responsible for her friend's death. Somewhere down below, in between the warehouse and the private airport, Zhang lay in a ditch. It was not the broken nose and cracked cheekbone that killed him, or the shattered kneecap from the bullet wound. The marks around his neck would soon give the tell-tale sign of the strangulation that caused his death. Chen took pleasure in knowing that the last thing Zhang saw before death was the eyes of a woman choking the life out of him. Chen decided that after everything Zhang had done to harm women by becoming an integral part in the human trafficking of thousands of Asian women, it was only fitting that the very life was choked out of him by an Asian woman.

Chapter 23
El Centro, California

The dirt crunched underneath Toro's boots as he walked out to face Leon. A wall of 15 trucks and SUVs blocked the road of any traffic coming or going. The remaining vehicles were further east on the road two miles ahead, ready to give the signal if law enforcement vehicles approached.

Having previously given $10,000 to each man, they were more than content to get paid for a ringside seat to what was sure to be a memorable battle between two of the most famous cartel assassins in recent memory. Each trafficker used the hood of his vehicle to keep his own gun, whether it be a rifle, AK-47, or a handgun, trained at the gas station in case the two feds came out shooting.

"I hope those feds know that nobody is coming to rescue them," Leon said, as he smiled confidently at Toro, knowing that all law enforcement personnel from the area was either transporting the seized cocaine to the DEA Laboratory in San Diego, or helping in the aftermath of the explosion at the El Centro Police Department.

"They won't need rescuing. You won't get that far."

"You sure are cocky for a man that's about to die." He rushed straight ahead and jumped in the air feigning a ferocious punch coming down with all the weight and power of a 220-pound man. Sensing Toro was going to again attempt to roll to the side and out of the way as he did during their first fight at the church in Mexicali, Leon started to twist his body as he was in the air and coming down, planning to land on his right foot and turn and explode with a vicious side kick or stomping kick depending on where Toro moved.

The older and smaller former assassin took one step to the left as Leon's body started to rotate, and then rushed straight ahead and past him, using the force of a football offensive lineman to explode up and into Leon's shoulders, causing the larger man to land off balanced on his right foot and fall to his right side, in the compromising position of being on the ground and having his back to his opponent. Realizing how vulnerable he was, Leon quickly rolled away, narrowly avoiding the stomping blows of Toro's feet.

All in one motion, and with the quickness of a cat, Leon did one final roll and planted his left foot on the ground as he attempted to stand. As he stood, Toro rushed at the larger man and jumped, putting all his power into his right knee strike as it hit Leon in the jaw.

The contact temporarily stunned Leon and knocked him on his back, again putting him in a vulnerable position.

Toro knew that he had to take advantage of Leon being on the ground, but at the same time did not want to rush into a position and make a mistake against the larger and stronger man. But Toro's momentary indecision cost him. Recovering amazingly from the knee to his jaw, Leon's giant hand grabbed a hold of Toro's left foot, and before either had time to react, Leon fiercely yanked Toro to the ground. Sensing his opportunity, Leon tried using his larger body frame to jump on top of Toro and pin him to the ground. He was successful in getting on top of Toro, but in doing so Toro jabbed four fingers directly into Leon's Adam's apple, again stunning the larger man and causing him to lose his breath and miss the opportunity to deliver the type of knockout blow that he had come to use so frequently during the street fights in Guadalajara.

Using a surge of adrenaline, combined with the lack of resistance from Leon, Toro was able to push the larger man off him as both moved apart and rose to a standing position. Toro rushed forward two steps, knowing that Leon anticipated that he would continue to be the aggressor while Leon recovered from the knee strike to the head and the finger thrust to the throat. Toro's plan worked perfectly, as he moved back to miss the side kick that Leon used to keep him away. Toro grabbed Leon's right foot as it extended to make contact. Holding it, he lunged forward and brought all his weight down in a kick at an angle on Leon's left ankle.

The bone breaking echoed in the night, heard by those paid by Leon to watch the fight, as well as those still waiting and watching from inside the gas station. The gasp that went through the group was usually the kind that immediately followed a crushing blow, and immediately preceding the end of a fight.

But Leon was not any average fighter, or an above average fighter for that matter. Despite his injury, even as Toro's kick came crushing down on Leon's ankle, breaking it instantly, Toro made a mistake that Leon took advantage of.

Toro got too close.

An instant before the searing pain of the snapped ankle shot through his body, Leon bear hugged Toro from behind, wrapping his large arms around Toro's neck as the two men fell to the ground. What would have normally taken seconds for Leon to choke an opponent out in a similar situation, was made more difficult with the pain shooting up and down his leg, in essence sapping the strength that he tried to use to squeeze Toro's neck until the lack of blood flow to the brain caused him to lose consciousness.

Fully aware of the precarious predicament that he was in, and how close he was to finishing this fight if he could escape Leon's death hold, the fully cognizant and juiced up Toro bucked his body with all his might while attempting to break free. He had never experienced an anaconda wrapped around him, but he assumed it could not be too dissimilar from Leon's giant arms squeezing the life out of him. Despite all the injuries Leon had suffered, still he held on, knowing that the fight was over if Toro was able to get to his feet. The men rolled and slid on the dirt as Leon maintained his grip from behind, even though his left foot dangled like a rag doll. Facing the gas station, Toro looked into the door and directly into the eyes of Victoria and Diego who stood like statues watching the fight.

During their previous fight when Leon was on top of him, Toro had been able to find a piece of jagged glass that he used to get the larger man off him. His hands reached out to grasp for a rock, or anything that could be used to get Leon off, but he could not find anything. Toro tried pushing himself off the ground, but Leon fell on top of him from behind with his body weight crashing down, even as Leon screamed in pain from the mangled ankle behind him.

Leon focused pressing the weight of his upper body against Toro and the ground, causing Toro's vision once again to blur, threatening to go out for the final time. Leon also pressed his knees into the back of Toro's upper legs, preventing him from raising up if he had had been able to get Leon's upper body off his own.

With his last remaining ounces of strength, Toro was able to move his feet below the knee. Knowing exactly which way Leon's ankle had snapped, Toro used both of his feet to kick against Leon's bum ankle in the opposite direction of how it had broken.

Not expecting Toro's counter to come from his feet, a new explosion of pain surged through Leon's body, momentarily loosening his grip, while Toro used that moment to thrust his head back and catch Leon directly in the nose, the crunch again audible throughout the crowd.

Toro moved to his left as best he could but was still mostly under the weight of Leon. Unable to stand because of the broken ankle or see clearly because of the broken nose that filled his eyes with water, Leon grabbed the back of Toro's head before he was completely able to slip out of his grasp. With a chunk of hair, Leon brought Toro's head up, and violently slammed it on the ground, again and again and again, until the onlookers were sure that Toro was no longer conscious.

Convinced that he had won, Leon rolled onto his back, looking up at the stars. With what little he could see, Leon turned to his right and looked at Toro, face down on the ground in the dirt a few feet away. Leon's vision prevented him from clearly looking at his former boss and determining if he was still breathing. But a knockout was just as good as death.

Leon raised his arms, triumphant. Rolling to his side, and looking at the army of cartel supporters, he roared, "I have defeated Toro.

Kill every person in that gas station. Leave the heads of the children for me!"

* * *

The explosion of activity that resulted caused those involved to be unaware of what was going on with others right beside them.

From inside the gas station Victoria let out a burst of automatic rifle fire aimed strategically at the lead vehicles. The cartel traffickers had planned to rush the gas station on foot, but that was soon clear that it would be suicide, and each man fled to the safety of their vehicles, entering the driver's seat, and hitting the gas, at least those that were not taken out by the initial onslaught of fire that came from the gas station.

Although four of five cartel workers unlucky enough to be on the initial end of the rifle fire were immediately killed, the remaining 10 roared toward the gas station, intent on crashing into the building and taking out the occupants any way possible.

As Victoria and Diego retreated to the rearmost location near the entrance to the hidden tunnel, the sound of an incoming helicopter from overheard was clearly heard. Stan from Los Angeles Field Division Group 5 hung from the side, just as he had done while in the military, raining down bursts of fire from a couple of machine guns that just happened to be in the back of the chopper. Having been assigned as the DEA agent responsible for collecting the seized kilograms from far away locations such as Victorville, Palm Springs, and Coachella, it had been decided that Stan would be the most responsible agent that could be trusted to fly with the pilot of the helicopter to the different locations, collect the dope, and then fly the dope to the DEA Southwest Lab in San Diego. When he received the urgent message from Victoria, and then Ana Lucia, explaining the situation, Stan knew that he could put his old military skills to use and help.

The Cartel members were completely unaware, not expecting an attack from the air, much less the fierceness with which the rounds came down, unmercifully plowing into the vehicles of all the remaining men trying to attack the gas station. Not a single vehicle made it to the gas station before being struck by more than 20 bullets each. The withering fire soon took out every Cartel member that had gathered for the purpose of watching the fight between Leon and Toro, and the murder of Julian Rodriguez' children. Once he was sure that all the enemy combatants were neutralized, Stan directed the pilot to set the chopper down in the flat lands beside the gas station.

* * *

With the surge of adrenaline that came from the belief that he had killed Toro, Leon attempted to stand, but his ankle was unable to hold his weight, and he crashed to the ground writhing in pain that now consumed his entire body. Leon's focus drifted away from everything else that was going on around him as he grabbed his leg and attempted to stabilize his foot to stop the searing pain.

Lost amid the action, Toro's subconscious willed him to wake when he heard Leon order the murder and beheading of Julian's children. With the world spinning in his vision, Toro placed one hand on the ground and looked for Leon. The larger man's back was to him after falling down clutching his ankle.

The roar of the overhead chopper masked the sound of Toro's footsteps as he approached Leon from behind. Bruised and bloodied, and still struggling for a deep breath, Toro grabbed Leon from behind by the top of the head and the bottom of the chin, and sharply twisted, snapping Leon's neck.

Chapter 24
El Centro, California

Victoria told Diego to stay inside the gas station as she ventured outside, rifle at the ready, just in case any of the cartel members had
survived.

"Special Agent Russo?" Stan called out as he rounded the side of
the gas station.

"Yes. Stan?"

"Yes ma'am."

"Let's check these vehicles and cuff anyone that is still alive," Victoria said, as she and Stan went shoulder to shoulder and carefully
inspected each body. It was soon clear there were no survivors. Stan
had not shown any mercy when faced with the group of vehicles that
were intent on killing the two DEA agents inside the gas station.

"Is Ana Lucia in there with the children?" Stan asked, as they
continued moving down the line inspecting bodies.

Victoria looked at Stan and gave a quick smile. "You worried
about her?"

Stan shrugged his shoulders. "I got her message first explaining
the situation, so since I had the chopper I came to help."

"Well, I definitely appreciate that help. Cut it a little close
though."

"Better late than never, right?"

"No kidding," Victoria said, as they finished confirming that all
the remaining bodies were deceased. "But to answer your question,
Ana Lucia is not in there."

"Where is she?"

"Well, at least she is not in the gas station. That building has a
door that leads to an underground tunnel that goes into Mexicali, a
cartel tunnel."

"So, what happened?" Stan asked. "Ana Lucia is in Mexicali with the children? And why does the Cartel want to kill a bunch of children? Other than the fact that they are homicidal maniacs."

Victoria spent the next few moments explaining how Leon had challenged Toro to a fight, instructing his followers to kill everyone in the gas station if he defeated Toro. "While those guys were fighting, Ana Lucia led all the children except for one back across the border. I didn't trust that the Cartel would let them live even if Toro won the fight."

"What is Ana Lucia supposed to do once she gets the kids to Mexicali?" Stan asked. "She needs our help!"

"Whoa, Ana Lucia is a big girl and can take care of herself, although we are both very glad that you arrived in the chopper with the big guns. I have a contact with the CIA in Mexico. He worked with me to set up this operation. I called him and he had a contact meet Ana Lucia and the kids and is taking them to a safe house in Mexicali as we speak."

Victoria and Stan had walked forward to look at Toro and Leon. After seeing the outcome of the fight, and what she thought was the ending, Victoria was surprised to see Leon's lifeless eyes as he laid on the ground on his chest with his neck turned at a weird angle. Toro laid beside him, remaining on his back. He slowly opened his eyes and looked at the sky, not sure if he was lucky to be alive or not.

Victoria and Stan stood over Toro. Both had heard the legend of Toro. Not all the stories were true, but most were.

"Is this really Toro?" Stan asked as they both kneeled to check him out. "The same guy that killed so many people for the cartel. The same guy that kidnapped Ana Lucia last year?"

"Yes, it's really him. Took a minor miracle to convince Ana Lucia not to take him out before this got started. I'm not sure what is going on and why Toro had a sudden change in heart, but the whole reason he was here was to protect the children.

"Julian Rodriguez was the father of each of those kids. Apparently, he fathered many children with women that were not his wife, and

204

although he did not raise them and acknowledge them as his true heirs, he did make sure they were provided for financially and given the best educations."

"But why did the Cartel want them all dead?" Stan asked.

Victoria shook her head as she contemplated the ever-present threat of violence that was part of the drug world, whether it was in Mexico, the United States, or elsewhere. "The oldest of Julian Rodriguez' children blamed his father's death on Juan Montoya. The teenager tracked Montoya to Hong Kong with the help of one of the local gangs, and murdered Montoya before being captured and killed. After Juan Montoya was killed, his son Carlos took over. Carlos gave the order for all of Julian's children to be murdered, to ensure that one of Julian Rodriguez' children would never come after the Montoya family again. They hired this goon," Victoria said, nudging Leon's shoulder with her foot, "who used to work in the same assassin group as Toro. Was Toro's right-hand man in fact."

"So, I guess the main question is why Toro cared about protecting those children," Stan asked.

"You can ask me yourself," Toro's voice from the ground came out raspy. "Despite Leon's best intentions, I'm not dead, although my head makes me wish I was."

Stan, never one to bend the rules, much less break them, took out his handcuffs and placed them on Toro. Victoria looked back at him, neither in judgement nor approval.

"You know this guy killed a DEA agent at the shootout in Juarez last year, right? Not to mention kidnapping Ana Lucia. I don't care if he saved 30 children, he deserves to go to jail and be judged by a jury of his peers to determine if he is guilty or not."

Toro made no move to get up but continued to remain sitting on the ground with his hands cuffed behind him. He looked at Victoria, and then back to Stan.

"Do you not agree?" Stan asked Victoria.

"He deserves to go to jail, no doubt," Victoria said, "and I'll make sure that he does. First and foremost, I need to get you back on that chopper to get all that cocaine to the lab in San Diego. The last thing we need is to get hijacked out here and let 800 kilograms of cocaine hit the street."

Stan looked at her suspiciously. He did not know Victoria, but he could tell that her mind was moving. She was up to something. But he had a mission, and it was his responsibility to see it through to completion.

"Look," Victoria said, as the sights and sounds of sirens from several miles away could be heard finally making its way toward their location. "The cavalry is on the way. You get out of here while you can. You know how the locals are going to be once they see all these people dead. They will not let you, or that chopper leave. I can't stress to you how important it is that those kilograms get to the lab, it is a matter of national security that the Deputy Administrator herself is keeping tabs on."

"I should stay on scene. I was the one that shot and killed these men."

"Normally I would agree. But for reasons that I will not get into right now, it is of the utmost importance that you get every single one of these kilograms to the lab as soon as possible. It is a matter of life and death. As the ranking agent on site, that is an order. If any fallout comes then I will take the heat."

"Yes ma'am, if you insist."

"I do. Now go, before they get here."

Stan complied, and walked back to the waiting chopper where the pilot stood waiting outside. Victoria stuck her head inside the chopper to get a peek at the eight duffel bags each containing 100 kilograms of cocaine. "That is a beautiful sight," she commented as Stan loaded up.

He agreed. "It sure is. Now you stay safe. Ask Ana Lucia to contact me once she gets back safely to this side."

Victoria nodded, sensing the budding possibility of an attraction that was unable to be hidden. As soon as the chopper began to take off, three local El Centro police officers arrived. They exited their cars, wide eyed at the carnage that had taken place. This level of violence was not supposed to happen on this side of the border.

Ana Lucia's supervisor also arrived on scene, almost frantic about his missing agent. Victoria spent several minutes explaining the situation and assuring the supervisor that Ana Lucia was safe, and likely on her way back to the US now.

As an ambulance arrived on scene and the EMTs met with the police officers, Victoria walked over to Toro, who had moved to the gas station and was sitting on the ground against the wall.

"I'm surprised you didn't try to take off," Victoria said, face to face with one of the most cold-blooded killers of their generation.

"I'm tired of running. Make sure Diego is safe."

"Of course."

"And the other kids?"

"With Ana Lucia at a safe location in Mexicali."

Toro shook his head. "What kind of world are we living in when an American DEA agent has to take 30 kids from the United States and into Mexicali to be safe?"

"Times are definitely strange. Speaking of strange times, I would like to request your help with something. Something very sensitive, and possibly dangerous. Are you interested?"

* * *

She had a good sense for detecting crap, and she did not get the sense that Toro was faking. Victoria trusted her instincts and told Toro something that only a few other people in the world knew. At this point, it was the least she could do. She had to find out what happened to Reuben.

After explaining the situation to the former assassin, the El Centro police officers walked over to her and said that they were going to need a statement, and to go back to the office. With more than 20 people dead, they wanted to avoid a potential situation in which the media might become aware and send dozens of reporters to document this scene that had obviously spiraled out of control while the local police officers dealt with the bomb attack at their station.

Victoria nodded. "Of course," as she walked away, looking over her shoulder at Toro, who had moved inside the gas station after being released from the handcuffs, unseen by the officers and forgotten about in the chaos.

Ducking into the tunnel, Toro's mind was set to right another wrong that he was responsible for, and possibly save a life, if the life was still left to save.

Chapter 25
Mexicali, Mexico

Luis Fonseca sat down across the table from Omega. The outdoor seating at the local restaurant was not yet crowded an hour before the noon rush, but still he did not want to be there too long, lest he be seen and recognized. Luis knew the chances someone in Mexicali recognized him were minimal, but still he wanted to be careful. Armed with the title, "Special Advisor" to the Chief of Staff for the President of Mexico, Luis was able to move with the power of the federal government, while still maintaining anonymity and a buffer to the leader of the country. As in every country throughout the world, some things a leader needed to be done officially, other things needed to be done unofficially. The unofficial tasks always required someone professional, trustworthy, and private to do the bidding of the leader in a manner that went under the radar for the media and public. In this role, Luis excelled.

Omega had proven to be exactly what Luis had hoped for: an unsuspecting killing machine that operated ruthlessly and efficiently. Able to use the new age of technology and social media to maximum effect to sow fear among the target portion of the population: rivals of the Cartel de Culiacan.

It was not that the Mexican President was corrupt, nor was he in the pocket of the Cartel de Culiacan, as was suspected by many Mexican citizens and believed by American law enforcement. While there were certain agreements in place between the President and the Cartel de Culiacan, it was no different than unwritten agreements that exist between every country's administration and the leading elements of the criminal organizations. They learn to coexist. If the criminal organization, or in this case the Cartel de Culiacan, goes too far one way or the other, then it was understood that there would be consequences. But for many years, there had been no need to direct government resources at the Cartel de Culiacan. After the group led by Toro had effectively ridden the western half of the country from all competitors in the drug trade and made the peace agreement with the GDG from the east side of the country, the number of deaths from the drug war had dramatically decreased. The decrease was lauded by both sides of the aisle, and as a result, the President's favorability ratings had skyrocketed.

The pending election was little more than a formality if the drug war did not reignite the vicious flame of deaths that had been present in the country during the late 1990's and the early 2000's. For that reason, the President of Mexico, and Luis as his unofficial representative, needed a strong Cartel de Culiacan. With no competing drug cartels in western Mexico, there would be minimal drug violence and no drug war. With no drug war, no deaths. No deaths meant an easy re-election. What the President did not need were rival cartels threatening to return to take control of the western Mexico drug trafficking routes by force from the Cartel de Culiacan.

For that reason, Luis felt no regret about his role in providing Omega with the intelligence needed to take out the budding rival cartels, those that threatened not only the Cartel de Culiacan, but also the peace that had somewhat settled over the country and assured the President of a second term. The intelligence provided to Omega about the location of the Tijuana and Juarez cartels had resulted in both rival cartel members being exterminated viciously. The social media aspect of the killings served only to intimidate any others that might be thinking of trying to upset the balance of power. Yet still there were some that wished to do exactly that.

"What do you have for me?" Omega asked.

"It's a startup group. The Cartel de Sonora. After what you did to the cartels in Juarez and Tijuana, these guys are obviously afraid and trying to avoid attention for the time being. That is why they have moved west, out of Sonora. They are trying to smuggle methamphetamine from Mexicali into Calexico *today*. In just a couple of hours."

"They already have the meth?"

"Yes, that's what our intelligence indicates."

Omega looked down at the ground, deep in thought. "This startup cartel, from Sonora, they were not around before. They have no previous issues with the Cartel de Culiacan. They do not have the history of battling against the Cartel de Culiacan like the Juarez and Tijuana cartels. They can't say that they are using this controlled territory because Toro killed their fathers and brothers in the past. They must be supported by someone else. Someone big. Who is supporting this start-up group, the Cartel de Sonora?"

"The President has asked the same question, and we are actively pursuing several different leads."

"No evidence yet?"

"Nothing verifiable."

"What's your hunch? Who is behind it?"

Luis rubbed his beard and leaned in, lowering his voice. "There are rumors that the GDG is trying to make a move, and that they already struck a bargain with the Cali Cartel in Colombia. What that agreement is, I don't know and won't begin to make assumptions. What we do not want...and must not have, is another bloody drug war. If a few people here or there must die to keep the overall peace and protect the masses, then that is an acceptable loss. But if the GDG is involved, I will let you know. At that point, we will have to reassess the situation, and our agreement. Taking on the GDG is different. They have thousands of workers compared to the dozens making up these smaller groups trying to establish control. Taking on the GDG would result in a long and drawn-out drug war. We can't have that."

"Interesting that you say the GDG might be making a play," Omega said. "Did you know that Carlos Montoya has married the daughter of the leader of the GDG?"

The Special Advisor to the Chief of Staff prided himself on staying in the loop, and there was rarely intelligence that caught him by surprise. This was one of those rare times.

"No, that I did not know," he said.

"You said this new cartel, from Sonora, has couriers that are trying to smuggle meth into the United States. If they are a new cartel, then they do not yet have contacts with the Asians to get the necessary chemicals to make substantial quantities of methamphetamine. They must be getting the chemicals from someone else, likely whatever group is supporting them financially."

It must be the GDG.

"Exactly," Luis said. "If you find these couriers working for the Cartel de Sonora, then you can find out who is supplying them with the chemicals to produce meth. That will be who is propping them up."

Omega nodded. The end game was near. "What information do you have on these couriers?"

"There are three. Each is crossing the border by foot sometime this afternoon. A location east of Mexicali. Each will have 50 pounds of methamphetamine in a backpack. They're going to cross somewhere in the desert, in an area away from the pedestrian and vehicular routes."

"Will it be patrolled by the American Border Patrol?"

"Possibly, that is a risk that is being taken."

"Where are the couriers leaving from?"

Luis placed several photographs on the table, with a longitude and latitude written on each picture. "This is where they are leaving from. Three men are supposed to leave from this house sometime this afternoon. The house is less than 20 minutes away from our location here."

"Thank you," Omega said, marveling at the government's ability to obtain such specific intelligence. Either they had an informant inside the stash house, or a wiretap on someone inside the house or both. "I will take care of everything else."

"Will you require the assistance of the drone again?" Luis asked.

"Yes, it is always good to have backup in case it is needed, especially being this close to the American border."

"Just as a reminder, while the drone does not have any connection whatsoever to me or my employer, we humbly request that you take all measures necessary to avoid using the onboard weapons system. It would be unwarranted attention and might cause the media to start asking questions that must not be asked."

"I know the rules. To this point, it has been used only for video. To give the viewer the eagle's vantage point. I will be careful with it, I assure you."

"I'm sure you will," Luis said, rising from the table. "Good luck this afternoon." Omega nodded as Luis left, already looking forward to the next assignment. Killing was starting to become fun.

Chapter 26
Mexicali, Mexico

The CIA safe house in Mexicali was in a quiet neighborhood nestled among several other similar houses. The remaining children of Julian Rodriguez, all except Diego, had managed to spend the entirety of the day under the roof, waiting for nightfall. Ana Lucia remained with the children along with the CIA case officer that stayed at the residence, a Hispanic female named Selina. When Toby arrived at the safe house in the afternoon, Ana Lucia bid the children farewell. Despite their limited time together, the children had come to look at Ana Lucia as a savior, one that led them away from the dangers that awaited in a foreign land at the hands of the vicious monster Leon. Even though Victoria had confirmed that Leon and all his men had been killed the night before, both women were still somewhat hesitant in moving the children too soon. Who knew if Carlos Montoya had employed someone else, or had other eyes watching and waiting for them to move? Ana Lucia and Victoria declared that they would not play into the hands of the madman.

At the same time, Ana Lucia knew that she had to return to the US, so that she could be interviewed by the local police, as well as the DEA internal investigators, to obtain her statement about the shooting that left so many members of the Cartel de Culiacan dead. Toby's arrival, and Victoria's confidence in his trustworthiness, convinced Ana Lucia that he had the children's best intention at heart. Toby assured Ana Lucia that he would coordinate transportation away from Mexicali, and to a safe location, for each of the surviving children.

Awaiting Toby's arrival, Ana Lucia sat on a stool peering around the curtain to the outside. The trained investigator noticed a flurry of activity in a house across the street that caught her attention. While she remained on the lookout for any possible threat to the security of the safe house, it was the undeniable movement of an ongoing drug transaction that kept her at the window, waiting and watching.

Lookouts left the house and walked around the neighborhood, peering inside all the cars parked on the street, constantly looking back and forth. It was the vehicle that showed up and pulled into a garage, only to leave 30 minutes later. It was the second vehicle that pulled in the garage five minutes after the first vehicle left. It too, left after 30 minutes. Finally, a third vehicle showed up, again pulling into the garage, and leaving just as the other two had done before. Finally, the lookouts had returned to the house.

The interesting part of this surveillance, not to include the fact that it was occurring in Mexico from a CIA safe house no less, was that there did not appear to be any vehicles in the driveway of the residence despite all the activity observed. Ana Lucia was certain that a substantial shipment of drugs had just been delivered to the house, but why were there not any vehicles at the house? How would the occupants of the residence get the dope into the United States?

As if by divine timing, further convincing Ana Lucia of what she must do, only minutes after Toby's late afternoon arrival, three males walked out the front door of the house with weighted back-packs. Each carried water bottles and wore hiking boots, convincing Ana Lucia of the fact that she had considered but dismissed as un-likely due to never seeing it before: these three guys were going to walk the dope across the border. Ana Lucia smiled to herself and made a quick speech to the children in the residence promising them that they were safe, and Toby would take care of them. While she cared deeply for their life and their right to live, like with most relationships, she tried not to get too close, and thus did not feel the need to cry or delay her inevitable departure.

Walking out the door with a couple of hours of sunlight remain-ing, Ana Lucia could make out the three men, all walking together out of the front of the complex of houses approximately 100 meters away. No good DEA agent can allow that much dope to enter the country, she thought to herself, as she began following behind the three men.

* * *

Two hours and several miles later, the trio of men had added a fourth person to their party, a pretty and seemingly fun-loving woman that wanted to cross into the US with them. There did not seem to be a leader among the three men, so when Ana Lucia asked to join their company, there was not any initial dissent, although one of the men did seem noticeably uncomfortable. However, Ana Lucia quickly used her womanly wiles to put the man at ease. It was nothing that could contend against the batting of her eyes, combined with a grasp of the hand, and ever so gently brushing of her chest against his arm. In no time, the one man that had initially seemed most reluctant to Ana Lucia joining their company, was the one speaking the strongest about offering her protection. He was no doubt incentivized by the promise that Ana Lucia made to rendezvous with him at her sister's apartment in Calexico at some point the following week.

Ana Lucia figured that it would be much easier to relay the movements of the three drug couriers to Victoria waiting on the other side of the border, by joining them rather than by following from a distance. Not to mention it would also be safer. How the three men intended to enter the US, however, was a surprise. They did not have access to the hidden tunnels belonging to the Cartel de Culiacan, and they did not yet dare drive the dope past the US Customs in Calexico. Their options were limited, and they intended to transport the methamphetamine into the United States the old-fashioned way, by crossing a 10-foot-high fence that ran east in Mexicali toward the international airport. Once on the US side of the border, the men would only be a mile or so from the US Customs checkpoint to the west, but with so much of the Americans' attention focused on incoming vehicles, the couriers hoped the darkness of night would provide the necessary cover to enter the country undetected.

Ana Lucia was not sure what to think of the plan. It did not matter.

Victoria was waiting for the traffickers on the other side of the fence in Calexico. She had remained in El Centro for the entirety of the day answering questions from local police as well as federal investigators regarding the shooting that took place the night before that killed over 20 cartel members. The fact that the DEA office in El Centro had shut down all operations and enforcement activities for the next 48 hours did not directly impact Victoria because she was technically assigned to the Headquarters Division and was not beholden to whatever policies were put in place by DEA management in El Centro, especially if those policies prevented additional seizures of drugs. It was not that the decision to shut down operations was for no reason. It was in response to the process of gathering information on the deaths of so many cartel members, not to mention the paperwork associated with the staggering seizures of cocaine throughout the state of California from Victoria's case. But what made Victoria excel as a DEA agent, was that her inner moral code would not allow her to stand by and knowingly allow drugs to enter her country, no matter how much dope she had just taken off the streets. The fact that Ana Lucia seemed to operate by the same moral code only confirmed to Victoria that the two women were doing the right thing.

* * *

As the three men ran across the road toward the border fence, Ana Lucia could not believe her eyes. A large section of the fence was missing. It was six feet across, easily wide enough for the men to enter the US.

How was the Border Patrol not monitoring this area more closely? Well, there are way more miles of border than patrolling agents.

As she looked through the fence, she could make out the shape of Victoria 50 meters away, deep into the dry desert ground that led away from the international border and further into California.

The border wall, more accurately described as a fence, was situated mere feet away on the Mexican side from a street with a considerable amount of traffic traveling east and westbound. For that reason,

Ana Lucia did not think anything about the sound of a motorbike approaching as the quartet of border crossers neared the Mexican side of the fence. However, the sound of the motorbike stopped just as the men slipped through the opening. Ana Lucia looked back as the individual got off the bike and walked through the gaping hole in the fence, blocking their exit back into Mexicali, had they been so inclined. The individual on the bike did not remove the helmet, but instead spoke to the three men as if they were well known, calling them each by name.

"Felipe, Raul, and Oscar, today is the day that you will pay for your betrayal of the Cartel de Culiacan!"

Ana Lucia's eyes grew wide. *These guys are NOT working for the Cartel de Culiacan? Then who are they working for?*

Just as surprising to Ana Lucia was that the voice that called out the three traffickers was not a male voice. It was a female voice. And the female did not have any type of backup as far as Ana Lucia could see.

Raul, the trafficker that had befriended Ana Lucia, stepped forward with as much machismo as he could muster. His bravado was enhanced by the realization that there was nobody around. It was 3 on 1. Three men against one woman.

"Perhaps you should have brought some reinforcements before you decided to confront us out here all alone, little girl," Raul said, as he walked forward and stopped six feet in front of the woman, whose face was still hidden by the motorcycle helmet. "Whoever sent you here all alone is a fool to send a soldier to her death. That is why the Cartel de Culiacan is going to crash and burn once and for all."

"Nobody sent me," the individual said. "I am here on my own. And if you knew who you were speaking with...perhaps you would not speak with so much confidence. You would speak with fear instead."

"And why would I be afraid of some...woman?" Raul asked, drawing two steps closer.

From several feet away, Ana Lucia looked over her shoulder, and noticed that Victoria had appeared from out of the shadows and was standing just 20 feet from the group, although all eyes were on the showdown between Raul and the mysterious and fearless woman that had appeared from nowhere. The next words out of the woman's mouth caused Ana Lucia to snap her head around in shock.

"Surely you've heard of Omega?"

Raul laughed and shook his head. "Yes, I've heard of Omega. You are not Omega. Now get out of here while you can." Raul moved forward, and with his right hand pushed Omega's left shoulder.

It was a mistake that he would regret for the rest of his life.

Before the man had a chance to withdraw his hand, Omega hooked her left hand around the man's wrist. Her right grabbed Raul's forearm, as she used his own weight to prevent herself from being pushed backwards. With surprising suddenness, Omega had the man's arm behind his back and his wrist pressed upward in such a violent fashion that the momentary shock quickly gave way to the pain shooting through his wrist and body.

If the spectators were impressed with that quick, but somewhat common move, they were left with their mouths open after what they witnessed next.

From behind, Omega used the pressure against Raul's arm and wrist to bring him to his knees. With the smoothness of an Olympic gymnast, Omega flipped from behind Raul to in front of him, never letting go of his arm and wrist.

The man's shoulder popped out of joint so grotesquely, Ana Lucia could have sworn that his shoulder was now coming out of his chest. She immediately turned around to look at Victoria, who stared at the unfortunate man that had decided first to work for a drug organization rivaling the Cartel de Culiacan, then foolishly challenged someone that he arrogantly thought he could overpower.

All the machismo that had been on display was gone, as Raul fell on his left side, already going in shock, yelling out in disbelief.

The Fight or Flight decision that goes through individuals in similar circumstances was also going through the other two couriers. Felipe decided to fight. Oscar decided on flight. It did not matter. Neither were successful.

Felipe pulled out a knife and ran toward Omega, not intending on letting her get the advantage with the first move. His lack of experience in hand-to-hand combat, or with any weapon for that matter, was clear. Pulling out a steel baton, with a flick of the wrist, Omega easily knocked away the knife. Rotating her body, and leaning over, Omega used Felipe's own momentum against him as she flipped him over and onto his chest. The dry Southern California ground was the last thing he would ever see, as Omega brought down the baton with the force of someone that had trained with it and was comfortable with the weapon in her grasp. The crack heard was the snapping of the man's spine where the skull met the neck.

In one fluid motion, Omega turned around, and with unbelievable accuracy, pulled out a six-inch blade, and sunk it deep into the head of the fleeing Oscar more than 20 feet away. The man fell to the ground with a thud.

Omega picked up the blade that Felipe had tried to use to stab her, and she walked over to the still suffering Raul, who was screaming in pain and clutching his dislocated shoulder. "Can't have you making so much noise and bringing the Feds over here," Omega said, as she used one hand to force open Raul's mouth, and grab his tongue. With the other hand, Omega used Felipe's blade to slice out the man's tongue, leaving him muted and in extreme pain.

Satisfied, Omega straightened and looked at Ana Lucia and Victoria, who had her gun out but at the low ready position, facing the ground.

"We don't have any problem with you," Victoria called out. "We were here for the men too, but for a different reason."

"Are you police?" Omega asked.

"Sort of," Ana Lucia said, "we're DEA."

Victoria and Ana Lucia were unable to tell what effect the revelation had on Omega, as she still had on the helmet.

After a moment's silence, Omega spoke. "Good to see some women finally taking over the playing field. It has been controlled by men for too long. Out of respect for you and what you represent, I am not going to do anything else besides walk back through that fence."

Victoria said, "What makes you think you could take us out so easily? We are US federal agents, on US soil. Sure, you just wiped the floor with three unsuspecting sloppy men, but I assure you we are much better trained and will not be nearly as careless as they were. They underestimated you. We don't."

"Good point. How about the three of us all walk out of here alive, and back to our respective countries?"

Victoria shook her head. "As much as I enjoyed seeing a woman beat the crap out of three drug dealers, as a DEA agent, I can't allow someone to walk free. Especially when I know that person is working for the Cartel de Culiacan. You are going to have to put your hands up and come with us." She raised her gun and pointed it at Omega.

Ana Lucia felt goosebumps on her neck as Victoria and Omega stared at each other.

Speaking to the microphone in her earpiece concealed by the motorcycle helmet, Omega said quietly, "Give me a little cover just in the area between me and the two women, but do NOT hit them."

A split second later, gunfire rained down from overhead, rounds pelting the ground in between Omega and the two DEA agents. Realizing that the threat did not come from Omega, Victoria had very carefully refrained from firing at her. Both women, despite the initial scare of gunfire at their feet, quickly realized that it was nothing more than a deterrent from overhead.

Ana Lucia looked up in disbelief. "Did that come from a drone?"

"Yes. And if anything happens to me, then both of you will be immediately taken out."

Victoria realized she was not going to take Omega into custody, at least not today.

"How do you have a drone?" Ana Lucia asked.

"Who are you?" Victoria said.

Omega finally took off her helmet. Ana Lucia did not recognize her, but Victoria knew at once who they were looking at.

"Maria Montoya," she gasped.

Maria, aka: Omega, smiled at the fact that she was recognized. With her father, Juan Montoya, as the second in command, and then leader of the Cartel de Culiacan, for an admittedly short time, and her brother Carlos as the new leader, Maria had always been overlooked, especially after she disappeared from the public spotlight following the incident in which she was raped by the son of long-time cartel leader, Julian Rodriguez. The night she was raped changed everything, setting into motion a series of events, from Juan Montoya ordering the poisoning of El Jefe's wife, to the cunning plan to displace El Jefe as the leader of the cartel, to Juan himself being killed in Hong Kong. But also, that night had forever changed the life of one Maria Montoya. Out of the spotlight, Maria Montoya had been forgotten, just a footnote as the woman that was raped by El Jefe's son.

She determined that she would never again be taken advantage of by a man. Her disappearance from the public spotlight was not out of humiliation and depression as most speculated. Instead, she used that time to travel the world, learning different fighting styles of different cultures. She became proficient with not only firearms, but all kinds of weapons. She learned hand to hand combat, as well as how to fight on the ground. She learned how to use her lighter frame to her advantage, with speed and decisiveness. During that training, Omega was born, and with it, a desire to take back her security, while at the same time defending the honor of her family that had gone to such lengths for her. It was more than enough for her to justify the use of her training to take out those that were now trying to usurp her family's power hold on the Cartel de Culiacan.

"Why have you not revealed your true identity?" Victoria asked.

"It will come out one day, I suppose."

"And would you really kill two federal agents, here on US soil, if we attempted to apprehend you?"

"I would...but I don't want to. Like I said, I have nothing against you two specifically. Now the DEA...that is another matter, but not you two."

Victoria thought to herself that it was a good thing that Maria/Omega had not heard the news about the massive seizure of cocaine from the day before. She was glad that she had ordered the news release to be delayed a few days. Had Omega known thousands of kilograms of cocaine had been seized from the Cartel de Culiacan, she might feel a little more offended about the presence of two DEA agents.

"Whose drone is overhead?" Victoria asked.

"Property of the government of Mexico. Unofficially of course. It is in their best interest that the Cartel de Culiacan squash this rebellion. Otherwise, another turf war will start. Thousands will die, and that might cost the President his re-election bid. The death of a few dozen is much more tolerable than the deaths of tens of thousands."

"Funny that you play God, you get to decide who lives or dies. If you use that drone on American federal agents, then the full force of the US government will come after you."

"I would be surprised if our paths don't cross in the near future," Omega said with a smile.

Victoria felt uneasy. Omega seemed to be referring to a specific point in the future. One that Victoria did not know about. Omega continued, "When that time arrives, maybe you will have the opportunity to play God...to determine who lives or dies. Until then..." Omega gave a quick nod and turned around, disappearing on the other side of the fence.

Chapter 27
Los Angeles, California

Remi eyed the heavily armed men surrounding the walls of the spacious warehouse. "We just went from a warehouse in one continent to a warehouse in another," she whispered to Chen who stood beside her. The contingent of women from China were added to dozens of other women already there. Some were still arriving. From what Remi could see and hear, there were women present from countries all over the world. She could hear Vietnamese and Japanese. She heard Spanish and was sure that many of the different countries in Central and South America were represented in the room. She also heard what she knew was several different Eastern European languages.

"There are at least 100 different women in this room right now," Chen said, as the remaining women from the violent ordeal in Hong Kong stood close to each other. "Where do you think they are going to take us?"

"I'm not sure. But we cannot make a move until we see Congressman Lightfoot. Otherwise, this will have all been for nothing."

The weariness in Chen's facial features was evident, but she still wanted to complete the mission for which they had traveled so far and endured so much. "How are you going to get a phone to get a call out?

Before she could answer, a man yelled and got everyone's attention. He spoke in English. "Listen up ladies. We are going to be leaving here in an hour. We will be going to a nice, private, secure mansion. There will be important men present. Those men are going to pay us money to spend the night with you. Maybe the week if they like you a lot. Your goal is to make them like you a lot. That makes us happy when our clients are happy. If we are happy, then your lives will be happy. Everybody will be happy!"

Remi edged through the crowd to get a better look at the man speaking. "I knew it," she said to herself. "I knew I recognized him."

"Who is it?" Chen asked from beside her.

"That's Romeo Sheffield. Best friend of Congressman Bobby Lightfoot." Remi remembered Romeo's face from when he was observed during the Group 5 surveillance, what seemed like years earlier.

"You think that's where we are going?" Chen asked.

"Yes, I do."

"Do you have any idea where that will be?"

"I think so...maybe. We followed them to a gated mansion in Westwood. I saw Lightfoot there myself. He took off in a helicopter with some women. I looked into that bastard's eyes. Yeah...he'll be there."

Chapter 28
El Centro, California

"You ladies seized 150 pounds of methamphetamine? The day after we hit 2000 kilograms of cocaine! You guys are rock stars! We might actually dismantle this criminal organization like we always claim to do in our priority target reports every quarter."

The ASAC of the DEA El Centro office was excited, and he could not wait to get his name on the Significant Enforcement Activity Report that would be sent to Headquarters later that day. He hoped that the results of the last few days of work would be the boost that he needed to get transferred away from the border and back closer to his desired location in the Mid-Western United States. The ASAC conveniently forgot that he had put an order in place restricting any operations, and that the seizure of 150 pounds of methamphetamine from the backpacks of the three couriers that had crossed the border was in direct violation of his order.

"Complete dismantling is the goal, sir," Victoria said respectfully. "But you have Ana Lucia to thank for this seizure. This was all her."

The ASAC smiled and looked from Victoria to Ana Lucia. He knew Victoria's close connection with the Deputy Administrator of DEA. He also knew Ana Lucia's reputation as someone quick to comment on the ineptitude or pandering of certain members in DEA management. The entire reason she was in El Centro was because of her comments directed toward the Administrator when others were present at an event in Headquarters. The ASAC did not want to risk the woman's wrath by saying something that would be observed by Victoria and might make its way to the Deputy Administrator, thereby creating a serious hindrance in his career progression and block any possibility that existed of obtaining one of the coveted

Senior Executive Service positions available, preferably in Chicago or St. Louis.

"Yes, of course! Very good work Ana Lucia! The El Centro office is glad to have you. You have proven yourself to be a very valuable resource."

"Thank you, sir," Ana Lucia replied, as her cell phone buzzed and she excused herself to take the call, leaving the ASAC a few precious moments alone to suck up to Victoria.

But Victoria could see things for what they were, and this ASAC was a man that had one thing on his mind, which was getting out of El Centro and moving up the career ladder. She could tell that the ASAC was hoping to get a transfer, so she politely continued with small talk until getting a tap on the shoulder from Ana Lucia.

"We need to get to the evidence vault. They've got something good."

Victoria nodded and excused herself, while the ASAC waved them away and encouraged them to continue fighting the good fight.

* * *

"Thanks for getting me out of there," Victoria said, as she and Ana Lucia walked toward the evidence vault. "What's up?"

"The Non-Drug Evidence Custodian was labeling and processing some of the exhibits from the three meth couriers. One of the couriers has an unlocked, old school cell phone. It has been ringing constantly and receiving text messages. The evidence custodian says we need to look because there is a message about another shipment of meth arriving."

"Wow, really?" Victoria asked. "I'm supposed to get back up to LA to meet with the US Attorney's Office this afternoon and make sure they don't go weak in the knees trying to prosecute the guys we arrested with the poisoned cocaine."

"Good luck with that," Ana Lucia said. "There are only one or two in that office that are worth the hassle of federal prosecution, the others are scared to prosecute a case without a full-blown admission

227

from the defendant. Statements from federal agents and intercepted wiretap calls aren't good enough anymore."

"I'll keep their feet to the fire," Victoria said, as the two women entered the evidence vault to speak with Kevin Tran, a plump and balding Vietnamese immigrant that was known to do his job well without complaints, which made him beloved among the agents that dealt with their fair share of complaints from co-workers, bosses, attorneys, and suspects.

"What's up, Tran?" Ana Lucia asked. "What do you have?"

Tran held up a plastic bag with a phone in it. "This phone belonged to one of your guys from last night named Oscar. According to the text messages coming in, Oscar was expected back in Mexicali this morning. A guy named Teofilo is telling him that the 'chino's' shipment is coming to the coast, whatever that means. Not sure if you can do anything about that, but I thought I would let you know. Would you guys like to take the phone for yourselves?"

Both women nodded. "Yes, Tran, thank you very much," Ana Lucia said, as she took the phone out of the bag and walked quickly out of the room. "Be sure to bring it back as soon as you can," Tran called out.

"Of course!" Ana Lucia said as she closed the door of the evidence vault and walked to an interview room so she and Victoria could speak quietly without being overheard.

"Who is Teofilo?" Ana Lucia asked. "Must be important the way your eyes lit up."

"He is. He runs meth production for the Cartel de Culiacan. I assume the Cartel is getting a large shipment of precursor chemicals from China that will be used to manufacture the meth. The Mexicans refer to anyone from China as 'El Chino.'"

"This courier from last night, Oscar, was definitely working for this new upstart cartel, the Sonora Cartel. But today he is getting a call from Teofilo, someone known to work for the Cartel de Culiacan?"

"Yep, he was playing both sides. Some men just can't help cheating."

"It's one thing to cheat on a woman, but on a murderous drug cartel?"

"Greed is a vicious thing. You're fluent in Spanish, right?"

"Yeah, what should I tell Teofilo?" Ana Lucia said, taking out the phone and preparing to type a response.

"Just let him know that you decided to spend the night in El Centro last night and see what he wants."

After 30 minutes of text messages back and forth, which Teofilo thought were safer than phone calls, yet another opportunity existed for DEA to make a huge seizure of illegal drugs. This time, at stake were tons and tons of precursor chemicals that would be used to manufacture enough methamphetamine to supply large portions of the Western United States. A container with more than 1000 tons of precursor chemicals was scheduled to arrive at the Port of Ensenada later that afternoon and driven to a garage located on the lonely 2D highway somewhere between Tijuana in the west and Tecate in the east, miles from the American border. The contents of the container, 1000 tons of chemicals, were being offloaded at the Port of Ensenada, and would then be transported to the garage later that afternoon. Oscar was supposed to receive a call from a person bringing the chemicals, and Oscar's job was simply to sit on the garage for 24 hours and lookout for law enforcement. This operation was going to be tricky though because Oscar was not provided the address of the garage. The longitude and latitude would be given to him by the driver transporting the precursor chemicals 30 minutes before arrival, and Oscar was supposed to be in the area and ready to respond.

Victoria and Ana Lucia had both overcome difficult obstacles in their careers, and they quickly set their minds toward another mission. The DEA had already succeeded in preventing the Cartel de Culiacan's poisoned cocaine from reaching its customer base in Southern California, thereby denying hundreds of millions of dollars in profits from the sale of those drugs. If the DEA could also take the chemicals sent from the 14K triad in Hong Kong to Mexico and used to manufacture methamphetamine, then it would leave the Cartel de Culiacan in a very precarious position. With the federal government seizing all the cartel's cocaine and methamphetamine, and the lack of revenue from the sale of those drugs, the Cartel de Culiacan would have no money to pay their own employees in Mexico, not to mention the cocaine suppliers from Colombia.

Conducting this operation on the Mexican side of the border would be sensitive. Only a limited number of DEA agents would be trusted with successfully conducting an operation of this magnitude on Mexican soil, even if approved by the Deputy Administrator. But the mission was essential. This seizure could eliminate the Cartel de Culiacan, once and for all.

Chapter 29
Los Angeles, California

Victoria walked off the elevator into the lobby of the Roybal Federal Building in Los Angeles and shook hands with Johnny. His own description as a "skinny Vietnamese guy with long hair and a long beard" made him easy to find. Johnny came highly recommended by Ana Lucia, who had worked closely with Enforcement Group 5.

Earlier that morning, the press had reported the deaths of two DEA Special Agents, one assigned to Hong Kong, and the other assigned to Los Angeles that was on TDY to Hong Kong. Also, the news reported the disappearance of Los Angeles Field Division Enforcement Group 5 Special Agent Remi Choylia. The reports also documented that SA Choylia had less than a year on the job.

Due to the death of one Group 5 member, and the disappearance of another, Johnny's normal jovial demeanor was replaced with a more serious vibe. Prior to the news breaking about Remi and Bear, Johnny's Group 5 partner Stan received the call to fly with the DEA helicopter to transport the poisoned cocaine to the DEA Laboratory in San Diego, making Johnny the only remaining member of Group 5 that had started working the investigation into Congressman Lightfoot. He was determined to see it through to the end and do whatever was necessary to find information that might lead to Remi's location. His gut told him that Remi was alive, and Johnny always trusted his gut. He hoped the information that would come out from the meeting with the Assistant United States Attorney and the recently arrested defendant from Victoria's investigation might shed some light into Remi's whereabouts.

"I'm very sorry to hear about Remi and Bear," Victoria said, as they moved through the lobby and out of the rear entrance to walk across the street to the ASUA's office. "Is there any update?"

"Not that I'm aware of. But there might be something that you can do to help."

"Really?" Victoria had been so consumed with her own investigation the last couple of weeks, she was not sure her investigation might possibly tie into the case being conducted by Group 5. "If I can help another agent, then I will."

"I know that Ana Lucia was Bravo Team Leader for your recent takedown. She provided the information that led to the initiation of this human trafficking case. Did she tell you anything about that?"

"No, she didn't. We were very busy down there, and she still is. Can you provide a summary?"

Johnny spent the next few minutes describing the operation that led to the identification of Romeo, and then Congressman Bobby Lightfoot, and the observations that led to Group 5 suspecting both men of being involved in the human trafficking of women. After explaining that the AUSA's office declined prosecution of Congressman Lightfoot or anyone associated with him, Johnny explained that Group 5 determined the only way to pin Congressman Lightfoot was to catch him in the act.

"Let me guess," Victoria said. "Bear took Remi to Hong Kong, for an off the books operation in which she was going to be introduced as a woman to be included in the group sent over to this human trafficking group in LA?"

"Yep."

"I've had a few investigations in Hong Kong. I worked with the other agent there that was killed. Kevin was a good guy. Willing to do whatever it takes to catch the bad guy, even if that means violating policy. Can come in handy sometimes. Can backfire others."

"Yeah, well this backfired big time. I have not been told anything that's not on the news. I know that Bear is dead, and Remi is missing. We must find Remi. We owe it to her."

"You're right. We do owe it to her. How can I help?"

"Well," Johnny said, as they entered the AUSA's office together, flashing their badges to the security personnel stationed at the front of the building. "For your operation, a few days ago, I was assigned as Foxtrot Team leader for the search warrant at Big D's residence in Compton."

"Oh yes, I remember Big D," Victoria said. "I'd love to see him again."

"Good. Because he wants to talk to you. He claims to have incriminating information on a white Congressman from California but won't give the specifics to anyone but you."

"You think he is referring to Congressman Lightfoot?"

"I think so. During our search of all the residences connected to other members of the gang, we found evidence which indicates some of the other gang members are also involved in human trafficking. We don't know what the connection is between a black gang and a white Congressman. I'm hoping you can find out."

* * *

Fortunately for Victoria, DEA Deputy Administrator Edmonds had made sure that this case was going to be handled by the best and brightest of the United States Attorney's Office in Los Angeles. Despite having more than a dozen Ivy League educated federal prosecutors to choose from, there were only two that were good at their job, and not afraid to prosecute a case out of fear that anything other than a conviction would tarnish their perfect conviction rate and ruin a possible political future, or even better, a huge salary with a high-paying defense firm. Ironically, of the 12 ASUA's in the criminal narcotics section, the one that was chosen especially for Victoria was the only one that was not Ivy League educated, but instead a California and Angelino native, born and raised in Los Angeles, played football at USC, and later attended law school there as well. Not only was Max the only non-Ivy League educated ASUA in the office, but he was also the only black man. Emboldened with a strong sense of justice, criminally and socially, he worked harder than everyone else because he knew that he would be judged more harshly than many of his other co-workers, because of the color of his skin and the school name on his degree.

When Victoria walked into the office to speak first and foremost to Big D, Max smiled with the anticipation that she knew something that could further their case.

Victoria quickly explained the circumstances of the case, assisted by Johnny when requested. Time sensitivity was the main issue, and Max wasted no time contacting the defense attorney representing Big D and telling him that he was going to speak with his client in an hour, and that he needed to be there.

Getting paid the big bucks, Big D's attorney was sure to drop whatever other appointments were on his calendar and an hour later he was seated in an interview room with Big D by his side, across the table from Max and the two DEA agents.

After giving Big D ten minutes to speak with his attorney, Max started. "I understand that you have made it apparent that you wish to speak to law enforcement."

"Not just any fed," Big D said. "I want to speak to her." He pointed at Victoria.

The defense attorney cut in. "Before my client says anything or divulges any information, we need assurances of an understanding in which charges will be levied against certain members...or certain associates."

Max leaned coolly back in his seat. He did not appear overly interested. Almost disinterested. "You know the game. It depends on the information you give. The better information, the more willing I will be to come to an agreement."

"First of all, I ain't no snitch," Big D said. "But I'll be damned if me and my boys are going to prison for 20 years while you got this crooked white boy congressman running hoes all over the world and selling them to the highest bidder. The feds catch us, but they ain't worried about the white crooks."

Max leaned forward in his seat, now fully engaged. "I assure you, that if you provide information about a US Congressmen, then that information will not be discarded. I will prosecute the case myself. Both agents seated by me have proven willing to investigate any lead

234

brought to them, regardless of who the target is or where they're from."

"Or skin color?" Big D asked.

"Of course," Victoria said, with Johnny nodding beside her.

"That's why I wanted to speak with you," Big D said, looking directly at Victoria. "I may not like you, but I got the feeling that you don't play around. I don't trust the feds. I don't trust any police actually, but I'm going to have to put my trust in somebody, and you're that lucky person."

All eyes turned to Victoria. "I don't care if you give me information on the President of the United States, if it checks out then I will investigate it. Whether it not it pans out is another question."

"Oh, it'll pan out."

Max worked his way back into the conversation. "So, what do you want in exchange for this information? Within reason, obviously," he said, looking at the defense attorney.

"Like I said, I ain't no snitch. If I get out early or even before any of my boys...I can't have that. I won't have that. I will plead guilty. I will give you this information that you need, but you *must* give my boys lighter sentences. My woman, the mother of my six-year-old daughter, I want her out. I don't care how you do it, but I want her out of jail and raising my daughter while I'm behind bars."

Max looked over at Johnny. "Remind me the details on his wife and the others that were arrested."

Johnny spoke up for the first time in the meeting. "Seven other members of this gang were arrested. His wife was in the front house of the residence. The dope was found in the structure behind the residence, on the same property."

"Okay," Max said, "and it was 200 kilos?"

"150," Johnny said.

Max rubbed his fingers together as he pretended to contemplate what he wanted to do, all the while knowing that he would gladly let the woman walk free and lighter sentences for Big D's associates in exchange for evidence that might lead to the arrest of a US Congressman.

"If you provide active intelligence, that these two agents can substantiate, then I can agree to those terms. But *only* if it results in information that can be used to charge this individual. You have my word on that," Max said, nodding his head at the defense attorney. The man simply nodded at Big D to give him his assurance.

"Who's the Congressman?" Victoria said, eager to not waste any more time.

"Bobby Lightfoot," Big D said. "Like I said, it isn't right that all my boys are about to go to prison while he gets to run free."

"And what criminal activity is Congressman Lightfoot involved in?" Victoria asked.

"Human trafficking. He is the head of a worldwide sex trafficking organization. Collects women from all over the world and sells them to the highest bidder."

"And how do you know all this?"

"Because...one of my boys provides women to his group. Mostly drugged up chicks that came to California to be a model or actress but never made it. Girls that got hooked on crack or heroin and could not go back home."

"And your associate delivers these women directly to Congressman Lightfoot?" Victoria asked.

"Hell no," Big D said, shaking his head. "He's too smart for that. He sends them to a friend of his named Romeo. I've been knowing Romeo since he was in college. He had a thing for this girl that was my neighbor. One thing led to another, and we started getting high together and he started flapping his gums and revealing all his dirty laundry."

"What can you tell us about Congressman Lightfoot, right now?" Victoria asked.

"I know he's expecting a shipment of girls at his warehouse in South Central as we speak. Romeo is going to pick them up and take them all over to Lightfoot's gated mansion in Westwood. They should be there by 7:00 p.m. tonight."

Remi could be there.

Everybody looked at their watches.

"We have three hours," Victoria said.

Johnny nodded. "We'll be there when they arrive."

"And you'll have your search warrant," Max confirmed.

Johnny sighed anxiously. "Let's hope Remi is there and still alive."

Chapter 30
50 miles east of Tijuana, Mexico

Slipping into Mexico was becoming something that Ana Lucia was more and more comfortable doing, despite the obvious restrictions in place about a federal agent doing so without having those plans approved by management. Victoria instructed her to not even let the DEA agents stationed in Tijuana know about their presence, because she had first-hand experience with the incompetence of the Resident Agent in Charge (RAC) leading the office. He was one of the few people that made Victoria snarl her lip in disgust, and Ana Lucia quickly understood that there would be no communication with the DEA office in Tijuana. They could not know about the operation out of fear the RAC would make an idiotic, unilateral, and unin-formed decision that would jeopardize everything. "It wouldn't be the first time...or the second," Victoria said.

Federal Highway 2D flows east of Tijuana and through a desert area with hills, mountains, and rocks as the backdrop for a beautiful landscape. It reminded Ana Lucia of some of her recent travels through Arizona. This trip, however, was business.

There were two lanes of travel in each direction. The east and west bound lanes were separated by a waist high concrete barrier. The location had plenty of rocks and hills off the main highway that Ana Lucia could hide behind as she waited for the conga line of ve-hicles bringing 1000 tons of precursor chemicals to be prepared for conversion to methamphetamine.

The earpiece was snug in Ana Lucia's left ear, and she spoke to Stan, a passenger in a DEA helicopter preparing to take off from a small private airport near San Diego, just miles across the interna-tional border.

"I knew you wanted to see me again, Stan, but you didn't have to volunteer for this dangerous mission just to prove how courageous you are," Ana Lucia said smiling.

"The way that Victoria explained the mission when she called, it didn't seem like there was much of a choice to volunteer. More of a command."

"Victoria can be convincing. But you are a grown man and make your own decisions, and I'm glad you decided to help. In all seriousness, my sincerest condolences for Bear. And I hope to God Remi is found soon."

"I don't usually make it a practice to violate my employer's policies, not to mention another sovereign nation's laws by flying into that country without approval, but if ever there was a time to take decisive action, it is now. DEA management in Los Angeles wants to shut us down at the exact moment we should be doing the opposite."

Despite him not mentioning their names, Ana Lucia could tell that the death of Bear Johnson and the disappearance of Remi was weighing heavy on Stan. This mission was his attempt to do anything to help the cause and get his mind off the death of his former co-worker.

"Are you clear on everything?" Ana Lucia asked from her position behind a rock on the east bound side of the Federal 2D Highway.

"Yes. We're going to fly low and avoid radar contact. If I observe the suspected line of vehicles transporting the precursor chemicals, then I will let you know so that you can do your thing."

"Exactly."

"What about the reinforcements? What's their location?"

Ana Lucia looked at her watch. "One of Victoria's contacts at the CIA is providing a team coming to help. They are coming from Tijuana. It's going to be tight if they make it in time. You know, there aren't a lot of trustworthy options available when employing Mexican law enforcement teams to take down Mexican traffickers."

"I understand. Every country has untrustworthy people in positions of power. The United States is no different."

Again, Ana Lucia could tell that Stan's thoughts were on Congressman Bobby Lightfoot back in the US, and how the mission to capture him had resulted in the death of Bear Johnson, and possible death of Remi.

"I know, Stan. We are here to do what we must until the Mexican forces get here, nothing more. If these precursor chemicals are seized, then the Cartel de Culiacan will be finished, forever."

* * *

The importance of the delivery of the precursor chemicals was as obvious to the leaders of the Cartel de Culiacan as it was to the DEA agent and CIA case officers working together to stop it. As with most drug operations, the individual that is truly in charge never lays a hand on the product, instead coordinating and overseeing from far away. In this case, Carlos Montoya was more than 1500 kilometers south in Culiacan while the 25 18-wheelers carrying 40 tons each of precursor chemicals made their way from the Port of Ensenada on Mexico's west coast to a large garage that did not have an official address, located just off the Federal 2D highway.

Montoya justified his decision to remain in Sinaloa while he dealt with the DEA agent pretending to be Vaquero, which had resulted in the American feds seizing all 2000 kilograms of cocaine that was sent out days before. The fact that his very first major shipment of cocaine had been seized by American law enforcement did not inspire much confidence in the Colombians or increase their willingness to supply his organization with more cocaine. With the Colombians unwilling to immediately send more cocaine, the cash flow problems the Cartel faced could be rectified with the production, manufacture, and sell of methamphetamine.

Praying to the patron saint of drug trafficking, Jesus Malverde, Montoya was sure that his prayers were answered when he finally received contact from the infamous "Omega," offering whatever form of assistance or protection necessary for the good of the Cartel.

The mysterious Omega had used a voice altering machine during the phone call, and even the leader of the Cartel de Culiacan had no idea who Omega really was. He did not suspect that Omega was his own sister. However, with Omega promising additional resources to protect the shipment of precursor chemicals, Montoya began to believe that things were finally going to work out.

* * *

Omega, on the other hand, was equally confident that things were going to work, mainly because she was responsible for ensuring the 25 18-wheelers successfully arrived at their destination. Having spoken with her contact in the Mexican government, Luis Fonseca, he was quick to provide a team of mercenaries to accompany the shipment of chemicals. In all, two dozen men were provided, all former military members or special operations officers with a background in protection. There were no connections to Mexican Federal Police or the Mexican Military, so they could not be implicated in this operation in the event something went bad. In truth, Fonseca told Omega that the Mexican President, nor anyone in the Mexican government for that matter, knew anything about the pending operation. Fonseca was not sure that the correct decision would be made, so he made the decision for them.

Fonseca instructed the two dozen men to provide whatever assistance was required by Omega. Her rules were simple, each man is responsible for the safety of the truck that he is in. If there is a problem, then they should contact Omega immediately.

Omega would be riding in the last truck in the conga line of vehicles, protecting the rear while also able to move up quickly and assist if necessary.

In addition, Omega had one more ace up her sleeve. The drone that had been provided by Fonseca and the Mexican government had come in handy on several previous occasions, from taking videos of certain missions that were then uploaded to social media for the world to see, or when the weapons system of the drone was used to make sure that the DEA agents were not going to attempt to detain her when she was caught on the American side of the border. Once again, the drone would be in the air. The individual that operated the drone, the only Mexican national that knew Omega's real identity, was a man named Ramos.

He was the only person that she trusted to fly the drone, and he listened to her instructions before making any unilateral decisions. Omega trusted him more than most men because Ramos was homosexual. As someone that experienced a traumatic rape in her youth, she knew Ramos' ulterior motive was not to get her to bed, and that instantly put her more at ease around him. Omega instructed Ramos to fly the drone overhead and be on the lookout for anything that would try to stop their progress.

With Ramos and the drone overhead and in front of the conga line of 18-wheelers, Omega in the rear, and the mercenaries spaced between, the future of the Cartel de Culiacan rested with the vehicles as they made their way east of Tijuana.

Chapter 31
Westwood, California

"This is the place," Remi whispered. "I've been here before, on surveillance, and personally witnessed Lightfoot leave in a helicopter
with four women that had just landed at the Long Beach airport."

"Maybe Lightfoot will be here, and we can finally identify him,"
Chen responded.

The two women were lost in a crowd of nearly a hundred that entered a large and spacious gated mansion in the residential area of
Westwood, about 15 miles west of Los Angeles. Most of the women
were impaired with their choice of readily available cocktails of cocaine, heroin, or some other opiate. In their impaired status, it
seemed their temporary presence in such a luxurious estate was a
dream come true, a clear sign that all the promises made to them
about a better life in America were coming true. For the moment,
most of the women were happy. Remi knew it would not last. Soon,
the women would be spread out, and a determination was going to
be made regarding which women would be sent to which city. She
had seen it with her own eyes, and knew it was coming.

With all the women gathered in the foyer, Romeo stood on the
second level at the top of a beautiful set of white marble stairs that
curved around to the top.

"The time has come, my lovely ladies, for decisions to be made.
There are many very willing and eager men in this country. These
men are anxious to consume the services that you ladies provide. If
you service the clients well, we will promise you physical protection,
financial reward, and an unlimited supply of your drug of
choice...within reason of course. So, continue mingling downstairs
while the decisions are made. We are awaiting one more individual
to arrive. He is running late, but soon we will get things going."

"He's got to be talking about Lightfoot," Remi said.

"Yes, now we have to figure out how to get you a telephone..."

"You!" a voice interrupted, roughly grabbing Chen by the arm. "Come with me. I like your look. Much like the boss, I too have an Asian fetish." The white man dragged Chen up the stairs, as she struggled to regain her balance, looking down at Remi.

Was this guy, a guard, really going to take Chen upstairs and rape her?

Remi could not think of any other reason for him to be going upstairs, and watched the man walk up the top of the stairs dragging Chen behind him. Another guard circling down at the bottom level saw Remi. "Are you jealous? Do you want to join your friend up top?" the man asked, laughing, and licking his lips.

"Yes, actually," Remi replied, looking lustfully at the man. "I was hoping to get that chance, but I guess that guy just wants to be with one woman..."

The guard's eyes got big and he stepped back as he yelled for the man taking Chen away. "Hey, Joey! Joey! Hey man!"

Joey stopped at the top of the stairs looking down at the man calling his name, still gripping Chen from behind. "This broad says she wants to join you with the chick you have now! I'm sending her up!"

"All right, buddy!" Joey called out, giving a thumbs up to the guard downstairs.

Joey turned his attention to Remi as she jogged upstairs. Remi gave Chen a smile and a look to convey that she knew what she was doing. After everything they had been through, Chen trusted Remi as much as anybody else in the world.

Remi's presence was calming. "Give him what he wants," Remi whispered as the man began to quickly disrobe while trying to undress both women at the same time.

"I want both of you on your knees, now," Joey yelled once they had removed their shirts and pants.

With Joey sitting on the bed, and closing his eyes in anticipation, Chen looked questioningly at Remi, who began talking seductively about what she wanted to do.

When Chen grabbed the man's crotch, he let out a satisfied groan and leaned back on the bed, exactly what Remi wanted. With the man's attention diverted, her hands reached for his jeans on the floor beside her. Searching the pockets quickly, Remi found the man's phone. She would need it to call her group to come rescue her, but more importantly, to record Congressman Lightfoot when he arrived.

Suddenly, without warning, a hand reached from behind and grabbed Remi's left arm. "What do you think you are doing, whore?" Romeo asked, glaring at Remi.

* * *

Romeo's hand came down hard and fast against Remi's face. Dressed in nothing but a bra and panties, she felt extremely vulnerable without a weapon, and was not sure what to do other than drop Joey's phone to the ground.

"Sorry, boss," Joey stuttered, "I was just sampling a couple of the girls before they were sent out. I didn't think it would be a problem."

Romeo frustratingly waved him off. "Moron! She grabbed your phone! Who knows what she was planning to do with it!" He grabbed Remi by the back of her hair and forced her to stand.

"I was just – I was just going to record us!" Remi stammered. "I thought he would like it. Sorry! I didn't even think about it, I swear."

Romeo pulled Remi's hair, forcing her closer to him, and grabbed her by the face, leaning in closely. "You do not do anything unless the client tells you to do it. Understand?"

"Yes, I understand!"

Romeo turned and waved his arm at the trio. "Enough fun. Pull your pants up, Joey. Both of your girls are coming with me. We have just moved the women into different rooms based on where they're going. I think I'll send you to New York," he said to Remi. Turning to Chen, Romeo told her, "I'm going to need you in Atlanta."

When Romeo turned around, Remi noticed a bulge in the back of his jeans, hidden by an untucked shirt. The man was carrying a gun, gangster style, tucked in the back of his pants.

"We need to get dressed," Remi protested as Romeo stood in the doorway.

"No, you need to listen to me!" Romeo shouted. "You belong to me now. You are my property. You must do what I tell you to do, and I'm telling you to come with me! Both of you."

"Of course," Remi said, lowering her head in reverence as she walked out the door, with Chen following and Joey still getting dressed.

Remi walked into the hallway and moved toward the wooden railing overlooking the hardwood floor below. Looking back at Chen, Remi nodded as she stumbled and fell to one knee, complaining of a turned ankle. Romeo again grabbed her by the hair, "I told you to get up!"

At that moment, Chen exploded from her position several feet away, hitting Romeo like a football player and knocking him against the waist high railing. Romeo's left leg did not land on the ground because it bumped into Remi, throwing him off balance as he landed against the railing. In one motion, Remi grabbed Romeo's right leg, and raised up from a kneeling to standing position, tossing Romeo over the side of the railing.

Before tumbling away from the railing, Remi deftly grabbed the gun tucked into Romeo's pants. Turning toward the stunned guard, Joey, Remi placed a single shot in his forehead.

The sound of Joey's body dropping to the floor was masked by the sound of Romeo's body crashing into the hardwood floor one level below. Remi dropped the gun on the floor by the railing, as she and Chen both looked at Romeo below.

He had landed directly on his head, and his lifeless eyes stared up as a pool of blood started to spread around him on the hardwood floor.

* * *

On cue, Chen started screaming like the distressed, strung out prostitute that she was pretending to be. Remi rushed to Joey's lifeless body and pulled out the cell phone which he had put back in his pocket, failing to lock it as he rushed to get dressed. Remi ran into the bedroom they had just been in, grabbed her clothes, and moved into the attached bathroom, shutting the door behind her.

Like most Special Agents that maintained contacts in a list saved on a phone, Remi did not know phone numbers for Stan or Johnny. She did, however, have the number memorized for the DEA Command Center in Los Angeles, which was staffed 24-7 every day of the year.

"DEA Command Center, this is Thomas."

"Thomas, this is Remi Choylia, from Enforcement Group 5."

"Remi! My god, everyone has been looking for you! We thought you were dead. Where are you?" Thomas yelled excitedly.

"I can't speak long, but you have to contact Johnny or Stan from Group 5. Tell them I have been taken to the residence in Westwood where we followed the target last week. They will know the spot."

"Remi, Johnny is on the way to that location right now. Johnny just dropped off the Operations Plan. They are leaving the Federal Building right now. They should be there in 25 – 35 minutes."

Screaming voices were now closer, and men had entered the bedroom and were approaching the bathroom as Remi ended the call. During the conversation, she had gotten dressed, and she now slid the phone in her panties underneath her black dress, as she sunk to her knees and put her head around the toilet.

"What are you doing in here? What the hell happened to Romeo and Joey?" The man grabbed Remi by the hair like Romeo had, dragging her out of the bathroom.

"I'm sorry! I'm sorry!" Remi yelled. "When I saw all the blood...all the death...I thought I was going to throw up! I had to go to the bathroom. I'm sorry." The three men at the top of the staircase appeared frozen. In shock or fear, Remi was not sure, but it was clear that they did not know what to do.

"I told you guys!" Chen yelled. "These two got into a fight over us. Joey pushed Romeo against the railing, and he lost his balance, but he took a shot before he fell over the side. They killed each other."

Remi marveled at Chen's quick thinking to explain the two deaths.

"And as Romeo fell to his death, he just happened to shoot Joey right between the eyes like a marksman?" one man asked accusingly. He clearly did not believe the explanation. It did not matter though, because at that exact moment, the front door of the mansion opened, and Congressman Bobby Lightfoot walked into the room.

* * *

"What. Happened. Here." The Congressman said slowly as he looked at the dead body of Romeo, his long-time friend, lying on the floor. One of the men from upstairs rushed down.

"We are trying to figure that out, sir," the man said. "Joey was upstairs with two women, when Romeo went up there too. Somehow, Romeo fell and hit his head, and Joey was shot in the head."

"Joey's dead too?" the Congressman asked.

"Yes, sir, it just happened, but we are questioning the two women involved upstairs right now."

"Leave them for me, I'll handle that. But first things first, we must get the other women out of here. We are on a very tight schedule. My contact with LAPD only gave me a 10-minute window in which we can be assured that the police will not be patrolling outside. Load the women up and get them to the airports. The drivers will know where to go, between the airports in Burbank, Van Nuys, and Santa Ana. The girls that are staying in Southern California will go to one of the hotels in West Los Angeles. Get them out now! But leave the two up there for me." Lightfoot looked up at the top of the stairs, and saw Chen and Remi standing beside the two men holding them. The two men, having received direction from Congressman Lightfoot, immediately ran downstairs, and to the rooms of waiting women.

Lightfoot slowly climbed the stairs as both women remained still. In a whisper, heard only to Remi, Chen said, "We can't let all these women get taken away. There are over 200 women. If we don't stop this, they are going to be sexually trafficked. We have to prevent that."

Remi shook her head. "Group 5 is going to be here soon. We can't make a move on Lightfoot until they're close. We did this to arrest him."

"Which means letting all these girls go." Chen whispered urgently as Lightfoot neared. "Who knows how many will even survive."

Remi looked at Chen. "We wanted the big fish, and here he is. I won't let him go. Not even for all those women down there."

Chen shook her head, disapproving.

Lightfoot got to the top of the stairs, while Remi and Chen stood near the doorway of the bedroom. "If we try to stop this now, there are only two of us. We might not be successful and Lightfoot might get away. If we let the women go, drag this out, Group 5 gets here before Lightfoot leaves. I don't like it either, but there are no good choices."

* * *

Congressman Lightfoot walked over to Joey's body and inspected the bullet hole in the man's forehead. "I never realized Romeo was such a good shot," he remarked, looking suspiciously at the two women. "It's funny, Romeo was my friend. But he was never really good at anything. Come to think of it, we even went to the range a few times in college. He could not hit the broadside of a barn. Yet, in his last act on earth he managed to shoot his attacker, someone he has known for years by the way, right in the forehead even as he was tumbling to his death. Rather amazing." He shook his head. "Follow me downstairs ladies."

They followed the Congressman downstairs and stood beside him near the door as he watched the progression of women making their way outside. "Sir," the first man told him, "these are the women that were selected to go to Atlanta." The women walked seductively by, with Lightfoot nodding in approval at the group of women, made up mostly of Eastern European blondes, and black women either from Southern California or West Africa. Also, a couple of Asian women were included, a very diverse group. Modern day slavery, Remi realized as the women went by.

"You," Lightfoot said to one of the Eastern European women. "You stay with me. I'll have you tonight."

"Okay, thank you, my name is Sletvana..."

"I don't care what your name is. We are not going to be friends, or romantic partners, so don't get any fancy ideas. Your sole objective from now on is to please the man you're with, starting with me."

In all, Remi counted 22 women in the group destined for Atlanta. Moments later, the group of women heading to Chicago walked by, and Lightfoot again nodded approvingly. "Yes, Charlie will definitely approve of this group," he said as the women walked out the door and to their own van. Two other groups walked past Lightfoot, and he gave the approval for the women to be transported to the chosen locations. All except for Sletvana and one other woman that had been scheduled to go to New York. They were staying with Lightfoot for the night.

Once everyone had left, Lightfoot spun around quickly and looked at Remi, Chen, and the other two women. "I will need to speak with you two privately, but you will also serve the purposes I need for the time being. Follow me, ladies," he said, walking toward the rear of the house, passing other living room areas, studies, and washrooms.

Before walking outside into the spacious backyard, Lightfoot called for Jorge, a security guard stationed in the back yard. "Clean up the mess downstairs and upstairs. There is not to be any trace of blood or anything up there, do you understand?"

"Yes sir," Jorge replied.

"And it goes without saying, but arrange to have the bodies disposed, preferably burned."

"Even Romeo, sir?" Jorge asked.

"Yes, even Romeo. I would have loved to give him a proper memorial service, but we must not have law enforcement searching around here. It would only be a matter of time before they uncover everything. Then the senior guys would have my head."

Remi looked at Chen, as they both realized the meaning of what they had just heard. Lightfoot might be the big boss in Los Angeles, and he even walked around and gave orders like he was the big boss. But there was a senior group to whom he reported.

Who was that group? How could they figure out who that group was? Would Lightfoot tell them if he was arrested?

All these thoughts ran through Remi's mind as Lightfoot walked towards the helicopter 100 meters away. It was from this exact location that Remi had seen Lightfoot depart on a helicopter during a surveillance that now seemed like a lifetime ago.

The pilot of the helicopter was waiting patiently as Lightfoot calmly approached. "All right, George, fire this thing up and take us to Palm Springs like normal," he said. The four women entered, with Lightfoot the last to get in, before he suddenly had a revelation. "Crap, I almost forgot!" he said. "Get the engine started," he told the pilot, "I'll be right back. I forgot the paperwork to provide to Charlie's people. Give me a couple minutes."

"Yes sir," the pilot responded as he began going through his pre-flight check list.

As soon as Lightfoot was out of the helicopter, Remi removed the cell phone from her underwear, and pressed the button to stop the recording that had captured Lightfoot's involvement in giving the final approval for which sex trafficking victims were sent to which locations. She quickly called the Command Center and instructed Thomas to patch her through to Johnny's cell.

With the whir of the blades, it was becoming increasingly hard to hear, but it was still a very welcome sound to hear the voice of her co-worker, who quickly told her that he would be there in five minutes, just to hold out if possible and they would be there.

The pilot, looking in his mirror, happened to see Remi on the phone, and shouted at her to put the phone away. By that point, Chen was accustomed to delivering death. She had already removed the belt from her clothes. Reaching over the pilot's seat she wrapped the belt around the pilot's neck, leaning back as far as she could with all her strength. The two stunned women looked on as the pilot struggled to breath, using his hands to try and provide space between the belt and his throat, but Chen had pulled it back so far there was not any slack. Within 30 seconds, the man was unconscious.

Lightfoot had nobody available to fly him away.

The shock on Lightfoot's face as he got back into the chopper moments later was one that delighted Remi. Still unbelieving that two prostitutes recruited from Hong Kong could be responsible for three deaths at the house that night, he realized all too late that he had misjudged the women in front of him.

Lightfoot attempted to snatch Chen by the neck and drag her out, but Remi had already removed her high heel shoe. With as much power as she could muster, she drove the pointy end of the shoe into the left side of the Congressman's mouth, puncturing the skin all the way through, but not causing any critical damage, other than shock. The surprise and trauma from the attack caused him to stumble backwards, and Remi and Chen collectively spent the next few moments enjoyably pummeling the Congressman who cowered like a scared child on the grass, trying in vain to protect himself from the blows of hands and feet that were coming down upon him.

At the point when Remi was near exhaustion, and sure that all the fight was gone from the obnoxious Congressman, she stopped when she heard her name yelled. Remi turned to look at Johnny, along with two other DEA agents that had scaled the fence and entered through the back yard, while another team was simultaneously assaulting the residence and detaining all occupants.

Remi hugged Johnny as a flood of emotions swept over her. Relief for her safety, satisfaction of accomplishing the goal of arresting the Congressman, grief over Bear and Kevin's death, horror at how easily she had killed so many men, and despair over the hundreds of women she had allowed to be taken away to a life of sexual servitude were all feelings that overwhelmed her senses as she finally let her guard down. She fell to the ground in tears. She did not want to appear weak, but at that point, the tears could not be held back.

She was safe, Chen was safe, and Lightfoot was going to jail.

Chapter 32
50 miles east of Tijuana, Mexico

"I see them," Stan said into his microphone from the passenger seat of the DEA helicopter flying low overhead a couple miles inside the Mexican side of the border. "25 trucks in all. From front to back they stretch out a few miles."

"Each one of those trucks is carrying 40 tons of precursor chemicals," Ana Lucia replied from her position hidden behind a large boulder, "and somehow nobody from the Mexican government is here to stop them."

"I don't think it's so much the Mexican government that is corrupt, as it is one important piece in the government that has a lot of power. Like the queen in chess. It is not the highest-ranking piece, but it is the most important piece. I would say most governments still in existence have a similar problem, it just so happens this one directly effects the citizens of our country."

"I wonder who inside the Mexican government is helping in this case."

"Not sure," Stan responded from the chopper, "but whoever it is, it is someone with enough clout to basically clear out all the traffic around here. Everything has been diverted. It's just going to be us and the 18- wheelers."

"How far are they from my position?" Ana Lucia asked.

"I'd estimate five miles. How far is the team helping us that the CIA guy got?"

Ana Lucia looked at her watch and shook her head. "They're not going to make it. They're at least 10 minutes out."

"What are you going to do?"

"We need to delay them."

"What do you have in mind?"

"The CIA team is coming from Tijuana. They will be able to catch up if we can slow this convoy down. If the chemicals get to the garage, and they realize Oscar is not there, then they will go somewhere else, and we'll probably never find them."

"Okay, but how are you going to delay them?"

"I might need a little help with that."

* * *

At a spot on the highway where the two east bound lanes curved slightly to the right, the DEA helicopter swooped across the road, delving deeper into the Mexican countryside. The chopper was at least a half mile from the lead 18-wheeler, just meters away from Ana Lucia's location behind the boulder. The chopper sweeping down had the desired effect, as the lead vehicle slowed considerably.

Peering out from behind the boulder, Ana Lucia looked and saw the driver of the lead 18-wheeler. What she was not expecting to see were two additional faces staring out the front windshield.

What were three men doing in the front cab of the truck?

Using her binoculars, Ana Lucia could see the two passengers speaking, likely relaying their observations to whoever was in charge. The response the individuals received must have been to continue, as the 18-wheeler never came to a complete stop and started moving faster.

"Come on back through again Stan," Ana Lucia said. Moments later, the chopper came back into view from around some hills, this time appearing to be returning toward the US side of the border. While all eyes were on the helicopter, Ana Lucia rushed down to the road and threw out a smoke bomb, covering the area in gray smoke.

It was readily apparent that the chopper overhead was not a coincidence, and the smoke restricted the vision of the driver, causing him to stop the vehicle in the middle of the two-lane road.

Before anyone inside the truck knew what was happening, Ana Lucia was across the road, and bounded up to the driver's side of the truck, ripping it open and pointing a stun gun at the driver. As an American DEA agent conducting a non-authorized mission inside

Mexican territory, delivering a lethal blow with a gun could possibly result in a long prison sentence, either in Mexico or the United States, and her agency would forget they had ever known her if the details came out to the media. The Taser stun gun was just needed to incapacitate the driver and delay the convoy. She was not interested in killing anyone unless necessary.

Making a quick assessment of the situation, Ana Lucia quickly noted that she only saw one passenger now instead of two, which she initially thought was a good thing because the Taser stun gun only had two barbs. She quickly fired the first barb into the driver, but as she turned to shoot the other passenger, her hair was pulled from behind, and she fell backwards and on top of the mercenary that had circled in front of the truck and come up on her from behind. The stun gun's barb missed the passenger, Ramos, hitting the window of the truck.

* * *

Omega had already yelled instructions to Ramos and the mercenary. She told the mercenary to stop the attacker, but to leave the attacker alive if possible. She told Ramos that the next time the chopper flew back overhead deeper into Mexico and away from the US border, to take it out with the drone's weapons system. Ramos pulsated with excitement, as it was the first time he was authorized to use the state-of-the-art weapons system to eliminate a target. That excitement grew as he could hear the blades of the chopper returning for yet another overpass. Ramos located the chopper on the computer screen in front of him.

The window of time to make the kill shot was very short, and the position of the drone did not provide the optimal angle for a direct hit that would undoubtedly take down the American helicopter, but it was better than nothing. The occupants of the chopper seemed to be focusing all their attention on the fight on the ground.

They never saw the hellfire missile come from the drone until it crashed into the tail of the bird, causing it to spin around violently, struggling unsuccessfully to maintain altitude.

Ana Lucia reacted to the mercenary even before she hit the ground on top of him. Moving her chin toward her chest during the fall to the ground, she used the momentum of their two bodies impacting the ground and drove her head backwards into the face of the man behind her.

The crunch of the bone breaking in the man's nose and the obvious pain that resulted was not enough to incapacitate the trained mercenary, who knew that he was now in a fight for his life. Despite the smoke and the blood and the tears blocking his vision, he managed to stand and wrap his right arm around Ana Lucia, attempting to put a strangle hold on her until she passed out. As she struggled to get the man's right hand off her, the mercenary used his left hand to deliver several blows to her back side. While each one hurt, she focused on getting out of the man's grasp and maintaining consciousness.

Mustering all her strength, she pulled her right arm forward, and then pushed it back quickly and as violently as possible, delivering a debilitating elbow strike directly to the ribs of the man behind her, again hearing a crunch of cracked or broken bone. Ana Lucia used the momentary release of pressure around her neck to move a couple steps forward, spin to her left, and side kick the mercenary in the chest to create separation.

Before she could turn back to address the mercenary, she saw and heard the impact of the missile from the drone striking the tail of the DEA helicopter. She looked on in horror as the chopper started spinning and spinning, away from their position, headed toward the desert floor deeper into Mexico. Ana Lucia's mind tried to process what she was seeing and why, until the realization dawned on her that the man sitting in the passenger seat of the 18-wheeler and staring at a computer screen was controlling the drone overheard.

Staring so intently at the computer, Ana Lucia was convinced that the man was planning one last missile strike on the downed chopper. A strike to completely destroy it. She knew that she must act quickly, otherwise Stan and the DEA pilot of the helicopter would die a fiery death. Ana Lucia drew her Glock .23 and jumped to the cab of the 18-wheeler firing two rounds into the man at the computer, just moments before he clicked the command to fire the second missile.

On instinct, Ana Lucia spun around on the step leading up to the driver's seat, just as the mercenary pulled out his own weapon.

Two shots rang out at the same time, and then a third came immediately after.

Ana Lucia was standing from a higher position on the steps of the big truck, and the shot from the mercenary hit her right thigh, a few inches above the knee.

She did not have to worry about return fire. While her first shot missed slightly high, the second shot of the double tap impacted directly in center mass.

Before she had an opportunity to express any sense of relief, she heard the crash of the DEA helicopter. Looking over the hood of the truck, she could see that the chopper had crash landed on the desert floor, still intact but inoperable and bursting with flames. Her only thought was to get to Stan and the pilot.

* * *

The quarter mile rush to the wreckage of the DEA helicopter was the longest and most painful quarter mile Ana Lucia had ever run. Her head was ringing. The bullet that went into her leg seemed to have exited without hitting a big artery, but her back was hurting equally now. As she put her left hand against the area that had been hit by the mercenary, she realized that it was not hits she had suffered, but stab wounds from a short blade. The blood on her hand confirmed the puncture, but she continued. Looking over her shoulder at the line of 18-wheelers on the highway behind her, she saw that they had started moving again, which could only mean that one of the men had come up to take over for the incapacitated driver and the other two men that Ana Lucia had killed.

A huge boulder provided cover from the line of 18-wheelers coming, but there was no way to disguise the crashed DEA helicopter.

Ana Lucia realized as she got closer that the chopper had been so low when it lost control and crashed, that the impact of crash did not destroy the aircraft.

Rolled on its left side, Ana Lucia leaped inside and found Stan, who had survived the crash, and remained conscious, unbuckling himself as he tried to move away. He immediately fell to the ground as soon as he put any weight on his legs, screaming in pain.

"Stan! Stan! I'm here!" Ana Lucia yelled. "Give me your hand so I can get you out."

Gritting his teeth through the pain, he yelled, "I can't put any pressure on my legs. I think I broke my hip!"

"Okay, let me pull you out of here in case this thing blows up."

She looked ahead and saw a fire blazing in the engine. She could also see the DEA pilot of the chopper unconscious and leaning against the controls. Taking care of one task at a time, she pulled Stan out of the helicopter, and then dragged him on the ground and leaned him against the boulder.

Priding himself on being a soldier and federal agent, Stan managed to fight through the jolts of pain that shot through his lower body as Ana Lucia dragged him from the chopper. He did so, appreciating her resolve to rescue him.

"There is a fire extinguisher in the front on the passenger side," Stan told her. "If you get it, then you can put the fire out before it gets too bad and blows the bird up."

"Okay!" Ana Lucia said, rushing back to the chopper as fast as possible, with the adrenaline surging through her veins causing her to temporarily forget the pain associated with the stab wounds in her back and the gunshot in her leg.

After a few moments, the fire was out, and Ana Lucia managed to unbuckle the pilot and drag him to the rock beside Stan. Collapsing in exhaustion beside the two men from the downed chopper, Ana Lucia smiled as she heard sounds of another chopper approaching from the direction of Tijuana. The reinforcements were arriving!

And not a moment too late. They would be able to get Stan and the pilot to safety, and...

She looked over her shoulder at the federal highway to see the line of 18-wheelers still moving by. She estimated that half of them had passed already. But as she looked for the end of the line of 18-wheelers, she noticed two forms approaching at a very fast speed.

Moments later, two dirt motorbikes stopped on the side of the boulder beside the DEA agents. The driver on the first bike did not get up but kept a gun out and pointed at the three agents. The driver on the second bike hopped off, also keeping a gun out.

"It seems like we just met," Omega said to Ana Lucia, recognizing her from the incident at the border a few nights before. Ana Lucia did not respond. Her gun was still at her side, but at this point, she was overcome with fatigue, and even she recognized the futility in trying to fight back. It would be at least a minute until the reinforcements from the CIA chopper would be on the ground. It had been a very tight window, and Ana Lucia had been convinced that everything was going to work out. She felt immortal, but the realization crept in that her life was now in the hands of another, Omega.

"Lucky for me, I had a motorbike in some of the trucks in case I needed to move forward quickly," Omega told her. "But when I saw the chopper crash, I just had to find out who was responsible for this operation. Was it the Americans? If so, was it the CIA? FBI? DEA? Well, I guess now I know. It is the DEA coming into *Mexican* territory, trying to conduct law enforcement operations on *Mexican* soil that violate *Mexican* laws. How arrogant do you Americans have to be to even contemplate an operation like this?"

Ana Lucia was never one to back down from an argument, and she was not going to start now. "Really? You are upset about the DEA breaking Mexican laws? The Cartel you are protecting has been breaking American laws for decades! Your selective outrage is hypocritical."

Omega stood in front of Ana Lucia, who was still leaning against the boulder behind her. "Would you like me to put you out of your pain, Mrs. DEA agent?"

Ana Lucia stared back defiantly, but it was Stan that spoke up, half delirious. "No! Don't hurt her! Don't hurt Ana Lucia!!"

Ana Lucia cut her eyes at Stan, imploring him to be quiet, but it was too late. Omega saw the emotion in the stare and could hear the emotion in Stan's voice. There was something there.

"We've got company!" the mercenary on the motorbike yelled as the strike force from the CIA helicopter approached with rifles out, pointing at them, waiting to see if it was friend or foe leaning against the bolder, or both.

Initially planning to use Ana Lucia as a hostage to get out of the situation, Omega instead grabbed Stan by the back of his vest and dragged him away from the boulder, putting her gun against his head as she looked directly at Ana Lucia. "If they are with you, then tell them to stand down right now or your boyfriend will have his brains spilled all over your lap. Tell them!"

The mercenary that accompanied Omega had now moved between the approaching team and Omega, shielding her as they moved closer. Ana Lucia stood up on a shaky left leg, holding up her hands as she yelled out, "Don't shoot! It's DEA!"

Toby, the CIA Case Officer that had met Ana Lucia at the safe house in Mexicali days earlier, was the leader of the tactical group. He held up his left hand as his right hand kept the rifle pointed steadily at the man. "Ana Lucia? Is that you?"

"Yes, it is! Toby, she has one of our agents. If you do anything, she will kill him."

"Who is she?" Toby asked, moving within feet from the mercenary protecting Omega.

"I'm known as Omega. My birth name is Maria Montoya, the sister of Carlos Montoya."

"Omega is Maria Montoya?" Toby asked, as he moved his rifle toward her.

"I am, and I am sure you might think you can get off a round quickly, but I promise you, I'm just as fast. If I am dying tonight, I'm taking this gringo with me."

Toby looked at Ana Lucia, who shook her head. She was not willing to sacrifice Stan's life for Omega's.

"You can have your life," Toby said, "but we are taking the precursor chemicals off those trucks."

"No, you aren't," Omega replied. "The same rules apply. If any of your men pass this boulder and come after us, then Stan will die. Let's load up," she told the mercenary, as they carefully moved Stan onto a motorbike, strapping him to the back of the mercenary.

"Just to make sure you guys don't decide to do something cute, like, say, shoot my man here driving the motorbike, I'm going to take out a little insurance." Omega removed a grenade, and pulled the pin, handing it to the man up front. She looked at Ana Lucia, and then at Toby. "You take my man out, then Ana Lucia's boyfriend will blow up. If you take me out, then he has permission to blow off your boyfriend's head, and then drag his dead corpse behind until he reaches his destination. Your call."

Omega straddled her motorbike as she moved behind her mercenary and the DEA agent strapped to the back. "Who's in charge? Who is going to make the call?"

Toby and Ana Lucia stared at each other. "That's your man on the back," Toby said. I won't give an order that will result in his death. Well, I could. But I won't."

Omega laughed. "A man with principles! A black American that will not allow a white American to die. Perhaps there is hope for your country.

"The DEA will pay for this incursion," Omega promised. "But *this* agent will not. If you allow us to leave, *this* DEA agent will be returned tomorrow morning. In the meantime, we will give him morphine and medical treatment. You have my word that he will live."

Despite all the weapons trained on Omega, all eyes turned to Ana Lucia. It was her call. Kill Omega and seize 1000 tons of precursor chemicals, effectively ending the Cartel de Culiacan, while allowing her friend, and possibly more than that, to suffer a gruesome death? Or sacrifice the chance to dismantle the Cartel de Culiacan for good for the life of one DEA agent?

Ana Lucia's hands were shaking as she looked at the ground, suddenly overcome with weariness and blurred vision from the loss of blood.

No good choices.

Human life was more valuable than any drug seizure, right? Especially the life of someone that had put his life on the line for his country already and was now serving honorably as a civilian federal agent.

"Let them go," Ana Lucia managed to feebly get out, her confidence and ego deflating even as the words escaped her lips.

"Very well," Omega said. "Now, Mrs. DEA agent, this is the second time I've been across from you and allowed you to live. You will not be so lucky a third time."

The two motorbikes zoomed off as Ana Lucia watched them fade into the distance behind the last 18-wheeler. Just like that, the Cartel de Culiacan had dodged the death blow that Ana Lucia had been certain that she was going to personally deliver.

Chapter 33
Rio Tamazula – somewhere between downtown Culiacan and Imala

Shattered glass on the linoleum floor crunched under the boots of Jesus Alvarenga as he paced around the three-bedroom cartel safe house located deep inside the Mexican state of Sinaloa. With the rifle slung over his back, Jesus nervously grasped and released the handgun in the holster on his thigh. He looked outside the window at the cartel guard watching the entrance to the property. The man noticed Jesus' glance and gave a nod to indicate that all was quiet.

Jesus turned to speak with the other two members of the four-man team, both of which were directing their attention toward the captive in the middle of the room lying on his back on a raised table. The captive's arms were above his head, secured to a post at the head of the table, while his feet were tied to a post at the end of the table. The security of the restraints was not in question. The captive was barely alive, having been beaten nearly to death, electrocuted, and waterboarded, all at the directives of Carlos Montoya, the leader of the Cartel de Culiacan. Jesus was impressed that the captive was still alive, despite numerous broken bones and even the painful removal of several fingers and toes.

But all that had stopped 30 minutes earlier with one phone call. The call came from a man in Jesus' past. The general population in small Mexican towns and the wealthy elites working in the big cities had all heard the legend of Toro. It had grown even more since the death of El Jefe, and Toro's rumored role in that death. But Jesus was one of the few people that had personally seen the extent that Toro had gone to in order to successfully carry out the duties of his job. As one of the members of the team that had also included Leon, Jesus was with Toro when they had crushed the smaller rival cartels in Tijuana and Juarez. He was with Toro during the shootout at the border in Juarez when Toro had killed one DEA agent and kidnapped another. He was with Toro at the shootout with the Mexican Federal Police at the bar in Tijuana. For those reasons, Jesus had a special knowledge of Toro's capabilities, but he had something that others did not, a relationship based on respect, born out of the trials and tribulations of past jobs. So, when his cell phone rang and Toro spoke, Jesus listened.

His former leader's voice sounded the same, albeit somewhat strained. He gave a simple and quick instruction: Do not kill the man in front of him, Reuben Valdez. Toro promised to call back shortly, and Jesus' pace and nervous twitches were the result of his momentary indecision and stress. Of the three men under Jesus' command inside the house, two were bloodthirsty, wanting nothing more than to kill Reuben. Preferably as brutally as possible. The one that did not seem to care either way was patrolling the perimeter outside the house. Jesus felt like he was holding back two ravenous pit bulls that were starved for food and salivating at a filet of steak just out of reach. Jesus could feel the two men's eyes on him, especially when the phone in his pocket vibrated. Jesus pulled it out, noting that the telephone number which was calling him was listed as unknown on his screen.

"Yes?" Jesus answered.

"Thank you for answering, Jesus," Toro said. "I understand you are in a very difficult position. I know that you are in charge of the other three men inside that residence, and I know that you recognize the man you've been ordered to torture and kill as the DEA agent that I met with at the bar in Tijuana the last time we saw each other."

"That's right."

"Do not kill that man."

"Why do you care? What does his life mean to you?"

"I'm trying to right a wrong."

"This man was a dirty DEA agent. Then, he came to Mexico, impersonating Vaquero, who we can only assume is dead. The DEA agent is not innocent. Much like you, the blood that I have shed is not innocent."

"That is right, Jesus, he is not innocent, but he does not deserve death at your hands. Not at the request of Montoya."

Jesus shook his head, turning around to look at the two other sicarios that were waiting for his instruction. He then looked at Reuben, who was unconscious but still breathing.

Sensing the hesitation in his former co-worker, Toro spoke quickly. "Tell the men with you that Toro is outside, and I have ordered the release of the prisoner."

"Here? You are here?" Jesus asked, peering out the window intently looking for any sign of the former hitman.

"Yes, I am."

"Toro, you know...you know *why* I can't allow this man to leave."

"Doing the right thing isn't always easy, Jesus."

"I...I can't risk it...you know what will happen if I don't follow orders."

The line suddenly went dead. Jesus looked at the phone. Toro had ended the call.

"Who was that?" Both of the sicarios inside the house looked at him for answers. Ignoring them, Jesus charged outside to speak with the guard responsible for watching the perimeter.

The house was set deep in a pasture. To the rear of the house was a fast-moving river, more than 50 meters across. The river snaked around the residence like a horseshoe, moving to the right and the left of the residence, but not completely encircling it before turning north. Based on the terrain, there were only two entrances. One over a bridge to the west of the residence. The other by land, a clearing about 200 meters wide, between the sides of the river.

Before Jesus even had a chance to question the guard standing outside, he heard it. The boom, and moments later, the shaking. "What was that?" the men yelled, looking frantically outside as the last remnants of daylight turned to darkness, restricting their ability to see, while simultaneously increasing their paranoia.

Jesus knew immediately. "The bridge. The bridge has been destroyed. Unless we go over the river, there is now only one way in, and one way out."

"Who would destroy the bridge?"

"Why?"

"What's going on?"

"STOP!" Jesus yelled in a commanding voice, peering intently to see if he could make out the form or figure of the man that everyone dreaded. One of the others was the first to see it.

"There! I see someone there!" the guard hollered, pointing his AK-47 into the distance, and letting out a long string of fire.

Jesus had not seen anybody and suspected that the young guard was possibly seeing things, confused as the shadows gave way to darkness. All four men stood in silence as they listened for any possible sound of movement to indicate a living thing remained between the residence and the only way out.

"Why don't we just go out there and kill whoever is out there?!"

"No, we can't," Jesus instructed.

"Why?"

"Because if we challenge the man out there, then there is a high possibility that all four of us will wind up dead."

"It's four against one!" the man said, with the others nodding in agreement. "Why are you scared of one man?"

Before Jesus could answer, a long line of fire suddenly blazed in the only remaining exit, from the grass on one side of the river, to the grass on the other side of the river, blocking the only exit from the property where the cartel safe house was located.

The eyes of the young guard went wide in amazement and fear, as they realized that they were essentially trapped unless they traversed the river behind them.

"Jesus, who is out there? And why do you think one man can kill all four of us?"

He turned and looked gravely at the young guards. "Because that one man...is Toro."

During the 30-minute time period when Jesus refused to allow the other men to finish the job and end Reuben's life, one of the men, Rogelio, stepped away. Having lost confidence in Jesus as the assigned leader, Rogelio suspected Jesus was being manipulated into not carrying out the task to completion. Rogelio did not want to suffer for Jesus not following directions, so he took out his phone, and sent a quick text message to Pelon.

* * *

Pelon cursed under his breath as he read the message. He looked out the window of his car in contemplation about what must be done.

Jesus had always been a good soldier. Rogelio confirmed that Jesus had carried out the torture and interrogation to the exact specifications that he had been instructed, so why was he now holding back when it came time to finish the job and kill the former DEA agent?

There was obviously a reason, and Pelon did not know what it was. But he also knew the leverage that he had over Jesus, so he pulled his phone back out and placed a call. The call was answered on the first ring.

"It's Pelon."

"Yes?"

"It's time. Take out Jesus' family. Kill them all."

* * *

Less than a minute later, the Uber eats driver gladly accepted a payment of Mexican pesos and began pulling food out of the white paper bag as three men gathered around him to receive their order. The men were standing around a truck stopped at the end of a long dirt driveway leading to a small residence 50 meters away. A sign on the side of the truck indicated that the trio was part of Lopez' Security Force, a group assigned to protecting the family residing in the house at the end of the driveway. Each of the three men had their weapons visible on their hip, back, or leg, appearing ready for a response or reaction if necessary. What they did not expect, was an attack from the individual disguised as an Uber Eats driver. By the time the quick and sudden attack was complete, all three men lay unconscious at the side of the car. Their bodies were dragged to the back of the car so that they could not be seen from the street.

The Uber eats driver calmly stepped over the last body and walked toward the residence. The family of Jesus Alvarenga was visible from the window. They were gathering around the table for dinner.

* * *

"I don't care if Toro is out there," Rogelio said. "We have to carry out our orders. The orders were to torture the DEA agent, and then to kill him. We have tortured him. Now it is time for him to die. I'm not going to put my life and my family's lives at risk because you are scared of one man. You should be more scared of the entire cartel than you are of one man."

"You don't know Toro. You haven't seen him work. If you had, then you would understand why I fear him more than the entire cartel. Don't let your youth and inexperience put you in an early grave. For now, we leave the DEA agent alive."

"We have to do what we are ordered to do."

"Montoya and Pelon are not here. They are not facing our circumstances. We are. I just need time. Find Toro, and then we can figure out what to do."

This time, both men's phones rang at the same time. Both men answered while the other two guards looked on uncomfortably.

"Why are you doing this?" Jesus answered, peering out the window to see if he could spot Toro.

"Jesus, I know why you feel forced to do this, but you're not. Listen."

A female came to the line. "Jesus? Is that you?"

Jesus' eyes bulged out from his head in realization.

"Carmen? Is that you? Where are you?"

"I'm home. I told you the Cartel has had three men outside our home for a week now, but this man is here. He says he used to work with you, and that you would trust him."

Toro took the phone back. "Jesus, I know the reason you felt like you have to kill that man is because you are afraid Montoya will have your family killed. I got past the cartel guards stationed outside their house. Your family is in my protection now. I will not let anything happen to them."

"But...Toro...if you're with my family at their residence...who is outside here? I thought you were calling from here. We are trapped and there is a man outside. We all thought it was *you*. You made it seem like it was you out there."

"It is someone else. An American. Black guy. Deliver the DEA agent to that man *alive*. If Reuben is alive, then the American will take you to your family and you will be given enough money to leave Mexico and go wherever you desire."

Jesus closed his eyes in shock, immediately realizing what had played out. Toro had pretended to be the one near their property to intimidate him into not killing Reuben. But Toro had known that Jesus was unable to disobey the cartel's instructions or else his family would be killed. While the American outside pretended to be Toro, the real Toro, speaking to him from another location, had disposed of the Cartel hitmen that were stationed outside his family's residence, prepared to massacre the entire family if Jesus did not follow through with the cartel's instructions.

While his eyes were still closed, Jesus heard three rifle shots ring out. He immediately dropped to the floor, seeking cover from the incoming fire. Slowly, Jesus realized he had nothing to worry about. The three men that he had been in charge of were all lying on the floor dead. Jesus raised his head and looked through the window. From the distance, he could see the American slinging his rifle to his back and walking toward the safe house.

* * *

The door of the safe house opened, and slowly, with his bulky arms draped around Jesus, a semi-conscious Reuben and Jesus made their way away from the residence. Toby attempted to put Jesus at ease with a comforting smile and speaking to him in fluent Spanish. The African American CIA officer quickly helped Jesus with Reuben. Toby pointed to the river, where a small motorboat sat against the river edge, on the other side of the destroyed bridge.

"Who are you?" Jesus asked. "And how do you know Toro?"

Toby helped put Reuben into the motorboat, and then gave the man a hand as he hopped in and directed the motorboat down the river.

"He's trying to right a wrong. I'm trying to pay a debt. Now let's get you to your family."

Chapter 34
Culiacan, Sinaloa

Pelon knew better than to call Carlos Montoya with the bad news that he could not reach any of the three Cartel members stationed in front of the residence of Jesus Alvarenga. The possibility that the cartel assassin had possibly broken Reuben Valdez out of the safe house would be very problematic.

That was why the Cartel boss trusted him. Pelon never called with problems, only with explanations or answers. When the Cartel members at the Alvarenga residence did not answer, Pelon knew that meant trouble, for each member knew to have their phones on at all times. Very rarely did one member miss a call or text. If all three did, then they had obviously been incapacitated. It made sense to Pelon, for he realized that there was no way that Jesus would have moved forward with protecting Reuben Valdez against Cartel instruction, if Jesus did not have prior assurances that his family was safe.

That meant that someone had told Jesus that his family was safe. Which meant that the individual was currently in the process of trying to extract Jesus' family. And if Jesus' family had been extracted, then it was a safe bet that the individual that extracted them was going to deliver the family directly to Jesus.

Pelon looked at the maps on his phone. The Cartel safe house where Jesus was responsible for watching Reuben Valdez was located along the Rio Tamazula, halfway between downtown Culiacan and the Cartel mansion based further north in the small neighborhood of Imala. He had a starting point for where Jesus was leaving from. Now he needed to determine where Jesus was going to meet his family.

Scrolling along the GPS, Pelon found the location where Jesus' family had been watched. It was a small residential neighborhood in the area of San Ramon, approximately 30 kilometers away from downtown Culiacan, traveling along Boulevard Francisco Madero. Whoever rescued Jesus' family, the most direct route to meet with Jesus would be to travel north up the Boulevard and meet somewhere downtown.

From his knowledge of the area, Pelon estimated it would take approximately 45 minutes to travel north up the boulevard and reach downtown Culiacan.

Pelon contacted Sergio, the Cartel contact working for the national cell phone company and asked him to see how long it had been since any of those three men watching the Alvarenga family residence in San Roman had made or received a call. Sergio quickly told him it had been 13 minutes.

I've still got 30 minutes, Pelon thought.

Pelon pulled up an app on his cell phone and put out a special message. He needed as many vehicles as possible to leave the downtown area of Culiacan and travel south on Boulevard Francisco Madero, stopping just north of Carrizalejo, the last town prior to reaching downtown Culiacan. If Pelon timed it right, he would beat the Alvarenga family there by five minutes.

The Cartel bodyguard finished the last of his beer, left cash on the table, and ran out the door to the Range Rover parked on the street.

* * *

From his iPad, Sergio tracked the location of Pelon's phone. Having been imbedded with the Cartel for so long, deep undercover as a CIA case officer, the amount of information instantaneously at Sergio's fingertips was staggering, whether he accessed his information from Cartel contacts, or contacts with the CIA. In this instance, after giving Pelon the information he requested, Sergio had an uneasy feeling. Watching the location of Pelon's phone stop just north of the town of Carrizalejo, Sergio checked the location of any other Cartel contacts located in the vicinity. His breath caught when he realized that there were more than 15 cartel workers in the area, all in the same location as Pelon.

Sergio had been fully briefed by his CIA counterpart, Toby, on the mission to rescue Reuben and Toby's work with Toro to reunite Reuben's captor, Jesus Alvarenga, with his family in exchange for Reuben not being killed. He was also fully aware of the escape routes being taken by both parties to facilitate the agreement and realized that Pelon and his men were waiting in an area to capture Toro when he arrived with Jesus' family.

Toro was famous for going radio silent on operations and discontinuing all forms of communication. Normally, that was good because it prevented anyone from tracking his location by phone. But now, Sergio desperately needed to warn Toro to turn around. The inability to communicate suddenly could now have disastrous consequences.

* * *

Toro's vehicle came to a stop approximately 30 meters from the long line of cars stopped in the middle of the road, blocking traffic in both directions. He looked in the rearview mirror. The way behind him was not blocked. He could turn around and drive south, but it would also be a dead give-away that he was trying to escape for a reason.

He turned and looked in the back seat. Jesus' wife sat in the middle of the back seat, clutching her children to her sides, realizing the meaning of the blockade. The fear was clearly evident in her eyes.

"Stay here, and get down," Toro said. He had promised to deliver Jesus' family safely if Reuben was not harmed. He intended to keep that promise, but for one of the first times in his life, he wasn't sure how to do it. The door of the old Tahoe creaked open and Toro slowly exited, walking down the paved road.

Closing half the distance, Toro now stood 15 meters away from the group of men that blocked the road. He stood there, waiting for the leader to step forward and speak. The man that stepped forward was someone that Toro recognized from a previous trip to El Jefe's mansion. Toro recognized the man from his position nearby Juan Montoya, presumably the elder Montoya's bodyguard. He wondered to himself if the man held responsibility for Montoya's death in Hong Kong.

The bald-headed man, Pelon, stood easily over 6 feet tall, and looked strong and thick chested. "Who are you? And what is your purpose coming through this area?" Pelon asked as Toro did not move any closer.

"I'm coming from my home to Culiacan. This is the shortest route. What is the meaning of this blockade and who are you?" Toro asked.

Pelon laughed and looked to his side, the confident and arrogant posture of a man assured that he was in complete control due to the amount of men and firepower at his disposal.

"I'm here at the request of Carlos Montoya and am a representative of the CDC. I'm looking for a family headed this way."

"A family? Like a woman and children? Or a man? What purpose does the cartel have with a family? Has the Cartel extended their threats of violence to women and children now? Publicly, I mean. We all know they do so privately."

"Watch your tone," Pelon said authoritatively, still confident that he was in control, but curious as to the confidence and lack of fear possessed by the man in front of him. He took several steps forward, and then his eyes widened with recognition. He too paid attention at the meeting at El Jefe's mansion several months earlier, and he now realized that the man standing before him was none other than the infamous cartel assassin, Toro. Still, the timing of Toro showing up at this spot, combined with the direction of travel, and the fact that no other cars were traveling in that direction at that time, only confirmed to Pelon that for whatever reason, Toro was transporting the family of Jesus Alvarenga.

Pelon turned back to the men still standing several steps behind him. "Weapons ready," he ordered. Each man immediately raised their firearm of choice and pointed it directly at Toro.

"I'm not sure what you're doing here, Toro, but I can assure you that if you have the family of Jesus Alvarenga in that Tahoe, you would be best served by surrendering and allowing them to come with me."

"Best served? In what way?"

Pelon looked around. Surely this infamous assassin wasn't by himself, all alone, this far away from anyone that could or would help, and was still this unafraid? Not seeing anyone or anything that could come to Toro's support, and confident that the army of men behind him could get off a shot before Toro could draw a weapon and fire a shot, Pelon answered.

"Your death here would serve no purpose, Toro. For all that you have done in your life, why end it on this desolate highway outside Culiacan? You have taken so many lives. Why do you suddenly care about saving these lives?"

"You have it wrong, Pelon. For too long, my *life* served no purpose. For as long as I remain alive, it *will* serve a purpose. And if that purpose is to protect an innocent family, then that is the purpose I will fulfill."

"Innocent? The Alvarenga family are far from innocent. You know that as well as anyone."

"The guilt of the woman's husband and the children's father does not transfer to them. They do not deserve death because of his actions."

"That's the way it works, Toro, you know that."

The two men stared at each other, neither blinking, for several moments, until finally Pelon spoke.

"In 15 seconds, my men are going to advance to the Tahoe behind you. If you try and stop their path, then you will be killed."

Toro assessed the situation, and realized he had few options. Surrender Jesus' family, or try and get a shot or two off before himself being killed. Both options would result in Jesus' family being captured and killed. An immense sense of disappointment and shame overcame him.

That feeling was disrupted by a sound Toro heard in the air. While the others looked in the air at the sound, Toro instinctively turned and ran as hard as he could toward the Tahoe. He had only made three steps, when an explosion rocketed behind him, completely incinerating the men in the blockade. The blast radius of the hellfire missile, the distance in which an individual is likely to be killed, extends between 15-20 meters. Toro was close to the 20-meter mark. The power of the blast at his back lifted him off the ground and into the air as he slammed into the side of the Tahoe.

* * *

Looking up from his iPad, CIA Case Officer Toby Phillips confirmed the Hellfire Missile from the CIA's Reaper Drone had an accurate target. Most of the cartel members were instantly vaporized. He studied the camera from the drone. Pelon's dead body was face down on the ground, on fire. Toby used the drone's camera to look for Toro and spotted him near the Tahoe. He watched for movement, then he turned the camera off. Toby contacted Sergio, and thanked him for the warning, confirming that the drone had taken out the cartel hit team led by Pelon. The fact that a CIA drone had taken out so many Mexican citizens was a battle for another day. For today, the Alvarenga family was still alive, and they would be able to meet with Jesus soon and leave this world behind them. Reuben was still alive and being transported to a location that would get him out of the country asap.

Still, there was one last mission that needed completing, and it was the riskiest and potentially impactful of them all.

Chapter 35
Culiacan, Sinaloa

Sergio Ramos appeared to work diligently at restoring the disabled server inside the mansion belonging to the leader of the Cartel de Culiacan. For several years, the Cartel had used their own special server to protect their conversations from being overheard by law enforcement officials that had connections to the major phone companies. This special server was only used by the highest-ranking members of the Cartel, to include the leader and the second command, along with the individuals placed in charge of drug shipment and transportation, and those involved in money receipt and remittance, in one of five major cities, to include Tijuana, Chihuahua, Guadalajara, Mexico City, and Culiacan. But the recent, and unexplained server disconnection had created a communication problem between many of the leaders of the Cartel, at a critically vital moment. The fact that it occurred shortly after the seizure of every single kilogram of cocaine that went into more than 30 different locations in Southern California only made the server disruption more suspicious.

As a longstanding asset for the Cartel working at the Mexican telecommunication giant Telcel, not to mention one of the individuals responsible for setting up the server in the first place, Sergio was the first person contacted and requested to immediately report to the mansion of Carlos Montoya in order to fix the server as soon as possible.

Sergio's deep cover was as solid as any CIA case officer or asset based in Mexico. The case officer had started off undercover with Telcel, and in no time earned the trust and appreciation of the Cartel, back when Julian Rodriguez was El Jefe, and he had proven his loyalty to the Cartel time and time again. If only the Cartel had known the amount of intelligence collected and passed on to the CIA during the previous eight years, then a fate as bad as any in the history of Mexico's previous violent drug wars would have befallen the courageous man. Yet here he stood, still trusted so much that he now found himself in the personal study of the leader of the Cartel de Culiacan, appearing to work diligently at fixing a problem that he himself had created the previous day.

As he moved back and forth from one room to another, attempting to seem busy, his assistant stood beside him taking directions. The assistant, unknown to those at the Cartel mansion, was able to enter the residence for no other reason than she was at the side of the trusted Sergio. The woman's dark complexion and dark hair gave the appearance that she was possibly of Hispanic descent, and while she understood some of the Spanish being spoken inside the mansion, most of it was too fast with too much slang for her to comprehend.

Nevertheless, she was there to complete the last phase of the mission that had been put into motion several days earlier. DEA Special Agent Victoria Russo realized that while the DEA had not been able to cut off the Cartel from all their dope after Ana Lucia's mission failed to capture the precursor chemicals arriving from China, there was still a mighty blow to be delivered.

Victoria had been undercover several different times over the course of her career, but none of those times had a prize at the end been as big as the one they were going after now...the leader of the Cartel de Culiacan.

* * *

Sergio was one of the last people to see Reuben prior to the wedding of Carlos Montoya and Fernanda Castillo. Victoria had thanked Sergio for risking his cover and getting Reuben out of being introduced to Montoya before the wedding. In addition to prolonging the man's life, Sergio's act had allowed the DEA to seize thousands of kilograms of the poisoned cocaine that were later transported into the United States, thereby saving many lives. Sergio only nodded, considering it part of the job, not needing any pats on the back for doing his job. Victoria appreciated that. Too many people in the federal government nowadays expected to be personally rewarded for doing their jobs, in addition to the regular salary that they received. But Sergio worked by a different set of standards, and now, he had one of his most important tasks yet to date, as he slipped into the closet attached to the master bathroom. Victoria managed to slip into a smaller closet in the master bedroom, and pulled the door closed.

Intelligence indicated that at 10:00 p.m. every night, the young lover Carlos Montoya took his new bride to bed. No matter where he was, Carlos stopped what he was doing for 30 minutes of passionate lovemaking. Afterwards, Montoya moved to the shower while Fernanda lounged on the bed. Victoria and Sergio were counting on that same schedule.

They were not disappointed.

At precisely 10:30 p.m., Montoya raised up from the bed, smiling blissfully as he slumbered towards the shower, pleased at himself for another job well done. Victoria peered through the opening in the closet door slit as Fernanda pulled on her underclothes and rolled over on the bed, turning on the television and not paying the least amount of attention to her new husband as he walked out of sight to shower off.

Before Carlos got to the shower, Sergio silently opened the door to the closet where he was hiding, and slipped behind Montoya, putting a rag of Chloroform against his face. Without knowing who was responsible, or why, Montoya fell unconscious. Sergio caught the man around the chest, and then, leaning down, released his grip, allowing Montoya's body to thud against the floor, making just enough noise for Fernanda to overhear in the bedroom.

"Carlos?" Fernanda called out. "Is everything okay?" Her question was met with silence. "Are you there?" Fernanda asked. Again, nothing. She contemplated returning her attention to the telenovela, but decided against it and got out of bed, pulling on her nightgown as she walked toward the bathroom to check on her husband.

As Fernanda crossed the threshold into the master bathroom, she was stunned to see her unconscious husband lying on the bathroom floor, naked, with Sergio kneeling beside him. He immediately injected Montoya with a sedative that would keep him asleep for several more hours.

"What?!" Fernanda started, as her eyes grew big. She turned to run out of the room and scream for help but was blocked from exiting by Victoria, who had slipped out of the bedroom closet and was now standing in the bathroom doorway, pointing a gun at her.

Fernanda's eyes flashed confusion.

"You? You are here for the server. What are you really doing here?"

"Since I know that you are fluent in English, let's switch, okay?"

Fernanda looked at Victoria and then back at Sergio, before nodding.

"First of all, if you scream or do anything to bring anyone else in here, then it is true, we will be captured, tortured, and ultimately die. All that will take place long after you die though, because if you raise your voice at all, you will have a bullet hole between your eyes in less than two seconds. Nod your head if you understand."

Fernanda nodded but her eyes were still defiant. "Do you know who my father is? If you kill me, then my father will bring all the resources of the GDG against whoever you are working for."

"Neither has to happen." Victoria said. "We are here to present you with a deal that I am sure you will not be willing to pass up."

"What kind of deal?"

"We know why you are here. We know that your father, the leader of the GDG, struck an agreement with the leader of the Cali Cartel in Colombia, to poison all the cocaine with lethal amounts of Fentanyl and sent it to Montoya and his associates in the Cartel de Culiacan. We know that your father was banking on tens of thousands of American drug users to die, and the American response would take out Carlos Montoya as leader, either by apprehension or by death, so that you, his daughter, could then rise to take control of

281

the Cartel de Culiacan based on the agreements and friendships you made with so many leaders during your brief marriage with Carlos Montoya. The Castillo family would have control of all the drug trafficking routes in Eastern and Western Mexico."

Fernanda tried to keep a straight face, but the knowledge of her family's sinister actions, and the realization that others knew of their actions, clearly unnerved her. She shook her head in a feeble attempt to deny the accusations. "You have no proof of these wild...lies," she tried to say, until Victoria cut her off.

"Actually, quite the opposite, Fernanda, you see, every kilogram of cocaine that the Cartel de Culiacan shipped to the United States on the day of your wedding was seized by the DEA. I know you are aware. All of those kilograms were tested at a DEA laboratory and confirmed to be positive for lethal traces of Fentanyl."

Finding her voice again, still defiant, Fernanda said, "That proves nothing."

"You're right. That alone does not prove you and your family's role in this matter. This on the other hand, does," she said, pointing at Sergio, who had withdrawn his mobile device, and played a recording that he had overheard in his role as a telecommunications expert at Telcel, in which the leader of the GDG introduced himself to the leader of the Cali Cartel in Colombia. The conversation that the two men had over the phone clearly painted out exactly what the plan had been from the beginning.

Fernanda shook her head, for there was no point in denying anything. "I always told my father to be more careful discussing such sensitive subjects on the phone. He was stuck in the old ways."

Victoria spoke up. "What if I were to tell you that there is another way? This recording will be lost. Carlos Montoya will be arrested, and you will become the leader of the Cartel de Culiacan. The Castillo family can control the entire drug trafficking route in Mexico, just as you wished."

Fernanda didn't hesitate in considering the proposal. "What would I need to do?"

"Get us out of here, unseen," Victoria said. "We take Carlos with us. We let the media know that all the cocaine recently imported by the Cartel de Culiacan was lethally laced with Fentanyl, but the media will leave out all reports that it was at the direction of Luis Castillo and the GDG. Instead, we create the false narrative that you found out that he attempted to kill so many of his customers in America, became outraged, and turned him over to Mexican law enforcement which delivered him to the Americans. Fernanda Castillo will be the hero. Everything that you worked for will come to pass."

"And you can do this?" Fernanda said, now all pretext of loyalty to Montoya gone.

"We can."

"And if I get you out of here, what assurances do I have that you won't arrest me and take me to American jail just like Carlos?"

"You have my word that we will not arrest you. You will never spend a night in an American jail." She extended her hand, which Fernanda shook.

"You give me your word that you will not arrest me or send me to jail?" She confirmed.

"That's right. My word. You will never spend a day behind bars. Only Carlos."

Fernanda smiled. "You have a deal."

* * *

Less than half an hour later, Fernanda led them out a secret tunnel leading directly from their bedroom, and to a small outhouse a kilometer away from the mansion. Victoria waited with Fernanda and the still unconscious Carlos while Sergio ran to get the vehicle that he left back at the mansion.

Fernanda's eyes flitted back and forth as they got outside. Victoria tried to calm her. "Don't do anything crazy," Victoria told her. "This is almost over. Carlos will be gone, just like you wanted."

The beautiful newlywed shook her head. "As long as my two feet stay in my homeland of Mexico, and I am the leader of the CDC, I will be happy."

"You shall never leave your homeland, as I promised."

Fernanda nodded again, crossing her arms as she waited for Sergio to return. "So, what happens next?"

"Sergio will get us out with the van. You will ride in the passenger seat and instruct the security guards at the exit that we can leave. We will go to another location to leave the area. You will not come with us from that point."

"Okay," Fernanda said, hoping that she was making the right decision. She did not want to die. And she did not want to leave Mexico. If agreeing to this operation with the American kept those options alive, then it was too bad for Carlos. Especially if the agreement produced the expedited result of the Castillo family taking control of both major drug cartels in Mexico. This was the entire reason that the decision was made to poison so many kilograms of cocaine and offer Fernanda's hand in marriage to Carlos, and now Fernanda had the opportunity to produce the result in a manner even quicker that initially thought possible.

Five minutes later, Sergio pulled up in the van. Victoria and Sergio loaded Carlos' unconscious body, wrapped in a set of sheets, and she entered the back as Fernanda got into the front passenger seat. She gave her permission and approval for the van to leave as they reached the exit.

For one of the first times in Victoria's career, the entire operation had gone exactly as planned. And it was the most dangerous mission of her career, no less. Had Fernanda decided at any point to alert security to their true identity, then they would have died. But she had counted on Fernanda's survival instinct to keep them alive, as well as her desire for the Castillo family to control both major Mexican drug cartels. Victoria's gut had been right.

Twenty minutes later, the van pulled to a small area, with several hundred meters of flat land cleared out. "We're here," Sergio called out from the driver's seat.

Fernanda opened the passenger door and walked out. Victoria opened the back door and met her at the front. "So, this is where I leave," Fernanda said. "You wanted me to get you here, and I have done that. Now honor your word and let me leave."

Victoria nodded, but took out her gun, and fired two shots into Fernanda's stomach. She collapsed to the ground, clutching her stomach in shock. "But...you...your word..." Fernanda tried to get out as blood pooled around her.

"I filled you head with exactly what you wanted to hear to get us out," Victoria said. "The word I gave you was that you would not be arrested and not spend any time in an American prison. I am keeping that word. You will never be taken to America, nor will you spend time in an American prison. You wanted to stay on Mexican soil for your entire life. For however many seconds of your life are remaining, you'll be in Mexico."

Victoria kneeled in front of Fernanda, whose life was quickly slipping away. "You and your father were content with killing thousands of Americans. I will not let anyone live that is morally okay with killing ten-thousand innocent people. I won't let it slide. Not with a clear conscience."

Those were the last words Fernanda heard, as she breathed her final breath, and closed her eyes.

Chapter 36
Culiacan, Sinaloa

"Hang on Reuben, we're almost out of here," Toby said quietly, as he parked the van in the lot of a small private airstrip east of Culiacan. At the end of the parking lot was the Fixed Based Operator, or FBO, a small one room building where pilots and passengers could go to the bathroom or eat something before or after a flight. It was simple and not excessive, designed specifically not to draw attention. A small six passenger plane was waiting on the tarmac 50 meters from the back side of the FBO. The plane's engines were on and it was ready to take off. The quickest and easiest way to the plane was through the FBO and then onto the pavement outside.

Unable to be in two places at once, the CIA case officer had put Jesus in a taxi and gave him exact coordinates where to go to find his family, instructing the former sicario to save his old boss Toro, if Toro was still alive. Toby knew that he needed to take Jesus there to ensure he was reunited with his family, and to confirm if Toro was still alive, but at that moment, he desperately needed to get on the private plane with Reuben and get out of Mexico. The unconscious former DEA agent had risked his life for the greater good of the country, redeeming himself and far outweighing the bad that resulted from his corruption with the Cartel while he was employed as a federal agent. But it wasn't just Reuben that needed to get out of Mexico as soon as possible.

Toby smiled wide with relief as he realized that there was another van also parked in the lot. His longtime partner from the agency, Sergio, exited the vehicle and gave him a fist bump. The undercover CIA case officer made sure to pull his hat low on his head. Even here, he was concerned with a roving satellite or unknown camera that might capture his face and blow the cover that he had carefully maintained for so many years.

Victoria exited the passenger seat and rolled open the side door, revealing the unconscious form of Carlos Montoya, the current head of the Cartel de Culiacan. With his hands zip tied behind him, and his feet tied together, there was no threat of escape. Still, they could not be too careful with the opportunity to remove the leader of the biggest Cartel from Mexico and dropping him on the doorstop of American authorities.

"I can't believe you really went through with this," Victoria told Toby as the two worked to place Reuben and Carlos Montoya on stretchers that had been stored in the van. "I'm not complaining, I just never thought I'd see the day that the US government approved an undercover mission to remove the leader of the Cartel de Culiacan, without a treaty or anything."

"Well, hopefully the story that is fed to the media will suffice," Toby said. "Months ago, I was responsible for the deal that ultimately set Carlos Montoya free from American prison when I tried to set up the removal of El Jefe. El Jefe was simply too dangerous, allowing the highest bidder free passage through their tunnels and into the United States. Bombs, terrorists, all kinds of things intended to destroy our country were being discussed and offered. I knew the only way to stop it was to remove El Jefe and put Juan Montoya in place and come to an agreement that if that happened, Montoya would restrict access of the tunnels to terrorists and others intending to destroy the US. Releasing Montoya's son from an American prison helped to incentivize Juan Montoya to follow through on his promises.

"The plan was *always* to eventually re-arrest Carlos Montoya down the road. That plan was expedited when Juan Montoya was murdered and Carlos took over the cartel for his father. My deal was with *Juan* Montoya. Fate intervened and took him out, so I had no one holding me to that deal anymore. Carlos was free game."

That answer satisfied Victoria.

"How is Reuben?" Victoria asked, as Sergio started rolling Montoya's stretcher to the FBO ahead of Toby who was pushing Reuben's stretcher.

"He's alive. If we can get Reuben to the US, I think he will survive."

"That's unbelievable."

"It is. Toro helped me pull it off."

Victoria smiled as she ran ahead and grabbed the door, holding it open for Sergio and then Toby to push their stretchers inside. "I love a good redemption story." After allowing the men to enter the FBO with the stretchers, Victoria moved to enter behind them, but dropped her cell phone to the ground and it bounced behind her. Stopping and stepping back to grab the phone, the door to the FBO closed behind Toby.

* * *

Hidden inside the FBO, Omega calmly observed two men enter the building, each pushing a stretcher. She figured that that at least one of the men on the stretcher was the former DEA agent that had impersonated Vaquero. Omega would make sure that he was dead. That was the reason she was there. She had no idea who the other individual was on the stretcher. Had she realized it was her brother, her red-hot fury would have burned even more, if possible.

* * *

Toby crumpled to the ground as 25,000 volts of electricity from Omega's stun gun connected directly with the right side of his neck. Not wanting to kill all of her prey at the beginning of the hunt, she decided to incapacitate one, saving that unlucky individual for a particularly gruesome torture session later that would be broadcast across many different social media platforms in an effort to thoroughly dissuade the rivals of the Cartel de Culiacan, along with any law enforcement agency, from interfering in the cartel's activities.

Knowing there was more than one active target still at large, she dropped the stun gun from her left hand and looked to her right, raising the pistol, and setting the sights on Sergio.

Victoria entered the FBO to Omega's left as she was transitioning from the stun gun on her left to the pistol on her right.

Witnessing the gun pointed at Sergio, Victoria moved with lightning speed, kicking out her right foot and striking Omega's wrist, knocking the gun out of her grasp several feet away on the floor. The bullet fired from the gun as it was kicked away smashed harmlessly into the stone walls of the building.

Victoria followed the kick with a right hook to the side of the head that knocked the stunned assassin to her side on the ground. She waited a split second too long to continue the attack, with Omega turning and sweeping her right leg, knocking the DEA agent's feet out from under her and sending her to the ground. This time, it was Omega that got the jump, pouncing from behind and working hard to place Victoria in a rear choke hold.

Victoria knew she was in trouble as soon as Omega was behind her. She reached for the gun on her left ankle but Omega immediately wrapped her legs around Victoria from behind, pinning Victoria's arms. Her eyes bulged, wondering where Sergio was, knowing that she had 20 seconds until she would be unconscious.

When the gun shot rang out from Omega's pistol, Sergio's initial reaction was to find cover from his exposed position. Since the gun shot came from inside the FBO, he pushed the unconscious Montoya on the stretcher out the door and outside the FBO, yelling for the pilot to come and retrieve the Cartel leader and put him in the plane. Sergio removed his weapon and peered back inside the FBO, realizing that Omega's rear choke hold on Victoria prevented him from getting a clean shot at the assassin. With Reuben still unconscious on the stretcher beside the two women fighting for their lives, and Toby incapacitated on the floor beside them, Sergio charged, realizing that in order to save Victoria he would have to go hand to hand with the female assassin.

Omega likewise realized that she was using both her arms and her legs to subdue Victoria and would not be able to stop the man running at her without releasing something. Letting go with her right hand, Omega swiped down to pull the blade attached to a strap on her right leg, flicking the blade open just in time to plunge the sharp edge into Sergio's stomach at he crashed into her with his full body weight.

There was no way to make up for the weight difference between the two, and the impact of Sergio's body, combined with the removal of her right arm from holding Victoria, caused Omega's grip with her left arm to loosen and knocked her to her side. As she fell to her left side, Omega jerked the blade in Sergio's stomach in several different directions, opening up a wound that required Sergio to use his own hands to keep his intestines from falling out to the ground.

The floor of the FBO resembled a war zone, with Sergio on the floor attempting to keep his insides from falling out, Victoria half-conscious from the rear choke hold that almost caused her to black out, Toby still suffering the effects of the stun gun, and Reuben slowly stirring from the stretcher.

Omega rose to get a look at Reuben, confirming it was the corrupt DEA agent that had been imprisoned and likely released by the Americans in order to impersonate Vaquero and stop the cartel's drug trafficking efforts. *But if this is Reuben, who was the other individual in the stretcher that just went onto the plane?*

Omega then heard two sounds. The plane's engine revved, and it rolled toward the strip for takeoff, attempting to get into position for a quick getaway. The reason it was rolling was because of the caravan of vehicles approaching the airstrip at full speed, lights visible from the front of the FBO 200 meters away. If Omega was going to stop the plane from taking off, she had to do it now.

Still clutching the blade in her right hand, Omega sprung over to Sergio, who was hopelessly trying to prolong his life by covering his fatal wound. The vicious assassin then plunged the blade into Sergio's ceratoid artery in his neck, spraying blood in all directions as the life seeped out of the man's eyes. Just like that, the CIA's longest tenured undercover case officer in Mexico, who had worked secretly inside the Cartel de Culiacan for more than a decade, was dead.

* * *

The death of Sergio, and the realization of the approaching vehicles belonging to the Cartel, spurred the surviving trio into motion. While Toby pulled himself to his knees, trying to shake free of the cobwebs brought on by the stun gun, Reuben rolled off the stretcher, realizing that he was going to have to carry himself to safety in order to survive the night. Victoria lunged for Omega, yelling in fury, spit flying and wild eyed.

Omega withdrew the blade from Sergio's neck and swung it at Victoria who caught the assassin's upper arm but was unable to stop the blade from plunging into her left shoulder. Victoria's weight, which was considerably less than Sergio's, did not have the same effect of toppling Omega backwards, but it did throw her off balance, as she hugged Victoria and wrapped her legs around the federal agent's waist, pulling her to the ground. Pressing Victoria to the ground, Omega raised her chest, withdrew the knife, holding it high above her head, intent on bringing it down in a vicious fashion that would instantly snuff out the life of an adversary that she now considered worthy.

From her position on the ground and on her back, Victoria used both hands to grab Omega's wrist, desperately trying to stop the blade from coming down. While Omega's right hand was struggling to bring the blade down, and fighting against Victoria, Omega used her left hand to choke the other woman and weaken her in any way possible.

With the pain in her left shoulder from the stab wound, and the restriction of air from being choked, Victoria knew that she was eventually going to lose the fight against Omega and die by either suffocation or stab wound.

The headlights from the approaching cartel vehicles suddenly filled the FBO, telling her that the cartel members were seconds, at most a minute away from flooding into the building. Victoria desperately looked to her side to see if Reuben or Toby would be able to help.

What she saw filled her with despair greater than she had ever experienced. Toby was already gone to the chopper, and Reuben was awake and stumbling from the FBO towards the waiting plane. She was moments from death by some gruesome means, whether stabbing, choking, or whatever the cartel members might do to her.

In that moment, Victoria felt let down. Let down by Reuben, who she had vouched for getting out of prison to help the DEA's cause. At the end of the day, he was a convicted felon, and he wanted to live, and had decided to save himself instead of saving Victoria.

That feeling suddenly led to another feeling. More of a desire. A desire to survive. Her survival instinct kicked in stronger than ever, and she screamed with all of her might as she used her strength and energy to push Omega's blade gripping hand away from her face.

Despite the struggle, Omega looked at her and smiled, telling her, "You're going to die tonight, one way or the other. Whether I do it or they do it."

Neither women saw it coming.

The form of Reuben Valdez launching himself into Omega, bear hugging her as he fell to the ground on top of her. Once again, despite her skill and strength, there was no way for Omega, who weighed no more than 120 pounds, to get off the man that outweighed her by more than 100 pounds.

Victoria was genuinely surprised to see that the ex-DEA agent had come back for her. She slowly stood up, looking at Reuben, who had Omega pinned to the ground in a stunning turn of events. Victoria made a step toward them, wanting to finish off Omega, but suddenly, rifle fire started hitting the FBO. The cartel members were outside and closing in, spraying, and hoping they didn't hit Omega, but not really caring.

"NO!" Reuben yelled. "They're here! You have to leave now or else we both die."

"But-" Victoria attempted over the roar of the gunfire and Omega's screams.

"But NOTHING! Get out of here! NOW! GO!"

Victoria and Reuben locked eyes one final time for no more than two seconds. She remembered the first time she met him at the federal prison in California months earlier and could not believe that it had come to this. But she had sensed that Reuben wanted redemption, and that he would die in order to clear his name and his reputation, and she realized that this was what he wanted. What he desired. He had never meant to come back.

Although her right arm was still pinned to her side by the heavier man that was on top of her, Omega still held the blade in right hand. For the first time in a very long time, Omega started to panic. Having a heaver man on top of her took her mentally back to a time long ago, when El Jefe's son Victor raped her. The moment that had changed her life and set it in motion to becoming the vicious killer that she was today. She plunged the blade repeatedly into Reuben's side, screaming at him to get off of her, crying in a fit of fury filled panic and rage.

Seeing Reuben suffer the stab wounds, and realizing she could do nothing to save him, more so, that Reuben had wanted to save her, Victoria gave one last appreciative glance, and sped out the back door of the FBO just as the Cartel members entered the front door. She rushed to the plane which was already taxiing down the runway.

Victoria looked back to the darkness of the FBO as the plane started to take off. She saw several men with AKs standing on the runway and shooting wildly at them from behind. From inside the FBO, in the area where she had last seen Reuben, the darkness of the room was lit up with the light from a string of gunfire.

Chapter 37
Los Angeles, California – Two weeks later

"There you go, Special Agent Russo," the court clerk said, handing over a single paged document. "The expungement is complete."

Veronica winced slightly with pain as she reached out to receive the Court Order clearing the criminal record of former Special Agent Reuben Valdez. The injuries sustained on the excursion to Mexico had not completely healed, but those injuries had not stopped her from immediately requesting Deputy Administrator Edwards to petition her contacts at the US Attorney's office to honor an immediate expungement of Valdez' criminal record. With a very limited amount of people on the need to know basis, Deputy Administrator Edwards had quickly arranged an in person meeting with the US Attorney in charge, quickly explaining the circumstances of the events that had seen Valdez risk, and ultimately sacrifice, his life. That sacrifice resulted in saving countless American lives from a Fentanyl overdose, along with the lives of several American federal agents.

In a normal situation, even someone with Deputy Administrator Edmonds' title might not be enough to move the wheels of justice that quickly, but she was a woman with extensive contacts, even outside the law enforcement arena. A certain call to an old friend working in a trusted position in the White House was all that was needed to grease the skids.

Reuben's parents were no longer living, and he did not leave behind any family. No wife. No kids. No siblings. That didn't stop Victoria from her strong desire to see the man's name cleared once and for all. Sure, he had made mistakes. Serious mistakes. But he had more than made up for those mistakes, saving many lives. Especially hers. Reuben could have easily got on the plane that left Sinaloa that night, leaving Victoria behind, but instead, he had returned, and stopped Omega, which allowed Victoria to escape.

The Expungement Order would not be delivered to anyone since Reuben did not have any family members. Instead, Victoria would keep it as a reminder of the importance of giving second chances to good people that had made bad choices in their lives. It was a memento to the man that had given his life to save hers.

* * *

Culiacan, Sinaloa

"My son!" Padre Miguel smiled, gently embracing the grown man that he had raised as his adopted son decades earlier.

Toro's expression acknowledged his appreciation to Padre Miguel for picking him up from the hospital.

After the Hellfire missile had taken out Pelon and the rest of the Cartel members that had blockaded the road in an attempt to capture Jesus' family, Toro's body was catapulted in the air and hit the car where the scared family members had watched the entire scene play out.

Although he had luckily been just outside the kill zone radius, he still suffered extensive injuries. Had he been alone, he would have died from those injuries. But perhaps because the family that he protected had personally witnessed the lengths Toro went to in order to save them, they also provided care for him in his time of need, pulling Toro in the car and then escaping along a road further south after Jesus showed up and led them away, dropping off Toro at a hospital to receive treatment.

Toby used his CIA contacts to make sure that Padre Miguel was aware of the hospital where Toro was admitted, and the elderly pastor's face was the first face that Toro saw when he opened his eyes.

But Toro sensed something in Padre Miguel that he had not noticed previously, a physical weakness. Despite his age, and his lack of physical size, the man had always seemed like the pillar of health. And although he had not seen the man more than a few times over

295

the previous 20 years, Toro knew Padre Miguel better than he knew anyone else.

The elderly pastor and the former assassin walked to a waiting taxi outside the hospital. As they entered the car, Toro looked at Padre Miguel. The old man smiled back. "You will be feeling better in no time."

"I will. But I sense something is going on with you. Tell me."

Padre Miguel nodded as the taxi driver started moving forward. "You have always been very observant. I can't hide anything from you, even after all that you've been through."

"Why would you hide anything from me? You have no reason."

"It's just, after missing you for so many years, I'm so glad that the Lord has finally brought you back into my life. You still might not believe in the Lord and His goodness, but the fact that you have turned from your previous life, committed yourself to helping save innocent lives, and are sitting in this car with me right now having a conversation, it is the answer to a prayer that I have prayed daily for 20 years!"

"Padre...I respect you. I respect your faith. But what you believe is not what I believe."

"Not yet."

"Not ever."

"We'll see. As long as you draw breath, there is hope."

"You didn't answer my question. What are you hiding?"

Padre Miguel's voice seemed to age years as he answered. "I remember how you reacted when you lost your sister and mother. It changed your life. You failed to see the goodness and hope that is in the world every single day. You were focused only on the negative and the evil in the world. I don't want that despair to overcome you again if you were to lose someone."

Toro's heart sank. He knew what was coming. While he had recently committed to trying to save others, Padre Miguel was the only person in the world that he truly cared about. The only person whose death would be tough for him.

"How long do you have?"

"Maybe six months. Probably less." In the back of the cab, the old man's wrinkled hand patted Toro's knee in reassurance.

Chapter 38
Arlington, Virginia

The previous gathering that brought Victoria, a still recovering Ana Lucia, and Remi together for the first time, along with fellow Los Angeles Group 5 agents Johnny Nguyen and a wheelchair bound Stan Jackson, was more of a somber note. The funeral for the former senior investigator in Group 5, Bear Johnson, was something attended by all DEA agents in Southern California, as well as law enforcement personnel from many different state and local departments. Regardless of whether those attending the funeral had met Bear through work or were simply paying respects to a fellow law enforcement officer that had placed his life on the line for his job, the Baptist church where Bear had attended in Chino Hills, California, was overflowing with well-wishers to his family.

To both Ana Lucia and Victoria, their spirits were remarkably uplifted by the presence of fellow Group 5 member Stan Jackson. Having survived the helicopter crash on the Mexican side of the border, and suffering a broken hip, Ana Lucia had worried that she would never see Stan again when Omega used him as leverage to escape, while also preserving the massive amount of precursor chemicals that were undoubtedly being used to produce large quantities of methamphetamine. But to her surprise, the ruthless female Cartel assassin had kept her word, and Stan was delivered to an emergency room of a hospital in Calexico, California. Despite immense pain radiating throughout his body, Stan had considered it his duty to attend the funeral of his fellow co-worker and pay his respects in the most honorable way possible just a week later.

As a part of the funeral ceremonies, both DEA Administrator Dennis Haskell and second in command, Deputy Administrator Cheri Edmonds, had been in attendance as well, with Edmonds giving an uplifting speech detailing the history and background of DEA's most recent fallen agent. With the approval of the more reserved, and nervous Administrator, Edmonds had described that the mission that cost Bear Johnson his life had ultimately been successful, resulting in the arrest of a sitting US Congressman for human trafficking charges as well as charges of drug trafficking, based on a couple of kilograms of cocaine and several ounces of heroin that were found at the location of Congressman Lightfoot's arrest. As a result, the Deputy Administrator stated that Bear Johnson, and those involved with the investigation, were going to be presented with the DEA Administrator's Award, the highest award possible in the DEA. Everyone from Group 5 was invited to attend the event at Headquarters the following week to accept the award in honor of their fallen comrade.

Following the funeral, Edmonds spoke with Victoria separately. She trusted Victoria's abilities as much as any other agent she had ever worked with or supervised, but most importantly, she had learned to trust Victoria's instincts, and those instincts had again proven right when she urged Edmonds to let her work the case with Toby from the CIA. The two agencies rarely worked together on such sensitive operations, but she had confided in Edmonds about her gut instinct telling her to trust the CIA case officer from Boston with the easily likeable personality, and it had paid off handsomely with the year's largest seizure of cocaine. The fact that the cocaine had been poisoned and would have potentially killed tens of thousands of Americans made the cooperation between the two different agencies seem much more worthwhile.

With the trio of hard-working female DEA agents standing at the forefront of the media room of DEA Headquarters, flanked by Johnny Nguyen standing beside Stan Jackson in the wheelchair, they all looked on with respect for what they considered would be the pinnacle of their career, as the Deputy Administrator began her remarks.

* * *

"Thank you all for attending today," Edmonds began, not just to the Special Agents in attendance, but also to the select few media personnel present in the crowd. "Most of you are aware of the recent loss of two DEA agents, Kevin Young based in the Hong Kong office, as well as Bear Johnson based in the Los Angeles Field Division. Both men were exemplary agents, and paid the ultimate sacrifice, their lives, to carry out the mission of their jobs. From speaking with Special Agent Remi Choylia, I know that both men went to great efforts to protect their co-worker. Although their lives were lost, they were successful in helping Special Agent Choylia survive the ordeal and continue the mission."

Edmonds looked at Remi as she delivered the next part of her message. "Special Agent Choylia, I pray that your career, and your life, will reflect the honor with which these two men dedicated their lives.

"I know that you are capable, for it was not their actions alone that led to your survival. Your own personal ability and quick thinking led to the identification and arrest of US Congressman Bobby Lightfoot. You displayed remarkable courage, loyalty, and determination in not panicking, and not giving up, but remaining focused to achieve the objective despite such a horrific loss.

"Group 5 was more than just a team; it was a family. It was made up of two other, equally talented young men in Johnny Nguyen and Stan Jackson. I know that both of you men were very important in the beginning stages of the investigation, especially during the surveillance aspect. Special Agent Nguyen, I thank you for getting to the residence in Westwood when you did and following up with the lead that got your team there. It was truly a team effort.

"Two individuals involved in the investigation that led to the arrest of Congressman Lightfoot were also involved in a second operation that will be discussed later, Special Agents Ana Lucia Rodriguez and Stan Jackson. But before we get too far ahead of ourselves, let us commemorate the impact of your actions. Not only did your actions prevent dozens, if not hundreds, of future sex trafficking victims at the hands of these predators, but you were able to identify the predator, a US Congressman no less! The actions needed to be taken to arrest and charge a US Congressman are next to impossible, yet destiny put Special Agent Choylia in the only position that would produce the desired result. It is no small feat to make any arrest. Much less that of a US Congressman. For that, everyone involved is to be commended. I would like to present a plaque from the Administrator's Office, recognizing the efforts of each person. Your names are forever engraved in this award. It is something you should be very proud of for the remainder of your career."

Smiling, Edmonds stepped back and nodded at Administrator Haskell, the leader of the DEA that was nothing more than a figurehead at this point, content with assigning all important tasks to Edmonds for completion. Haskell moved forward to the microphone and invited each of the agents onto the stage and shook hands, while the DEA photographers, as well as some of media present, took photographs of the event.

After several minutes of private congratulating and pats on the back, Remi, Ana Lucia, and Johnny exited the stage, while Stan used the wheelchair ramp to roll down to the floor. Edmonds again strolled up to the podium.

"Our final award for the evening is going to be given for another operation that was also responsible for saving tens of thousands of American lives. Nothing we do could be of any greater value to our country than to save the lives of its citizens, and that is what this operation accomplished, led by Special Agent Victoria Russo."

Several of those in attendance clapped at the conclusion of the strong opening remarks from the Deputy Administrator regarding the final operation being recognized. "Unknown to all but a few, several weeks ago DEA intelligence, working with other federal agencies, came across information that indicated the GDG from Mexico had secretly agreed with the Cali Cartel in Colombia, to lethally poison thousands of kilograms that were going to be provided to the Cartel de Culiacan for shipment into the Western United States.

The reason for this treachery, was the belief held by the GDG and their leader, Luis Castillo, that with the death of so many Americans, law enforcement in both Mexico and the United States would force out the Montoya family as leaders of the Cartel de Culiacan, creating a vacuum which would be taken up by Fernanda Castillo, the daughter of the GDG leader. Castillo even went so far as to marry off his daughter to Carlos Montoya attempting to appear like he was brokering a peace deal between the rival Mexican Cartels, all the while intending to stab him in the back when the time was right.

"Fortunately for Americans everywhere, Special Agent Victoria Russo led an operation that resulted in the seizure of thousands of kilograms of lethal fentanyl laced cocaine in a single day, not to mention the arrest of dozens and dozens of violent drug traffickers throughout Southern California. Unfortunately, all the individuals involved in this operation can't be recognized, for their own safety, but their contribution to the safety of our country through the seizure of lethal drugs and the apprehension of violent drug dealers is greatly appreciated."

Edmonds looked directly at Victoria, knowing she was thinking about the efforts of Reuben Valdez, the former Special Agent that had been arrested for corruption but jumped at the opportunity for redemption despite realizing the high probability that he would not survive. "Thanks to Special Agent Russo, as well as others, these efforts were not in vain. A great tragedy was avoided. And thanks to the immense pressure put on the Mexican cartels, events unfolded which resulted in the death of Fernanda Castillo, and the delivery of Carlos Montoya to a police station in the United States. It is not clear who was responsible for delivering Carlos Montoya to American law enforcement, but these efforts were a direct result of the pressure put on by Special Agent Russo and her operation."

Edmond's statement denying knowledge of Fernanda Castillo's killer and Carlos Montoya's bounty hunter was an obvious lie, but one that was necessary. The DEA could never, ever, admit to running an operation in Mexico that resulted in the murder of a Mexican citizen, even if that citizen had plotted to kill thousands of Americans. Just as risky, the DEA could never, ever, admit to running an operation in Mexico that resulted in capturing the leader of the Cartel de Culiacan, on Mexican soil, and taking that leader to the United States to face a myriad of drug trafficking charges. An operation of that sort would have flown in the face of legal extradition treaties, an insult to the working relationship between the governments of Mexico and the United States. Lucky for Edmonds and Victoria, Montoya had no recollection of being knocked out, nor did he have any idea about who was responsible for delivering him to the Americans, although a dirty, hand written note with just enough local Spanish slang inherent only to Mexico, was provided to the police station where Montoya's unconscious body was delivered, thoroughly convincing those that read the letter that the responsible party for delivering Montoya to the Americans was none other than the GDG.

Edmonds managed to avoid looking at Victoria as she delivered the line, remembering that there were several media outlets represented that might interpret a knowing look between the two women at the mention of an understandably questionable gift like the arrest of the leader of the Cartel de Culiacan.

After several more compliments were paid to Ana Lucia, Stan, and other individuals involved in the investigation, the agents were called up to the stage to receive their award. Handshakes were given. Pats on the back were plentiful.

Before the awards ceremony was over, Administrator Haskell moved to the podium to call everyone's attention for one last item. "Once again, I, along with Deputy Administrator Edmonds, are honored to present the best and the brightest the DEA has to offer with these well-deserved awards. Seeing these agents receive these awards is very satisfying for me as the Administrator, perhaps one of the most satisfying experiences I have had in management with this organization. I am proud that you agents are making the most of your time. This is your time. I have had my time. And I realize that my time is passed, and I would like to pass the torch on to the next in line. Deputy Administrator Edmonds has shown a remarkable ability to lead, and I am naming her as the Acting Administrator, effective first thing tomorrow morning. I will strongly advise the President of my support for Mrs. Edmonds and advise him that I believe he should officially appoint her as the next Administrator of the DEA. I have already turned in all the necessary paperwork, and Mrs. Edmonds has been made aware of this pending outcome for a few days now. I would like to thank the DEA, and I wish you all nothing but the best in the future."

Without taking any questions from the media in attendance, Haskell walked off the stage and out the door. Wide-eyed, Victoria looked at her mentor, who was less than 24 hours away from being the leader of the DEA.

Chapter 39
Washington D.C

"There he is. That's him," Ana Lucia said, as the form of a short, stocky, white man in his mid-30s entered the Georgetown bar, dressed in an untucked polo shirt and blue jeans, the familiar attire of a DEA agent. As the man's eyes scanned the bar, they connected with Ana Lucia. A slight, reserved smile was on the man's face as he approached the table of DEA agents that had gathered in celebration to mark the end of the operation that had cost several good men their lives, but also saved countless others.

"Tyler!" Ana Lucia exclaimed, as she hugged the former DEA Agent that had worked closely with Reuben Valdez prior to his arrest. "Great to see you again. I wish it were under different circumstances, but the DEA is lucky to have you back."

The trajectory of Tyler Jameson's career had taken a sudden and unexpected nosedive after the arrest of his partner for corruption, and the revelation from the FBI that Jameson had gone into Mexico to rescue Reuben during a meeting in which Reuben had delivered information to representatives of the Cartel de Culiacan. The information Reuben delivered during the meeting in Mexico had been used by the FBI to charge him with corruption. However, a shootout at the location of the meeting had resulted in Reuben being wounded, and he would have died if Tyler had not traveled into Mexico, without telling his other DEA counterparts, and brought the larger Hispanic agent back into the safety of an American hospital. For his part in saving his partner and friend, the FBI had insisted to the DEA Administrator that Tyler resign his employment, effective immediately, or face the prospect of disclosure of his actions to the outraged public, and then have the everlasting mark of termination on his separation papers. The decision to sign the letter of resignation was the low point in Jameson's life and career, a career that had otherwise distinguished him as the best agent in the entire Southwest United States, and possibly in the entire agency. He had never thought he would have the opportunity to be reinstated, especially less than a year later. But here he sat at the table with Ana Lucia, the proud holder of new credentials and a new badge.

Ana Lucia went through the introductions, first with Victoria, then with Remi, then Johnny, and finally the wheelchair bound Stan. "Everybody, this is Tyler Jameson," Ana Lucia said.

"Sit down for a drink with us," Johnny said, as Tyler took a seat at the high table the other agents had gathered around.

Before even asking how or why he was there, Tyler looked at Ana Lucia. "You know, Reuben and I did everything we could to try and get the information requested when Toro kidnapped you last year."

"I heard about that," Ana Lucia said. "I heard that you two were even involved in a shooting in LA."

"That's right," Tyler said. "And I would have been killed if not for Reuben. He saved my life that day. I owed him."

"So that's why you risked your life and your career to go into Mexico to save him," Victoria said, sitting to Tyler's left.

Tyler nodded. "Yes. That and because he was my friend. He was a good person that did a bad thing. But that didn't make him a bad person."

"No, it didn't," Ana Lucia agreed.

"Actually," Victoria said, "Reuben was a great person. He was able to redeem himself. And all he asked for in return, was one thing. Your reinstatement as a DEA agent. You must have meant a great deal to Reuben."

"You're referring to him in the past tense," Tyler noticed. "What happened?"

"Why don't I get another round, while you explain," Ana Lucia said to Victoria.

Almost 30 minutes later, Tyler sat quietly at the table as he contemplated his friend, Reuben, sacrificing his life for the greater good, and asking only in return that Tyler be reinstated. They all had another round of drinks in Reuben's memory.

"The only question I have left," Tyler said, "is about Toro." He turned to look at Ana Lucia. "Is this the same guy that kidnapped you? The assassin that had all the narco ballads written about him? I do not buy this guy suddenly turning into a good guy. I mean he killed a DEA Agent for god's sake."

"It's the same guy," Ana Lucia said. "I saw him myself. I would not have believed it otherwise. He saved me, Victoria, and about 30 kids that would otherwise be dead right now."

"And you were okay with letting him live?" Tyler asked, surprised.

"Everybody deserves a second chance, don't you think?" Victoria asked. "We gave Reuben a second chance, and he was able to redeem himself. Maybe it's not too late for Toro."

Tyler shrugged his shoulders. "Maybe. I have never met the guy, so I couldn't say. It's hard to believe Toro went back to Mexico to look for Reuben. Where is Toro now?"

Victoria answered. "Toro just got released from a hospital in Mexico. I have his number. I told him to keep it so we could stay in touch. He said he would. We'll see."

* * *

Two hours into the evening, and the effects of the continuous flow of alcohol were beginning to have an effect. Remi sipped a drink and danced by herself in the middle of the bar, Johnny had already asked and received more than ten phone numbers from different college age and young professional women, Ana Lucia sat in a chair and chatted up Stan, whose normal level of pain was subsiding somewhat, and Victoria's usually tight natured lips were flapping more than normal with Tyler, the newest-veteran-DEA agent.

The night would not be remembered for the good times had during the two hours of drinking and comradery, but for what happened afterwards.

The bad news, which would later snowball, began with Johnny. As he was busy inputting women's phone numbers in his phone, he received a phone call from Dana, an Intelligence Analyst in Los Angeles that he had established a friendship with since his first week as DEA agent.

Johnny rushed back to the tall table, coming between Victoria and Tyler, putting his hands on both of their shoulders to steady himself so that he could relay the news.

"Victoria, I need to talk to you. I'm sorry to interrupt," he said, looking back at Tyler. As the DEA agent at the table that had consumed the least amount of alcohol, Tyler was not even tipsy compared to his DEA counterparts.

He shook his head and urged Johnny to speak. "I got a call from an Intelligence Analyst back in LA. She is good. Knows her stuff. Apparently, you really pissed off some white biker gang out in San Bernardino County when you were running UC with Reuben. One of the leaders of the group has just put out a hit on you."

Victoria laughed. The one outstanding thing on her to-do list was to arrest the white biker gang that had received the methamphetamine. "What is the source of this information?" Victoria asked.

"Coming from a wiretap at the Division, according to the Intel Analyst. Also, she said she debriefed an informant that mentioned details about the hit as well."

"Wouldn't be the first man that's wanted to kill me. Good luck to him if he can find me."

"It's not just that," Johnny said. "They know that you're on the east coast, so they reached out to some white supremacist and KKK members in the south. Told them to be on the lookout for you. There's a $25,000 reward for your head!"

"Twenty-five k? That's it?" Victoria asked. She patted Johnny on the shoulder. "I do appreciate the intel. I'll be careful, but I assure you I will take care of myself."

Seemingly relieved that Victoria was not as scared as he was initially, Johnny shrugged it off and continued his quest at identifying the most beautiful women in the bar.

A familiar voice broke in before Victoria had a chance to return to talk with Tyler. "Well, it looks like you are a highly sought federal agent," Toby said, moving to the stool at the high table across from Victoria.

She smiled at the sight of the CIA case officer, leaning over the table to give him a hug in a rare display of outward emotion for Victoria. Sensing that Victoria was slightly intoxicated, Toby flashed a look across the table at Tyler who was sitting by her side. Victoria made the introductions and assured Toby that he could speak in Tyler's presence.

"So, you're the guy Reuben wanted to be reinstated?" Toby asked.

Tyler nodded.

"Well, I'm glad I got the opportunity to meet you. I'm not sure if our paths will ever cross again, but if they do, then you have a friend in me."

Tyler nodded his appreciation again.

Toby's expression immediately turned serious. "Unfortunately, the tidings I bring aren't great. The racists white guys in San Bernardino aren't the only people that want you dead."

"Who else does?" Victoria asked.

"We're collecting more intel as we speak, but I overhead a conversation that caught my attention during a debriefing today while I was back at Langley. Apparently, information indicates that Congress-man Bobby Lightfoot was not at the top of the food chain for the human and sex trafficking ring that DEA discovered."

"Who was?" Victoria asked.

Toby shrugged his shoulders. "Not sure yet, but some of our officers that are more knowledgeable about the situation seem to think there is an entire group of politicians, both Congressmen and Senators, that are involved. Republicans and Democrats. They know that

Lightfoot will not dime them out because of previous agreements that were made, but they are deathly afraid that the feds will find information implicating them in Lightfoot's activities. It would be very embarrassing to them and the country if their involvement was discovered, and they are determined to not letting that happen."

Victoria smiled. "I can understand their panic, but I think you need to pass this information on to the cute Asian girl dancing over there," she said, pointing toward Remi. "The Lightfoot case was her deal, not mine."

"I know," Toby said. "but...somehow the awards ceremony you guys had today at DEA HQs was leaked already before an article even came out about it, probably by someone from the press that was in attendance. The source of information that we have made it sound like you were at the top of the pyramid. For whatever reason, they believe you are pulling the strings for the investigation."

"That's weird," Victoria said, both to herself and to Toby. "There were only a few, select media invited to the event today. I can't believe anyone selected by the Administrator would have been responsible for leaking that information. Something isn't right."

The cobwebs around her mind began to evaporate as she shook her head and began to think clearly and process the information she had just been told. At that moment, her cell phone sitting on the table began to vibrate. She looked at it and saw that Deputy Administrator Edmonds was trying to do a video message by Facetime, something that she had never done before. Victoria's brow crinkled in worry at the unusual circumstances, but still hit the button to answer the call.

It was a call that Victoria would remember for the rest of her life.

Chapter 40
Washington D.C

The day before the awards ceremony, journalist Veronica Valdez
had an unexpected visitor knock on her DC apartment door. As one
of the brightest foreign correspondents for a new Mexican television
network hoping to compete against Univision and Telemundo, Veronica was establishing a reputation as a fearless reporter that was not
afraid to ask tough questions of those she interviewed. Her best qual-
ity, according to the viewers, was that she was one of the only members remaining in media that did not pander to one side of the political aisle, giving softball questions to one political party, while ham-
mering incessantly the other side. She had watched CNN and Fox
News just like the next person and had come away disgusted by the
blatant hypocrisy on both sides.

Veronica knew that she had a great career ahead of her, and she
told herself that she was never going to sacrifice her morals to appease a certain political agenda. She never dreamed she would likely
have to sacrifice her morals for another reason, her own personal
safety, and that of her family. Veronica thought she had escaped that
aspect of life so common to many law-abiding citizens of Mexico that
were confronted by Mexican cartel members. She never considered
that the long arm of the Cartel would reach her in the American capital.

Yet when she answered the door of her apartment that was exactly what she faced. Upon opening the door, a smiling Hispanic woman, remarkably similar in physical features to her own, stood in the
doorway and boldly walked into the apartment without being invited
in, closing the door behind her.

The woman identified herself as Maria Montoya. At the mention
of the Montoya name, the journalist's eyes went wide at the realiza-

tion of who was standing in front of her. Much like often happened in rural farmlands throughout Mexico, two options were presented to the journalist.

The first option presented was Montoya's request for the opportunity to use Veronica's media credentials for the next two days, after which point they would be returned. To make it appear that Veronica had not been complicit, she would be tied up and left in her own bedroom, and later she would be found and rescued by law enforcement. Also, and most importantly, Veronica would be emailed the access information to a bank account in the Bahamas containing five million dollars. When Veronica asked what Montoya planned to do with her media credentials, the only response was that one person would die, but no more. Montoya gave Veronica her word.

Knowing that the next option presented by Montoya would be much less attractive, Veronica asked for it anyways. If Veronica refused Montoya's request, then she would be tortured, and slowly killed. Her family living in Guadalajara, however, would all be immediately massacred. The killings would be recorded and played on a loop for her while she was being tortured. Pictures of all 26 of her immediate family members were laid on the table in front of her. The faces of her grandparents, parents, uncles, aunts, cousins, nieces, and nephews all stared back at her.

Veronica knew that she had come to a pivotal moment in her life. A crossroads. Her morals told her to never go along with this plan, but the faces of her loved ones haunted her. Maria Montoya knew that she had Veronica when the journalist looked up from the pictures and said, "Only one person has to die?"

* * *

Maria Montoya looked so much like Veronica Valdez that the Cartel assassin doubted the journalist's own family would have been able to tell them apart. Montoya used Veronica's blush, foundation, eye shadow, perfume, and clothes. The two women already had the same height and weight, and Montoya adjusted her hair color and shape to match that of the journalist. She also had contact lenses that changed the color of her eyes to identically match that of the journalist. Posing as Veronica Valdez, Maria Montoya had appeared as one of the few select reporters at DEA HQs for the Awards Ceremony the day before. It had been an eye-opening experience. In a room full of federal agents, none realized that one of the most dangerous cartel members still alive was mere feet from them, taking everything in. Victoria, Ana Lucia, and Stan had each come into close contact with Montoya, but none gave her a second glance, so confident they were in the building's security.

For the moment, Maria had to put aside the persona of Omega that had risen to such recent fame. There was no way that Omega could have gotten a weapon inside the heavily guarded DEA headquarters, nor could she have taken out more than a couple of the agents with only her hands before she herself would have been killed or captured. Instead, she was patient, basking in the disguise of a media reporter, one that she had watched frequently since the journalist began her career several years earlier.

Following Haskell's retirement announcement and the end of the press conference, Montoya the reporter had managed to slip out of the media room at Headquarters and catch the DEA Administrator before he was able to escape to the confines of his office. Montoya confidently displayed the credentials of Veronica Valdez and said that it would be the honor of her lifetime if the DEA Administrator would give an interview to her over dinner, reflecting on the proudest accomplishments of his career, as well as his thoughts about what was necessary in the future for the governments of Mexico and the United States to accomplish to combat the influx of drugs and finally end the long drug war.

Administrator Haskell was not one for bravado, but in this instance, he did not see the harm in speaking to this attractive and young Mexican reporter over a nice meal which he assumed would be paid for. Haskell did, however, temporarily worry over the possibility of revealing some information that might be confidential, so he requested the presence of the Deputy Administrator for the dinner. Montoya smiled. Of course, it would be okay.

* * *

The location for the dinner meeting was a recently renovated restaurant in the Adams Morgan neighborhood of Washington D.C. on 18th Street, just a few miles away from the group of DEA agents celebrating at the Georgetown bar. Montoya was already waiting in one of the back rooms when Administrator Haskell and Deputy Administrator Edmonds arrived, flanked by a group of 8 DEA agents assigned to provide security for the top two ranking officials in the organization. The security team did a preliminary sweep of the mostly empty restaurant that did not result in any unusual observations, so the leader of the security team walked into the back room with the two highest ranking members of the DEA, where Montoya was sitting patiently at a table. Montoya greeted the trio as they opened the door and entered the room. The lovely smile on Montoya's face had the desired intent of immediately putting them at ease.

As Haskell and Edmonds looked for a seat at the table, Montoya urged them to try the delicious salsa, as authentic as any found in Mexico, she claimed. While they reached forward to test the salsa themselves, Montoya remained focused on the lead security agent that remained at the door.

No more than 30 seconds later, the lead security agent cocked his head toward the door, straining as if he had heard a noise and was not sure what it was.

At that moment Montoya's "Veronica Valdez" persona disappeared, and Omega re-emerged.

With lightening quick reflexes that surprised the older Haskell and Edmonds, Omega pulled out a stun gun and fired it at the security agent. Completely unaware of the threat from inside the room, the shock of the stun gun paralyzed the agent, and dropped him to the floor. Omega dropped the stun gun and pulled out two handguns from her purse. Holding one in both hands, she pointed one at Haskell and the other at Edmonds. Omega did not take her eyes off the targets. She backed towards the closed door, and maintaining her gun on the two, she kicked the door with the back of her foot, and then walked back closer to the table.

The door to the backroom slowly opened. The mercenary team appeared that she had used to escort the precursor chemicals from the Port of Ensenada to the factory where they were converted into methamphetamine a couple weeks earlier. Dressed as staff members at the empty restaurant, they had been overlooked and underestimated by the security staff. It had not taken long for the mercenaries to strike, using non-lethal weapons to incapacitate the seven members of the team that had remained outside. The leader of the mercenary team directed his associates to make sure each DEA agent was zip tied and placed into the freezer, along with the actual waiters and waitresses that were on staff at the time. Assurances were made that they would be in there no longer than 45 minutes, and the mercenaries closed and locked the freezer door.

A blow to the side of the head with the gun knocked out both Haskell and Edmonds for a short period of time, during which, their unconscious bodies were taken out the back door and loaded in a utility van.

Ten minutes later, Omega and her team were in their own safe house in the middle of the American capital. Helping the two high ranking DEA officers wake up, Omega pulled out Edmond's phone, which she had snagged at the restaurant to make sure that it did not go into a locked mode. Using the Deputy Administrator's phone, she placed a face time call to the individual that was the star of the Awards ceremony earlier that day.

* * *

Victoria's stomach knotted when she saw the incoming Facetime call from her mentor, Deputy Administrator Edmonds. It almost started convulsing when she answered the call, and instead of seeing Edmond's face, saw the face of Omega staring back at her.

"Hello, Special Agent Russo," Omega said as she looked at the phone.

"How did you get the Deputy Administrator's phone?" Victoria asked.

"Good to see you too. You know, the last time we met, you raced off to the safety of a helicopter and allowed that traitorous former DEA agent to stay on top of me. If it makes you feel better, he died a very violent and painful death."

Seeing the reaction of Victoria, Ana Lucia rushed to her side to look at the phone. "Good, so you two girls are together right now," Omega said. "I'm glad you are here for this, Ana Lucia. If it were not for you, I might not have ever figured out that it was the DEA that was responsible for many of the hardships bestowed on my family recently. My father's death in Hong Kong, the impersonation of Vaquero that led to the seizure of thousands of kilograms of cocaine, the arrests of all my family's clients in the US, the attempted seizure of precursor chemicals by Ana Lucia, and last, but not least, the invasion of my country, and the unlawful kidnapping of my brother and violation of the US and Mexican extradition treaty."

Omega stared intently at the phone as the screen showed Victoria and Ana Lucia looking at each other. "We had nothing to do with your father's death in Hong Kong," Ana Lucia responded after a few seconds of silence.

"But you admit to illegally entering Mexico, kidnapping my brother, and delivering him to American law enforcement?"

"That was the Castillo family," Veronica said. "They've been gunning for your family since Day 1."

"I know that, but they had nothing to do with my brother being delivered to American law enforcement. I saw two stretchers at the airport that night. I know Reuben was on one. Now, I know my brother was on the other. He conveniently was delivered to American authorities the next day. By the GDG? Please. Don't insult me."

Victoria did not respond. She only stared at Omega. Victoria moved to the side to speak to Remi and Johnny who had also come over, "Call HQs and see what the Deputy Administrator had on her calendar tonight. Tell them to get there immediately."

"You can just tell your partner there that there is no need to run off," Omega said. "They will want to see what is about to happen. Your two bosses were scheduled for a dinner meeting at a restaurant, but they are no longer there, or anywhere close to there actually. You won't find them in the next couple of minutes."

Victoria breathed deeply before asking, "What do you want, Omega?"

Omega turned the phone to show the kneeling forms of both Haskell and Edmonds. Both were on their knees, as forced by the mercenary team, with their hands still tied behind their backs. "As you see, Special Agent Russo, I have kneeling before me the two highest ranking members of the DEA. Deputy Administrator Edmonds, your friend and personal mentor, who is scheduled to become the Administrator next week. And Administrator Haskell, as of tomorrow he will be retired from his role as the leader of DEA. Both have a lot to look forward to in the coming weeks. Unfortunately, only one of them will get to live that long. You, Special Agent Russo, get to decide which one that is. Who lives, and who dies?"

By that time, everyone had gathered around the phone, staring over Victoria's shoulder. Ana Lucia, Remi, Tyler, Johnny, Stan, and Toby waited beside her, entranced at the impossible decision being asked of Victoria.

"I'm going to need a decision within the next 30 seconds," Omega said, "or else they will both be shot in the head."

Victoria shook her head. "You can't make me make that kind of a decision. There is no good choice. I won't do it."

"I told you what will happen if you don't. They both die. Is that your final answer, Special Agent Russo?" Omega moved both guns behind the heads of Edmonds and Haskell, as one of the mercenaries held the phone to record.

"No!" Victoria shouted. "No! I'll decide, just don't shoot both."

"10 seconds," Omega declared. "Who dies?"

Looking down at her feet, and unable to look at her co-workers, the seconds crept by.

"Haskell."

Before acting, Omega leaned in close to the camera.

"Victoria, and Ana Lucia, believe me, I know what this means. I know that war will be declared on the Cartel de Culiacan. I invite that war. But just so you know and are aware, my family still has control of this cartel. Now, I am leading the cartel. I spent the last two weeks establishing alliances with customers, contacts, and sources, and I have formed an agreement with the GDG. You killed the daughter of the leader of the GDG, and he wants you dead as much as I do. And there is no longer any Cartel rule stopping the murder of American agents on American soil.

"You came into my country. You thought you could take all our chemicals to make meth. You illegally kidnapped my brother and delivered him into the United States. You killed my sister-in-law, Fernanda Castillo. You delude yourselves into thinking you made a serious impact in the drug war, but really, you only inflamed that war. The Cartel de Culiacan and the GDG are going to bring that war to the American streets, so that the American people will have a front row seat.

"And Victoria, you, and your team there, everyone that was at that Awards Ceremony today, you guys are going to be *first* on the kill list. The time for the Mexican cartels to be reactive is over. We are now being proactive. It will provide us with the added incentive of taking your time away from arresting our people and seizing our products, and instead focusing it on not being viciously murdered in your own bed while you sleep at night. The hunters have now become the hunted, Victoria. Get ready, it's coming."

The mercenary holding the phone switched off the video recording but left on the sound.

A single gunshot rang out, and a thud indicated that a single body had dropped to the floor.

CPSIA information can be obtained
at www.ICGtesting.com
Printed in the USA
LVHW101623160423
744495LV00020B/344